The Chatelaine of Mallaig

Castle

Diane Lacombe

First published in french in 2003 under the title La Châtelaine de Mallaig

Translated from French by Brenda Logue

Cover design by Kerry Ellis

Proofreading by Ana Joldes

Formatted by Noman Shahid

Produced by Jean-Baptiste Lacombe Lavigne

To Laurent…

…companion, literary agent and first fan of this medieval

fiction.

Table of Contents

Chapter One The Exile 6

Chapter Two The Meeting 35

Chapter Three The Wedding 61

Chapter Four The visit 87

Chapter Five The Revelation 111

Chapter Six The Death 138

Chapter Seven The Tide 165

Chapter Eight The Vote 189

Chapter Nine Ne'er Day 216

Chapter Ten The Siege 238

Chapter Eleven The Hunt 264

Chapter Twelve The Forest 295

Chapter Thirteen The Tournament 326

Chapter Fourteen The Plot 357

Chapter Fifteen The Plague 384

Chapter Sixteen The Return Home............................413

Chapter Seventeen The Trial...................................432

Chapter One
The Exile

It had rained for most of our journey from the valley of the Dee to Mallaig on the west coast. Everything in our party, which had been kept to a bare minimum, gave off an overpowering smell of dampness: our clothes, the canvas and oak of the carriage, the horses' wet, muddy coats, our headdresses, and our trunks. The constant drumming of the rain on the dripping-wet canvas roof of the carriage intensified the gloom which had hung heavily over us since our departure. It was as if the misty, grey weather was set on matching the despair into which my heart was slowly sinking. Each stone clipped by the horses' hooves carried me a little further from my family and the castle they had built on the shores of the river Dee at the dawn of time, or so it seemed to me.

So, what is so dramatic about leaving your parents' home when you are nearly twenty years of age? I pondered.

Five days of uninterrupted travelling on muddy mountain tracks, and there I was: the third daughter of prosperous Aberdeen ship-owner Nathaniel Keith, given in marriage to the second son of Baltair of Mallaig, clan chief of the MacNeils. I was heading in abject despair towards my destiny with only my two servants and a four-man escort as support. I could not resign myself to the heartbreak, as complete as it was permanent, of leaving my home. If this marriage had all the appearances of an utter disaster to my loyal and as yet untried heart, I had to acknowledge that it had a highly strategic significance for the opposing clans it was bringing together.

Indeed, in this year of grace, 1424, the long-standing quarrel between our fathers and grandfathers over the use of similar coats of arms had been brought before the courts and settled in favour of the MacNeils. For the Keiths to be able to keep the falcon with the three gold stripes on their coat of arms, the two families had to be united through marriage. In addition, the Grampian forests, gifted to the MacNeils by the king, represented a potential, incalculable source of raw timber for my father. Since the MacNeils were only interested in the forests for hunting, the income from the felling rights constituted a powerful argument for the two families to come to an arrangement. The MacNeils' sole heir was a bachelor, and I was the last unmarried daughter in my family. So, it was decided that I would be sacrificed for the sake of this alliance. Such was the conclusion reached by my father and his rival from Mallaig in the spring, for nothing suited these two proud men better than to conceal their differences behind the union of their children. However, from the very beginning, this agreement had been accepted neither by me nor, as I learned later, by the one for whom I was intended.

For one thing, marriage had never appealed to my independent nature and for another, it was extremely difficult for me to enter into a marriage with a man I did not know and about whom I was told next to nothing—except that he belonged to a clan from the Highlands, a region with the reputation of being wild and rugged. I was ill-prepared to fit into such a society. Being the youngest, I had been pampered and mollycoddled until the moment it was decided to send me to continue my studies in France, where my uncle, John Carmichael, was the Bishop of Orléans. I had already completed four years at the convent school when diplomatic relations with France deteriorated, and my father called me back to Scotland, where I spent what was to be my last autumn as a young girl at Crathes Castle, my childhood home.

As far as my father was concerned, the idea behind this marriage contract involved more than a coat of arms. My family needed the wood from the MacNeils' forests to build new ships, and such an alliance would ensure a steady supply of raw materials for his business. Therefore, these had been the terms of the contract: Since the MacNeils were contributing more to the alliance than the Keith clan, it was Lord MacNeil who would gain a daughter and not Lord Keith who would gain a son.

What a stressful time I had just spent at Crathes with my parents, my two brothers, my two sisters, and their husbands! Not a single week went by without my trying to reverse this decision, which hung over me like the sword of Damocles. But, in the end, all I managed to do was to irritate my father by opposing his plan. He had been infuriated by my stubbornness and had refused to hear even one word of my arguments. Even though she usually sided with me, I had not had my mother's support either, given that she never opposed her lord when it came to clan matters. This marriage was indeed a 'clan matter' and had little to do with my personal happiness or what I imagined that to be. So, throughout the autumn, I had rebelled and fought on my own and in vain. In the end, not only had I failed in my attempts to reverse my father's decision, but I made him so angry that, just before Christmas, he sent me off to meet my fate alone, accompanied only by a small retinue of men. So, neither he, nor my mother, nor my brothers, Daren and Robert, and certainly not my two pregnant sisters, would be at my wedding. I think that this rejection was the final nail in the coffin that my exile had become.

In the back of the carriage, Nellie, my old nurse, and Vivian, my young maid, were quietly humming dance tunes. Not knowing whether I was in the mood to join in, they would risk these little musical interludes from time to time to relieve their boredom and soothe their bitterness of soul. This exile was certainly no more pleasant for them than it was for me, and it was only their deep affection for me that had kept them in my service. *What was to become of the three of us in this part of the country, said to be wild and unforgiving?* I asked myself the question every time I looked in their direction. Their loyalty at this momentous turning point in our lives weighed heavily upon me, and I did not dare share my apprehensions with them for fear of adding to their unhappiness.

The carriage came to a halt, and it was a few minutes before Lieutenant Lennox informed us that we were stopping for the night. Since morning, the rain had enveloped us in so much darkness, we had not realised that the day was drawing to a close. It would be dark in an hour, and we would have to set up camp for the third time since our departure. In fact, we had been able to spend two nights in an inn before taking the road through the Grampians, which stretched across Scotland.

Tomorrow, we shall sleep in Mallaig Castle, my future home. Tomorrow, I will know what my husband looks like, I said to myself, with an obvious lack of enthusiasm or even simple curiosity.

I quickly stood up and stepped out of the carriage, only too happy to stretch my legs. The rain had finally stopped. Large clumps of heather were growing here and there, providing patches of hard, dry ground. I felt a desperate urge to run off down the road, which dropped sharply towards the valley of the Dee.

What is the use? Will I even have the possibility to return one day? I thought gloomily.

Suddenly, I became aware of the isolation all around us. I could not make out a single road either behind or ahead of our little group. We were in the middle of the sparse vegetation of a plateau, following what appeared to me to be no more than a path.

'But where is the road, then, Lieutenant Lennox?' I shouted.

'There is no road in the north-west, milady. There is no bridge either nor a staging post. These are the Highlands,' he replied with a look of resignation. Then, trying to sound reassuring, he added, 'Fortunately, I have been here often, and I know the way. Otherwise, we would have needed an escort from Mallaig.'

I could not have been more disappointed. I had grown up in the middle of towns, streets, thoroughfares, and ports, which were, for me, symbols of business, commerce, and even life itself. They represented tangible proof of civilisation itself. And here I was, not only given in marriage into a clan my family did not know, but on top of that, shipped off right into the middle of nowhere. A shiver went right through me. I pulled myself together on meeting the lieutenant's apprehensive look, and I raised my head defiantly. *I will face it*, I thought. *I owe it to myself. I owe it to Nellie and Vivian, and despite everything, I owe it to my family. The Keith family honour depends upon my attitude towards the clan MacNeil!* So it was that, when it was time to leave, I climbed back into the carriage with a look of determination on my face. Under grey skies, amidst a dreary and misty landscape with the smell of impending snow in the air, the rest of the afternoon passed without incident.

While Nellie and my guards were preparing our modest evening meal, a group of four men, three on mules and the fourth leading an ox-drawn cart, arrived. I barely had time to look at them before Lieutenant Lennox told me to get back in the carriage. Although the road we had been travelling from the beginning of the journey was not deemed to be dangerous, since King James had arrested the highland rebels, he preferred me to remain hidden from the view of any passer-by; this was clearly in accordance with the strict code of escort duties adhered to by this dependable and mature man who was unstintingly loyal to my family. As I was fond of him and did not wish to upset him, I always followed his advice. I was all the more willing to do so as I knew I could count on Nellie and Vivian to faithfully report back to me whatever they had learned from the few people we met during our journey.

They ended up bringing me my meal to the carriage, for the other travellers seemed set on imposing themselves on us, and indeed, they did not leave our camp until dawn the next day. I, too, would have so liked to dry my skirts by the fire and chat all evening with the strangers. When at last they returned to the carriage for the night, I wasn't asleep. I could not wait to find out what news they had, and I questioned them as soon as they had wrapped themselves in their cloaks.

'Well, my lovely,' answered Nellie dolefully, 'they were only some peasants looking for work and a master glazier from Inverness. He travels around the Highlands repairing the windows in castles and churches. One of them is his son, and he is learning the trade. Decent men, I think.'

My nurse had turned away, and she seemed to want to end her brief account right there. Was it the late hour and the tiring day, or was it a general lack of interest in the meeting that caused her to have so little to say? I could not say. It was too dark for me to make out her features, which were usually so revealing.

However, Vivian, after a moment of silence, declared with a laugh, 'It is true that they have a terrible accent, but I don't think I am far wrong when I say that two of them would not have turned their noses up at some female company for the rest of their journey. In any case, they had a really good time at Mallaig Castle last month, when they were replacing the windows in the great hall.'

To my great surprise, Nellie sternly ordered her to be quiet, allegedly because she wanted to sleep. Yet, she was not in the habit of interrupting my maid, whose chatter she particularly enjoyed. I immediately suspected that the information she had gleaned about the residents of Mallaig Castle was worth hearing. So, I immediately got Vivian started again, encouraging her to tell everything. From Vivian's disjointed account, I learned that the lifestyle of the MacNeil chiefs was totally devoid of dignity or good manners. Carried away by her pleasure at giving her report, she did not spare me the disparaging comments that the travellers had made about the MacNeil heir, who, they had all but said, was good-for-nothing.

At that point in the story, I understood what my faithful nurse had wanted to protect me from by her reluctance to speak. The less I knew about my future husband, the better I could face his family. As far as my faithful friend was concerned, remaining ignorant about the personality of the man to whom I would be bound for life was the surest way to peace of mind. Therefore, all she could do was hope that the latter would gloss over the more sensitive details. Well, her hopes were dashed. Once Vivian had embarked on her tale, she could not be expected to differentiate between what should be told and what was best left unsaid. And it was only when she ran out of breath and things to tell that my maid finally fell silent and wished me good night without the slightest idea of the alarm that her account had stirred up in her mistress's heart. Suddenly, there was total silence in the carriage. Vivian fell asleep right away, and Nellie followed suit soon afterwards. I, alone, remained awake until dawn, torn between anger and fear of what was waiting for me. I was incapable of doubting for a moment what four strangers, totally unaware of my situation, had to say about a family who had hired them in good faith and given them lodgings for several weeks.

Clouds heavy with snow were unravelling towards the horizon against which the craggy mountains of Mallaig headland stood out. The dull, grey weather would continue for a fourth consecutive day. Perhaps there would even be snow. Iain turned away from the window and fell back onto the rumpled bed. A familiar pain had been gnawing at his stomach since he woke. With her back to him, Beathag was sleeping soundly and her satin-white shoulders rose and fell regularly with each breath. Her long, red, curly hair spread out over the pillows, and her naked body left him strangely indifferent. She usually got up in the middle of the morning. It would take all the willpower he had for Iain to immediately begin a day, which, more than any other, he wished were already over. The first thing he had to do was to drag himself out of Beathag's bed, get dressed, and return to his own room or go down directly to the kitchens and eat as much as his stomach would allow. A heated argument with his father and yet another drinking session had been added to the long list of excesses he had been indulging in for a while and in which he took no real pleasure or pride but which, on the contrary, left him with a deep sense of uneasy despair.

There was a deep hush across the keep. The windows in the great hall were closed and allowed no direct sunlight or noise to enter from the courtyard or the guardroom beyond it. Only muffled sounds could be heard coming from the adjoining kitchens situated in the west wing of the castle. Together with the cook, Anna was wearily seeing to the fires. Her plumpness and advanced years prevented her from moving quickly. Her physical slowness was coupled with a despondency which had held her prisoner for the five

13

years since her mistress's death. She thought of her first thing every morning as she prepared the breakfast trays to be taken upstairs: one for Lord Baltair in his bedroom, which he rarely left, one for Guilbert, the secretary, who no longer came downstairs in the morning, and one for Lord Iain, who might not even be back in his own room yet.

A young maid, still not quite awake, quietly entered the kitchen and enquired about her first task. Anna knew she dreaded having to take Lord Iain up his tray. They had lost count of the maids who had left the castle service in the past year because of the incessant harassment from clan members and their men. Anna took pity on her and, half-smiling, gave her Lord Baltair's tray, which she usually kept for herself, all the while wondering how many months the girl would last at the castle.

Lord Baltair, chief of the clan MacNeil, was entering his sixty-third year. God had been more gracious to him than to other highland chieftains, who had left this world before reaching the age of fifty. *Why am I still here?* he had asked himself every morning since the death of his wife, Isla. Her loss had been all the more painful since it had come a few months after the tragic death of his eldest son, Alasdair. Why, indeed, go on living come what may with this deepening wound inside him, and at the same time helplessly watch the decline of his clan? Misfortune had struck down what was dearest to him, leaving him completely bereft of what had once been his strength and greatness: an exceptional wife and a gifted son who had been respected by all.

Moreover, the exact circumstances surrounding Alasdair's death had never been revealed to the clan council, and the suspicion which fell on Iain, his heir, ate away at his heart more fiercely than any affront could ever have done. He was perpetually haunted by the question: *What had Iain done to his brother at the end of that fateful tournament of the islands in 1419 when death had taken him?*

Sitting in front of the black stone hearth, where a good fire was crackling away, Lord Baltair struggled to get out of his armchair when the young maid arrived with his breakfast. 'Put it down next to the bed,' he said in a tired voice.

'Are you not going back to bed, my lord? I can hear you. You are having trouble breathing. Were your legs very sore last night?' she asked him, with a genuine note of compassion in her voice.

Servants rarely addressed him without first being invited to. This one could not have been on the staff too long. She wasn't fifteen, was not aware of his habits, and clearly had not known life at the castle in its hour of glory.

'Bah! What does it matter, little one? It is the price I must pay for the advanced age I am being granted. Tell the secretary that I am waiting for him to go over the business of the day and tell Anna to come and get her instructions for receiving Nathaniel Keith's daughter.'

The efficient young maid set the tray down on the sideboard opposite the bed and immediately slipped out quietly, surprised that her master had not asked to see his son. Was it not from Crathes Castle, the Keith family home, that Lord Iain's future wife was to come? It was a good three weeks ago that a messenger had come to bring news of this extraordinary agreement with Lord MacNeil. Suddenly realising how unusual this day was and overcome with the desire to share her excitement with some member of the staff, she rushed back to the kitchens. She tore down the spiral staircase, tightly gathering her skirts around her. The prospect of Lord Iain's marriage aroused a lot of curiosity among the female servants in the castle. Curiosity, certainly, but also a faint hope. The hope that a wife would succeed in curbing the indiscretions of a man of such loose morals and also, that the castle, left with no one at the helm since the death of Lady Isla, would find in the new mistress from the east coast a hand capable of restoring order. It was a lot to hope for. In fact, life at Mallaig Castle could hardly be worse, whoever its next chatelaine might be.

When she reached the kitchens, the young maid stopped dead in her tracks. Lord Iain was there, dressed in breeches and an open shirt. He was sitting at the table in front of a steaming bowl of broth, his tousled hair loosely tied back with a leather cord. Anna stood imperturbable in the centre of the smoke-filled room, immediately handed her the secretary's tray, and motioned her to take it upstairs. It had not been worth the trouble rushing. Her chat with the housekeeper would have to keep. Tray in hand, she nimbly did about turn and disappeared into the great hall. Iain had not even looked up. He was engrossed in the cloud of steam rising from his broth and fiddled with a chunk of bread, which he dunked in the broth from time to time. Without wanting to admit it to himself, the housekeeper's preoccupied look bothered him. Anna had been his and his brother's nurse. She was certainly the only person at the castle who had any time for him. The only one who did not hold his bad behaviour against him. The only one who saw him as the child he had once been and who understood him as he was now. He hadn't yet exchanged a word with her since entering the kitchen, but he had felt the weight of her gaze as she served him. It was clear that she was worried about the kind of reception he was planning for Gunelle Keith. Besides, everyone at the castle shared her concern. There was no one who didn't know about his fierce opposition to this arranged marriage, which he had expressed as soon as his father had informed him of it. But to go against Baltair MacNeil's opinions got one nowhere. Iain knew it. Indeed, he had always known it, but neither

16

was he in the mood to keep his opinions to himself when it concerned his own future, the way he lived his life, and the choice of the woman he would have to sleep with. Each of his violent outbursts against his father over the past few months on the matter had one theme: opposition to the plan. And this conflict, the outcome of which was never in doubt, drained Lord Baltair every bit as much as his son.

It was precisely because of this constant fighting between the two men that Anna suffered in silence. Her devotion to Lord Baltair had been unstinting for the thirty years now that she had been in the family's service, but the affection she had for the churlish heir was sometimes beyond folk's understanding. Lord Baltair's grief distressed her and, each day, plunged her a little deeper into despair. Her old master's heart and lungs were worn out. He was crippled with rheumatism, and his mind was completely swamped with regrets of the past. It was a source of great sadness to watch this masterful man gradually fail: he who had succeeded in keeping his clan away from the fraudulent practices against the Crown in which all the other highland chieftains had indulged during the twenty years King James I had been a prisoner of the English.

The truth was, Baltair MacNeil no longer led his clan; he no longer held clan councils in his castle, and he managed the family estate through his secretary without ever visiting his lands or his lairds. It was now up to the MacNeil heir to take over the estate, as the serfs had the right to expect and to defend it against the frequent attacks by enemy clans. Only very rarely did the father consider the need to groom his son to take over as clan chief. He had to admit defeat in the face of the spectacle the young man presented, that of someone sinking into a life of alternating apathy and rebellion. It seemed to Anna that, at twenty-three, Iain was as much a stranger to his father as the sons of the clan lairds. *These two men could love one another so much. They are so alike*, she often said to herself. The old woman bit her tongue to stop herself from passing a remark and shook her head as if to chase away the gloomy thoughts that plagued her.

The hot broth was gradually having a soothing effect on Iain's upset stomach. He stretched his legs out under the table, brushing against his big, long-haired, red dog, which responded to his master's touch with an energetic wag of his tail.

Iain looked furtively at Anna, and then, looking back down at what was left of his meal, he muttered, 'She will be here tonight. I wonder if she wants to get married as much as I do. If that is the case, it is going to go well, and you'll have nothing to fear from the next MacNeil chief, even if I am still the family's second choice!'

'You're not going to jilt her at the altar, as you threatened your father yesterday, are you?' enquired Anna immediately.

As she always did when she was afraid of annoying him, she had asked her question in a tone that was at the same time tender and gruff. Like most of the servants, she had heard the quarrel between father and son at supper the night before. It had been one of the rare meals the two men had shared in weeks. She glanced at the young man's angular profile. Iain was saying nothing. She would get no answer from him, and that hardly surprised her. Her young master had already revealed a lot in very few words. Such was this strange young MacNeil: taciturn, impetuous, and evasive.

Having gulped down the last mouthful of broth from his bowl, Iain stood up slowly. He gave his nurse a hint of a smile, which was meant to reassure her, took his leave, and with a quick nod by way of thanks, he left the room, his dog close on his heels. What was he really going to do at the altar if they ever reached that point? Wasn't there always the possibility that the young Keith girl would refuse

18

him as a husband? That idea made him smile to himself. *It would be the act of a sensible woman if she did so*, he thought. Immediately he was brought back to reality. If he, determined as he was, had not been able to break his father's will, how could she, a slip of a girl fresh out of a convent school, be expected to succeed with hers?

That is what he was thinking when he heard footsteps on the stairs. He looked up. It was the young maid coming back from taking the secretary his breakfast with a tray under her arm. Their eyes met, and Iain was amused to see she was flustered. She stopped dead, and, deliberately looking down, she pressed against the wall to let him pass. Her face had turned a pretty shade of pink. Iain suddenly felt a surge of energy within. He made as if to move towards her, but, with a great deal of agility, she ducked under his arm and dashed down the last few steps leading to the hall. Iain didn't even have time to grab hold of her. He shrugged his shoulders and continued up the stairs, his brow furrowed with worry about the day ahead. He had a sudden urge to go riding on the moor, to flee.

Upstairs, Mallaig's secretary, Guilbert Saxon, was standing in front of his master, waiting for him to point to a chair. In his late fifties, thin-faced, and immaculate in his black doublet, he had succeeded his father as secretary to the MacNeil family. Unstintingly loyal to his master, he had also been very attached to the late Lady Isla and still mourned her secretly in his heart. Never having married, he had no heir and, therefore, no one of his own to follow in his footsteps. He saw himself as being at the end of his career and planned to retire after the death of Lord MacNeil. Estate business was certainly deteriorating, but more than anything else, he felt unable to serve under Iain, who would inherit the land as well as the title of clan chief. There was no doubt, he would have felt able to continue managing things under the elder son, for he had had great respect for his qualities as a person. However, as far as the younger was concerned, that was another matter altogether.

Baltair MacNeil looked up from the dimly lit parchment, sighed, and motioned to Saxton to sit down on the chair on the other side of the sideboard where the breakfast tray was still sitting.

'Have you finished examining the contract, and do you have a clear idea of what the felling rights in the Grampians will bring in, Saxton? If we keep aside a good part for hunting, could the forest make up for our losses on the livestock?'

'Certainly, my lord, as long as we limit the concessions you make. On the other hand, your herds have done very well this summer, and we will be able to sell more than in the past two years. According to my estimates, Nathaniel Keith will pay for the rights on seven acres the first year and another four the following year, which will bring in a total sum of seven hundred pounds to the house of MacNeil before the autumn of 1426. In addition, your lordship will then be able to allocate the newly cleared land to your knights and lairds, several of whom, as you know, have sons who have reached the age of taking on a tenancy.'

Baltair MacNeil moved slowly in his armchair. His bones were sore, and no position was comfortable. Overall, he was satisfied with the terms of the marriage contract, but he was annoyed that his secretary was giving him a long-term view of the situation. His state of health did not allow him to look to the future, not even the immediate future. The idea of a round of oath swearing ceremonies for the serfs really depressed him. He pictured Iain carrying out this noble duty: men all older than him, kneeling before him to take their oath of allegiance to him. He could not stop himself from grimacing at the scene. He tried to get a breath for a moment.

20

'How will my son succeed in having the MacNeil name respected if he refuses to behave like a man worthy of that name? Why is he hell-bent on remaining this adolescent agitator, always eager to take part in tournaments, brawl, and hunt and fiercely opposed to any kind of education and decent behaviour? It is certain his men admire him for his exploits, and his enemies fear him, but the serfs are wary of his impulsiveness, and the lairds just try to ignore him. Nobility is hereditary, but respect can be earned or lost and is indispensable for a clan chief. Iain will have no one's respect if he persists in his ways. God willing, marriage will settle him down!' said Baltair MacNeil.

The old chief turned wearily to Saxton and started discussing the business at hand. The mere thought of going into business with Nathaniel Keith made him uncomfortable. He had always been able to get on with men in business. Barely a year ago, Keith was his enemy. His secretary's steady, slightly nasal voice had a calming effect on him, so he walked around the room as he listened to the report. On reaching the window, he watched the snow falling, a fine, light snow that would melt as soon as it touched the ground. Then, looking into the distance, he saw a horseman galloping towards the plateau, with a big dog right behind him. There was no doubt it was Iain. He was riding alone, which was surprising. The hope that his son might be going to meet the Keith party made his heart beat a little faster.

Our horse and carriage were beginning a slight descent as we left behind the woods which had surrounded us since early morning. Melting snow had momentarily covered the ground and was disappearing, leaving large black patches here and there. I suddenly looked up. I had distinctly heard the lieutenant pointing out Ben Nevis. I sat up and immediately to the north-east I saw the famous peak, the highest in this part of Europe, as I had learned in my geography classes at the convent school in Orléans.

Suddenly, all that seemed so far away. In my mind's eye, I could see my four years at the convent unwind like festive ribbons. The passion for learning that gripped me as soon as I arrived at the convent in the middle of my fifteenth year; the eagerness with which I had thrown myself into my studies and life in a French convent school; my insatiable desire to make friends, which was evident right away; and finally, my great disappointment at being called back to Scotland following the defeat of my fellow countrymen in the battle of Verneuil-sur-Avre on August 17th last year. My father had thought it best to bring me home after this military setback. The fate of the Scots in France seemed less secure than when the expeditionary force was first sent to lend support to the Dauphin Charles, who was at war with the English. All the same, the three years of Scottish success in France had proved very profitable for my father's business. The entire family praised his astuteness in aiming to conquer this southern market of France, which the Scots were still happy to call the 'auld ally'. My own accomplishments at the convent school had gone unnoticed.

Vivian and Nellie stuck their heads out from under the canopy that covered the carriage and looked toward the mountain. I could see that the mass of granite, which was Ben Nevis, did not make much of an impression on them despite its snow-covered peak. They were more interested in the herds of cattle grazing in the dark glen that stretched far into the moor. They began counting the number of head of cattle and the quantity of meat it represented. Their comments made me smile. 'What could they possibly know about livestock? They can't watch a chicken being plucked without squirming.'

The wind had died down, but the cold forced us to cover ourselves up more or return under the canvas top. For my part, I wanted to see every tree, every stone, and every cloud of this setting that would soon be mine. The landscape before me was grey, wet, and vast: the Highlands. On the horizon appeared the almost black sea and the wild kingdom of the Hebrides. My heart stopped. What fate awaited me in this trouble-torn part of the Highlands, where each inhabitant took after his Viking just as much as his Pict ancestors: bearded, drinkers of whisky, eaters of turnip and mutton, always looking for a fight, and, according to some, savages?

Later, my lieutenant came to inform us that we were stopping for a few minutes to water the horses in the stream that ran alongside the path. As I stared at the countryside beneath us, I noticed a horseman followed by a dog, galloping towards the north. He was skirting the herd half a mile from where we were. I could also make out three other riders who seemed to be rounding up the animals. *Why are there no fences?* I wondered. I was used to the small, enclosed pastures of Deeside, where there would a dozen cows at most grazing. Here, there were at least about fifty head of cattle. The first indications of the excessive size of this region were dawning on my anxious soul. I took a deep breath in the cold air and waited in silence for our party to set off again towards its destination: Mallaig Castle.

Late that afternoon, at a turning in the forest, I finally saw it at the far end of the peninsula, between the two lochs, its back to the sea. It was imposing. The whole building stood on a promontory, which, from where we stood, seemed impregnable. The keep, with its thirty-foot-high walls, and the guardroom were both made of red sandstone, which looked striking in this grey setting. There did not seem to be a village built against its walls. It was surrounded by field after field—some used to grow some cereal or other, others as grazing. I counted seven thatched cottages dotted around and a mill to the east. That was all. And that was how the Mallaig peninsula and its castle appeared to me for the first time.

Lennox had had the horses pull up. He was giving instructions for the announcement of our arrival to Lord MacNeil. It was Nial, our young guard, who was to go ahead of us to the castle. We had all stepped out of the carriage to admire the view.

As if she had read my mind and come to the same conclusions as me, Nellie sighed, 'That is one place that is desolate and deprived of any social company! A chatelaine had better enjoy needlework, for she will not see many troubadours at her court.'

'It's true that the hustle and bustle of the port of Aberdeen offers more opportunities for amusement,' I answered, 'but there are castles with a lot of life about them thanks simply to the people who live there. Who knows, maybe the MacNeils have their resident poets and musicians?'

'Milady, do you think that they hold parties, banquets, and contests like we do?' interjected Vivian dreamily.

'I have no idea, but we are definitely going to have a wedding reception, is that not so?' I answered, trying to sound cheerful.

Nellie gave me a cautious glance, then turned her eyes away to avoid mine. She had no illusions about the festivities we were going to experience. As for me, I was divided between the little-founded hope of discovering a rich and busy life and the fear that the austere appearance of the castle was a true reflection of the atmosphere that prevailed there. In the distance, I could see Nial galloping ahead. Despite the fatigue, the hunger and the dirt that clung to us after six days of travelling, I was suddenly in no hurry to reach our destination.

Father Henriot was a small, attractive-looking young man with a monk's tonsure. A slight nervous twitch made him shrug his shoulders from time to time. He was standing motionless in the huge courtyard of the castle, mentally going over the words of welcome that Lord Baltair had dictated to him. He was beginning to feel the cold, and he was in a hurry to be done with it all. Next to him stood Lord Tomas, visibly uneasy at being part of Mallaig's scant welcome committee for its future chatelaine. Slender and well dressed, with blond hair and very blue, intelligent eyes, the young man had a look of nobility and sobriety about him. As Lord MacNeil's nephew, he had quite naturally been chosen to present the family's respects. Lady Beathag, draped in a red cape trimmed with otter fur, was trying hard to conceal her curiosity by looking uninterested, her scarlet lips pursed in a half smile. She wore, what turned out to be a permanent look of disdain on her milky white face, with its perfect lines and framed by a mass of flame-red hair neatly arranged under a hennin. Last in the reception line, young Nial stood a bit away from the others, eager to return to his place in his lady's escort.

At the rear of the courtyard, the castle guards and the grooms stood waiting. Hidden in the passageway inside the great door, other members of the castle staff were standing, excited and curious. Among them, Anna, who would surely be the first to be introduced to her future mistress, was worried sick. She absent-mindedly stroked the red hair of a little girl snuggling into her skirts. The wait seemed endless to everyone. Then, at last, the party slowly entered the courtyard. One carriage escorted by three men-at-arms—that was all. Inside the well-built carriage were three smiling ladies: two young ones and an older one.

'Which one is Gunelle Keith?' eagerly wondered the members of the household.

Father Henriot shook himself out of his daze and moved forward to greet the party. The guards had dismounted, and the oldest of them was helping the ladies out of the carriage. With great dignity and respect, he introduced the first lady to the priest: Lady Gunelle Keith. She took his proffered hand in hers, and he reeled off his welcome speech. She had pushed back her hood, revealing her light-brown hair, which was braided and tied back at the nape. There was nothing remarkable about her looks: freckles, a high forehead on which she wore a blue velvet band, strong cheekbones, thin lips, darting brown eyes, and a focused gaze. She was no taller than the priest to whom she smiled and confidently returned his polite greeting. The second lady, who had more sparkle and charm, looked embarrassed and stared at her shoes. The eldest lady, who followed, was tall and looked stern.

Lord Tomas, whom the priest immediately introduced, walked up to Gunelle Keith. He greeted her with a slight bow, his right hand on his chest, as was the custom of the northern knights and, in a deep voice, conveyed the respects of the MacNeil family. He then introduced Lady Beathag, Lord MacNeil's daughter-in-law, who made as if to curtsey but did not open her mouth. Lady Gunelle accepted the welcome, returned the compliments, and turning to her staff, she quickly named them, and each one, in turn, gave a slight nod of the head by way of a greeting.

So, the round of introductions was thus complete. Lord Tomas gave a quick, clear signal to the grooms, who immediately took charge of the horses and carriage and headed towards the stables. He invited the ladies and their escort to enter the keep, going in front of them with Father Henriot and Lady Beathag. They proceeded through the vaulted corridor without stopping to greet the waiting servants. They were now making their way in silence along the passageway that led to the entrance hall. It was dark and damp.

I looked up at the blackened stone walls and ceilings. *What a gloomy interior!* I thought. Lennox was walking by my side, looking composed, his right arm brushing lightly against my shoulder, his left hand resting discreetly on the pommel of his sword. I could feel he was tense, on his guard. What is going on? I said to myself. I felt slightly uneasy. I should have spoken to my hosts, who were walking in front of me, but I could not find anything to say. Besides, they had their backs to me, and they seemed in a hurry to get me to wherever they were taking me. No doubt, to meet the masters of Mallaig. I was disappointed by their absence in the courtyard. It seemed to me that it showed a serious lack of the most basic of good manners. Maybe they were out, or busy, or suffered from some disability. That was what I was in the middle of thinking when we crossed a huge entrance hall and came to the great hall itself. An impressive, beautifully sculptured stone fireplace, deeper than any I had ever seen before, occupied the far end of the large room and gave off a welcome heat that hit us as soon as we entered. There were no straw mats on the stone floor, which meant there were large, dark, wet patches here and there. Two of the walls were decorated with frayed tapestries. The blackened wooden ceiling had at one time, perhaps, been painted a light colour, but because of its height, it cast a deep shadow on the whole room. In contrast, the windows were of generous proportion. Coloured stained glass panes—real luxury—decorated the windows on the south side of the room. To me, that seemed surprising in a dwelling so far from any town. I recalled the meeting with the master glazier, and his disturbing remarks about the castle's inhabitants came rushing back to my mind.

Lord Tomas had turned towards me and, unaware of the significance of the frown on my ever-watchful lieutenant's face, he firmly took my arm and led me to the fireplace in front of which several armchairs were lined up. It was then I noticed a man who could only be old Lord MacNeil. He rose to his feet as I approached him. Under his dark green hat, of the same velvet as his long, embroidered cloak, I could make out a full head of white, still remarkably thick hair. He was of medium height, and he looked drawn. Was it fatigue, pain, or simply old age?

Letting go of my arm, Lord Tomas immediately introduced me, 'Uncle, this is Gunelle Keith, daughter of Nathaniel Keith, brother of the king's Marshall, William Keith, and brother-in-law of John Carmichael, Bishop of Orléans. She is accompanied by her servants, who are delighted to accept your kind hospitality.'

'Welcome to the castle, Lady Gunelle,' he said very simply, taking hold of my hands to interrupt the curtsey I was about to make. 'We have been impatiently awaiting you, you and the members of your family.' He looked around the room then added, 'We are sorry to see they were unable to accompany you. The roads through the mountains are not yet blocked, but they can be bad at the beginning of winter. Did you have a good trip? No mishaps on the way?'

'Everything went admirably well, thank you, my lord,' I replied. 'My father sends his regards, as does my whole family. He can rarely get away in November, for several shipments pass through Aberdeen before winter. So, it was agreed that my entire family would remain at Crathes.'

He accepted this explanation without seeming too concerned. He pointed to an armchair and sank back into his. He listed the things at the disposal of my servants: lodgings, food, facilities for as long as they chose to stay at Mallaig. I could not take my eyes off his stern face. His features were regular, his jaw square, his eyes very blue, and his thick eyebrows cast a shadow over his harsh expression when he bowed his head. He spoke Scots with the same accent as Father Henriot and Lord Tomas, but his words were more carefully chosen and refined. The skin of his gnarled hands, which rested on his knees, was almost transparent and covered with calluses, his fingers shrivelled up. He continuously slowly opened and closed them with some difficulty. Baltair MacNeil was older than I had imagined.

There was, of course, a question I was dying to ask: *But where is the son?* I had discreetly scanned the hall, and there was no man who could have been him. My servants had sat down on a bench and were conversing quietly. Lady Beathag and Father Henriot had left the room. Lord Baltair had stopped speaking and was calmly staring at me.

Feeling uneasy, I let slip, 'My lord, is your son not at home at the moment? I was not introduced to him in the courtyard a little while ago.'

'My son is not at the castle, but we are expecting him. He will join us very soon... for supper, which will be in one hour, if that suits you,' he answered in a voice that betrayed a certain irritation.

That was surprising, to say the least. Lord Baltair showed no desire to justify his son's absence, yet he confirmed that our party was indeed expected that day. I stood to my feet, indicating that I would like to go to the rooms designated for me and my servants. He agreed and called his housekeeper to show us upstairs. She was a kindly-looking woman by the name of Anna. As I left the room, I walked past Lennox and caught his look of anger. I smiled to reassure him. Of course, it had been a very cold welcome for the future chatelaine of Mallaig, but neither he nor I could do anything about it.

'Everything is fine, Lennox,' I whispered, to which he replied with a less-than-convincing nod of the head.

We climbed the two floors of the keep by means of particularly steep stairs. The bedroom was at the far end of the east wing, forming an angle tower. It was remarkably well lit. At this level, two tall gothic windows fitted with plain glass let in a soft light. Three large tapestries hung on the west and north walls, and an alcove dug out of the back wall contained an oak bathtub. The floor was completely covered with woven rugs. In the middle of the room stood an imposing bed draped with heavy damask curtains. Our trunks had been left beside two other beds placed at an angle in the corner opposite the door. It was a really elegant room. I could see that Vivian and Nellie shared my appreciation of our quarters. Later I was to learn that it was the late Lady Isla's room.

The housekeeper checked that there was water in the pitchers and in the basins, which were heating up in front of the hearth for the bath. On a low table was a pile of several neatly folded, white towels, a lovely pewter tray with some apples, a carafe and goblet, and some dried thistles in a dish. Everything had been provided to greet exhausted and worn-out travellers, as we were. I felt the tension in my neck and back ease: For the first time since my arrival at Mallaig Castle, I could breathe freely. This foresight on the part of the housekeeper showed a courtesy and thoughtfulness, which were, indeed, particularly welcome. I was happy and relieved to note that Anna knew her job. We had not understood a word she had said to us. She spoke Gaelic, as, no doubt, all of the castle domestic staff did. None of the three of us spoke or understood this language of the Highlands. Of our party, Lieutenant Lennox was perhaps the only one who could.

As soon as Anna had finished her duties, she left the room, closing the door behind her. Heaving a sigh of relief, we fell as one onto our beds. We burst out laughing. We had reached our destination and had a whole hour just to be our old selves again. By the time someone came to take us to supper, darkness had completely fallen on the castle. The passage walls cast heavy shadows that the golden yellow flames of the candles could not soften. We entered the great hall, where a mouth-watering smell of meat filled the air. A good-sized table had been laid. Making a quick count of the number of places set and the number of guests, I realised that Nellie and Vivian would not be joining us. They, too, realised this, and we parted company without a word. Of our party, only Lennox would join me for my first supper at Mallaig. He was standing waiting, motionless and tense, a little back from the fire. The other guests were waiting for me in silence.

Standing near the table was Lord Baltair, who, as soon as I arrived, held out his hand and signalled for me to come forward and take the seat in the middle. Opposite an empty place on my right sat Father Henriot. Lord Tomas was right across from me, and, next to him, a tall, austere-looking man, dressed all in black, who was introduced as Guilbert Saxon, the family secretary. The person opposite him was Lennox, looking inscrutable and determined, and then there was another empty place at the far end of the table. *Lady Beathag's or the MacNeil son?* I wondered. They had not yet arrived, and while we waited, I was able to examine the table at leisure. It was covered with an impeccable, white tablecloth; flowers, whose name I did not know, floated in a bowl of scented water; in the centre were plates full of hazelnuts and thick slices of bread. Once again, I noted a certain elegance, which—I could not say why—seemed so incongruous in these parts.

Nellie and Vivian had sat down on the benches by the entrance. I looked in their direction when I heard a ripple of laughter that preceded the appearance of Lady Beathag and a servant, who left her to join us on her own. Beside me, I heard Lord MacNeil pass some bitter-sounding remark in Gaelic. Then turning to me, he whispered an apology which I quickly accepted. I immediately concluded that Gaelic was the first language spoken by everyone at Mallaig Castle, including the MacNeil clan chief.

With a fixed smile in my direction, Lady Beathag sat down opposite Lennox and gave him a puzzling look. Lord Baltair immediately ordered his servants to begin serving the meal. I gave a start and could not help staring at the empty place on my right. So, we were about to begin this meal of welcome without the son being present. However inconceivable it might seem, I soon realised that Iain MacNeil had not yet returned to the castle. Lord Baltair kept the conversation going and systematically avoided the subject. throughout the entire meal. He was visibly upset, and no one dared to broach the subject for fear of provoking his anger. I began to shudder with dread. In the space of one hour, this old man had become a tough clan chief. During the entire meal, not one word of Gaelic was spoken, even between the people of Mallaig. Obviously, an order had been given to that effect. Since Lady Beathag neither said a word nor listened to any conversation, I concluded that she did not speak Scots.

We were served beef and mutton, boiled vegetables, and quince pastry. Mead and beer flowed freely, and it was Lord Tomas who made sure that my cup was never empty. I was starving and did the meal justice, putting out of my mind the unease the son's absence

32

stirred in me. Lord Baltair was polite enough to enquire at great length about my family, life in Aberdeen, and my impressions of the Grampians, the MacNeils' newly acquired lands, which I had crossed during our journey. He also addressed Lennox with great courtesy. However, the atmosphere remained tense until the end of the meal. Baltair MacNeil behaved as the perfect host. Furious, but perfect.

After supper, the people of my party re-joined us, and I was relieved to have my servants by my side again. Then, in the space of a few minutes, the great hall was filled by a continuous stream of the Mallaig residents, some of whom were introduced to me. Knights, guards, servants, various tradesmen who worked within the castle walls, their wives and children of all ages mingled together in merry mayhem. The noise soon became deafening. I noticed among all these people a predominance of redheads: coppery red. The women wore plain coloured dresses, but the style suggested neither elegance nor wealth. All the Mallaig men had beards, except Lord MacNeil, his secretary, Tomas, and the priest. From time to time, I surprised folk looking curiously at me and heard coarse laughter ringing out on all sides. My ears were buzzing with the Gaelic language, and I was beginning to feel my head spinning. Two men, each looking very concerned, didn't take their eyes off me: Lieutenant Lennox and Lord Tomas. Near the door, Lady Beathag was surrounded by a particularly lively group of admirers. The priest and the secretary had isolated themselves in a corner and were deep in conversation. Anna, the housekeeper, looking distraught, was hovering around her master's armchair. I would have liked to congratulate her on the meal, but I was too far from her and could not easily get away. Soon, I could not hide signs of tiredness. Fortunately, Lord Baltair retired early, content just to greet me with a nod of the head. With a sigh of relief, I returned his nod. I was going to be able to go back to my room. I quickly went round and wished my own folk and my hosts good night. When I finally left the room with my servants, Iain MacNeil had not shown up. He did not come home all night. Neither that night nor the two following nights.

Chapter Two
The Meeting

That first day, Father Henriot had not really been surprised to see Lady Gunelle and her servants at the morning service in the chapel nor, indeed, for that matter, the men of her escort. In fact, the evening before, each one of them had impressed him by the dignified way they had behaved. The sobriety and nobility they displayed contrasted with the excesses and coarseness of Mallaig's inhabitants and, particularly, the lords. Without question, these were honourable and pious Christians who faithfully served their God. On the other hand, the deep grasp of Latin Lady Gunelle had shown during their conversation after the service had surprised him and made him a little uneasy.

She had quite simply come to have a chat with him and find out about his ministry in Mallaig, the schooling of the village children, and the medical provision in the area. The priest did not often speak Scots, and as he looked for his words, Lady Gunelle had quite naturally slipped into Latin. The conversation had immediately flowed. Despite himself, he was fascinated by the young lady; her confidence, her bearing, and the intelligence displayed by her questions. The priest had also been impressed by the great interest she showed in the MacNeil book collection. Since the deaths of Lord Alasdair and Lady Isla, no one at the castle opened a book anymore. He felt rather ashamed of that in front of such an apparently well-educated person. The chapel library was sparse, for most of the books had been taken to Lord Alasdair's room, which was now only open on rare occasions. But one such occasion was about to present itself; Lady Gunelle had expressed a wish to see the collection.

So it was that the good father found himself given the task of leading the young woman up the floors of the keep to the elder son's bedroom and giving her a tour of the premises on the way. He preceded the response to every question the young woman asked with a shrug of the shoulders to which Lady Gunelle, who was totally engrossed in her visit, paid no attention. He spent a good part of the morning with her until it was time for him to return to the village for his next service, and then Lord Tomas took over.

Lord Tomas, too, felt uncomfortable in the young lady's company, but his discomfort had an altogether different origin. He liked her and had done so since the first moments of their meeting in the courtyard. Although he was the same age, he felt rising inside him what seemed to be almost a need to protect her. He was captivated by her words, her expressions, and her deportment. He dreaded finding himself alone with her, but fortunately, Lieutenant Lennox accompanied them for the remainder of the visit, which consisted mainly of the ramparts. Lady Gunelle's two servants joined the group, and their incessant chatter quickly filled the silences which invariably arose.

The icy wind gusted through the ladies' skirts and made walking difficult. With one hand, frozen stiff from the cold, they tightly held the hood of their cloaks around their necks. By common consent and in keeping with Lord Baltair's wishes, none of the party mentioned Lord Iain. The sky was low, but shafts of sunlight broke through to cast yellow bands of light across the moor. From each crenel of the parapet, you could clearly make out the herds of cattle and blackface sheep, which were foraging for food while trying to avoid the bogs around the castle. The entire west side of the edifice was encircled by a double wall.

From the summit, a fast-flowing torrent now ran with the pleasant sound of a stream between the rocks of the moat separating the two walls. It escaped through a grating built into the south wall and fell as a veritable waterfall into the sea which was crashing against the rocks below. The rocks, mainly gneiss and schist, formed the promontory on which the castle stood. The spray gently splashed the faces of the visitors as they moved closer to admire the panoramic view. It was when they arrived at this viewpoint that they discovered the village of Mallaig—a group of thatched houses nestled beside a little harbour.

'This is Mallaig, my lady,' explained Tomas. 'The village has thirty-five homes, two fishing boats, one for whaling, a salting, a tannery, and salterns. This year they produced more than five hundred pounds of salt, but they are only worked in the summer. Along with beef, salt is Mallaig's principal export. However, it is also the reason for a lot of the damage our enemies inflict on us. We have to deploy a group of several men to guard the harbour and the salt marshes all year round to protect our stocks.'

'I can well imagine, Lord Tomas,' replied Gunelle. 'In Aberdeen, my father has to arrange special surveillance for the cargoes of salt which pass through on the ships. It is a commodity worth its weight in gold, and therefore a great temptation for pirates.'

Tomas would have liked to ask Lady Gunelle a lot of questions about the commerce in Aberdeen and the ships which dropped anchor in that important Scottish port. Although he had studied in Edinburgh and was better acquainted with the commercial trade with the south of the country, he had a keen interest in the trade routes which crossed the North Sea to Denmark, Germany, and Holland. In his capacity as guide he contented himself, however, with pointing out the particularities of Mallaig, its trades, and its problems. He decided not to bring the conversation round to Aberdeen.

Having visited the ramparts, the party returned to the courtyard, where Tomas caught Gunelle making a quick curtsey in the direction of one of the towers. He immediately understood why: a little red-haired girl who had scampered off as soon as she saw the young lady's gesture.

'So, who is that timid little person hiding over there?' Gunelle asked the surprised Tomas. 'She has been watching and following our party for nearly an hour. I would like to get to know her.'

'Ah, that is little Ceit,' replied Tomas, rather hesitantly, noticing the child's game for the first time. 'She is a little orphan whom Lady Isla took under her care when she was still a baby. She is a little unsociable and does not speak. We think she is unable to speak despite what Anna, who is bringing her up at the castle, has to say about it. She maintains she can talk.'

The explanation left the young lady puzzled. As for her two servants, they were smiling and nudging each other, delighted to have witnessed an amusing incident in the middle of a tiresome visit in the strong wind. Lord Tomas quickly led the party back indoors.

As she had done earlier with Father Henriot, Lady Gunelle had thrown herself into Lord Tomas's guided tour, asking him all kinds of questions and thereby making this first full day at the castle an experience rich in information for all her party. Her hosts were delighted by the lively interest she showed in castle life. In the evening, she was seen deep in conversation with her servants and sharing some hours of relaxation in the great hall. All that day, Gunelle Keith had appeared calm and attentive to everyone, showing no sign of annoyance at the non-appearance of the MacNeil son. It did not seem to worry her. On the other hand, Lieutenant Lennox did not appear to share her calmness on the matter.

Lady Gunelle took all her meals with her servants, Lieutenant Lennox, and her guards. Lord Tomas sat at their table, but he was the only representative from Mallaig. In fact, old Lord MacNeil had made it known after the morning service that he was not well enough to come down from his room. So, he had charged Anna to entrust his nephew Tomas with the task of looking after the Nathaniel Keith party.

On the floor above, Baltair MacNeil, leaning on his walking stick for support, paced up and down his bedroom. He slowed down when he passed in front of the fire so as to catch some of its heat in the folds of his long blue tunic. He had slept badly the night before and so had spent the whole day in bed. In fact, it seemed as if he had not slept a wink the whole night. He was choking with rage. As often happened, his rage had manifested itself in real difficulty in breathing. He had coughed and spluttered so much and so strongly that in the morning, he was literally exhausted, worn out, and shattered. He did not want to see anyone all day—neither his secretary, nor the priest, nor even his doctor who called daily at the castle. He would only have Anna at his bedside. There was no need for conversation between the two of them. She knew how to look after him well, and most important of all, she respected his need to be left alone.

As night fell at the end of Nathaniel Keith's daughter's first day in his home and with still no sign of his son's return, he asked to see her. She appeared before him wearing a fitted dark red dress. Its broad sleeves hung down by her narrow hips. She was wearing a pure white touret,[1] and the ribbon tied under her chin defined the perfect oval shape of her face. He found her at the same time slight and plain, although her style of dress displayed a certain graciousness. With his daughter-in-law, Beathag and, indeed, his late wife, he had been accustomed to seeing more flamboyant finery. They cultivated a strong predilection for jewellery, hennins,[2] intricate gold threaded embroidery and damask velvets. With Gunelle Keith, you thought you were in the presence of a convent girl. He found a certain charm in this youthful austerity. It appealed to him. He greeted her with a great deal of gentleness and pointed to the armchair beside his in front of the fire. With signs of concern in her voice, she immediately inquired about his health.

'I am as well as I can be in the circumstances, thank you, my lady,' he replied. 'I do not intend to keep you long, but I would like to speak to you.' A fit of coughing interrupted him. The young lady waited patiently for him to continue.

'First, tell me, how was your first day? Did my nephew Tomas carry out his duties as your guide well?'

'Really, my lord, we could not have had anyone more enthusiastic to show us around.' replied Gunelle. 'He did a good job of informing us about the village, so much so that I would like to visit it tomorrow if the temperature allows and the opportunity arises, of course... Your nephew loves this area, it would appear.'

---

[1] Woman's veil covering the forehead.

[2] Cone-shaped or cylindrical headdress for women.

'The truth is that he is passionate about Mallaig. He is like a son here in the castle. My young brother Aonghus, his father, died in '21 on French soil at Baugé, fighting the English alongside the Regent's son, Robert d'Albany. Tomas was studying in Edinburgh at the time with the view to becoming a knight here, at Mallaig. He has been living with us for two years now and will be knighted in the spring. He has chosen Iain as his master at arms and parrain[3].'

Lord Baltair suddenly stopped speaking, his face tense with rage. He would have liked to avoid any mention of his son. Lady Gunelle guessed as much right away, for she had the presence of mind to change the subject.

'I also had the benefit of another excellent guide in the person of Father Henriot. He was very willing to show me the books you have in the castle. You possess some magnificent ones, my lord. The illuminations of some of them are of rare quality. I am thinking particularly of the work on Greek mythology which I leafed through. I would like to take another look at the library if you have no objection to giving me access to it.'

'No objection at all, my lady. Besides, it is hardly my library. In its time, it was my wife's and our son Alasdair's, the only erudite people in this house. They died five years ago, as you no doubt know. Father Henriot is a good man and he knows the theological books well, but his scholarship does not go much beyond that. The bishops are not in the habit of sending their most well-educated priests to the Highlands. In their eyes, we still give the impression of being savages in many respects…'

---

[3] A Knight of rank enough to train and dub a new knight: sponsor.

Seeing the young lady give a start at this assertion, he corrected himself immediately. 'As far as Europe is concerned, the north of Scotland, my lady, is a distant and wild land, and is barely aware that people live here. But it is the same for the Lowlanders, especially those gentlemen from Stirling, Glasgow, and Edinburgh, who no more know the difference between a broch[4] and a tower than between a claymore and a rapier. As for our monarchs, they have hardly ever come to the Highlands and rarely send their top functionaries. Besides, what would they come here to do? We look after our own affairs… our way, the northern way. A little hasty occasionally, but oh how effective! All the Highland clans agree on that. That is at least one vision we have in common!'

The old man was caught up in his own game. He had sent for Gunelle Keith to come and see him out of duty and politeness, but his conversation with the young lady had stimulated him. Rediscovering his former drive, he vigorously broached political topics he had long since given up discussing. He explained, without even stopping for breath, everything Gunelle Keith wanted to know about his clan's position with respect to the other clans, the battles he had fought and the family's relationship with King James. He kept gesturing with his hands, he raised his eyebrows, and his eyes were sparkling. As a result, when Lady Gunelle retired for the night, thanks to his meeting with her, Baltair MacNeil had once again become the vigorous clan chief. He slept soundly that night.

---

[4] Iron-Age Scottish Stone Tower with hollow double-skinned walls

What an astonishing man, I said to myself as I came out of that strange meeting. *One minute a sick old man, the next the great clan chief very much in control*. I did not know what to think of him. When he had sent for me, I thought for a moment that he was going to broach the subject of the wedding. I would obviously have felt a certain amount of embarrassment. After our conversation, I was at pains to see his real objective. In fact, in the end, it did not really matter. It had been another opportunity to learn about the MacNeil family, and I had to admit it had satisfied my burgeoning curiosity.

Closing Lord Baltair's bedroom door behind me, I found myself in the total silence of the corridor. Not a sound from any of the rooms reached my ears which were straining to listen. Not having much idea of which direction to take to reach my bedroom, I advanced with caution. Leaving the halo of light thrown by the two torches hanging on either side of the door, I was plunged into almost total darkness. When I had left my room, I had taken neither torch nor candle with me. I stopped. I was shaking like a leaf. Suddenly I heard footsteps coming from the opposite direction. I turned on my heels and saw a circle of light grow bigger on the angled wall of the corridor. The footsteps, brisk and agitated, were getting closer. That is the sound of a knight's footsteps. I immediately thought. My throat tightened, and I gulped, stupidly rooted to the spot. As soon as he turned the corner, I recognised him.

'Lennox!' I sighed with relief.

'My lady, he said, hurrying to meet me. What a long time Lord MacNeil kept you.'

I gratefully grabbed his arm. Of course, what else could I have expected from this unfailingly vigilant man? He had probably followed me up from the great hall and spent our entire meeting standing in the nearest corner he could find. When he heard the

43

bedroom door closing, he had started to run. Showing complete disregard for any semblance of discretion, he questioned me as he led me firmly towards my room.   'What did his lordship say about his son's absence?'

I knew that this question preoccupied him more than any other. His mission, as far as I was concerned, would only end on my wedding day. The fact of the matter was that the bridegroom was not in the castle.

'He didn't speak to me about it,' I said. 'I do not think there is any question of it being mentioned. Do they even know where Iain MacNeil is at this moment?'

Lennox suppressed an oath. He declared that he found the conduct of their lordships MacNeil totally unacceptable and considered it an affront to the Keith family.

'What!' I exclaimed. 'Have they not sent men to find him? If he has not come home, it is because he has been delayed somewhere because of some problem or other. Come now, Lennox, Lord MacNeil has surely sent a guard to fetch him. If he is not here, it is because they have not found him yet, that is all.'

The longer I continued my reasoning, the more sullen Lennox became. I looked at him out of the corner of my eye and realised he knew more than I did on the matter. I urged him, therefore, to tell me everything. We had reached the wing where I was staying. He slowed down, glancing briefly at the various closed doors we passed, looking for a place away from listening ears. Not seeing any, he confided what he knew in a low whisper tinged with notes of barely stifled anger.

'One thing is sure, my lady, wherever he is, Iain MacNeil is not in danger. The morning of our arrival, he went off on his own, apparently with no intention other than to stravaig his property. His father probably knows where to find him, but he will not send anyone. Why, my lady? Because the MacNeil son does not want to come back to the castle. There, you have it. Since he is not the kind of man you bring home by force, you will have to await his good pleasure.'

I was dumbfounded. I knew that Lennox's information, probably gleaned from the knights of the castle bodyguard, had to be true. After all, it was his duty to keep himself informed, was it not?

But why the devil would Iain MacNeil flee from his own castle? I asked myself. The answer was simple, and it suddenly came to me in a blinding flash: Iain MacNeil was not fleeing from his castle; he was fleeing me! I took a deep breath; my heart was pounding. *That is all it can be...*

We had arrived at my bedroom door. I turned towards my companion and looked him straight in the eye. I thanked him for his kind attention and wished him good night in a voice which I tried to keep calm. I must not reveal any hint of anxiety to my people. That was what it would take for things to go well at Mallaig. And that was very much the way I wanted it. Lennox bowed his head slowly and returned my goodnight before heading, candle in hand, towards his own quarters, his footsteps now more measured. When he had disappeared round the corner, and I could no longer hear his footsteps in the darkness, I entered my room. My heart had started beating regularly again. Nellie and Vivian rushed into my arms, twenty questions on their lips, their words peppered with nervous laughter. They, too, had been concerned about my conversation with Lord MacNeil. However, I did not feel like sharing my latest impressions with them. I reassured them as best I could, and they were happy with that.

That night I did not experience the rest of the night before. When I was alone in the darkness and the freshness of my sheets, a thousand thoughts assailed me. A thousand doubts tormented me. I ended up falling asleep with Lennox's puzzling words going around in my head: *'We will have to await his good pleasure.'*

The next day, at the end of the morning service, Lord Tomas approached me with deference and offered to go for a ride with me to the village. I could not help smiling: Lord Baltair, who did not overlook a thing, had given his nephew his orders for the day.

'Unfortunately, I am not a very accomplished horsewoman,' I replied. 'But if we could go on foot, that would please me very much. That way, my servants could go with us. I am sure they would be delighted.' Seeing his look of surprise, I added, 'I have always had a fear of horses, and my father did not insist that I learn to ride as a child. As I spent the past four years in a convent, I have had little contact with the noble beasts.'

His radiant smile which revealed his strong white teeth immediately touched my heart. From that moment, I felt a great deal of affection for him. I considered him to be a sensitive and very good person. In this wild Highland world, to admit one's incompetence as a rider was the equivalent of admitting to having a handicap, if not even an infirmity. I had no doubt about that. In these parts, even the women must be excellent riders. I do not know why, but at that moment, I got the impression that Tomas did not feel as comfortable in the saddle as most of the other knights. A thought came to me... just as his cousin and parrain, he must be a real expert when it came to horsemanship. *Is someone ever going to speak to me about Iain MacNeil?* I thought anxiously.

As soon as our little party of Nellie, Vivian, Lennox, our young guard, Nial, Tomas, two of the MacNeil guards, and I left the castle by the draw bridge, I breathed in as much as I could of the invigorating air. It was a mixture of the smells of the moor, forest, and sea. I was strangely happy to leave the castle. My shoulders were relaxed, my cape seemed lighter, the winter wind was less sharp on my face, and my eyes were dazzled by the first sunlight for almost a week. The prospect of this walk to the village literally filled me with joy. So it was that I realised just how heavily the atmosphere in the castle had weighed on me. While circling the castle to go down to the harbour, it was with a certain apprehension that I noticed the height of its walls. Over generations of MacNeils, rows upon rows of stones had been built up around what had probably originally been a simple tower. One thing was for sure: The people of Mallaig were well protected in the event of an invasion or attack. I shook my head as if to rid myself of these dark thoughts and return to my state of happiness of the moment before. Tomas, who was watching me, furtively noticed my gesture, which he undoubtedly interpreted as a sign of impatience, for he reassured me about how long the walk would take. I immediately rediscovered the intelligent and attentive guide of the day before with his countless details or anecdotes inspired by the things or people we saw on the way.

That morning was just the same as the previous afternoon: a wealth of information about life in Mallaig. We had the opportunity to meet some of the people we had seen at our welcome party in the great hall on the evening of our arrival: here, the blacksmith, there, the saddler, or the mason, but also other men, women, and children who lived in the village. The curiosity our group had aroused two days earlier showed no sign of dying down. All the looks cast in our direction, all the time, proved it.

This first examination of the harbour and its houses revealed a poverty that was greater than any I had encountered in France or even in Aberdeen. Despite the winter cold, which had formed a frosty cap on the tops of the shrubs, several villagers were going about almost barefooted and with their clothes in tatters. I saw many toothless mouths and, eyes, which, for the most part, showed signs of fever. However, a quick glance in the direction of the members of our group revealed that I was the only one to pick up on these details. I noticed nothing in their looks that even hinted that the sight disturbed them. So, I refrained from sharing my observations with Tomas, who had started talking about the movement of ships to and from the little port of Mallaig.

Going down the road, I saw a long, thatched cottage built onto the little stone church. It seemed abandoned, and part of its thick thatch had collapsed. I learned it had served as the school before the chatelaine's death. I remembered what the priest had told me the day before about the children's education; he had lost a young teacher and had been unable to replace him. We finally reached the oak pier, thrust out between the wet rocks, where our walk came to an end. In the distance, out on the water, I could see the shiny black heads of the seals going up and down in time with the waves. I turned to look back at the castle. Once again, my heart froze on seeing its granite mass dominating the little village. *This landscape is too vast*, I thought. A falcon flew over the turrets for an instant and then disappeared in the direction of the mountains. I gave a start: Lord Tomas was asking me a question I had not even heard. His blue eyes gazed at me attentively. A wayward lock of hair blew at the whim of the north wind and covered his brow from time to time. He was standing straight, his arms dangling relaxed by his long, lithe body. He was wearing light weapons tucked into a magnificent pale leather belt buckled with a heavy golden clasp. His tight-fitting dark-green tunic moved up and down to the rhythm of his heartbeat. At that moment, I found him handsome. I must have smiled at him, for he looked away in embarrassment.

'Excuse me, Lord Tomas,' I said. 'I do not think I understood your question. Would you be kind enough to repeat it?'

'I have a terrible accent when I speak Scots. I was told that a hundred times in Edinburgh. Pay no attention, I beg you, my lady. I was simply asking if your father's ships have had occasion to drop anchor on this side of Scotland, in the islands, for example.'

'Do you mean Rhum or Skye or both? Either way, my lord, I doubt if our ships have ventured there. I think I am correct in saying that the isles do not have a good reputation. They are the private property of the Clan MacDonald, and honest traders hardly ever venture there.'

'You are perfectly correct, my lady. I see that the clan MacDonald's exploits are known throughout the whole of Scotland. Truth be told, these people are first in line among our many enemies. You see, Mallaig is the last enclave south of Loch Ness, which supports the king. In fact, one wonders why the MacNeils have remained loyal to the monarchy for generations. They were so all the way through the regency and swore an oath of allegiance to James I in April when the English freed him. I imagine the MacNeil sense of loyalty has always won the day over any clan wars. In any case, it paid off this time. We were gifted Cameron land which covered a great deal of the Grampians.'

While I remained silent after these worrying revelations, Lord Tomas was deep in thought all the way back up to the castle with our little group following behind. I was struck by the moderation he showed in his comments. There was no possible comparison with Lord Baltair's fiery speech the day before. *Tomas is gifted with judgement of a rare quality*, I thought. I was eager to know his general opinion of the hill folk, the Highlanders, so I dared to ask the ultimate question which was tormenting me.

'There is something which concerns me, and no doubt my question will seem very childish to you. So, excuse my silliness if it appears so. Lord Tomas, do you consider Highlanders uncouth and barbaric?'

Staring deep in concentration towards the horizon, he did not look at me straight away. I sensed that he would choose his words carefully in answer to my question, thereby demonstrating the seriousness he attributed to it.

'It would be difficult for me to describe as barbaric people to whom I owe what I am and from whom I come. They are uncouth, certainly, for the most part uncultivated, no doubt, but I do not know of a people more energised in the face of trouble, more resilient in the face of the harshness of nature, or more passionate lovers of song, music, and dance. However, they are not given to making great speeches. They speak far more readily with their weapons, and spilled blood is a joke to them. That is the problem with depending on weapons and armour: Highland clans are quite happy to kill one another. The English have begun to realise that it is only a matter of time till they can use that to their advantage.'

His reply did not call for comment. Something told me he was right. The MacNeils' political opinions were at the very least unique: One could neither openly contradict nor ignore them. I looked up at the sky. Large snow clouds were gathering above the mountains. I pulled up my collar. Enjoyment of the walk had completely deserted me. I wanted to return to the castle and continue to wait. To wait 'for his good pleasure.' It was then that I saw three horsemen coming to meet us on the road. As soon as they were close enough, I recognised

Lady Beathag with two of the Mallaig knights. She was wearing a bright orangey-red suit and a large damask hat from which some ringlets of fiery red hair elegantly escaped. The spectacle she presented with her guards, who were dressed in black, was striking. I had not seen her since our first meal, and I had almost forgotten she existed. With a dazzling smile, she greeted the whole company in Gaelic. I thought I noticed a glance in Lennox's direction. Then she turned her horse around and galloped off towards the moor with her guards following some distance behind her. This sudden appearance started our party talking again. In the men, one sensed a certain excitement. It was obvious that Lady Beathag did not leave any of them undisturbed. She only had to appear for a few moments for the sap to rise. Only Lord Tomas seemed not to have been touched by this gift she had. He continued on his way with an indifferent, relaxed, almost offhand air about him. Today's assignment as my guide was coming to an end. In fact, we reached the castle about twenty minutes later.

As on the day before, we had an intimate supper with the folk from Crathes. Tomas did not join us. Neither did Lord Baltair, who had stayed in his room for the second day in a row. In the evening, I caught sight of the man I was told was his doctor, Mister Kenneth MacDuff: extremely tall, about forty, and looking very professional. He stayed almost an hour at the old chief's bedside. Afterwards, I could find no one to give me news of his state of health. Those living in the castle seemed in a hurry to get to bed that night. The wind sweeping the moor came in gusts to shake the shutters and lightly lift the curtains covering them. The cold air from outside entered the rooms wherever possible. The evening was gloomy, and we went up to our quarters early.

It snowed all night, flurries at first, then towards morning light flakes. The three of us were huddled together in my bed for heat and for consolation. Vivian, whom the visit to the village had disgusted, had complained about it for a good part of the evening. Sensible Nellie had really tried to look on the bright side, but it was no use. It was then I began to think that Vivian, a social animal, would not cope with life at Mallaig and that she would want to return to my mother's service at Crathes with Lennox. I sighed. My heart was suddenly overcome by a deep heaviness. I did not want to lose Vivian. I was already sad at the thought that I would miss Lennox when he left my service. From my world in Aberdeen, I would only have my maid Nellie left, and I did not feel ready to make any more sacrifices.

The next day after morning service, I surprised Anna and little Ceit, who were busy making honey biscuits in the kitchen. The child, engrossed in her work and her face covered in flour, had not seen me come in, which gave me the chance to watch her at my leisure. She was a sickly child with a thin face. Her features revealed a slight deformity. At first glance, it was not noticeable, but her eyes, which were very blue, were not at the same height on her face. She had a strong chin which seemed out of place in this little person marked rather by fragility. Nellie, who was following on my heels, made a more obvious entrance. Ceit jumped, dropped the lump of dough she was kneading, and, with the swish of her flour-covered skirt, fled as fast as she could through a little concealed door that led to the wine cellar. The three of us stood dumbfounded. Anna passed a remark in Gaelic. To my great astonishment, Nellie replied with a few words in Gaelic. I turned and stared at her. She shrugged as if to say there was nothing more natural than learning Gaelic in two days. Downcast, I sat down on a stool and listened to the two women as they conversed slowly in Gaelic and helped one another out with exaggerated hand signs as they looked for their words. Their resemblance to each other struck me at that moment. Did all the nurses in the world have that same homely face, those same generous body proportions, and that same self-assured voice, when they reached a respectable age? I would not have known how to prove it, but those two seemed to form a double rampart of protection against the hurts, which, no doubt, my life at Mallaig held in store for me.

I let my gaze wander towards the door leading to the garden. No one had ever taken me there, having no doubt assumed that I would not be interested in its abandoned winter state. All the same, I wanted to explore it and went outside. The snow had almost all melted away. I was first struck by its size; you could just make out about ten paths under the rotting vegetation that carpeted the ground. I counted seven fruit trees that did not seem to have been pruned for years: apple trees, a plum tree, and a sweet chestnut. At the bottom of the garden, a pond which might also be a fishpond, occupied an area bordered by rosebushes. It all seemed a bit out of place in this part of Scotland. The rosebushes, too, had not been looked after for a while. I examined the mounds of frozen earth but could not work out what summer produce could have been grown in them. Nellie and Anna joined me, and I immediately asked Nellie to find out what was planted there. The response came hesitantly. Was Anna looking for her words, or did she simply not know? Gardening had been the late chatelaine's favourite pastime, and no one had been capable of carrying it on in the way she had done it.

The library, the garden, the village school, so many things abandoned since the death of the chatelaine of Mallaig. *How many others would I discover?* The more I discovered about the place, the more I was forming a picture of Isla MacNeil's personality in my mind. This chatelaine had been held in high esteem by her people. She had influenced them greatly with her knowledge and her initiatives. I felt a strong urge to speak to Anna, who, at that moment, was walking along, sadly looking around her. It must have grieved her to recall the memory of her mistress. Her tear-filled eyes bore witness to that, and she was miles away, distractedly wringing her red hands.

A noise from the kitchen made all three of us turn around at the same time to have a look: It was little Ceit who was hiding. She had no doubt noticed Anna through the open door and had wanted to rejoin her, but she had not seen Nellie and me as we were further on in the garden. She must have retreated at the last minute when she saw us there. The two women laughed at the child's game and went in to see her. Before following them inside, I took one last look at the garden in its sorry state. *Yes*, I said to myself, *it must have been a magnificent place at one time, and Isla MacNeil must have been a marvellous chatelaine. Oh, that God would enable me to be equal to the role which awaits me!*

Another day was coming to a close. It was the beginning of Advent. I had attended the evening service without Vivian and Nellie, for I greatly felt the need for quiet contemplation to calm my troubled soul. I took great comfort from the very simple liturgical prayers recited quietly by Father Henriot. So, it was with a more serene spirit that I went to rejoin my servants in my bedroom and get ready for supper. So absorbed in my meditation, I went the wrong way and ended up in Lord Baltair's wing on the floor above mine. A strong smell of wet dog filled the passage. I immediately noticed a large red dog I had never seen before lying outside the old man's closed door. I stopped dead, rigid with fear. The dog had lifted his head and was looking at me. He got up slowly and came towards me. I was paralysed. I would have loved to have fled, but my legs were not doing what I told them. I calmed down and forced myself to take a good look at the beast. His muzzle was long, his ears slightly floppy and with black edges. The long hair on his paws and his tail was dripping wet. There was a gentle look in his very black eyes. He sniffed my hands, then my feet, and, obviously satisfied, he was returning to his position when the sound of a man shouting came from old Lord Baltair's bedroom. A second voice, which I recognised immediately as that of the old lord, replied. The tone with which the two men spoke to each other left absolutely no room for doubt; it was an argument in Gaelic. The dog, too, had stopped dead and was staring at the door. He growled. I was about to take advantage of the opportunity to beat a hasty retreat when suddenly the door opened. A man came out and stopped when he saw me. Of medium height, long hair, a beard which was very dark brown, almost black, broad shoulders shown off by a tight-fitting, soaking-wet tunic, boots, and black leather gaiters: That was my first sight of Iain MacNeil. For it could be no one else but him. The icy-cold shiver which had gone down my back had told me so. His gaze met mine. His eyes, the same blue as Lord Baltair's, were still full of anger. Before I had the time to utter a sound, he had turned around, whistled to the dog, and disappeared with great strides in the opposite direction.

In front of the open door, a pool of water marked the place where the dog had waited for his master. Straining my neck, I saw another left by the master's boots. From the evidence, the two of them had not been back long. From the room, I could hear a fit of coughing, which turned quickly into a sound of choking. I bounded in. Lord Baltair was crouched over in his armchair, breathless, his hands gripping a walking stick. I rushed to him, grabbed him by the shoulders, and made him sit up. He raised his head and recognised me; his eyes were bloodshot, and a trickle of pink saliva ran down onto his chin. He was turning grey. I called anxiously for help in a voice that stuck in my throat. Of course, no one could hear me here. I would have had to shout for that to happen. The stick fell to the floor with a thud. Trembling, Baltair MacNeil grabbed hold of my hands. I felt an extraordinary strength in this gesture of despair. He got his breath back for a few seconds. It was enough to bring him back to life a bit. He sank into the armchair, and I dropped down at his knees, our hands still locked tightly together. I lost all sense of time. Was it twenty minutes or an hour before Anna arrived? I could not have said.

'Everything is all right now.' I sighed on seeing the good old housekeeper arrive. I closed my eyes with relief.

I returned to my empty room and collapsed exhausted onto a chair. Deep within me, feelings of fear, despair, and rebellion were struggling with each other for supremacy. What kind of man could mistreat an old man as ill as Lord Baltair without giving it a thought? What kind of son was he? I was choking with rage. I took a long time to calm down again, and it was with at least a semblance of self-control that I appeared later in the great hall for supper.

Apart from Lord Baltair, the whole family was there. Silence fell when I arrived. I remained hesitantly in the doorway, looking for a friendly look of support. Tomas understood my silent appeal, for he was at my side immediately. On seeing his anxious look, I knew that the difficult task of introducing me to his impossible cousin had fallen on him. I gulped and held out my hand. He took it. His was clammy and cold. I raised my head and met the icy glare of Iain MacNeil, standing in the centre of the room with his arms crossed and scrutinising us as we approached. He had changed into a jet-black doublet worn over a long red linen tunic. His hair had dried in dark patches on his head. Strangely, he had not removed his weapons which were still hanging from his belt. Tomas did not have time to name me, for Lord Iain did it for him. As he pronounced my name, I noticed a note of what sounded like scorn in his serious voice. I stiffened immediately.

'My lord,' I murmured while giving a curtsey which I wanted to be the absolute minimum required.

There was a heavy silence in the hall. The only sound was the crackling of the torches hanging in each corner. Everyone was holding their breath, not wanting to miss a single detail of what would prove to be a real spectacle. Imperturbable, Lord Iain began to walk slowly around me, the only sound, the thud of his boots on the ground. I felt his sharp gaze eye me up and down as he would a broodmare. It was unbearable. My cheeks were on fire. To my stupefaction, he addressed the company in Gaelic as he walked towards them. It would appear he said something amusing, for several of them burst out laughing. I saw Tomas clench his fists. He looked tense. He was not laughing. Lennox, whom I noticed standing close by, looked outraged. I realised that Lord Iain was making a less-than-flattering comment about me. It was too much.

Trembling with rage, I shouted at him, 'Would you not speak in Scots, my lord? I am not fortunate enough to understand what you are saying, and it appears to be amusing.'

On hearing me speak, the MacNeil son turned slowly towards me, one eyebrow raised. His whole demeanour oozed self-importance. Without taking his eyes off me, he nodded in Tomas's direction and waited. I was shocked: Was it possible that the MacNeil son neither spoke nor understood Scots? Apparently, yes, for Tomas caught my eye and a half-smile formed on his lips. In a voice which was strangely composed, he uttered a sentence in Gaelic to his cousin. Was this sentence the translation of what I had just said? It appeared so. Laughter broke out. The look Lord Iain gave me hardened. The laughter died down. I understood that this time, they were laughing at him. I turned towards Lennox, my eyes pleading with him. I just had to understand what was being said. He was just waiting for a sign from me to intervene, and with two strides, he came and stood behind me and quietly translated Tomas's words.

'Lord Tomas said, "How happy I am to finally meet you, my lord. I am just love   bearded noblemen who know how to keep people waiting for them."'

Dumbfounded, I quickly turned towards my interpreter. I saw a wicked glint shining in his eyes. When I caught Tomas's eye, the same expression lit up on his face.

'They are making fun of the young lord!' I said, bursting out laughing. Iain MacNeil was not a man to lose face. Like the crack of a whip, he fired what seemed to me to be an oath into the stillness of the atmosphere. Then, with a threatening glance at Tomas, he came quickly towards me and shouted Lennox's name as he threw him an icy look over my shoulder. I trembled. His breath stank of whisky. Behind me, my lieutenant braced himself. Then, looking down at me, his face hard and impassive, Iain MacNeil gave me a stinging reply. He looked in Lennox's direction and repeated his name. He had just retaken control of the situation and was clearly indicating who would be the intermediaries in the discussion. I could not take my eyes off his tense face with its hard features.

Lennox obeyed and said in a muffled voice, 'Lord MacNeil says, "For my part, I am not mad about ladies who learn Gaelic by eavesdropping at doors."'

That was like a knife going right through me. To my own surprise, I heard myself replying in a tone of voice that bordered on insolence.

'My lord, if you are referring to our meeting a short time ago, I would have you know that I was not eavesdropping, I was introducing myself to the canine language in the company of your very obliging setter. When it comes to attractiveness, I prefer the canine language to Gaelic.'

I had hardly finished when peals of laughter burst out from Tomas, the priest, the secretary, and my servants—in short, all those who understood Scots. I turned to look at Lennox to invite him to translate, and, imitating Lord Iain, I accompanied my gesture with a resounding, 'Lennox!'

Meanwhile, Iain MacNeil was seething. I saw him clench his fists and flex his neck and shoulder muscles. Behind me, Lennox was performing his task in Gaelic in a steady monotone, and the end of his reply was received with a thunderous outburst of hearty laughter: By the looks of it, more of the people in the audience spoke that language. I did not wait for the MacNeil son's reaction before rejoining the nearest group, and, all a tremble, I began to greet each one courteously. Here and there, I noticed admiring glances being thrown in my direction. They were very much enjoying this long-awaited meeting, although it was already three days into Advent.

The supper which followed very much resembled a tournament where the opposing teams each occupied one half of the arena. I had taken my place at one end of the table with the 'Scots,' in other words, the priest with his constant shrugging of the shoulders, Saxton the secretary, a light of self-interest in his eyes, a beaming Tomas; an outraged Lennox, our three bodyguards, and my two servants all in a state of excitement. Lord Iain sat down at the other end with his knights and Lady Beathag and deliberately faced me. We carefully avoided looking at one another, conscious of the fire which was smouldering in the situation. Conversations began, ended, and died in an atmosphere that was generally subdued.

At one point, I noticed little Ceit with her arms around the setter's neck as she whispered secrets in his ear. I noticed her lips were moving: Was she really talking? My annoyance had greatly sharpened my attention to detail. I was tense all the way through the meal, my senses on the alert, taking in a huge number of insignificant details. Tomas gave me smiles of encouragement, but to no avail; I could not settle. The end of the meal was rushed; I did not know why. The MacNeil son and his followers all rose from the table and noisily left the room. Some knights were staggering, and pouting Lady Beathag was clinging to her brother-in-law's arm. She had obviously missed him a lot. After their departure, a heavy silence fell over the room like a stone falling to the bottom of a well. The storm was over. I looked around the table. Everyone was looking at me in alarm. Unable to contain myself any longer, I started sobbing.

Chapter Three
The Wedding

The day after her meeting with Lord Iain, Lady Gunelle shut herself away in her bedroom. She did not go down to the service, and she asked her servants to leave her on her own. This meant Nellie spent a good part of the day with Anna, in whom she found a real friend. Anna did not approve of her young master's unspeakably bad behaviour and showed a great deal of sympathy for Nellie's young mistress, scorned by the way she had been treated. She slipped little treats onto the trays she had taken up to her at mealtimes. The two nurses were dismayed and concerned when they saw these were returned, untouched.

As for Lennox, he was outraged at Iain MacNeil's complete lack of respect and several times was almost on the point of demanding an audience with the father to seek an explanation of his son's behaviour. But, to do this would have gone beyond the remit of the task Nathaniel Keith had entrusted to him and would have put Keith's daughter in a delicate position. Was the clan MacNeil chief even up to dealing with the situation? Lennox had to force himself not to intervene without receiving the order to do so. He realised that the order could only come from Lady Gunelle herself. So, despite what Nellie had told him about their mistress's wish to be left alone, he resolutely decided to keep watch all day in the hope that she would ask him to do it.

It was Guilbert Saxton who had the delicate task of reporting the he entered the room as Doctor MacDuff was leaving. The two retainers greeted one events of that gruelling evening to Lord Baltair. His master had asked to see him for that purpose, and another coldly, and each went on his way. Saxton had little time for the doctor, and the doctor held the secretary's position in contempt. Knowing that the symptoms would be deliberately exaggerated, Saxton did not enquire about the chief's state of health that day, the day after the crisis. Baltair MacNeil's doctor was as proud of his knowledge as of his ignorance, which, in fact, were evenly matched. When Saxton stood in front of his master, however, he was annoyed that he had not inquired about his master's health. Baltair MacNeil looked pale. He was wheezing, and his hands trembled constantly. He was in bed, propped up with pillows. It was the first time the clan chief had received him in bed. Anna, sitting by his bed, a cloth in her hands and a basin of cold water on her knees, rolled her eyes in dismay.

On the arrival of his secretary, Lord Baltair turned his head towards his housekeeper and asked her, in a faint voice, to leave them, which she did reluctantly. Then, addressing Saxton, he continued slowly, carefully articulating each of his words.

'Please forgive me, Saxton, for receiving you like this, but I must know exactly what happened yesterday. I want to hear it from you, for I consider your reports to be accurate. There is no point in me getting out of bed to hear you. I beg you to take no notice of my weariness. And finally, do not try to be gentle with me by hiding from me things of which I should not be ignorant.'

Saxton tried to strike a balanced note in the account he was being asked to give. His master had complete confidence in him, and he was not going to disappoint him at such a crucial moment for the MacNeil family. So, he gave a concise account of what was, as far as he knew, one of the worst moments Mallaig Castle had experienced. His old master had closed his eyes, so Saxton did not know if he was sleeping or simply listening. When he finished, he just about heard Baltair MacNeil's murmur of thanks. He waited a few seconds to receive his instructions, but his master said nothing. He left the room exhausted.

While Saxton was giving his account of events to the father upstairs, Doctor MacDuff was giving his to the son in the study on the ground floor. Iain MacNeil did not hold the doctor in high regard either but that morning, he was paying attention to what he said. That was because Anna had told him about the turn his father had had before supper the evening before. He had been very shocked; he had no idea his father was so ill. In fact, he had seen so little of him these past months that the deterioration of the old chief's health came as news to him. The doctor's prognosis was alarming, but how much faith could he put in it? However, Anna's concern about his father's condition undeniably backed up MacDuff's report.

He quickly dismissed the doctor, and when alone, he nervously paced up and down the room where there was no fire. He felt rising within him something resembling a sense of guilt. There he was, no sooner back at the castle than he was in the middle of a row with his father. The wrath the old chief had displayed, his look of hatred, the fixed grin that distorted his marked face, the hard and hurtful words he had uttered, everything accused him. Especially the reproaches, always the same ones, but which seemed to become harder each time. The doctor had confirmed that Baltair MacNeil did not have long to live. Iain wondered if he would be given one last chance to explain himself, man to man, to his father, before the latter joined his mother and brother in the hereafter. The way things were going, he had serious doubts. His stomach was in knots, and for a few moments, he had difficulty breathing.

During the week following the meeting of the MacNeil son with the Keith daughter, Mallaig Castle was astonishingly quiet. Lord Baltair, who was accepting only the attentions of his housekeeper, was gently regaining his strength in the quietness of his bedroom. He did not want to face his son, who had not visited him once since his return to the castle.

The weather had turned mild, but there was no sign of the sun. The snow had melted, and Lord Iain went out as often as possible, thus carefully avoiding Lady Gunelle. He would leave in the morning to hunt with the knights of the castle and only return in the evening. On several occasions, he accompanied Beathag on a ride across the moors. However, not once did he go riding with Tomas during those days. He resented him for having taken sides with the young Keith woman at the time of their fateful meeting. As for Tomas, he seemed in no way intimidated by this sulk. On the contrary, he was delighted to be free to remain at Lady Gunelle's beck and call.

Since his cousin's return, Lord Tomas dreaded that Gunelle Keith would ask to return to Crathes. Neither he nor anyone at Mallaig would have been surprised if she did, and Lieutenant Lennox, who was as angry as ever, would certainly have been relieved. In fact, it was a completely different wish the young woman expressed that morning when she returned from a walk on her own. Looking sad and almost pleading, she asked him hesitantly if he would teach her Gaelic. The request astonished him, but he was even more moved to hear her explanation.

'I am very conscious of the difficulties it may cause you as the family representative. I admit I first thought of Lieutenant Lennox, but his knowledge of your language is too limited, and I want to learn as many words as possible. Otherwise, I will never be able to converse with your cousin without an interpreter. With your cousin, nor indeed with most of the folk in Mallaig. And that is not an option as far as I am concerned. Do you understand?'

64

'I understand perfectly, my lady,' he replied eagerly. 'I am flattered you thought of me, and I will not shirk the responsibility. You know very well that I am at your service here. So, you do me an honour in asking me to do this. I am not aware of any gift I may have for the art of teaching, but I will do everything necessary to acquire them. Show me simply where to begin.'

Lord Tomas had not reached the end of his astonishment and admiration for this young woman. The days passed without him even noticing. Gunelle Keith had a gift for learning. She was blessed, in part thanks to her studies in France, with a remarkable memory. Everything he taught her was immediately assimilated, and she could put it into practice without any form of reminder from him. She had the rudiments of German, and he noticed the link between it and Gaelic. For days on end, they went out walking wherever the mood took them; around the castle, in the village, or on the cliffs, talking about subjects she chose. That was how she came to know the merchants, fishermen, artisans, and castle servants, indeed, everyone who lived around Mallaig very well.

In the space of two weeks, Gunelle Keith mastered the basics of the young man's language, and he took great pride in that.

During the day following the MacNeil son's return to the castle, I was tempted to flee about twenty times. As soon as I closed my eyes, I relived the harrowing moments of my meeting with him. Each time I trembled with indignation. So, what had I done to deserve such contempt? What could he have learned about me that was so terrible that he passed judgement on me without even knowing me? Of course, no satisfactory answer came to enlighten me. I reached the point where I began to look at things as an outsider: The MacNeil son had decided to keep us waiting for three days, at the end of which he had faced the justifiable wrath of his father, an upright man. Then, he had been openly arrogant and discourteous to my face when we were introduced; then, he had hidden behind bitterness and silence. All his arrogance had done was to reveal his inexcusable ignorance of the Scots language. As for me, considering my state of anguish as a result of Lord Baltair's attack just before the difficult moment of the introductions, the pain of separation from my family and the three-day wait I had just lived through, I could not be expected to suffer such an affront without being upset. I came to the conclusion that I had done nothing worthy of such punishment.

It was then that the certainty dawned on me that Iain MacNeil had nothing to reproach me with other than that I was the one being forced upon him in marriage. He was displaying this arrogance to put me off from marrying him and put the odious burden of refusing the marriage on me. Through his good offices, the Keith family would once again be in the wrong. But he was mistaken. *I shall not flee Mallaig, thereby causing my father to fail to keep his promise,* I said to myself. *I shall explain myself to Iain MacNeil, even if it means studying his language day and night until our next meeting.*

I was relieved by Tomas's kind response and very quickly discovered that I enjoyed my Gaelic lessons. I was so excited that I would wake in the early hours of the morning without being able to go back to sleep. Not wanting to disturb Nellie and Vivian, I would get dressed quietly and go out onto the ramparts to watch the day breaking. I had found a little spot at the top of a turret where I was sheltered from the winds. Through its three amazingly wide arrow slits, there was a great view of the mountains and the two arms of the sea which surrounded the peninsula. I would lean on the cold stone and contemplate the splendour of the Hebridean Sea. I silently composed messages for my family, whom I missed so much. Those

66

moments of solitude, stolen from sleep, brought me more peace than those spent in prayer in the chapel, comforting though they were.

One morning when I was deep in one of these meditations, I was startled by the unexpected arrival of the MacNeil son's dog. I immediately froze, not out of fear of the animal but of fear of meeting his master. I turned around and immediately noticed him watching me from a crenel on the battlement walk. How long had he been there? I had no idea, but I had the unpleasant feeling of having been spied on. I had literally not set eyes on him since the day of the introduction and had almost come to think that he had once again left Mallaig.

He abandoned his observation point and came to join me. He was dressed for hunting: short tunic, leather breeches and boots, his claymore in his belt. He was not wearing a hat, and his tousled hair lay tangled on his shoulders. I thought I detected a hint of curiosity when his eyes met mine. Not knowing what attitude to adopt, I looked straight back out to sea. I heard him more than saw him come over and stand beside me. He gave me no greeting and remained silent. Barely turning my head, I noticed that, like me, he was staring at the horizon from the same arrow slit. I shuddered when, without turning his eyes away from the sea, he finally opened his mouth to quietly address me in Gaelic, 'You must miss your family a lot, I suppose, my lady. Your family and life in Aberdeen. Unless it is Orleans and your friends at the convent.'

'Certainly, my lord, I miss all of them.' I was aware of my poor pronunciation, and I was blushing. 'I left one part of the country to discover another. I hope the loss of what I had there will be compensated for by what I find here.'

'And what do you hope to find here, apart from a husband, of course?'

The question was impertinent, and I pursed my lips in annoyance. I despairingly searched for my words and felt myself getting flustered when I heard him continue in a conciliatory tone, 'Let us put the question another way. What do you like most about Mallaig?' This time, he was staring at me. I closed my eyes a moment to concentrate. Was he setting a trap for me? What answer was he expecting? What was he getting at? I immediately reproached myself for having such thoughts. He seemed sincere with his third question. I had to give him an answer. Looking back at the sea, I found a neutral spot and walked forward carefully.

'I admire the scenery around Mallaig very much. This area is so… so…' I could not remember the Gaelic word for 'vast.' Giving up the cause, I stretched out my hand, shaking my head to show that I did not know the word. We were cramped in the turret, and my sleeves brushed the pommel of his claymore. He stepped back. His beard moved; he was smiling broadly.

He opened his arms, imitating my gesture, which started his dog barking, and he left with a loud laugh while retorting, 'I see. We will continue this pleasant conversation when you speak the language of this vast region better! The truth is I see my cousin has a lot to do. Either he is a mediocre teacher, or you are a mediocre pupil.' Turning on his heels, he added over his shoulder, 'Or both!'

He disappeared as he had arrived, his dog running ahead of him. In the seclusion of my deserted turret, I was seething. Tears were stinging my eyes. Later, when I came out of my hiding place, I caught sight of little Ceit, who was scampering off towards the ramparts. The sight of her little red head brought a smile to my lips that did not leave me throughout the morning service when I returned to the keep.

In the evening, I had more success with the father with my Gaelic than I had been with the son in the morning. For the first time since his last crisis, Baltair MacNeil had asked to see me and I expected the conversation to be in Gaelic. I was afraid of finding him extremely poorly, for the news Nellie gave me regularly was not encouraging. I was relieved to see him sitting in his armchair, in ceremonial dress, head held high, colour a bit pale, but his breathing regular. *This man has amazing powers of recovery*, I could not help thinking, remembering the crisis that had had me rush to his aid. The same memory must have crossed his mind too, for he took my hand, held it tightly in his, and invited me to sit down in front of him.

'Gunelle,' he said in a voice full of emotion, 'I have neglected you. I was not well enough to receive you.' After a brief pause, he continued, 'No one here is ignorant of the fact that I owe you my life. Unfortunately, all I have to offer you in return is a son who does not deserve you.'

I read deep hurt in his eyes and was immediately moved.

'Iain is not all bad, but he has locked away the best of himself somewhere deep in his heart. You have excellent reasons to think of him as wicked, but I tell you the opposite is true despite the way he received you. Gunelle, I want you to know that I respect you too much to allow a union in which you risk being ill-treated. I know that Iain will never beat you. Even if that is the norm here in the Highlands, it is not the way the MacNeil boys, Isla MacNeil's sons, were raised.'

Deep in thought, for a moment, he said nothing before continuing gravely, 'Well, as we know, the deadline fixed for your marriage is Christmas! That is eleven days from today. I had a conversation with my son this morning, and he does not want to use this time to get to know you better. Gunelle, the decision is yours: Postpone the

69

wedding and take as long as you want to think about it or refuse my son in marriage. Rest assured; I will respect your choice whatever it is.'

It was obvious that this last phrase had cost him. I took a deep breath and laid my head on our hands which were still clasped together. So, the son was accepting me. That put me in the position where I could not refuse him, despite the option of doing so that the father had just given me. I, therefore, forced myself to announce that I was not renouncing this marriage. I expressed myself in Gaelic and was pleased to see the surprise in his eyes, which encouraged me to continue. Without too much thought, I began to recount in detail the last weeks spent in the company of his nephew Tomas. I told him of my happiness at rediscovering what I loved most in the world—learning. The words came easily, and at no time did I stutter. I was proud of myself and Tomas. The old clan chief was looking at me with admiration. I made no reference to his illness or the life-saving role which, according to him, I had had during his last attack. From then on, I felt a great deal of respect and affection for this remarkable man.

In the end, I decided not to delay the marriage needlessly. Since Iain was ready, I would be too. My mother's birthday was the 18th of December, Saint Marchan's Day, and that was the date I suggested for the wedding. He approved immediately, saying that he would entrust the preparations to Anna under Nellie's direction. By doing so, he wanted things to go according to marriage customs in Aberdeen. *Four days. In four days, I will be the wife of Iain MacNeil, chatelaine of Mallaig*, I thought with apprehension as I left the old chief.

Anna had been very impressed with the chest of spices. It was a present from the Keith family for their daughter's wedding. Lieutenant Lennox had brought it down to the kitchen after supper. A good number of the spices it contained were unknown to the housekeeper. While looking through it, Nellie told her their uses.

One thing and one thing only counted as far as Anna was concerned: The marriage was to take place. She had very little time to make the preparations, but the simple fact that she did not have to organise them by herself took a great weight off her shoulders. Vivian, Lady Gunelle's young servant, was going to take charge of the reception and the dressing of the bride, while Nellie was going to supervise the banquet. With the profusion of spices, which were worth a fortune, the dishes were certainly going to be very rich. Anna rejoiced at the thought. In her time, Lady Isla had favoured spicy cooking. Her knowledge on that score surpassed that of all the Highland chatelaines, and her table was the most highly esteemed by the lairds.

As her young master's old nurse, all that remained for her to do was to see that he was beyond reproach on this occasion. Suddenly, it seemed that that was, perhaps, the most onerous task of all. It seemed to Anna that, for years, she had dedicated herself untiringly to answering to the father's needs and the son's whims, both sources of countless worries for her old heart.

However, the plans Nellie came to show her the next day were so well laid out that, spurred on by her growing sense of excitement, she felt years younger. Mallaig was going to experience a marriage feast! Music and dancing were essential. So be it. She would have to let the troubadours, flautists, fiddlers, harpists, and pipers at Arisaig know. Since the deaths of Lady Isla and Lord Alasdair, there were no longer any musicians living at Mallaig. They did not hold soirees anymore. The castle walls had once and for all stopped resounding to the sound of sentimental ballads and lively reels.

Her young master had been a great dancer at the age of sixteen and seventeen. Even now, in the Highlands, his reputation as a dancer almost equalled his reputation as a fighter. Ever since parties at the castle had stopped, when he had a notion for dancing, he would attend a party in the home of one of the lairds, and she no longer had the opportunity to admire him. How many evenings and even nights had she spent watching him dance! Tireless he was! Without fail, Iain MacNeil would keep the momentum going until the musicians and other dancers begged for mercy. The immense pleasure written all over his face was a great source of comfort for Anna. When he danced, Iain revealed a completely different character. He beamed and was cheerful and pleasant to everybody. Anna sighed with relief. All that would be restored to him on the occasion of his wedding. One question arose, however: Would Iain agree to dance?

The narrow chapel was full on the morning of 18th December 1424. The religious ceremony, very simple but full of solemnity, took place at the castle, and everyone had wanted to be there. Hiding under a bench, Little Ceit watched Father Henriot's bouncing robe as he read the genealogy of the future couple in Gaelic, accompanied as always by a powerful shrugging of his shoulders. But it was the broad, richly embroidered border of Lady Gunelle's dress, the magnificent gold thread tassel hanging from her belt to the floor, and her shoes trimmed with otter that captured the little girl's attention and filled her with sheer delight. Right next to the otter-trimmed shoes, the motionless, black velvet shoes and the point of a claymore hanging just above them left her more indifferent. She could not suppress a pout of disappointment when the three personages went out of view.

Vivian was nervously hopping from one foot to the other despite the looks of exasperation that Lieutenant Lennox, standing beside her, was giving her. The couple were at the exchanging of the rings, the part of the ceremony which subjugated her. Her mistress was perfectly ravishing in her dress of moiré velvet, very fitted at the waist and spreading in large tails from the hips. A very long red cape, embroidered with azure-blue stars, fell from her narrow shoulders. Around her freckled neck hung a sapphire necklace given to her by her father when she left Crathes. She wore an embroidered satin hennin.

The young bride looked serious and a little tense. By her side, head and shoulders above her, stood a motionless Lord Iain.

Vivian, who had always been very susceptible to masculine charm, could not take her eyes off him. 'What bearing,' she muttered.

It was obvious that Anna the housekeeper had had her way: The young man's hair and beard had been trimmed, and his dark-blue doublet interlaced with black silk braid showed off his powerful chest and broad shoulders; underneath, he wore an ochre, ankle-length tunic.

Vivian quivered on hearing the young lord's deep voice as he repeated the traditional vows in Scots and slipped a ring onto her mistress's fourth finger, 'With this ring, I thee wed and with my body I thee honour.'

It was now her mistress's turn to recite the vow, this time in Gaelic and accompanying it with the same gesture. The priest's task was coming to an end. All that remained for him to do was to bless the couple, which he hurriedly did when he noticed that Lord Baltair, whose duty, along with one of his knights, was to hold up the purple veil above the couple's heads, was showing signs of weakness. A group of knights then sang a Gaelic hymn. The majestic anthem rose solemnly from the back of the chapel and marked the end of the ceremony.

'That is it! They are husband and wife,' said an emotional Vivian, who found it hard to believe. She hurried to fall in behind the newlyweds, who were now leaving the chapel arm in arm. On more than one occasion, it had come close to disaster between her mistress and the indomitable MacNeil son, and she had come to the point of doubting that the marriage would ever be celebrated. She still had a lot to do for the reception that was to follow. She had never had such an important role to play in her life.

Suddenly, she was jostled by a woman standing in her way, Lord Baltair's daughter-in-law. Looking superb in her finery of garish colours, Lady Beathag was determined to have the best seat in the great hall. All smiles, she hurried towards the old man, who was walking slowly behind the couple. Vivian could not stop herself from giving the haughty and vulgar woman a dirty look. At that moment, her attention was drawn to Lord Tomas, standing close by. Pain was clearly written all over his face. She knew only too well what feelings her mistress, despite herself, had sown in his loyal heart.

Under Anna, Nellie, and Vivian's direction, the great hall had been completely transformed. It had found its former cachet. Each windowpane had been polished and the red and ochre glass, on which the bright sunlight danced, was casting spots of colour on the stone walls and tapestries. Bouquets of branches and dried flowers had been hung on each pillar and underneath the windows. Five large tables had been magnificently laid, and knights, assigned to serve wines, beers, mead, and meats during the meal, were standing on duty near the side boards behind the tables. The space in front of the huge fire had been kept clear to allow jugglers and musicians to move about freely and to be easily seen by the guests. The air was filled with the odours of spices which whetted burgeoning taste buds even more.

All across Mallaig, there was sheer and total delight at the thought of a celebration. It had been a long time. Several personalities from the diocese had made the effort to attend the meal given in honour of the couple. All the lairds connected to the clan and their wives were present. The ten or so family knights, tradesmen from the village, and all those from the castle had been invited too. In a continuous coming and going from the kitchen to the great hall, servants and servant girls, laden with trays, circulated among the groups of enthusiastic and curious observers. A cacophony of laughter and lively conversations filled the room as the people arrived. The serving of the meal began as soon as all the guests had taken their places, and so did the songs and the music.

The members of the Keith party sat at the first table with the knights of the household. The second table grouped together the lairds and their ladies. The top table was naturally presided over by Baltair MacNeil. As well as the newlyweds, there was Father Henriot and the clergy, Guilbert Saxton, Lennox, Beathag, the Marshall of Kyle and his wife, and Tomas. The fourth and fifth tables accommodated the craftsmen of the village and the castle with their wives.

Anna nervously stood behind her old master, constantly bending down to his ear to receive instructions and pass them on to the people concerned. Throughout the meal and the entertainment that followed, she watched the young couple's behaviour out of the corner of her eye. Her concerns regarding her young master were growing.

Lady Gunelle was sitting very straight, her expression fixed and her elbows tight against her body. Every one of her movements was measured so as not to have any contact with Lord Iain beside her. Relaxed and with an enigmatic smile on his lips, he was having a lively conversation with the Marshall of Kyle. With singular regularity, he signalled over his shoulder for the knight to fill his cup.

Anna, who saw what he was playing at, bit her lips. 'He is going to get drunk if he continues at that rate,' she said to herself. She suddenly had an idea: the custom of sharing the cup and the bread between newlyweds. *Yes, that is it!* she thought. *The newlyweds must share the same cup and the same bread. And Iain is going to moderate his drinking if he drinks from the same cup as Lady Gunelle.'* Moving behind her young master, she reminded him of the custom.

Iain smiled. Then, turning to Gunelle with a malicious glint in his eyes, he took her hands from the cup from which she was going to drink. In a slow movement, he put it down in front of him and held his cup out to the young woman while quoting the well-known formula, 'It appears that drinking, eating, and sleeping together are what makes the marriage.'

Silence fell over their table. Gunelle, dumbfounded and blushing, took the cup from Iain's hand and rather hesitantly lifted it to her lips amidst a burst of applause. The mouthful she drank almost choked her.

'My lord,' she whispered to Iain, 'that's not wine you are drinking.'

'No, my lady, it is whisky. I drink very little wine. It is not good here. The local whisky is much better!' Glancing at Gunelle's cup in front of him, he went on in the same sarcastic tone, 'Although that wine must be very much better than average since it comes from the wine cellar of your generous father. Three barrels of wine and a chest of spices… what a generous dowry he has paid for you, my lady.'

By this time, Gunelle's cheeks were burning. Choking with anger and embarrassment, she kept looking down, unable to give any kind of reply whatsoever. Fortunately, no one around them had heard the remarks exchanged by the couple. When she forced herself to lift her head after a moment, she realised that conversations were flowing easily, and only her husband was paying her any attention. He was watching, eager to see her embarrassment spread like ripples formed by a stone thrown into calm water.

'Now, the bread, my lady,' he said, raising his voice. 'What are you going to have on it? Elk, wild boar, grouse, bear, and reindeer are all excellent, and they are the results of my hunting. You choose, please. I do not have any preference.'

'Since you allow me to choose, my lord, we are going to have lamb. I have been told that it is very tasty, especially when spiced up with cumin from our chest.'

The knight, who had come forward on Iain's signal to take the lady's order, burst out laughing when he heard Gunelle's reply. He was rewarded with a dirty look from his master, who, unable to hide his irritation, gave the order, 'Bring some lamb on a piece of bread, for my lady and myself.'

From that moment on, Lady Gunelle relaxed. Lord Iain continued his conversation with the Marshall without touching the piece of bread left in front of him and his wife. Gunelle cut herself a piece and joined in conversation with those around her. The musicians had taken over from the singer, and she heard the powerful and haunting sounds of the pibroch for the first time. She suddenly felt a little tightness at the waist. Glancing under the table, she discovered little Ceit crouching at her feet and playing with the golden tassel of her belt. She whispered her name, but the child, caught red-handed, suddenly turned and, as quick as lightning, wriggled her way through the guests' legs to escape to the back of the hall.

Towards the end of the meal, an important piece of news was announced to those at their table by the Marshall of Kyle, who was very surprised that the MacNeil chief had not already heard it: King James had arrived by ship at Dunvegan, the home of the MacLeods on Skye with a bodyguard of twenty men and intended to return to Scone by land.

'Lord MacNeil,' he said in conclusion, 'it seems very probable that the king will stop off at Mallaig. As you have the best stables on the whole of the west coast, his Majesty will most likely acquire some horses at the same time.'

In utter surprise, Baltair MacNeil answered, 'What the devil is he coming to do in the Highlands, Marshall? He made himself very unpopular with Murdock's execution and the arrest of the lords of Angus, Douglas, and Mar. They say he is going to release them, but the harm has been done. He is taking a big risk coming to these parts at this time. Of course, if the king of Scotland chooses to stop off at Mallaig, he will be welcomed here at the castle

Rising to his feet and raising his glass in Lady Gunelle's direction, he added loudly, 'Our King James I will be even better received here at the MacNeils' now that the castle has a new chatelaine, who is a lady of great qualities and who is very capable of organising grand receptions. Friends, raise your glasses to my daughter-in-law, Lady Gunelle! Sláinte!'

The music had stopped, and the great hall suddenly resounded to the sound of a magnificent cheer uttered by a hundred voices in unison.

Nervously, Gunelle stood up, took the cup still sitting in front of Lord Iain and raised it in the direction of Lord Baltair, pronouncing in a clear voice, 'Here's to you, my dear father!' Addressing the gathering, she added, 'Friends, let us drink to the health of the chief of our clan, Baltair MacNeil, and his son, Iain, my husband from today. Sláinte!'

Once again, the toast was followed by a huge shout. Iain had stood up for the toast, and when Gunelle had swallowed a mouthful of wine from his cup, he took it in his hands and drank in his turn. He screwed up his eyes as he looked straight at her. She sat down slowly and listened in on the animated conversations which were starting up again all around her. Iain sat down, put the cup well out of reach of his wife, and put the cup of whisky, which had just been refilled, back down in front of her. The singing and music were starting up again. Since the coming and going of the servants and serving girls had finished, all the musicians except the harpist approached the tables and encouraged the guests to get up and dance.

Anna, who was standing to the side with Nellie, named the reel that the musicians were beginning to play and nudged Gunelle's nurse. 'That's my young master's favourite piece,' she whispered. 'Watch him closely, Nellie, and you will see how well he knows how to skip and whirl!'

Looking alarmed, Nellie replied, 'But Lady Gunelle cannot dance to that! She has not learned these dances…' Her companion did not hear her protests, for the din of chairs and benches being pushed back drowned out everything else. Delighted at the chance to stretch their legs, several knights, lairds, young ladies, and servants congregated in front of the tables, and were starting to dance in a merry scramble in the middle of the musicians.

Lady Gunelle's eyes were wide open in amazement. In a frantic rhythm, each musician seemed to want to compete with the others. The skill of the dancers and the complexity of the steps and figures they were performing left her speechless with admiration. She had never seen or heard anything like it in France.

Lord Iain, his face impassive, had sat forward on his chair, and his eyes were scouring the room. Only the sound of his wedding ring tapping out the beat of the reel on his cup revealed his love of the tune being played. His dog, which had lain peacefully at his feet throughout the meal, popped his head out from beneath the table and placed it on his knees, brushing against Gunelle's dress. She was startled and instinctively grabbed the nearest arm: her husband's.

He turned his head in her direction, then, looking down at Gunelle's hand, which she withdrew right away, he smiled wickedly and spoke to the dog as he stroked it with one hand, 'Good old Bran, you will have to avoid touching my lady. She is very sensitive and does not like hairy beasts … unless they are teaching her to speak their language.' He addressed Gunelle sharply, 'In fact, my lady, how is your canine language coming on?'

'I have stopped the lessons, my lord.' As she too stroked the dog, she continued in the same relaxed tone, 'I was not abandoned by my tutor. For the past two weeks, his services have been required for hunting trips. On the other hand, I have worked on my Gaelic. What do you think of it now? Have I made progress, in your opinion?'

'There has certainly been some, my lady. What I am wondering is, to whom is the credit due? Has the pupil improved or the master?'

'I think both, my lord.'

Lord Iain was furious at finding himself at a loss for words. This little game with his wife was beginning to exasperate him. It would be better to make her drink rather than talk. So, with a big smile, he held out his cup to her.

I could not get out of it. With a smirk on his face, he waited for me to take a drink. The very smell of the amber drink made me feel a little sick, but I took a sip and then drank a mouthful which had less of an effect on me than the first. I gave him back the cup, which he emptied in one go and lifted it above his head to signify he wanted it filled up. I noticed his movement was unsteady; the cup was swaying at the end of his arm before someone took it from him. *He is drunk*, I thought.

The next instant, I saw Lady Beathag come towards us in a flurry of skirts and veils. She addressed me in a flattering but pompous voice, 'Very dear chatelaine with great qualities, would you do me the favour of lending me your husband for a dance? My brother-in-law is the best dancer here, and it would be a shame if he could not show his new wife what he can do.'

'Please, I replied, relieved at the prospect of seeing Iain move away. Unfortunately, I do not know any of the dances they are doing.'

I had no sooner finished speaking than Iain MacNeil got to his feet, and with a brief nod of the head in my direction, he left the table to make his way confidently towards the group of dancers, followed by Lady Beathag. It was then I witnessed the most incongruous spectacle ever given to a newlywed wife to see: that of her husband moving with grace and exquisite pleasure in the enveloping arms of his sister-in-law. In fact, the series of fast and furious reels and jigs had made way for a ballad that was not unknown to me. I tried to take my eyes off the fine couple Iain and Beathag made, but it was no use. They exhibited such togetherness, such understanding. Each of their movements and the looks they gave each other was proof of the relationship between two people who had known each other for a very long time. *Or who know each other intimately*, I could not help thinking to myself. The idea made me very uneasy, and I quickly turned my head. As I did, I caught Tomas's eye as he was standing not far from me. I saw the rage in his eyes. I looked down; something told me that he had read my thoughts. *It is mad! I am too emotional.*

He appeared at my side right away, his hand outstretched, and he invited me to dance. 'My lady certainly knows this dance. I know it is very popular on the east coast of Scotland. As it is slow, neither your dress nor your cape will restrict your movements. I beg you, Lady Gunelle, it would be better if you danced.'

It was the first time I heard him say my name. He was perfectly right. I could not remain seated during the whole reception given in honour of my marriage and with my eyes riveted on Lady Beathag's hand as she stroked my husband's beard. I must give myself a shake. Why not dance even if I knew I was not very good at it? I glanced briefly at my table companions as I stood up and noticed a nod of approval from the Marshall's wife and Lennox, who had not missed Tomas's invitation. I resolutely took the proffered hand. It was hot. Tomas clasped mine firmly and led me towards the couples at the end of the formation. My husband and Lady Beathag were at the opposite end. This way, it was impossible for us to be part of the same movement. I was relieved and could fully enjoy the music as much as the dancing skill of my cavalier. We danced several sets before they began another series of jigs, which, by the looks of it, were more popular with the Mallaig folk.

Tomas led me back to my seat and, quite naturally, took my husband's. He knew that Iain was not going to re-join me any time soon. At the far end of the room, he was taking part in what seemed to me to be a sort of dancing competition for men. Seven knights formed a circle in the centre of which they had laid their claymores. Their gleaming weapons shimmered in the light of the candles now lit everywhere. Most of the other dancers had gathered in groups to see better, careful not to block the view of those at the top table. The piper moved towards them. All the other musicians had moved away. A kind of frantic reel escaped from his impressive instrument.

Arms raised to shoulder height, hands open and extended, the tips of their fingers almost touching, the seven men were tapping the ground in time to the music. They crossed their legs and, on every second beat, brushed the handle of their respective claymores with the point of their foot and then the heel. Keeping their upper body straight, they were not looking at the ground but at each other. Soon the rhythm of the pipes quickened and a first knight gave up, saluted the piper, picked up his weapon, and left the circle. The other dancers stopped and moved towards the centre, moving their claymore with their feet as they did so. They raised their arms again: This time, their hands were touching. They joined hands, and the music started up again. The same move was repeated each time a dancer dropped out, the circle getting smaller and the claymores' tips getting closer until they formed a perfect star. The men held one another by the forearm, then by the elbows. When only four were left, they put their hands, fists clenched, at the height of their belt. Their hair was soaking wet with sweat. Large circles of dampness marked their tunics. To my great astonishment, my husband showed no sign of tiredness. His chest stuck out as he filled his severely tested lungs with air. His feet were skipping with an amazing lightness and without missing a beat. His face was wet, but lit up with a genuine smile, completely devoid of malice. A smile of pure delight. I think that was the first time that I found him handsome. He remained the last one standing, to the hearty applause of the audience. Had the knights deliberately let him win? Impossible to say for certain. The fact remains that no one around me seemed surprised at the outcome of the competition.

Lord Tomas had retired. I could not say at what moment. My husband came back beside me. Without even taking the time to sit down, he immediately took hold of the cup, which he emptied in one go. Turning quickly towards me, he shouted, 'Good grief, my lady. What is in that? Water?'

'That's right, my lord.' I said calmly. 'I felt like a drink of water. Since we must drink from the same cup, I had some poured into your cup. Water is very refreshing, and I think it will quench your thirst better than the whisky after the efforts you have just made in that magnificent dance.'

Dropping heavily onto his chair, he replied, 'My lady, what do you know about that dance, since you do not dance it, and what do you know about whisky since you do not drink it? I would have you know that this drink quenches my thirst better than any water.' Then, glancing disdainfully at my throat, he added huskily, 'Besides, you drink too much water. It is making you rust.'

I left the room before the tears began to flow. My heart was suffocating. Like an automaton, I made my way to the door. There was nowhere to be alone. So, with wet cheeks, I hurried to the staircase leading upstairs. I was not in my room five minutes before Vivian and Nellie arrived because they were worried. I must have been a sorry sight. I had torn off my hennin. My hair, matted with sweat, was hanging woefully on my shoulders, and my face was tear-stained; I could not stem the flow. Nellie took me in her comforting arms and rocked me gently from side to side. As she held me, I gradually relaxed to the soothing rhythm of her tender words of affection. When I was completely calm and had stopped crying, she asked me what had upset me. At that moment extreme weariness took hold of me. How could I explain? What was there to explain? I walked over to the cheval mirror beside the window, took off the necklace my father had given me and looked at my neck, cheeks, and nose. The freckles were pale in colour, delicate, and thinly spread. I remembered the comments of my dormitory companions at the convent in Orleans. Some said that they became more obvious with age, others that they were a sign that I had been conceived in a field, others that men hated freckled skin. The latter were right—I knew that now.

I did not want to go back down to the great hall. I felt unable to do so. I felt particularly incapable of facing Iain MacNeil's look. To my great distress, Nellie sent Vivian back down to the party, declaring that she would get me ready for my husband's visit. I let her undress me without saying a word. The silence was gradually broken by her gentle voice telling me everything a newlywed needed to know. Just to picture Iain MacNeil performing his conjugal duties with me was torture. Contrary to all the practices and even the precepts of the church, I began to hope that he would not come up to my room. He must have heard my unspoken prayer, for he did not come. I lay in bed waiting impassively for him for the rest of the evening and part of the night. Nellie and Vivian had discretely arranged to sleep in the servants' quarters. So, I spent my wedding night completely alone, in despair, my heart on tenterhooks, my ears straining, listening for the slightest sound outside my door.

I must have dozed off, for I did not hear Nellie come in, in the early hours of the morning. She was going back and forth in the room, preparing my bath, and getting the day's clothes ready. When I put my head out of the curtains, I blinked at the light filtering gently through the two windows. She made signs in the direction of the bed; she wanted to know if I was alone. I answered in the affirmative. She rushed towards me to help me with my morning wash. I caught her looking closely at the crumpled sheets as I got out of bed. Meeting my gaze, she hastened to add confidently, 'You do not always lose blood the first time, my lovely. It does not mean anything. Lord Iain did not comment, I hope?'

'No, of course not, Nellie. Do not worry about it.'

Noticing that I turned my head so she would not see my face, she added, worriedly, 'He hurt you; he was not gentle! My dear, these things happen sometimes. Young men are often too rash in these circumstances. Highlanders probably more so than all the others. It will sort itself out after a few times…'

Interrupting her more abruptly than I would have liked, I told her I did not want to talk about the subject of my wedding night for the moment. She did not say another word and gave me my bath in silence. The hot water on my skin soothed me like ointment on a wound. I stretched out for a long time, relaxed, and enjoyed my nurse's pampering. In the end, I felt I had to allay her concerns and said frankly, 'I have nothing with which to reproach Lord Iain, Nellie.'

Chapter Four
The visit

I t was late morning. From the courtyard rose the usual sounds of water being drawn, horses being led to the stables, carts being shifted according to the provisions they were carrying. The icy air entered the bedroom through the half-open window. Iain sat up slowly. His head hurt when he moved. Beathag had left the room. He was alone. With great difficulty, he got out of bed, looked on the sideboard for something to drink, and, finding nothing to quench his thirst, he dressed, fastened his belt, slipped his claymore into it, and left the room. Bran made a great fuss of him, licking and jumping up on him. Iain went to his own bedroom at the end of the corridor.

'What a wedding, what a wedding night. Only it was not with my wife,' he brooded. He had difficulty piecing together his memories of the day before.

First of all, after Gunelle's sudden departure, he had been hassled by that impertinent Tomas, who had asked him what he had done or said to his wife.

'A bit too quick to come to Gunelle's aid, that one. I will have to keep an eye on him if I do not want to be cuckolded,' he said to himself. Then, it had been the turn of his wife's young servant, who came to tell him a little while later that her mistress had gone upstairs to get ready, and she was waiting for the moment when he would decide to leave the wedding reception. She had spoken solemnly, and her pinched expression had annoyed him. He had almost grabbed her by the waist and put her on his knee. To round off the evening, several cups of whisky at the knights' table had knocked him senseless and stifled the reproaches that were beginning to well up within him.

'After all, what have I done that is so bad?' he asked himself. 'I have inherited a wife who not only drinks water but tries to get me to drink it, prefers reading and praying to horse riding, does not dance and does not like game.'

Sometime later, his father asked to speak to him. He had been conducted to the arms room next to the great hall. Baltair MacNeil was on his feet, and Iain had been struck by how tall he looked. Very few words had been exchanged. In fact, the father had simply instructed the son to return to his room, splash cold water over his face, and honour his wife before daybreak. No shouting, no recriminations. A simple, clear order with no room for discussion.

On the clan chief's signal, two of his friends, who were waiting for the conversation to end, had stepped forward, grabbed Iain under the arms, and dragged him to his room by the staircase facing the door. For him, the party was over. The walk had been enough to bring Iain back to his senses, and he had sent his friends away as soon as they reached his bedroom. He had collapsed onto his bed and had stayed there long enough to sober up. One thing was clear: He was neither in the mood nor in a fit state to take away the virginity of a less than attractive young woman, even if she was his wife.

An hour later, having come to completely, his throat was on fire, he had looked in vain for water. He had smiled at the thought that he would certainly find some in Gunelle's bedroom. He left his bedroom. The whole castle was asleep. In the corridor, Bran was stretched out at the door, and Iain stroked his head as he passed and continued on his way. At the end of the corridor, a door was wide open—Beathag's, of course. He had carried on walking without stopping but had heard his name being called; she had recognised his footsteps and those of his dog and asked about his success in his wife's bed. He had stopped, his arms hanging by his side, and she come to join in the corridor. The last memory he had of last night was of Beathag, with her tongue exploring every crevice of his mouth, one hand running through his hair and the other trying to unbuckle his belt.

Iain adopted an air of disgust. He looked at his room and immediately noticed that Anna had been in. Steam was rising from the hot water in the basins in front of the hearth. There were clean towels, his clothes spread out on the bed, and there was a carafe of cold water, which he emptied. Then he started to have a wash. He felt greasy and dirty. *Filthy as a rotten swine, which has been wallowing in the mire. he* thought bitterly.

Lieutenant Lennox did not know what to think of his mistress when he saw her looking so pale and frail as she prayed in the chapel that morning. No husband by her side, which hardly surprised him. His opinion of Iain MacNeil had not changed since their first meeting: It was even lower since the wedding reception the day before. Inside he was seething. How could a man worthy of that name, an heir, and a future clan chief get so drunk at his wedding that he could not perform his conjugal duties?

Looking again at his young mistress, he thought it was probably better that way. In fact, Lieutenant Lennox had not taken his eyes off young MacNeil all evening and had even discreetly watched his door in the early hours. He had also witnessed the groom's escapade in his sister-in-law's bedroom. That had sickened him. Thinking back to Lady Beathag's seduction scene in the corridor, he wondered if he himself would have been able to resist. He remembered the glances she had sent his way from the first moment of his stay at the castle. Only the circumspection that his position demanded had enabled him to keep the woman at a distance. *She is a witch, and he is scum*, he thought.

Of course, he could not do or say anything. He was suffering with his young mistress. During the time he had been responsible for her, more than a month now, he had come to protect her as if she were his own daughter. One thing for sure, he would not have given her to Iain MacNeil! In this whole affair, his master, Nathaniel Keith, had proved to be more of a businessman than a father because he was not unaware of the kind of people the MacNeils were. The previous day, Nathaniel Keith's part of the contract had been fulfilled: His daughter was married. As soon as he had received confirmation, Nathaniel Keith would be able to send his team of woodcutters for the winter felling in MacNeil's forests. Lennox was determined to be a part of the team of men responsible for guarding the site and thus be close to Mallaig. He could not reconcile himself to the idea of leaving his young mistress behind, even more so because Vivian had expressed a wish to return to Crathes. He knew that Lady Gunelle would not stop her from leaving even though it would cause her a great deal of distress. *How many more heartaches await this young woman?* he wondered with a sigh. He came to a decision: He was going to leave that very day. Best not to prolong his stay at Mallaig.

While the morning service was going on in the chapel, little Ceit was ferreting around in the bedrooms upstairs. From the height of her six years, she could not quite reach the windowsills and was in the habit of rummaging in the shady areas underneath them. Her little feet, shod with felt slippers, meant she could explore in complete silence. In fact, no one took any notice of her roaming all through the castle and particularly so that day when everyone had a lot to do after the festivities.

As she slowly opened Gunelle's bedroom door, she knew that her visit would be successful; the room was empty, and the wonderful belt was hanging there within reach. She went in, grabbed it, and wound it around her waist several times. Then she sat down on the floor and, dreamily, began to stroke the fine gold threads of the tassels, letting them run through her spread-out fingers. She did not hear Gunelle enter.

The young woman advanced quietly into the room, captivated by the little girl crouched at the foot of her bed. She made a movement that gave away her presence, and Ceit jumped to her feet, her panic-stricken eyes feverishly looking for somewhere to hide. The only thing within reach was the bedspread. She dived under it. Gunelle smiled as she went over, lay down on the floor, and began to speak gently to the child. She talked about the wedding, the clothes the ladies were wearing, the feathers on the gentlemen's hats, and the good things served up for dessert. After a while, seeing that Gunelle did not present any danger and more so because she was trying not to look at her, Ceit finally ventured to come out at the opposite side of the bed to where the young woman was sitting. Immediately, she began to undo the belt. Then she heard Gunelle say to her, 'Do not take it off. It suits you very well, and I am giving it to you.'

She thought she had misunderstood. She could not hope for such a gift. No one had ever given her such a gift. She walked around the bed and came to stand behind one of the curtains, which she grabbed to hide her face. Gunelle saw the little redhead shake her head and picked up a faint 'no.' She asked the reason for the refusal but received no reply. Then, after a moment, she heard the tassels of the belt fall to the floor with a thud and watched as the little girl escaped out into the corridor.

Outside, it was a dull, grey day. The low tide had left a lot of debris on the short strip of sand in the harbour. There was a strong wind. Lord Tomas was watching the gulls and fulmars fighting over the sea's leftovers. He dismounted, and, tying up his horse, he stepped on to the quay, which was deserted at this time of the day. He had left the morning service before the end as he could no longer bear seeing how miserable and unhappy Gunelle, flanked by her two servants, looked. A desperate need to move and breathe in the fresh air had led him to go riding like the wind for an hour. Now his hands were frozen, and he was clapping them against each other to warm them up.

Scouring the horizon, he was looking for ships coming from the tip of the Isle of Skye. If King James was coming, it would be from that direction. He turned to survey the harbour and check the lookout positions. He did not see a single lookout. He was angry.

'Another problem to sort out,' he grumbled.

Since the end of the summer, the regular changeover of the guard had left a lot to be desired. They were either not turning up at their posts on time or leaving early. More and more often, indiscipline resulted in breaches in the protection of the castle and the village. The king's visit, if there were a visit, would highlight this weakness. He would take care of it.

He remounted and headed towards the pastures half a mile away. On the way, he met several shepherds and cattlemen who greeted him heartily. The wedding had put the whole of Mallaig, even those who had not attended, in a festive mood. Lord Tomas could not prevent his thoughts from turning incessantly to Gunelle and his cousin. He was outraged at Iain's behaviour, but what could he do? There was nothing he could do. Iain was his master at arms as well as his uncle, and he was his subordinate. He found himself with no room for manoeuvre, his hands were tied. Lady Gunelle was out of reach of his heart and his aid. He sighed deeply. Was life about to become pure torture?

The morning was drawing to a close. Having seen everything, he had planned to see, he turned his horse around and returned to the castle by the plateau. Entering the courtyard, he stopped dead. A team of horses was being prepared for departure. He guessed rather than knew that a new crisis was being prepared for Gunelle. He got down from his horse and bridle in hand, walked towards the man in charge of the escort who informed him of the imminent departure. He learned that Lieutenant Lennox was leaving that very morning and was taking young Vivian with him. That was what he had been dreading since daybreak. Today, Gunelle would have almost all of her ties with Crathes cut.

As soon as their party had crossed the drawbridge, I rushed as fast as my skirts would allow to the staircase leading to the battlement walk. I wanted to watch them for as long as they remained in view. I had managed to put on a face throughout the goodbyes. My lieutenant had rushed his own goodbyes, knowing full well that it was all very painful for me, and I was secretly grateful to him. When he had shaken my hand, his tear-filled eyes had almost made me burst out sobbing. Crying as though her heart would break and unable to speak to me without taking refuge in her handkerchief, Vivian had not helped the situation. Of the MacNeil household, the only ones present at the farewells in the courtyard were Tomas, Saxton, and Father Henriot, who wanted to bless the return journey. This meant we had been able to embrace and speak to each other in Scots for the last time.

Up here, where they had had the sensitivity to leave me alone, I could at last give way to my misery. My hands were resting on the parapet, and through my tears, I could see the knights waving to me, as they took it in turn to turn around on their horses, all the time getting further and further away. I waved in response, shaking as I sobbed. In the end, unable to bear it any longer, I slid to the ground, crouched up in a ball, wrapping my cape round about me to protect myself from the wind. How long did I cry like that? I did not know. Later, I felt a hand trying to push back the straggly locks of hair out of my eyes. I opened them and saw Ceit. She was kneeling close to my face and was looking at me, her eyes full of sadness.

'Gone,' she said.

I sat up immediately, looking all around me. We were alone. The position of the sun on the towers told me that the afternoon was well advanced. I looked back at the little girl. Her fine hair had been plaited, and she was wearing a bonnet tied under her chin with a strange blue ribbon. I could not help but smile. Pointing to the ribbon, I told her it was pretty.

She took one of the ends of the ribbon and tried to repeat the word 'pretty.' Then, with a gesture of extreme tenderness, she wiped away the traces of tears from my face, repeating very softly, 'Gone, gone… Gone.'

I had difficulty holding back a fresh flood of tears. I took her little hand in mine and raised it to my lips, murmuring, 'Thank you, my lovely little Ceit. My friends have gone, but I still have one. You.'

From that moment on, Ceit did not run away when she saw me. She even seemed to search out my company, which far from displeased me. She stopped me from thinking too much about Crathes and Orleans. I gradually realised that Ceit was not mute but simply a little deaf and this had prevented her from learning to speak. As well as this, her slight facial disfigurement made her want to hide from people. It was just one step removed from there for her to behave like a little wild animal. The fact she was an orphan had done the rest.

That evening, despite Nellie's repeated offer to have her meal with me in my bedroom, I was keen to dine with the family in the great hall. She assured me that the whole family would understand my need to be alone, and she was certainly right, but I had decided to put aside how I felt and face my new life head-on.

As soon as I entered the room, my husband came to meet me and without a word greeted me in the style of the northern knights, his open hand on his chest. I stared at the ring on his finger, trying not to meet his eyes. He took my hand and led me to the table, where he had me sit down beside him. As we proceeded, he had enquired about my health in very courteous terms, showing he was aware of the pain the departure of my own folk had caused me. The tone of his voice was neither haughty nor cold. On the contrary, he displayed sincerity and compassion.

This change of his behaviour towards me took me by surprise. I had been prepared to avoid him as much as possible. I realised that his absence from my room, the previous night, was an affront—not to his father this time, but to me. What I did not understand were the reasons behind it. Obviously, I do not appeal to him physically very much, and he just as much to me… But we had both consented to this marriage. Therefore, we had to act like a married couple and do what had to be done.

The decorations were still up in the great hall, and near the fire, the clarsach was resting on its base, its brass strings glistening in the light of the flames. So, the harpist had not left the castle. I looked at the table, which was garnished as beautifully as the day before. They were serving wine and beer. There was no whisky. The members of the MacNeil family were sitting opposite each other. Only Lord Baltair was missing. Since Iain had had a long conversation with him during the day, he gave me a detailed report of his father's state of health. He told me that the wedding had used up what little strength he had. As well as that, there was the anxiety caused by the prospect of a visit from the king. The visit was the talking point among the guests. Iain often asked my opinion on one matter or another, sometimes etiquette and royal receptions in France, sometimes the customs in Aberdeen. This was the first time we conversed in Gaelic in a spirit of good-natured agreement. He was careful not to broach the subject of the wedding or the wedding night. But that left Lady Beathag out of the equation. In fact, with a little scheming look of mischief which exasperated me, she passed several remarks, which fortunately were not picked up by anyone. It certainly was not Lord Tomas, Father Henriot, or Saxton, the secretary, who were going to show any interest. However, her little game did mean that I realised that Iain and I were the only ones who knew what had really happened in my bedroom the night before. The intensity of my husband's expression confirmed it. And in it, I read the message: 'Let's not talk about it.' *So be it*, I said to myself.

After supper, I was pleasantly surprised to see the harpist come and sit down and begin playing some ballads and laments. Nothing could give me more pleasure and put me at ease. As the rest of the company prepared to play cards at the table, which was being cleared, I went over to the musician and sat down to watch him play. One other person was fascinated by the music which flowed from his nimble fingers—it was little Ceit. She had slipped in once the supper was finished and sat down at my feet. Then I felt a sense of great calmness. I was no longer thinking of my dear absent friends, and I became unaware of the people around me. The music was winding a gentle path towards my heavy heart and soothing it. I caught myself stroking Ceit's hair. She was motionless with delight. I caught my husband's puzzled expression as he watched us.

The harpist did not seem to know the words of several of the songs he played, even though he played them well. When I commented, he replied that he never sang, for his croaky voice was an insult to the beauty of the songs. He graciously invited me to sing instead, saying that he knew I would be a good singer because of the length of my neck. This simple but flattering comment melted my reserve. I asked him to play a piece he had played earlier. It was a French song I had learned from my school friends in the convent, and I was particularly fond of it. Hesitantly, at first, I began to sing along and then my voice grew stronger and rose clear and pure in the great hall. The sound of my voice took me by surprise. I remembered something my mother said about tears purifying the voice, or so she thought. It seemed as if she was there by my side and had seen me sob all day long. When the song was finished, Tomas left the card table and came over to congratulate me. As I had sung in French, he asked me to translate the lyrics. It was a song about leaving on a journey: A lady was saying her goodbyes to her lover, who was leaving for the Crusades. So, line by line, I translated the whole declaration of love the lovers had made. Tomas was listening intently as if each word were meant for him.

The rest of the company had gathered around to listen. Lady Beathag showed a great interest in the topic of courtly love, and she questioned me on how ladies held their *cours d'amour* in France, where the fashion had originated. Since my French experience was limited to what was taught in the convent, I could not satisfy her curiosity. However, I learned that the former Lady of Mallaig had held such a court the year before her death. The troubadours, knights, and the female gentry of the Highlands had mingled in this very room using the refined language of court and discussing in oratorical jousts the amorous affairs of the heart. This picture did not fit in well with the castle where I had been living for a month. Besides, nothing belonging to Lady Isla Mallaig seemed to have endured after her death.

The conversation had cast a cloud over my husband. I sensed that the mere mention of his mother was painful. His look of utter dejection did not suggest so much a sadness at the loss of a loved one as a certain anger or powerlessness. That gave me food for thought. I was the first to show a desire to retire at the end of the evening.

My husband responded immediately and accompanied me to the staircase leading upstairs. He wished me goodnight before saying dryly, 'I beg you, do not wait up for me. Not tonight or in the nights to come.' He handed me the candlestick without the slightest explanation and returned to the hall.

There was nothing left for me but to go up to my room alone. I did not know what he meant by this piece of advice. One thing was clear: I was spared living through such a wait. *His own good time has been made abundantly clear*, I thought.

For Lord Baltair, King James's visit could not have come at a worse time. His son had come to give him the news a little before midday: The king's ship was in sight off the Mallaig coast, and taking advantage of the high tide, would arrive before supper. The old chief had been gasping for breath since he woke and he had difficulty speaking. He was in despair and dared not admit it. It was a great disappointment to him not to be able to appear before the king of

Scotland. He also entertained a thousand fears about what kind of welcome the king would receive without him. Lord Iain completely shared his father's worries but took care to hide them from him. For the first time, he could call upon his wife's reputed talents for organising such a royal reception. So, in order to reassure his father, the son found himself in the strange position of having to sing the praises of someone whom he was taking great care to belittle elsewhere.

When he was sure his father would rest, he left him in the care of a servant girl and went down to inform the household of his plans. He had had everybody gather in the arms room. As soon as he entered, his eye was drawn to the clan coat of arms engraved in stone above the fireplace: an escutcheon of stone with the inscription, *Vincere vel Mori - Vanquish or die*, a motto which went back to the sixth chieftain Neil Og MacNeil, who had fought with Robert Bruce against the English at the famous Battle of Bannockburn in 1314. At that moment, he felt the whole weight of his ancestors and their loyalty to the Scottish kings on his shoulders. He looked again at his people, who were looking slightly concerned as they waited. He must not let them down.

In a clear voice, he explained the situation: The castle had to welcome the king of Scotland within its walls without the presence of its master, Lord Baltair. He listed the tasks to be carried out and distributed them one by one. When he came to the preparations for the reception, he entrusted them to Anna and Nellie under the guidance of their mistress, his wife.

It was then that Lady Beathag interrupted to propose herself instead, arguing that she was more accustomed to directing the castle personnel and had more experience when it came to organising such celebrations and receptions. 'My lord, let us give your wife the time to become perfectly acquainted with the ways of the house and thereby get the best out of our people. It is well known that convent life differs greatly from life at court, and Lady Gunelle's talents, though certainly very great, will definitely not be a great help in the programme you are setting out. Entrust me with all of that. I will see to it. No one could do it any better.'

'Dear Beathag,' said Lord MacNeil calmly, 'immediately after your marriage, when you left the islands, which you had never left before, you came and shut yourself away in Mallaig. What you know about receptions is probably limited to the correct garment to put on or take off, depending on the circumstances. You could have become the chatelaine of Mallaig, but my father decided otherwise. The king of Scotland will be received here according to family tradition. In other words, by the first lady of the castle, Lady Gunelle. If my wife requires your services, she will ask you herself, and I would ask you to comply with her wishes.'

He had turned towards Lady Gunelle as he uttered this last sentence. Anna felt her heart swell with pride on hearing his words: she was proud of young master and of her new mistress. Lord Iain had just put his wife before his ingenuous sister-in-law in front of the entire castle personnel. She gave a look of victory towards Nellie, standing beside her. Lady Beathag gave Gunelle a broad smile to which her eyes full of scorn gave lie.

Totally absorbed by the size of the task which had just been entrusted to her, Gunelle was paying no attention. She looked at her husband, waiting for the rest of his instructions, but she realised that he seemed to be waiting for something from her. With a little nod, he handed it over to her.

'The rest is up to you, my lady. It is up to you to tell us what you expect from each one. For my part, I have nothing more to add.'

Gunelle turned towards her people, took a deep breath, and named the men and women from whom she required help. Then, after a brief nod to her husband, she led them towards the kitchens, her mind on the plan she was already drawing up in her head. Without even a look at Lord Iain, a furious Lady Beathag left the room like a whirlwind. When everyone had left, he took Tomas with him and left the castle in the direction of the harbour where a guard had to be organised.

Guilbert Saxton had never met the king. The event which was being prepared surpassed all those he had attended during his service at the castle. He was anxious to see how Iain and his young bride would acquit themselves. That day he had paid a brief visit to his master and had found him much weaker. He had spoken for a long time to Anna about the old chief's state of health and he shared her concerns. Baltair MacNeil was dying. He probably was not looking forward to another spring at Mallaig; he would not see the New Year. He no longer wished to see his doctor, and it was agreed that from now on, Anna would spend all her time at his bedside and gradually hand over her role as housekeeper to Nellie under the direction of the new chatelaine as they were both now mastering Gaelic.

The secretary, as, indeed, all the castle staff, had come to hold the young chatelaine in very high regard. Lady Gunelle had won the respect of everyone with her dignified behaviour and her extraordinary gift for adapting to life at Mallaig. He was even more delighted to discover in the young woman so many talents that he saw the moment rapidly approaching when he could leave his post as secretary at the castle and pass the keeping of the books to someone competent. He had no doubts about Lady Gunelle's knowledge of arithmetic and her ability to organise. Like many educated wives of her day, this young woman had received a full

101

education and was more than capable of keeping the estate's books in order.

The MacNeil son, who had vehemently refused any education whatsoever, could not have a better helpmate. Unable to read or write, let alone speak Scots, Iain MacNeil's roots were in the Highlands and he only ever conversed with the lairds of his own clan and the chieftains of the neighbouring clans. Apparently, up until now, that had been enough to enable him to maintain order on his estate, become a renowned fighter, and incontestably the tournament champion of the whole of the north of Scotland, including the isles. He had to be recognised for what he was, a practical, down to earth man. Despite his lack of education, Iain MacNeil was certainly the stuff clan chiefs were made of: he displayed great competence in commanding his men and enjoyed a great deal of respect as a horseman and battle strategist. He was cunning, a great expert in handling weapons, a very skilled horseman, and inexhaustible in a fight.

Guilbert Saxton had observed him closely over these last years, and despite this tormented young man's countless faults, he had been impressed by his ability to stand up to his father, authoritative and stubborn man that he was. The latest episode in the struggle between father and son over the marriage had all but broken Lord Baltair's heart but seemed to have hardened his son's. The king's visit was going to highlight the new strengths now present in the castle: the young lady and his future master. A frisson of curiosity ran through the phlegmatic secretary as he went towards the great hall to welcome the Scottish king.

Every torch in the hall was lit and gave off an unpleasant smell of sulphur and brought out the pink of the stone walls. Several guards had taken up position at each door leading to the various wings of the castle. The door of the great hall was flanked by a line of armed men, mostly members of the household company. Silence reigned in the ranks. Each man looked serious, grave, staring straight ahead. Beards and moustaches were motionless on intimidated faces. In the great hall, woollen rugs formed a path from the entrance to the fireplace. Several armchairs had been brought down from the bedrooms and arranged close to the fire. Nearly every candlestick in the castle had been requisitioned, and they formed a vast circle of light all over the room. Lady Gunelle had on the magnificent dress she wore at her wedding and was standing in the doorway, her head held high. The members of the household, standing in a group behind her, waited in tense silence for the entrance of the royal party.

When he entered the great hall, all the king of Scotland could see for a long moment were the tops of heads and the backs of necks. The men had placed one knee on the ground, and the ladies, curtsying deeply, were staring at the floor. He turned to his party, following two paces behind and looked for Lord Iain, who, as it happened was right behind him. Pointing to Lady Gunelle, he asked in Scots, 'My lord, is that your wife?'

Iain guessed the meaning of the question and rushed to pass in front of his king in order to present Gunelle to him. He held out his hand towards her and beckoned her to come forward, calling her by name.

Relieved at last to see the heads and bodies of those present as they straightened up again, the king slightly bowed his head as he met the young lady's eyes and murmured in French, '*Mes hommages, Madame,*' to which Gunelle replied in the same language with a simple, respectful '*Votre Majesté.*' The king smiled at her and looked at the members of the household whom he scrutinised one by one as he waited for the introductions to be made. After a quick glance in her husband's direction, the young lady cleared her throat and began introducing each one in Scots.

King James of Scotland, aged thirty, was a fine-looking man. He had the physique of an athlete, a royal bearing, refined manners, and a strong English accent. To relax the atmosphere, he had a friendly word for each one which did not call for an answer. Once the presentations were over, he signalled to a man from his own party to come forward. Without any ceremony, he made the introduction himself, addressing himself principally to Lord Iain, 'Lord MacNeil, this is Sheriff Darnley whom I have just named as Crown Officer in the Highlands. Let us say that he is your sovereign's eyes, ears, and hands here in the north. My visit has no other purpose than to introduce him to you and ask you to assure him of a temporary place of residence here at Mallaig. Let us say for the moment a stay of seven months.'

James Darnley was standing in front of Lord Iain. In his forties, he was a tall, stout man with a ruddy complexion and thinning hair. He constantly screwed up his eyes, which were small, very dark and scrutinised everyone and everything. He barely bowed his head towards Lord Iain, who returned his greeting with the same economy of movement. The king continued without waiting for them to say anything else. 'That is what has been decided, my lord. I knew we would find loyalty and faithfulness to Scotland and the Crown here. Mallaig is a stronghold par excellence and by far the best place in the north of the country to introduce the new tax law. I am counting therefore on the clan MacNeil to protect and support my representative as if it were I, myself.'

Thereupon, he walked towards the entrance hall, taking hold of Lady Gunelle's arm as he did so. Lord Iain, whom the sheriff was still staring at with his piercing eyes, made as if to step back towards his guard. The voice of Darnley, addressing him in Gaelic, stopped him in his tracks.

'Lord Iain, am I mistaken or do you not speak Scots?' Receiving no reply, he continued, 'Just as I thought. Well, let me explain what the king expects from you.'

Iain was seething. He stiffened as he felt the sheriff's hand on his arm to draw him aside. He waited impatiently for the latter to end his report on the royal wishes at Mallaig. He felt rising within him a wave of antipathy for this officer with his condescending tone of voice.

It was torture for me to hear the king address my husband without getting any response apart from a nod of the head. I was concerned that such a lack of respect would be noticed and the honour of the MacNeil family tarnished forever, but to my great relief, I quickly realised that the king was in the habit of holding forth on his own. In fact, King James, affected by fatigue or the strain of the sea journey, showed a greater need to talk than to listen. That was why he bombarded me with a thousand comments about his journey to the Highlands with no other aim than to furnish the silence. Then, comfortably ensconced in the best armchair and after having drunk the mulled wine he had been offered, he slowly began to relax, and his chatter dried up.

I had planned to have the whole company dine quite early, for I had been informed that the king wanted to leave Mallaig at daybreak the next day. I gave the signal to sit down at the table. The monarch did not seem to want to talk to anyone but myself, and he began by asking me about Lord Baltair's health. He invited Lord Tomas to join in the conversation since it was he, who had informed him of Lord Baltair's illness when he disembarked. Tomas sat opposite me and next to the king, who occupied the place of honour at the head of the table. To my left was my husband, then Saxton, the secretary; opposite them sat the sheriff and Father Henriot. As a result of this seating arrangement, Iain found himself right in the middle of people who were speaking Scots. His sullen look spoke volumes about his unease. I glanced furtively at him, and I was concerned. I did not know by which turn of his conversation with Lord Tomas, the king had learned that I spoke fluent French. I was stupefied, therefore, to hear the king use the language to speak to me about his wife, Jeanne Beaufort, daughter of the Count of Somerset and their little two-year-old daughter Marguerite. He spoke clearly and had perfectly mastered this language which all the monarchs in Europe spoke fluently among themselves. He was kind enough to congratulate me on my knowledge of French, and we laughed about it. I think it was at that moment that I was won over by his affability.

As if it were a great secret, he told me that he spoke French with his wife in public when he did not want what they were saying to be understood. He confided that theirs was a love match which was very rare in royal houses. What simplicity, what candour in such a confession so unexpectedly coming from a king! I was, to all intents and purposes, smitten by the time I suddenly realised, half an hour later, on noticing Tomas's admiring glance, that the king had kept me to himself. And that we had been conversing in a language only the two of us spoke. The king, too, must have realised it because he began to speak to Tomas in Scots and asked him about the studies undertaken by the young northern lords in the Edinburgh colleges. I was relieved to no longer be engaged in conversation with my sovereign, and I could devote myself to my other duties as hostess, particularly the service of the rest of the meal. My orders had been carried out to perfection, and the flavours of all the dishes did justice to the combined efforts of the kitchen staff during the day. I overheard a discussion in Gaelic between my husband, Saxton, the secretary, and Sheriff Darnley. It was about taxes and new laws. I knew from having heard a lot of talk about it at my father's house that, since his return from England, King James had earned the reputation of being a great law maker. His very numerous royal edicts had regulated the military training of young men, the parity of the English and Scottish currency, the suppression of public disorder and vagrancy, salmon fishing, and the export of gold. Almost no part of Scottish life had escaped his statute books. Evidently, this desire to legislate for everything met the need to restore order and prosperity in the land which twenty years of regency had made bankrupt. Observing and listening to the stern Sheriff Darnley, one realised that nothing would be accomplished without constant surveillance of the northern clan chiefs, who historically had always been more than ready to question royal authority.

This declaration made me uneasy. Would Lord Baltair and Iain agree to subject the clan MacNeil to the sovereign's new policy? When I managed to catch my husband's steely blue eyes, I knew that anger had begun to set in.

The reception was a success. The king expressed his appreciation which I promised to convey to my people at the earliest opportunity. He expressed the wish to retire early, which he did as soon as the polite exchanges that usually followed a meal were over. Before leaving the room, he had a friendly word for Tomas too. My husband, who was deep in conversation with Sheriff Darnley, was unable to greet the king, nor was he greeted by him.

After the sovereign's departure accompanied by his own escort and some of our knights, I remained sitting quietly by the fire and shared my impressions of the royal visit with Tomas. I was delighted with the intelligent and pertinent comments Tomas made. We shared the same ideas, and we asked the same questions about the exceptional man who King James was: We must have spent nearly an hour talking this way, quite naturally in Scots. That was the first mistake. Iain, who had soon tired of the sheriff's company, was standing behind us and harangued me dryly.

'My lady, what is it that is so interesting that you can tell my cousin, but I do not get to hear it? This evening, you are enjoying using all the languages of your impressive repertoire but not a word in Gaelic.'

I was speechless. Tomas jumped to his feet, with a look of outrage on his face and answered his cousin on my behalf. That was the second mistake.

'Look here, Iain! Your wife spoke the language chosen by the king to address her. She is the one who save the family's face, and you hold it against her? She covers up your own ignorance of the Scots language in front of your sovereign, and you dare to reproach her?'

'Get out!' Iain ordered him in a tone that did not invite a reply. 'You are not the king, and she has been talking to you in Scots for an hour.' Then, giving me an icy look, he added, 'From now on, I forbid you to speak Scots in the castle. Do I make myself understood, my lady?'

'Perfectly, my lord,' I muttered in Gaelic through tightly closed lips. I sensed that I must not provoke him. Everything about his demeanour indicated that he was spoiling for a fight. I gulped and looked down at my hands, hoping with all my might that Tomas would leave the room without saying a word. I breathed freely when I heard his footsteps move away.

I looked up. Almost everyone had already left the room for the night. My husband sat down in the armchair that Tomas had occupied beside me and asked for a drink of whisky. He was served a cup immediately. The silence between us became heavy, palpable, suffocating. He broke it with a gentle voice that took me by surprise.

'How strange, my lady. You have nothing to say. Do not tell me you are looking for your words.'

'No, my lord. I am ready to discuss whatever you wish.' After a moment's hesitation, I continued, 'I have nothing to hide from you. Lord Tomas and I did not notice that we were speaking Scots after the king left. We were sharing our impressions of our sovereign in particular and the reception in general.'

'I imagine you are waiting for me to congratulate you on this reception, are you not?'

'Of course not, my lord. I merely did my duty to the best of my ability.'

'Of course… Your duty…' He emptied his cup in one go and added with obvious annoyance, 'Just how far are you ready to go to do your duty? I would like to know.'

I did not know what to reply. Where did he want to go with this? I could not work it out. However, I had to speak to him and, if possible, for as long as I had spoken to Tomas. I forced myself to use a rather conciliatory tone, full of restraint, to broach the subject that had engrossed me minutes earlier with Tomas: the king. I repeated, this time in Gaelic, what I thought of the sovereign. From time to time, Iain looked at me inscrutably then plunged again into his contemplation of the fire in the hearth without saying a word. I spoke to myself like that for quite a while. He was not giving me the slightest hint of whether my comments were of any interest to him. He sank deeper into the armchair and stretched out his legs. Bran came cautiously and laid his head on his feet. When a servant came to refill his cup on his signal, he offered me some. Contrary to all his expectations, I accepted. He sat up and stared at me. Then, moving forward in his armchair, he moved his head close to mine and asked with a sneer, 'Tell me, my lady, is it also out of duty that you are accepting to drink whisky with me?'

'I am tired of talking to myself, my lord. Since you seem to be in the mood for drinking and to be in my company, I might as well drink with you. The interesting thing about drinking is that it does not need conversation, and drinking is drinking in any language. Do you not agree?'

'You have just said it, my lady, drinking can do without conversation.'

Grabbing the cup which was brought for me, he held it out to me and then touched it with his, which he gulped down. He did not say a word but did not take his eyes off me the whole time I drank my whisky. That was a very long time. Each mouthful burned my throat and my insides. Exhaustion enveloped me like a lead coat. I almost fell asleep after twenty minutes, and I would have done so if my husband had not burst out laughing when he saw my head nodding. He stood up, took the cup from my hands, pulled me up, and gently advised me to go to bed. As I was picking up a candlestick to leave the room, which was almost empty by that time, he added very quietly, 'The reception was perfect. You came out of that admirably well, and the whole MacNeil family owes its success to you.'

Chapter Five
The Revelation

The weather had changed for the better since the departure of the king and his entourage. The men hunted all day, returning in the evening with their bag of game to be dressed. Now, when I went up on the ramparts with Ceit, I no longer needed to protect my face from the biting cold. I went there every day and took advantage of the solitude to tutor my little protégée. In fact, I had noticed that when I managed to be alone with her, she was very receptive. In the strong wind I could speak loudly without worrying about disturbing anyone. That way, I was sure that the little girl heard each syllable I pronounced so that she, in turn, could repeat them. Her progress was extremely encouraging, and this activity kept me well away from the unpleasant company of Lady Beathag and her maid. I had not been able to stir up any interest in the tapestry they spent the whole day doing, and their inuendo strewn idle chatter exasperated me. I avoided their company as much as they avoided mine. We only conversed, so to speak, at mealtimes, and the conversations were always disappointing.

I had also formed the habit of spending a few hours in the afternoon in the library, which had been the late Alasdair's bedroom. Occasionally, Ceit accompanied me, but she did not stay long. In the daylight which flooded in through the south-facing window, I would get lost in the perusal of the manuscripts and books. I selected works that I could propose as reading material for Lord Baltair. Since the old man no longer got out of bed, I visited him regularly and entertained him by reading aloud to him. He was delighted. He welcomed me with great joy and listened to the stories I read to him as long as his strength allowed. I had noticed that he was not very familiar with the collection of books gathered by his wife and elder son over the years and concluded that he had not been a great reader. I was delighted to watch him discover the richness of the books he owned.

It was the 24th of December, and the joy of Christmas filled me from the moment I got up. The morning service, which for me was the one form of happiness possible at Mallaig, had brought peace to my heart. The day before, I had picked out a book about the life of King Arthur, and after the service, I was heading towards Lord Baltair's bedroom to read to him when I was stopped by Mairi, a young servant who had joined my service after Vivian's departure. Mairi was carrying my fur cape and gloves on her arm, and she handed them to me. Breathlessly, as if she had been running, she informed me I was awaited in the courtyard.

'You are going out this morning, my lady. Lord Iain sent me to fetch you. He told me to watch for you coming out of the service and to take you to him immediately. Everyone is waiting for you.'

It was just like my husband to demand my presence for some activity or other without asking my opinion. I handed the book to Mairi and put on my cape and gloves. When I went outside, I realised what kind of trip it was. A horse ride! The sweat began to form in drops on my brow, and a chill ran down my spine. Lady Beathag, her maid, Sheriff Darnley, Tomas, and four household knights were waiting on horseback in the middle of the courtyard. Beside my husband, who was holding his horse by the reins, an equerry was standing with a white horse, which was obviously meant for me.

I immediately stepped backwards and confessed in a voice in which I had difficulty overcoming the note of fear, 'My lord, did no one mention it to you? I do not ride. I do not know how to ride. I…'

'I was told, my lady, but the sheriff wishes to go for a ride over some parts of our estate, and you are going to take advantage of the opportunity to visit them too. I should have done it sooner, I know. It is inadmissible that the chatelaine of Mallaig does not know her estate. Do you not share this opinion?'

I was panic-stricken at the idea of going near the horse the equerry was holding and was incapable of saying a single word. Since my husband was not getting an answer, he let go of his horse, walked over, and took me by the arm to help me into the saddle, all the time talking to me about the animal as if it was a member of the staff.

'Good old Melchior is as gentle as a lamb and as slow as a crab. We are very fond of him, but he hardly ever has the chance to get out. I am sure he will be unaware that he is carrying an inexperienced rider. He will hardly even notice you on his back.'

I must have shouted as I escaped from his grip, for he jumped. I ran towards the porch, but he soon caught me. Grabbing me by the wrists, he made me turn to look at him. He must have seen my distress and fear, for his look of anger turned to one of concern when I tried to explain myself. I was pleading. 'It is impossible for me, my lord. I am too scared of horses to ride. I beg you, do not make me. I am begging you. I will go by carriage… or on foot!'

'What on earth, my lady? That is insane! Our estate extends for fifty miles, and not even eight of those are practicable by carriage. You will never be able to cover that distance on foot. You are going to have to conquer your fear and get on that horse.'

'I am going to try to learn, my lord. I promise you, but not today and not with these people watching me. I will visit the estate another time. It can wait,' I pleaded quietly.

'The king of Scotland's representative will not visit the MacNeil estate before the chatelaine of Mallaig,' he declared by way of reply.

He let go of my wrists and, addressing the horsemen and women waiting for us, told them to go ahead by the south shore. The group moved off immediately, with Tomas at the front. Iain sent the equerry and the horse back to the stables and began to unsaddle his mount. I had no idea what was happening. What did he intend to do? He left the thick blue woollen cover and the bridle on the horse.

He turned towards me, took my hand, and drew it gently towards the nostrils of the animal which he was holding with his other hand and, looking straight into my eyes, simply said, 'Let him get your scent, my lady.'

My hand was enclosed in his. I could not pull it away. I closed my eyes so that he would not see my terror and went along with the game for a few seconds, which seemed like hours to me. What happened next was very sudden. Grabbing the horse's mane, Iain mounted and, leaning sideways, took hold of my waist with one hand and lifted me up from the ground as if I were a wisp of straw. The next instant, I was sitting in front of him, a leg on either side of the animal's neck and my skirts covering part of it. He was holding the reins in his left hand and had his right arm around me, pinning me back against his chest. My hips were pushing against his knees, tight against the horse's flanks. With my two gloved hands, I was desperately clinging to the arm around me, squeezing it so tight that I could have almost broken my fingers. I was holding my breath. My ears were ringing. *I am going to die*, I thought. The animal moved forward slowly, obeying some signal I would not have been able to identify. Then he began to trot and moved onto the drawbridge. I closed my eyes again, petrified with fear.

'There, my lady, you are on horseback,' said Iain. 'Please open your eyes, or you will miss the view.' Probably noticing that I was not taking his advice, he calmly added, 'Do you feel securely held, my lady?' Not receiving a reply, he continued, 'Do you think I intend to let you fall?'

I felt his grip tighten as he repeated his question. I opened my eyes.

'Answer me, my lady. Do you think me capable of letting you go?'

'No!' I murmured.

'Good. Now, do you think that I could fall off this horse?'

I had to make a great effort to formulate the first answer which came to mind, 'Many consider you to be one of the best horsemen in the north of Scotland. I would imagine that no horse of yours would even attempt to throw you.'

'Excellent! Then, in that case, my lady, seriously, what could happen to you this morning as you go riding, with my arms wrapped tightly around you.?'

Obviously, I had no answer to that. Absolutely rigid, I stared at the thick black ears moving backwards and forwards in front of me each time my husband spoke. The horse's nostrils regularly gave released a white vapour which formed as frost on its neck. The tangled black mane swayed to the rhythmic movement of its strides. I risked a glance towards the horizon. We were already a good distance from the castle but still half a mile from the group ahead. I slightly turned my head to the right and saw the glint of the sun in the distance; then, on the other side, the dark outline of the mountains spread out like a fan. I took a deep breath. The cold air that entered deep within me acted like a lever that thrust out the fear lodged inside. I felt the tension in my arms ease.

My husband must have noticed, for he murmured with a voice that revealed his sense of satisfaction, 'Now, you are going to enjoy this ride, my lady. You will not be disappointed. You own the finest estate in the Highlands.'

We rode that way for more than an hour. My husband did not seem to want to catch up with the rest of the party and was happy to follow at a good distance. He talked to me throughout the ride. First, he explained why he had to insist that I make this reconnaissance trip that morning and not later. It was then that I learned of Sheriff Darnley's precise role in the affair: He was to check the accounts of all the Highland clans and introduce new taxes for each one. Iain informed me that Saxton, the secretary, was not prepared to put up with this intrusion into his work and had asked to leave the castle service as soon as possible. It turned out that I had been appointed as his replacement.

'Do you understand, my lady, why you must never know less than Darnley about the MacNeil estate? You must have seen, read, and heard everything he will see, read, or hear about us. Do you understand, my lady?'

'I understand, my lord,' I replied.

'You see, my lady, I am not forcing you to go for a ride for the pleasure of forcing you. I owe it to myself to escort you this morning, and that is why I am doing so. I would like you to know that I shall never force you to do something you hate unless I must.'

This clarification dissolved the lump I had had in my throat since we left. I could not have any resentment against him for his behaviour towards me. It was totally justified. Deep down, I had to admit that I trusted him and agreed with his decision. From that moment, I began to relax. I felt a strange sensation inside at the sound of his voice from behind my head, the touch of his face on my hood when he leaned forward and the security of his arm around my waist. The scenery of the promontory we were skirting soon occupied my attention. The shore was made up of bare black rocks as far as the eye could see. The sea was rolling in with great breakers throwing a pure white spray up into the air. My husband scoured the coastline and the invisible isles in the distance, pointing out everything which had a direct link with the MacNeil estate and which he thought I should know. Sometimes there were historic anecdotes, sometimes, the yield of the land or fishing, sometimes methods used, sometimes about people too. Compared to Tomas, my husband was a very concise guide, explaining things to me as if I had always lived in the Highlands. I liked that.

Towards the end of the morning, we caught up with the others, who had stopped in a cove. The wind had risen and was gusting through my open cape. I did not dare let go of my husband's arms, even with one hand to hold it closed. My eyes, stinging from the cold, were streaming. I must have been a sorry sight for, when the horse stopped, Tomas, no doubt, worried about me ever since we left, hurried over to help me down. As soon as I was on the ground, he wrapped me in his own cape and led me to the shelter of a rock under my husband's look of annoyance. The ladies and Sheriff Darnley were all already there, busy warming their hands over a little makeshift fire of driftwood. The sheriff half-smiled at me and spoke to me in Scots. I could not help stiffening up and glancing at my husband, who was coming over to us.

'I almost forgot, Lady Gunelle, you have only been married a week. That explains your sharing your husband's horse.'

The remark was coarse, or at least I found it so. I decided to ignore it, but the sheriff repeated it in Gaelic for the benefit of Iain, who was now within earshot. Lady Beathag and her maid both burst out laughing with the same impertinent laugh.

Lady Beathag, turning towards my husband, continued mellifluously, 'I was never fortunate enough to ride in such a loving, romantic way with your brother Alasdair, for I already knew how to ride when I came to live at Mallaig, if you remember, my lord.'

'Even if you had not been able to ride, dear Beathag,' replied Iain, 'you could never have mounted the same horse as my brother. I do not know of any horse capable of carrying both your weights for more than a mile.'

'Ah, your brother was indeed a man of exceptional height. Tell me, my lord, he must have been a good head taller than you, was he not? As I am better built than Lady Gunelle…'

'Keep quiet, Beathag!' Iain cut in dryly.

'Look at that. Men are all the same! They never admit to being inferior to others. Come on, my lord, I did not say you are not a fine piece of manhood.' Turning to address me, she persisted and stressed, 'Lady Gunelle, have you not got a fine specimen of a man there?'

I did not have to answer, for once again, my husband interrupted her, his voice becoming more and more exasperated.

'Dear Beathag, when will you stop thinking of me as a stallion always ready to cover the first rump which offers itself?'

Lady Beathag guffawed. My husband's reply brought a smile to the lips of everyone except Tomas. As for me, I was embarrassed and all the more so because certain words my husband had said were new to me, and the context indicated that they must have been coarse. Lady Beathag had risen to her feet and was going towards the horses with the eyes of everyone fixed on her. She stopped, and turning towards us, she hurled a reply to my husband's question, which cracked like a whip.

'When you stop behaving like one!'

This time, there was complete silence. Apart from Darnley, no one was smiling. My husband swore as he kicked the fire. His face contracted into a scowl full of hatred, and he said between clenched teeth, 'Rotten bitch!'

I shuddered on hearing those words. What was the relationship between my husband and his sister-in-law? Sometimes they behaved as if they were close; sometimes, their exchanges were cutting and full of utter contempt. A shiver of unease went down my spine. My husband must have noticed, for he gave the signal to leave. One of the knights came and put out the fire and everyone remounted. The wind was twice as strong now, and I could hardly stand when I left my shelter. My skirts were blowing so much they were hindering my walking.

Iain signalled to Tomas, who came and retrieved his cloak. He said to him dryly, 'Help her up behind me. I will shelter her from the wind.' Then to me, in a gentler tone, 'The view will not be as good, my lady, but if you think you can hold on, you will not be as cold behind me. Do you think you will manage?'

I was not sure at all, but since I was determined to show as much goodwill as possible, I did not want to say no. I nodded. He jumped on his horse's back and held out his arm, which I grabbed without any hesitation. I immediately felt myself being lifted by Tomas, who set me down behind Iain. I leaned instinctively against his back; my arm tight around his waist. Tomas gathered my cape here and there under my legs so that I would be well wrapped up, then gave the horse's rump a slap, and it began to move off. I clung even more tightly to my husband while suppressing, with great deal of difficulty, a cry of sheer terror. Iain wedged my arms under his own and, with a move of his body, signalled to his mount to trot.

The journey back was much more silent than the one going. With my cheek squashed against my husband's back, I heard the orders he gave the other riders as if through an ear trumpet. Watching the landscape go past sideways was making me dizzy. I protected myself from the attacks of the cold wind by screwing up my eyes and burying my nose in my hood. The smell of the warm leather of Iain's jacket soon filled my little enclosed universe. Not a word was spoken between us all the way to the castle. And so, it was for the rest of the day. The opening which had been momentarily created between us in the morning was closing, and, once again, I was incapable of working out the exact cause.

Father Henriot would have been unable to say whether he was fond of Lord Baltair or not. He had asked himself the question since he had gone to give him communion that Christmas Eve and had foreseen the imminent prospect of giving this man of faith the last rites. The last time he had had to do so at the castle had been for the late chatelaine. Henriot had not known her well since he had begun his ministry at Mallaig in spring 1417, just two years before the tragedy which had befallen the MacNeils.

Life at the castle had changed completely as a result of that event. When Lady Isla had fallen ill, he had noticed that the family's faith had begun to wane. They had come to the point of deserting the chapel altogether, leaving him totally at a loss as to what to do. He had fervently spent whole nights in prayer asking God to come and help him to support this family, which was being sorely tested, and for whose souls he felt responsible. However, the passing of Lady Isla had closed the hearts of the two lords to the teachings of the church once and for all. He knew that their religious practice was only a facade. Within a few months, Baltair MacNeil had become distant and unapproachable, and his son almost a stranger.

During his visit to Lord Baltair, he had accepted that one of these two lost souls was about to appear before his God. Would he be able to find the right words to make this final journey easier for him? Of all the tasks in his ministry, that of accompanying the faithful in death seemed the most difficult. Father Henriot suddenly felt too young to understand an old man like Baltair MacNeil. He shrugged his shoulders and heaved a long sigh as he closed the door of the old chief's bedroom. At midnight in the well-lit chancel of the chapel, as he raised the host above his head, a deep sense of peace flowed through him and he knew that grace would be given to him to serve God at Lord Baltair's side.

The singing of the knights and ladies of the castle rose clear and hearty at midnight mass. The whole MacNeil household was there. For the first since their wedding, the newlyweds stood side by side in the front row. Lord Iain, his face inscrutable, was barely making the responses. By his side, his wife was praying reverently, and the joy of Christmas was obvious in every trait of her face. Looking at her during the benediction, Father Henriot began to hope that divine faith would win back the Lords MacNeil through this chatelaine just as it had disappeared with the departure of the former one.

As tradition demanded, Nellie and Anna had prepared a light meal which they served at the end of the service. Trays of cakes, oat cakes, honey biscuits, and marzipan sat side by side on a table with cups of mead and pitchers of posset, a mixture of mulled wine and curdled buttermilk. The harpist, whom Lord Iain had retained at the castle, had set up his clarsach in front of the table and was playing airs taught in the monasteries to accompany the Christmas liturgy. The ladies, maids, and servants were thoroughly enjoying his programme and sang throughout the meal. Lady Gunelle knew the Latin words and smiled at how the Highlanders had translated them into the local dialect.

Little Ceit, who was holding on to the young chatelaine's skirt, had put on a white dress with a finely embroidered bodice and wound the belt from the wedding dress several times around her waist. Lady Gunelle had a protective hand on the frail shoulders of the little girl and leaned over to whisper little secrets in her ear. Ceit would smile for a few seconds, then hide her face again in the silky material of her guardian's dress. On seeing Lord Iain coming towards them, she stiffened. He had been watching them out of the corner of his eye for some time. When he was very close to his wife, he noticed the little girl's game and his face lit up with amusement.

He bent down to her level to ask her in a serious voice, 'Tell me, Ceit, since you can speak now, how do you find little Jesus tonight?' Not receiving an answer, not even a look, he broached another subject, 'This is the first time I have seen you so prettily dressed. Especially the belt. I think I have seen it before. Were you wearing it at the wedding?'

'No! It is Gunelle's!' she answered promptly, looking straight at him.

Iain caught her by the chin and gave her a long, sad look. Then letting go of her, he said slowly, 'You must say, "Lady Gunelle."'

Ceit broke away from the couple and ran out of the room. Bran, who was just wandering about, took off after her, thinking she wanted to play but was called back by his master. Then Iain turned uneasily towards his wife. He felt he should talk to her about Ceit when he saw her questioning look. He cleared his throat and asked, 'I imagine, my lady, you are waiting for me to talk to you about Ceit?'

'No, my lord, why should you?' she asked him calmly.

'Because she has benefitted a great deal from her contact with you, I suppose.'

After a brief silence, he continued with a bitter smile on his lips, 'It would appear you have a real gift for languages. You speak Latin, French, German, and no doubt English. You learn a language in two weeks. You teach a little girl who cannot speak to speak in only one. Well then, tell me, my lady, how long would it take you to teach me Scots?'

'That depends on you, my lord. What kind of pupil are you? Have you a good memory? Can you concentrate for long hours? Can you read and write quickly? You know it requires all of that to learn a language in a short time.'

'My lady, I do not know what kind of pupil I am, for I have never been one. Since you still seem to be unaware of it, I shall inform you that I can neither read nor write. I have always refused to be educated. I left that whole domain to my brother, who excelled in it, and I devoted myself to weapons, which is more akin to my character. With the results that you see. No one attacks Mallaig when I am here, but I cannot acquaint myself with any documents concerning the estate without an interpreter. With my father's illness and a representative of the king in the house, I am afraid my talents as a fighter will not suffice.'

'In that case, my lord, I cannot answer your question precisely. I can, and I am going to teach you Scots if that is what you wish. We will see if you are a good pupil. If you are, you will learn the language and read and write it before the New Year. You will have to give all your free time to it and lift the ban on me speaking Scots in the castle.'

'Obviously, my lady. It goes without saying, the ban is lifted but only with me.'

However, the Scots lessons could not begin. The days after Christmas extinguished all joy and hope in the castle. Firstly, a new health crisis for Lord Baltair caused the spectre of death to hover for forty-eight hours. Insensitive to the distress that this caused the castle folk, Sheriff Darnley monopolised Saxton, the secretary, for the auditing of the books, which ended in a violent disagreement between the two men. Despite his best diplomatic efforts, Lord Iain was unable to resolve the dispute in favour of his secretary and had to accept his resignation.

Guilbert Saxton would have wished to remain in the service of the MacNeils until chiefs' final breath, but his professional pride would not allow him to bow to the sheriff's wishes. The hours spent discussing estate finances with the young chatelaine at her husband's request had convinced him that the changeover was in safe hands. Lady Gunelle was alert, intelligent, and a thinker who would very effectively represent the family's interests. She would know how to adopt a better approach to the problem with Darnley. The feminine approach. He smiled as he remembered the many talents of the preceding chatelaine, one of which was to obtain exactly what she wanted from people, even if they were enemies. Something told him that Lady Gunelle was acquiring the same gift. When he announced, he was leaving to old Lord Baltair, it was in the presence of the MacNeil son and his wife. He watched Iain and Gunelle carefully, standing at either side of the bed in a common attitude of respect and love for the old chief. He thought he detected a certain harmony between the couple, and there was a definite improvement between father and son.

'It is going to work out,' the secretary reassured himself. 'These three people so desperately need to get on with one another. The future of Mallaig depends on it. We must have confidence in them. May God help them!'

He, therefore, left Mallaig with a sense of duty accomplished. Lord Iain gave him an escort of six men as far as his destination, the monastery at Dornoch on the North Sea coast, where he came from and where his brother was still a bishop. The goodbyes exchanged with the castle folk had shown Guilbert Saxton that the bonds of friendship woven over so many years were by far the most precious a man could possess at the end of a career in the service of a clan. Father Henriot came to bless this, the second party to leave Mallaig in two weeks. All that remained was to hope that the start of January would be clement for the travellers who set off, under the MacNeil banner.

For Tomas, the imminent death of Lord Baltair aroused the same pain he had felt on his father's death. Unable to sleep because of the doubt and anguish which struggled against each other within his soul, he rose early. He was constantly afraid his uncle would succumb to the next crisis and was always on edge. All that left him exhausted. He would have liked to share his anxiety with someone. None of his fellow knights were close enough to be his confidant, and his cousin was still rather hostile towards him. The only person, in whom Tomas felt he could confide, was Lady Gunelle. However, he had forced himself to avoid her company as much as possible. He must not make the slightest move which might aggravate the extreme tension between himself and Iain, and the attention he paid to Gunelle was a part of that. Tomas was sorry about that, for the days spent teaching her Gaelic had been the most enriching experience of his life.

One morning when sleep deserted him in the small hours, he went to the chapel. It was plunged in half-light, and a smell of incense and dampness floated in the air like some sort of presence. He did not take a candle and knelt to pray in one of the corners for a while. As he stood up, his foot touched something. Leaning down, he found a psalter, probably forgotten by Gunelle. He picked it up and left the chapel. It would be better to return it to the library rather than give it to the young lady. He went straight upstairs. The library wing had three bedrooms looking out onto the south face of the keep—the first was Lord Iain's, the second Alasdair's, and the third Lady Beathag's. Tomas noticed Bran wandering in the corridor but did not pay any attention and went into Alasdair's room where the family's entire collection of books was kept. He placed the psalter in full view on the table and perused the rows of perfectly arranged books for a few minutes. He took out several books, put them back, and took out others and leafed through them. He began to browse here and there and realised how little he had read since leaving Edinburgh. At Mallaig, his training to become a knight with his cousin took up all his time, so much so that he had never had the opportunity to visit Alasdair's room as he did that morning. He spent an hour among the books until he heard the bell for matins ringing in the courtyard. His escape into the books had brought him serenity and calm. He replaced the books one by one and left the room. At the door, he stopped: Lady Gunelle, a book in her arms, which were

126

crossed on her chest, was standing motionless at the end of the corridor, her eyes staring straight ahead. Tomas turned his head to see what was captivating her attention at the other end of the corridor and understood immediately. There was Bran stretched full length outside Lady Beathag's bedroom door, fast asleep. He scarcely had the time to turn towards Gunelle than she was already fleeing up the staircase leading to her bedroom.

'Good grief!' he murmured between his teeth. 'Is there nothing he will spare her?'

He went down to the chapel, his heart full of contempt for his cousin. Contrary to her usual habit, Gunelle did not turn up for morning mass.

Tomas felt at a loss: He wanted to help the young woman, but he did not know how. Having a word with his cousin would be a move doomed to failure since the thorny question of the relationship between Iain and his sister-in-law was a taboo subject at the castle. He automatically set off in the direction of his uncle's bedroom to enquire about his health from Anna, who, he knew, was at his bedside. In fact, she was there with Gunelle, who got up as soon he entered and made to leave.

He attempted rather clumsily to stop her. 'I beg you, my lady, do not go! I just came to get some news.'

'The health report is good, nephew,' Baltair MacNeil answered immediately from his bed. 'Thank you for your visit. Come and sit down and find out for me what is wrong with these two women. They have nothing to say this morning, and I cannot find out what is on their minds.'

Thomas cast a furtive glance at Gunelle. She stubbornly kept looking down.

Anna was the first to break the silence and said, as she fixed her master's pillows, 'My lord, come now, you are making your visitors feel uncomfortable. We have nothing to say because the day has hardly started, and we are not quite awake yet. There! And of course, we are worried about your health.'

'Of course,' he replied. 'That is very understandable. Do you not think it is upsetting to see young people wasting their time at the foot of my bed? Tomas, you would do me a favour by taking Lady Gunelle out to get some fresh air this morning. That makes two whole days in the study, and the air must be polluted there. Take her out! That is an order!'

Tomas made a gesture of helplessness towards Gunelle, who had watched him throughout this broadside. The authoritarian tone of the patient allowed for no discussion: They had to comply with his wishes.

Gunelle understood, for she left the room murmuring, 'As you wish, my lord.'

Without a word, Tomas caught up with her. Outside the closed door, she arranged to meet him on the north side of the battlement walk and went up to fetch her cape and gloves from her bedroom.

From the top of the castle, Tomas looked at the mountains where clouds, heavy with snow, were gathering. The wind was blowing north-northeast, which meant snow would cover the village. He repressed a frown: Several poorly situated houses offered little protection for their inhabitants. He tried to take his anxious mind off the thought of talking to Gunelle alone. He failed. When he saw her

128

coming towards him in the strong wind, his heart missed a beat. How worn out she looked! He knew that the conversation would turn to his cousin.

'Lord Tomas,' she said in Gaelic, her voice under control, 'you do not have to say anything. You are aware of what I discovered this morning and the conclusions I have drawn. I know by now that no one at the castle will broach the subject.'

After a moment's hesitation, she continued, 'It is very painful for me to note that I am the last person to know what everyone seems to have known for a long time and particularly since it concerns me.'

While she spoke, she had gathered the edges of her fur-lined hood around her eyes so that it was impossible to see them. Only her fine nose was visible.

'My lady, I am not bound by any oath of secrecy where my cousin is concerned, and I disapprove of the way he conducts his private life. On the other hand, I hold you in very high regard, and if I can be of any help, I would be delighted to help in any way I can. I am prepared to tell you what you have the right to know about the man you have married. Do you wish to hear my revelations, my lady?'

Lady Gunelle moved forward slowly. She took the arm Lord Tomas offered and fell in step with him. For a long moment, she said nothing with the result that her companion wondered if she would accept his offer of help. However, he heard her begin to speak in a whisper.

'My lord, I am perplexed. I do not know how to react to all this. I am not an expert when it comes to men…'

'My lady, let me tell you about my cousin.' After a moment of silence, which he took for consent, Tomas continued, 'When I came to Mallaig for my apprenticeship two years ago, Lady Beathag was already his mistress. I was stupefied to see that their liaison was common knowledge and was indeed tolerated by his father. I have never been aware of any discussions on the matter between my uncle and Iain, and God knows he reproaches him with a lot. How my cousin and his sister-in-law can live with this sin, I have no idea. Evidently, it does not weigh heavily on their consciences. You yourself must have noticed that neither is a very fervent Christian. However, they are both tormented and unloved beings. You may be astonished to hear me say that, and I am not saying it to try to excuse them. They are not happy together. What they give to each other has nothing to do with love. Beathag is an insatiable woman, and my cousin is a disaffected young man. I think Alasdair's death has a part to play in this liaison, but I would be incapable of explaining how.'

'I am touched by your revelation. There are so many things I do not know, which prevent me from understanding your cousin, Lord Tomas. He is unfathomable. I do not understand Lady Beathag's behaviour any better. Why did she remain at Mallaig after her husband's death? Should she not have returned to her family, who still live on Skye?'

'Listen, at that time, I lived in Inverness with my father and did not have much contact with my uncle and aunt. But I do know that Lady Isla greatly appreciated her daughter-in-law's presence, which contributed much to the castle in its heyday. Even though she had been declared infertile and thus deprived the family of an heir, at the time of Alistair's death, my aunt asked his widow to stay on at the castle. Besides, Lady Beathag would not have returned to her island for anything. To be happy, she needs to be surrounded by admirers. Mallaig offers her that. Not one man has passed through here without her seducing him or at least trying to do so. If she spoke Scots, I am sure she would have tried to seduce the king.'

'Did she seduce you, Lord Tomas?'

The young man squirmed at this question, which was straight to the point. Lady Gunelle's voice was firm and showed none of the uneasiness of the beginning of the conversation. They had reached the guards' tower and were now sheltered from the wind. Since she had let go of the edge of her hood, Gunelle's face was now visible. Her expression revealed her intense curiosity.

He looked away as he replied, 'Let us say she tried and did not get what she wanted. Lady Beathag is not my kind of woman.'

'My dear cousin,' Lord Iain's voice thundered suddenly from behind them. 'Would my wife be your kind of woman?'

Shocked, Tomas and Gunelle turned around as one. Iain MacNeil, whom they had not heard arriving, was standing fifteen paces from them, straight, motionless, and menacing. He was dressed in battle armour: helmet and short chain mail, claymore in his belt, sgian-dubh at his ankle. Instinctively, Gunelle moved back towards Tomas, which made her husband laugh cynically. Tomas had difficulty controlling the fit of anger which had taken hold of him. A deathly silence fell over the group.

It was Iain who broke it, addressing his cousin curtly, 'Enough! I will wait for you in the courtyard. We are resuming your training this morning. Fighting with the claymore. Go and put on your chain mail!'

As if in a dream, I watched Tomas go around Iain and briskly leave the ramparts in the direction of the guardroom. I could only see my husband's eyes under his helmet. They were staring at me, full of hardness. I froze with fear. It was no use thinking back to Lord Baltair's assurances that the MacNeil son did not ill-treat women. The terror my husband awoke in me at that moment intensified. I turned around and fled in the opposite direction to the guardroom. I almost bumped into Bran, who was passing behind me. I let out a cry of surprise, and gathering up my skirts, I made off as quickly as I could. My mind was blank as I ran off. I was frantic. Tears of bitterness, intensified by the cold wind, were streaming down my face. When I finally reached my bedroom, I threw myself on my bed. I was exhausted. *"What am I going to do now?"* I thought in despair. Then I heard a gentle knock at the door and saw Mairi enter, looking worried.

She came towards me without a word and helped me take off my cape and gloves. From the look on her face, I realised she had been told of the drama unfolding. Without being too sure why, I asked her what she thought of my husband. I realised right away that her answer ran the risk of receiving a reprimand, but I saw in her eyes such sympathy and trust that I knew she would speak frankly. Indeed, she did just that. With a great deal of simplicity, she painted a picture of a man transformed since his marriage. A man who no longer hassled the servant girls, a man who no longer got drunk, a man who no longer spoke ill of his father, a man who concerned himself with the people of the castle and their well-being, a man who received the King of Scotland with dignity.

At first, that description of my husband appeared most incredible. What was most disconcerting was that she gave me all the credit for such a transformation.

'Come now,' I said to myself, 'this dear girl is living in a land of make-believe.'

Then, thinking about it carefully, I had to admit that what Mairi had told me probably did correspond to the picture of an Iain MacNeil, who had been transformed in the space of two weeks. Before our marriage, my husband had been in the habit of flirting with the servants, quarrelling with Lord Baltair, neglecting the castle folk, and getting drunk. I suddenly remembered what the men we had met on the way from the Grampians had said to Nellie and Vivian—that he was good for nothing. I had deliberately buried this picture in the back of my memory so that it would not interfere with my meeting with the MacNeil family, and here it was resurfacing with power. I had to think about it. After stirring up the fire in the hearth, a content looking Mairi left me. I went towards the window. Long flurries of fine snow were covering the landscape with a veil of white. The north point of the promontory was gradually being hidden from view. A shiver went through me. I went over and knelt in front of the fire. As I looked into the blue flames, I could see my husband's eyes so full of wrath.

'Iain MacNeil, who are you?' I asked the question over and over without getting an answer. It looked as if I would not have the opportunity to speak to Tomas again. Why had he referred to Iain and his sister-in-law as tormented and unloved people? Why would my husband be a disillusioned man at twenty-three years of age? How had the elder MacNeil son's death affected his young brother?

I was determined to speak to Anna about my husband at the earliest opportunity. Who would know the events that had shaped a man better than his nurse? Without a doubt, she, apart from Lord Baltair, was the only one who could answer my questions. And it was out of the question to alarm the old chief with the questions which were tormenting me.

Anna, someday soon, will you speak to me about your young master without feeling you are betraying him? I wondered.

By the time Lord Iain went down to the courtyard to join his cousin, his anger had disappeared. His wife's look of terror haunted him. He saw a deep chasm being dug between them and understood it was he himself who was doing the digging and that he was not in control of the situation. He took a deep breath. The dog came to touch the back of his hand with his cold muzzle. Iain stroked him and told him to wait with a curt, 'Lie down!'

He was almost disappointed to see his cousin, in his armour, standing waiting in the middle of the courtyard, a look of determination on his face. The household knights had come to watch the exercise and had gathered in a group near the guard house wall. There had been no training sessions since Gunelle's arrival at the castle. During this time, the men had been busy hunting and had missed watching the bouts. But Iain MacNeil no longer felt like fighting. He had had the idea when, from Beathag's window, he had seen his cousin and wife on the ramparts. Now he found his reaction unworthy of a knight, but the challenge had been thrown down and had to be honoured.

He stepped determinedly towards his cousin and was surprised to see him draw his claymore. Instinctively, he drew his. The weapons held in the bare hand by the two men began to sway gently above their heads.

134

A thrill of excitement ran through Iain. *My cousin is an interesting one*, he said to himself. *He is a quick learner and is fearless.*

Their feet were slipping on the hard ground. In silence, the adversaries began to move, tracing an imaginary circle, each waiting for the movement which would give the first opening. From their open mouths, little wisps of steam rose in time with their measured breathing. When the first clash of the weapons resounded in the cold air, there was total silence in the courtyard.

Iain quickly realised that his cousin was going to attack. Each of his blows counted. Iain did not have time to parry them before the following blow was already underway. *Well, he wants a fight. So be it!*

Dry snow, swirling in the strong wind blowing up in the courtyard, had begun to fall and cover the ground. Everything would soon be dirty and slippery. Iain had moved on to the attack. He knew he was stronger and more skilled; all he had to do was keep attacking. He increased the rhythm and put more power into his blows. Tomas jumped quickly from side to side, avoiding his cousin's blows, which ended up in mid-air. The two men began to slide on what had become compact mud under their feet. The fight was taking a dangerous turn, and Iain thought of ending it when he heard Tomas murmur between his teeth.

'Keep going, you swine!' he said as he looked straight into Iain's eyes.

Iain shook on hearing the insult. It was against the rules to insult one's opponent. 'What did you say?' asked Iain with a direct blow.

'You heard,' Tomas answered as he sidestepped the swipe of Iain's claymore.

'And am I allowed to know what makes me a swine?'

'Because you cheat on her every night with your brother's wife.'

Iain saw red. Without even thinking about it he struck Tomas's shoulder and with the sound of a clash of metal, split his fine chainmail. Immediately, a trickle of blood dripped onto the fresh snow. Under the force of the blow, Tomas dropped his weapon and jumped backwards. Iain lowered his weapon, and he, too, took a few steps back.

Threateningly he shouted at Tomas, 'That, dear cousin, is no concern of yours. I advise you to mind your own business and leave me to conduct mine, my way. Pick up your claymore again. The fight is not over.'

At the far end of the courtyard, the knights were startled to hear the words. Lord Tomas had been struck and Lord Iain should have stopped the contest immediately, but there he was, goading his injured opponent. That was unheard of.

To their great surprise, they suddenly saw Lady Gunelle arriving in alarm in the courtyard. One of them rushed towards her, explaining that it was a training exercise and it was better not to get too close. He blocked her path, but she broke free, shouting in a piercing voice, 'Are you all blind? Can you not see that my husband wants to kill him?'

At that moment the knights were dumbfounded to see the young chatelaine, her hands outstretched, rush towards her husband, who had resumed the fight, unaware that his wife was behind him. He raised his weapon above his shoulder and ended up gashing the young woman's hand. Time suddenly stood still. The ensuing seconds were a nightmare for the two cousins, who were petrified with horror.

Nellie ran from who knows where, cloths in her hand, shouting, 'Murderer!' She rushed to attend to her mistress.

Somewhere, in a hidden corner of the courtyard, little Ceit was screaming. Some of the knights had grabbed the weapons, and others were pushing Lord Tomas towards the guard room. Lady Gunelle had collapsed on the ground and was staring with tear-filled eyes at Lord Tomas's tunic dripping with blood as they led him away.

Lord Iain closed his eyes. When he opened them, he went over to his wife, whom Nellie had helped up and was supporting her bleeding hand. Giving her an icy look, he said: 'Never do that again!'

Chapter Six
The Death

I saw my husband's lips moving as he stood in front of me, but I did not hear a single word. The deafening sound of drumming was banging inside my head. The cloth Nellie had wrapped around my hand was completely sodden with blood. That was the last thing I saw before I passed out.

When I came round, I was lying in bed in my nightdress. Nellie spoke gently to me as she soothed my face with fresh water. I tried to move the fingers of my right hand, but I could not feel them. I looked down with concern and saw my hand swathed in a clean cloth from which only my thumb was visible.

'Am I going to lose my hand?' I asked Nellie right away.

'Your husband looked at the wound and said the blade did not slice off any flesh or cut the nerves. You gave us a real fright! I am still completely bewildered! You must not get involved in exercises of that kind. Your husband is right. What were you thinking of, my dear?'

I closed my eyes. So, my husband had examined my hand and declared the wound superficial. I was strangely relieved to hear that. He would know about sword injuries, and I trusted his diagnosis.

'And what about Lord Tomas, Nellie? Is he going to be all right?' I murmured.

'I do not have any news of him. Your husband is with him at the moment. Let us hope that his injury is not too serious. What a lot of blood there was all the same!'

'Good old Nellie.' After a long silence, I asked her, 'Will you please leave me on my own? I think I am going to try to sleep.'

'Of course, my dear. I will send Mairi up in an hour. Sleep well. You are very weak after losing all that blood.'

She left my bedside and gently closed the bedroom door. I was alone with the crackling of the fire as the only sound in the room. I stretched my eyelids which were swollen from all my weeping.

'Almighty God,' I pleaded 'come and help me! I do not know what to think anymore.'

One question haunted my tormented soul: Had Iain intended to kill Tomas, as my instinct had warned me, or was it simply a fighting exercise as everyone had agreed to say? If the first hypothesis was correct, I had to conclude that I had married a monster. I began to weep silently. I no longer had the strength to stem the flow of tears. It was thus that I fell into a deep sleep which lasted several hours.

When I opened my eyes, I noticed golden shadows moving on the curtains around my bed, reflecting the redness of the flames of the fire. Night had fallen. Mairi was sitting quietly spinning at my wheel. Her slight form was silhouetted in the half-light of the room, lit simply by the glow of the fire. She had not lit any candles. I gently moved my hand and felt the pins and needles go through it. The feeling had returned, and with it, the pain. I must have groaned, for my servant looked round and stopped spinning.

'How do you feel, my lady?' she enquired anxiously. 'You slept all afternoon. Nellie told me not to wake you, and little Ceit has been asking for you.'

'Thank you, Mairi. I feel better. I am not going to get up right away. My hand is too painful. But will you go and fetch Ceit and bring me something to drink, please?'

'Right away, my lady. Lord Iain will be pleased to know you are awake.'

Lord Iain... pleased, I thought bitterly as I watched my servant scurry from the room. Little odds that my husband was worried about my fate. Was he at least looking after with his cousin? I sighed and sat up against my pillows. I had a visit from my little Ceit, who snuggled up beside me, her face all smeared with dried tears. All she did was mutter reproaches against my husband, whom she described as a 'bad knight' and 'dragon killer.' It made me smile to think of Tomas as a dragon, he who was as gentle as a lamb.

Anna brought me something to drink, a hot infusion of pain-relieving herbs mixed with honey. Her expression revealed her fondness for me, but also her unasked questions. She would have liked to know what had made me rush to the aid of Lord Tomas and expose myself to danger in that way. She gave me news of the latter and when I asked her, also news of Lord Baltair. Both were well. I was greatly relieved to hear these words. It was agreed that I would not go down for the evening meal, which would instead be served in my bedroom. Ceit asked if she could stay with me. In the evening, at my husband's request, the clarsach player came to entertain me. He played a series of very gentle and melancholic melodies, typical of the north of Scotland. I discovered the beauty of these airs, which were full of emotion, and I had the notion as I listened to them that perhaps it was Iain who had suggested them to the musician. That thought made me feel strangely uncomfortable.

Iain MacNeil had completely lost control in front of his knights during the training session. Such a thing had never happened to him before and he had difficulty composing himself. When he entered the guardroom, every look in his direction confirmed his fears: He had not gone up in the estimation of his men. His cousin was lying bare-chested on the bed near the window, surrounded by knights. He walked slowly over to the bed. His men stepped back to let him through. When he was alone with his cousin, he tried to get him to look up.

'Show me your wound' he said gravely.

Tomas did not look at him, but, grimacing in pain, he lifted up the dressing which covered his wound. Iain leaned over and examined the damage done by his weapon. It was a deep gash. A nerve might have been cut. Strangely there was little blood coming from it.

'Can you move your forearm and your fingers?' Iain asked in the same deliberate tone.

Tomas silently did as he was asked, still without looking at his cousin. He bent his arm and clenched his fist to close his hand. His wound began to bleed again.

Iain placed his hand on his cousin's fist and then lifted it. He sat down on a stool and, with his elbows on his knees and his head between his hands, stared at the ground in silence. His hair was still wet and matted with perspiration. After a long moment, he looked up and, facing his cousin's ever inscrutable expression, began to speak intensely, 'Tomas, I made a mistake during that fight. A serious mistake. Just as you did, I let myself be carried away by my feelings. What happened should never have happened and could have proved fatal for you or for her. I accept full responsibility.' After a moment's hesitation, he continued, 'As from today, I can no longer be your parrain, but that does not mean you have to leave Mallaig. You can choose any of the household knights to continue your training. I wish you to be knighted here in the spring as was agreed with my father.'

Since Tomas was maintaining a stubborn silence, Iain rose to leave. It was then that he heard his cousin say behind him, 'I am leaving. Tomorrow, if I am up to it. I do not wish to stay at Mallaig any longer.'

'As you wish,' muttered Iain before hurriedly leaving the room.

Old Baltair MacNeil was having difficulty breathing. At the beginning of the evening, he had nevertheless asked Anna to help him out of bed and into the armchair and prepare him to receive his son. The morning's events in the castle had developed into a crisis, and he could not ignore it. His failure to welcome Sheriff Darnley, to familiarise himself with estate business or the accounts, was just about acceptable. But if his son was coming to blows with his nephew and the young chatelaine suffered because of it, the situation was becoming intolerable and demanded his intervention. When Iain appeared before him, he knew at a glance that his rebel of a son was suffering. He sat down opposite his father. He looked lost, his jaw was tense, and he did not speak.

Once again, he is denying his pain, Lord Baltair thought immediately. *When he is hurting, he withdraws into himself and closes his heart. He will not speak to me. But I can speak to him.* He studied him for a long time before saying anything. When he finally decided to speak, his voice was gentle, and his breathing became easier.

'Son, what are you planning to do about your cousin now? Would it not be expedient to send him away from the castle for a time? Let us say until your relationship with your wife is… less distant.' After a short pause, he continued, 'I think that what happened between Gunelle and Tomas was bound to happen. You gave your cousin plenty of space beside her from the start, and at a time when she needed someone to make things easier for her at Mallaig. That could have been and should have been you. You chose to run away from that role. I know you have your reasons, although I do not understand them. Listen to me carefully, son. For a month now, I have known that I am dying and that you have taken over the running of the clan. I know, too, that I have no authority over you. So, I must be content with looking on, when I would so wish to be able to help you.'

'Why would you help me, father?' Iain interrupted with a muffled voice.

'Because I, too, almost destroyed myself in the past, and I would like to save you from that. I knew a life of mayhem in my youth. I pillaged, stole, and raped as much as my madness allowed and I defied paternal authority for the sheer hell of it. But I had the extraordinary fortune to meet a woman. A woman who loved me, and it was that love that saved me. That exceptional woman was Isla MacGugan, your mother.'

'And it is not difficult to imagine that you see my mother in Gunelle,' replied the son.

'It little matters what you reproach Gunelle Keith with, I know one thing… that young woman is your wife, even if you did not choose her. I know her well now, better than you perhaps, and I also know you. She is made for you, son. Win her love, and she will reveal the real Iain MacNeil.'

'Father, you have become like a romantic troubadour, and you are talking as if you were in a court of love! I have nothing with which to win the pure heart of Gunelle Keith, even if I wanted to.'

'If your claymore is all you possess with which to win her, you are right. She will learn nothing about your heart. Leave it locked up as it is at the moment. Do not let her see it. That would be better.'

Lord Baltair's remark had the effect of a resounding slap in the face for his son. Iain jumped up and covered the distance between him and the door in a few strides.

Before opening it, he turned towards his father and said to him in a tone he wanted to sound offhand. 'You asked me a question, father. What to do about Tomas? I am going to take your advice and send him to lead Sheriff Darnley's escort. Our eminent constable is leaving for the isles for a month to examine the books of the MacDonalds and company. Your nephew will have a thousand opportunities to wield the claymore, and it will do him a world of good.'

Tomas's shoulder was healing well, thanks to Anna's ointments and tight bandages. What was recovering with much more difficulty was his broken heart. How could he burn his bridges with Mallaig, which he loved? How could he leave his sick uncle? How could he refuse

144

to shake the outstretched hand of his cousin, whom he still regarded very highly as a master at arms? The MacNeil family was his only family, but with Gunelle at the heart of it, he had to move away; he knew that. So, he accepted Iain's proposal to accompany Sheriff Darnley to the islands. For two days following the accident, he exercised his arm without leaving the guardroom. Through patience and tenacity, he achieved a satisfactory result. On the morning of the departure, he went out into the courtyard and waited for the end of the morning service to say goodbye to the folk of the castle. He intended to leave for the harbour as soon as possible.

A radiant sun was already rising in the clear blue sky, and the wind coming in from the sea had calmed down. Tomas was bareheaded with his long blond hair tied back, and he was wearing a red tunic lined with fine fur. He was in a hurry to board his uncle's ship and set out to sea. The view of the castle from the sea had always thrilled him. Lord Tomas had felt a desperate need to escape. His goodbyes to the members of the family demonstrated his impatience. Lady Gunelle shuddered on hearing of his departure. She had come down from her room for the first time in three days and heard the news when she was passing the chapel. She did not have the chance to say anything at the moment of the goodbyes, which Lord Tomas seemed to wish to rush through, and that hurt her deeply. She also saw her husband for the first time since the accident, for he had not visited her once in her bedroom, contenting himself with the news people gave him.

Another surprise that morning was that he had attended the service. His beard was neatly trimmed, and he was wearing a long tunic. Lady Gunelle deduced that he would not be going outside or accompanying the sheriff's party to the harbour. She watched him when he said his goodbyes to his cousin and was astonished to see no hint of emotion on his face. When he asked kindly about her

145

hand, she hid her bandage inside her sleeves and replied tersely without looking at him. Lord Iain had chosen that day for his first Scots lesson, and he informed his wife, who replied less than enthusiastically. They agreed to meet in the library after breakfast which was served in the great hall. In a bad mood, Lord Iain rushed to the study to have a final conversation with the king's representative.

I had been waiting for an hour and was becoming very impatient. My heart was in utter revolt against this flagrant injustice towards Tomas. According to the evidence, my husband had arranged to have him sent away from the castle because he could not bear for any family member to show me the affection, he himself was incapable of feeling. When he finally arrived, I could not hide my annoyance. I had no wish to work with him, and he must have realised that, for he apologised for keeping me waiting.

Then he politely asked, 'Where do you wish to begin, my lady?'

'With your claymore, my lord. I would like you not to wear it during the lessons. It is pointless to appear armed before me. I have no intention of attacking you. Besides, who would do so within the walls of your own fortress? You are the only one in the castle who does not remove his weapon.'

'My lady, this claymore was a gift from my father when I was sixteen, and since then, I have worn it wherever I go. I only take it off to sleep or to have a bath. I fear no one here, least of all you. In the Highlands, no castle is totally impenetrable when an enemy has you in his sights. If such an enemy comes looking for my father, he will find me armed. If a robber seeks to take advantage of one of

146

those who benefit from my protection within these walls, he will have to go through me first. If a man is looking for my wife, he will find me first.'

'Indeed, my lord! You gave us a very clear demonstration of your protection… I am going to have an everlasting reminder,' I replied, beside myself with rage, as I raised my bandaged hand. His expression darkened. He turned his head, walked towards the window, and stopped. I could only see his straight back, his thick brown locks with occasional red tinges highlighted by the sun. When he began to speak, he did not turn around right away. His voice revealed great tension.

'I came to you this morning for a Scots lesson. I note that you are interested in different matter. I am ready to discuss it, my lady.'

Doing an about turn, his eyes searching for mine, he added, 'I very much regret having injured your hand. I am equally sorry for having wounded my cousin, but those are the risks of combat. What disconcerts me is the readiness with which you threw yourself into the fray to protect him. I could have done you more serious harm. You could even have lost your life.'

It was my turn to turn away. I was embarrassed. He had the right to want to understand my thoughtless action, which was so dangerous. I had to give him an explanation and show the same willingness to discuss the matter with him. But what was I to say to him? That I had not come down from my bedroom with the intention of being present at the fight? That, like all the inhabitants of the castle, I could not help looking out to the courtyard at that moment? That the sight of Tomas's blood had put me into such a state of shock that clear thinking was out of the question? That I was convinced that the two cousins were really fighting?

147

'My lord,' I said syllable by syllable, 'I have never seen a contest using claymores. When I saw you, I really believed for an instant that it was not an exercise. I felt something which is difficult to explain. I was convinced you were going to win, and I was afraid of the consequences for your cousin.'

I found the silence which followed this confession extremely difficult. After a long moment, he came towards me. He stood so close to me that I could not avoid looking at him. I looked into his eyes and was astonished to see pain.

'Tell me, my lady, if it had been your husband who was in danger, would you have risked your life in the same way to protect him?'

I was unable to bear his gaze and had to look down. What answer could I give to such a hypothetical question? I did not know what reaction my heart would have dictated in those circumstances. My duty certainly would have been to try to protect my husband. But can duty alone dictate an action which puts one's life in danger? Did that mean that the feelings I had for Tomas were deeper than I imagined?

My husband must have guessed my thoughts, for receiving no immediate answer, he concluded, 'Do not reply, my lady. There is no point. I have my answer. It is written all over your face.'

He moved away a few steps and continued in a voice full of hurt, 'I must admit something to you. Your instinct did not deceive you. When you intervened, the training session was no longer just that. We were fighting for real. For some reason I am not aware of, my cousin insulted me, and I lost my self-control. What happened is entirely my fault.'

I was outraged at hearing that. So, Iain could have killed Tomas. What kind of a man was he then? A surge of violent anger was rising within me, and I clenched my fists. Immediately my right hand began to hurt.

'And I imagine that it is thanks to you that Tomas has been sent off to the islands, afflicted with an injury which will probably prevent him from defending himself properly if there were an attack by those barbarians?' I hissed as I looked up at him.

'Do not exaggerate, my lady! There are no more barbarians in the islands than there are in Mallaig! I would remind you that my cousin is travelling under the standard of the King of Scotland, and because of that, his life is less at risk than if he were going there under the MacNeil banner.'

'If you had a little more courage, it would be you escorting Sheriff Darnley, not your cousin.'

This last remark of mine was thoughtless, but it had slipped out. He grabbed me violently by the shoulders, squeezing them until they hurt. His piercing gaze searched the very depths of my soul.

'I see,' he retorted with rage. 'Now you are going to tell me clearly which one of us you would have for a husband if you had been given the choice. Me or him?'

In the face of his aggression, I was gripped by the same terror I had felt on the ramparts, the only difference being that this time I could not run away. I groaned with pain. He was crushing my shoulders with his hands. In horror, I heard him declaring that he would let me go when he had a reply.

I closed my eyes to hold back the tears I felt welling up and answered in a whisper, 'Him.'

He let me go so forcefully that I almost lost my balance, and he left the room, leaving the door open. I collapsed onto a stool, worn out and completely distraught. Would every discussion between us always end this way? Could I not achieve anything with this man other than to incur his anger? Once again, I gave in to my pain. And again, it was my little Ceit who came to coax me out of my numbness.

The castle's arms room which adjoined the chapel, stretched the whole length of the east wing. The walls were lighter in colour because the fire was lit less often than in the other rooms. It had three windows in a lancet arch, giving it a touch of elegance. Iain MacNeil had always felt comfortable there. The proximity of the weapons, the sound of the workmen's tools as they worked on them, the coats of arms and the history they recalled made it a refuge for him. The ladies never came there; for that reason, too, he was guaranteed solitude. In fact, in his life every one of Iain MacNeil's conflicts had begun with a woman. He could count on the men's silence when he entered the arms room. There he could lay down the burden of what was pre-occupying him and gather himself together even better than in the chapel.

When he burst in the morning of the sheriff's departure, there were only three knights who were busy admiring the quality of various blades which had recently been sharpened. They were the unwilling witnesses of one of the young MacNeil's rare excesses of rage. Without even noticing their presence, Iain, claymore in hand, pounced on a block of wood used for splitting the firewood and dealt blows of such force that chips flew off it in all directions. When his rage had passed, he fell to his knees, drained of a good deal of his strength. His weapon slipped from his hand and dropped to the ground with a thud. Without a word, the men at the far end of the room had stopped what they were doing. They were flabbergasted to hear the young man curse the castle of his birth.

'What have I ever done to this accursed castle for me never to have found love in it? First there was Alasdair, now Tomas, and after Tomas, someone else will come to take my place.'

The knights, no doubt embarrassed by this spectacle, left him on his own. Iain stayed shut up in the arms room for the rest of the day without eating, and no one came to disturb him. In the evening, when the castle was asleep, Iain heard Bran's whimpers from behind the door and got up to open it. The animal, who had sensed his distress for hours, rushed to his master. Iain took the big dog in his arms and buried his haggard face in its warm coat.

The next day, the young lord slipped in at the back of the chapel for the service. Lady Gunelle only noticed him as she left and could not hide her surprise. He caught up with her and casually asked her to resume the Scots lessons. She, too, feigned casualness and gave him the same rendezvous as the day before. This time she did not have to wait. When she went into Alasdair's room, her husband was already there, sitting at a table and leafing through a book, turning its pages with care as though the paper was made of silk. He rose to his feet when she entered. She immediately noticed his belt. No weapon hung from it. She lowered her head in embarrassment and had to make an effort to sound natural when she addressed him. Iain did not lose his inscrutable demeanour once throughout the whole morning. It was the same all through that first week of lessons, and he arrived punctually at the library every morning. Lady Gunelle showed a consistent coldness towards her pupil. She was, however, relieved to see that he learned quickly, which would make the task considerably easier.

Iain MacNeil had a prodigious memory, an above-average level of concentration, and unstinting determination. The serious atmosphere which settled immediately between teacher and pupil favoured the learning process. So much so that after a month, the couple achieved very gratifying results: Iain surprised himself by discovering a taste for study, and Gunelle was happy to bring out his aptitude for learning. The young chatelaine put her heart and soul into the activity and reached the point where she forgot the man behind the pupil. She had opted for the simultaneous teaching of reading and writing in Scots, which suited Iain's temperament as he was happiest when doing something. She had him choose books from the library which she could use to teach him. Thus, she became familiar with books on brewing beer, whisky, falconry, navigation of the North Sea, and the principles of architecture for the construction of walls of defence. This was the longest time the couple had spent in one another's company since their first meeting. They were both perfectly aware that several subjects risked leading them onto dangerous ground, and they had the wisdom to avoid these.

Within a short time, Lady Gunelle had regained the use of her right hand. The bandages and ointments had been effective, and it was time for the skin to be exposed to the fresh air. A long scar ran along the side of her hand from the little finger to the wrist where the blade had touched the first veins. As often as possible, the young chatelaine hid her hand in her sleeve, particularly when she was with her husband. The afternoons were free for one as for the other. Iain hunted or went with his knights to deal with disputes on the estate, and Gunelle divided her time between Lord Baltair, little Ceit, and running the castle. She still was not at ease keeping the accounts and had to make a commendable effort to master all the skills needed for the task. As she had promised, she had had a few riding lessons from her husband and these also demanded a lot of effort. As for Iain, he displayed great patience and congratulated himself on managing to get his wife over her fear of horses and thereby allowing her to use the only possible means of transport in the Highlands.

After some weeks of this programme, the relationship between the two co-habitants had changed. Each one stuck to the task in hand with total application. The evenings took a particularly pleasant turn when the chatelaine asked the clarsach player to play during supper and to accompany her afterwards. Nellie, who had a very nice voice, joined in with her mistress, and the two singers delighted the audience with Lowland ballads and laments. The musician taught them several northern songs, and soon, Anna, Mairi, and Finella, Lady Beathag's companion, ended up performing with the two ladies from Aberdeen as a small melodic choir of female voices. The men of the household, who were in the habit of spending the evenings in the guardroom, lingered more and more often in the great hall to listen to the ladies' singing.

The couple kept their distance from one another in a mixture of reserve and respect. One evening at supper, several of Lady Beathag's remarks to Iain revealed to Gunelle that her husband was neglecting his sister-in-law's company. Had he deserted her bed? She could not say, nor did she want to know. Deep nausea overcame her every time she thought of her husband's reprehensible behaviour. She could not help looking for reasons for his refusal to perform his conjugal duties with her. She had heard about young noblewomen being dropped by their husbands in favour of men, but that was obviously not the case with hers, who had the reputation of 'a stallion always ready to cover.' So, what was so unpleasant about her that a fit, strong man could not bring himself to perform the marital act? That question tortured her more than she would have liked to admit and fuelled her resentment towards her husband, so she resolved to forget it as much as possible.

Nellie, Anna, and Mairi knew about the state of the physical relations between the newlyweds but kept a discrete silence about it. The reasons for Lord MacNeil's avoidance of his wife's bed were not known by them, so they could not understand. They could well imagine that their mistress suffered because of the situation. As for Iain MacNeil, the more time passed, the more difficult it became to imagine intimacy with his wife. The dislike he had quite intentionally inspired in her ever since their first meeting had turned to hatred, then quite recently to coldness. They had reached the point of hiding behind a screen of polite indifference. The young man had never taken a woman by force, nor had he slept with a woman who did not feel a certain attraction for him. With his many adventures, he had acquired the rare talent of always arousing and satisfying desire in his conquests. But with his wife, things presented themselves badly. He had turned her against him so much that he was sure she felt nothing but contempt for him.

Sheriff Darnley returned to Mallaig at the end of February. He was furious because his mission to the islands had not had the results he had hoped for. Tomas had not had to fight. No one wanted a quarrel with the members of the escort of the king's representative when they were MacNeils. The royal policy against those who had betrayed the Crown was beginning to have an effect on the rebel clans.

Getting away from Mallaig had matured Tomas a lot. He had also found romance with the daughter of the secretary at Duart Castle on the Isle of Mull, and this love affair had enabled him to distance himself as far as Gunelle was concerned and to bring into question the unconditional affection he had for her. He adopted an attitude of reserve towards her while still maintaining all his friendliness. The tension between the two cousins greatly decreased. All it would take to rediscover the pupil-master relationship was for the two men to have the opportunity to fight side by side. This opportunity was given to them. During a ride in the Grampians, the Lords Iain and Tomas, along with seven knights and men of the MacNeil household, drove back an attack from some of Clan Cameron's men. The nine of them fought against twelve and had to use a lot of skill to scatter their assailants. The incursion onto their land was hardly surprising. The Camerons were trying through intermittent skirmishes to take back what the king had confiscated. If they succeeded in getting rid of the MacNeils, they would regain ownership of that part of the forest. The Mallaig men had not worn their chain mail for the trip, but the Camerons were only too aware of what they were coming to do in the Grampians and had dressed accordingly. Less encumbered by their ordinary clothes, the MacNeils had been lighter and more agile in their movements which gave them the advantage. However, they were returning home visibly wounded by their adversaries' claymores. Iain, always the prime target of such attacks, often found himself facing two opponents at a time. He always came through it, but it invariably cost him a jacket, if not a badly gashed limb. This time, he had been struck between the shoulder blades. He had a deep flesh wound about the length of a hand down to his ribs. The journey back to the castle was a long slow one, for he was losing a lot of blood and had difficulty staying in the saddle. The party had to make several stops to tend to him. Night had fallen on Mallaig when the men finally crossed the drawbridge.

Iain was immediately carried to his room, and they sent for Doctor MacDuff. As she sat at her master's bedside, Anna, who was used to these bloody returns from such expeditions, was not overly concerned. She had seen many other such injuries with this intrepid young man and knew exactly what to do. She made everyone leave the room and thoroughly cleaned the wound. The bleeding had to be stopped. She applied a coat of ointment around the edge of the wound to draw the flesh together then carefully dressed it. Iain continually asked for a drink. The men had given him whisky to stop him from losing consciousness during the journey back, and he was parched. When the doctor arrived, the necessary had been done. He gave Anna a dirty look and she left the room with a shrug of her shoulders. The chatelaine, Lady Beathag, and her servant had accompanied the doctor into the room to see the wounded man. They found him sitting on a chair naked from the waist up, his chest wrapped in bandages. He did not even look up when they entered. With no reason to stay, the doctor chose to chat with the chatelaine and asked for news of his patient Lord Baltair, whom he had not examined for quite a while. Then he asked about her state of health, asking if a child was on the way. He was astonished to see her blush profusely. A brief glance in the husband's direction told him the question was not appropriate.

In an attempt to apologise for his indiscretion, the doctor felt obliged to explain that a young woman was not always fertile in the first year of marriage. He added that prayer helps many young couples produce an heir.

Lady Beathag, who was intrigued by her lover's sexual relations with his wife, allowed herself an acid comment, 'My dear Mister MacDuff, as far as prayers are concerned, there is no need to worry about our chatelaine. She spends more time in the chapel than in her husband's bedroom.'

Iain, from whom they had heard nothing yet, shouted that he had had enough and ordered everyone to leave. Gunelle was now crimson with rage. How could her husband allow his mistress to accuse her for a situation for which he was entirely responsible?

The stinging reply aimed at Lady Beathag and her husband just came out. 'The great advantage of the chapel over my husband's bedroom is that in that sacred place, you are sure to find what you are looking for!'

She left the room in such a rush she bumped into the doctor, who almost fell over. The poor man had understood nothing of the conversation but realised the trouble his remarks had caused. He apologised and left. Iain dismissed Lady Beathag and her servant with a shout which brought Anna running back. One look told her that her young master had a fever. When she was alone with him, she put him to bed and decided to watch over him, a cold cloth in her hand to wipe his brow. Iain turned to her. He felt sorry for his old nurse, whose face was ravaged by fatigue because of the sleepless nights spent at his father's bedside. He asked her to leave him on his own, reassuring her that everything would be fine. From experience, Anna knew there was no use insisting and so left.

Each breath cost Iain a great deal of effort, for his lung was pressing on his injured ribs. He wanted to change position, and proceeding very gingerly, he turned over on his side. It was then he noticed the fresh young face of Ceit in the half-open door. He invited her to come in without letting the dog in. After thinking about it for a long moment, she accepted the invitation. Her eyes wide open with curiosity, she quietly entered the room.

When she was in front of him, she asked quietly, 'Have you a sore stomach?'

'No, it is my back,' he answered.

'Is your hair hot?'

'No, I have a temperature, and that wets your forehead.'

'Are you bored on your own without a song?'

'Yes,' he said, smiling tenderly.

'I am going to get Gunelle. She will sing you a lullaby.'

'You say *Lady Gunelle*,' Iain reminded her when she had already gone.

He must have dozed off for a moment, for he did not hear his wife coming in. When he opened his eyes, she was standing in front of him. Her expression was inscrutable. He wanted to sit up, but the burning pain in his back reminded him of his injury. He groaned and fell back down, closing his eyes. The words his wife had spoken in the doctor's presence came back to him, and he was overcome by a wave of shame.

'I'm in no position to apologise to you,' he slowly began but was immediately interrupted.

'I have not come to hear any apology, my lord. I have come to sing to you at the request of little Ceit. That is if you wish me to, of course!'

'My lady, nothing would do me more good at the moment than to listen to you sing.'

158

He closed his eyes and become again as he was a minute earlier: a man dripping with sweat, swarthy around his beard, muscular shoulders, and his chest as white as the bandage which completely covered it. I looked around the room. Lady Beathag was correct. I had never seen my husband's bedroom. It was sparsely furnished like those used by travellers who are just passing through. The light came from a single window and the fireplace was narrow. The badly situated bed had no curtains; above it, a large standard in the MacNeil colours was stretched across the north wall. There were no carpets on the floor, and several weapons, including his claymore, were stacked in one corner. It had not been cleaned and was spattered with dried blood. I shuddered.

I had no idea about what it is like to fight. Everything to do with fighting and war seemed unreal to me. I realised that if I did not understand this aspect of the Highlanders' way of life, I would never understand my husband. The smallest object in this bedroom told me that its occupant first defined himself as a fighter. I sat down on the chair he had occupied during the doctor's visit and began to sing the first song which came to mind. It was a lullaby I had learned from my mother. An old, very gentle lullaby. Then another came to me, and I moved on to a ballad. The songs were coming to my lips, and all I had to do was sing them gently and clearly. Singing melted every trace of anger in my heart and sent the injured man, burning up with a fever, to sleep. In his sleep, my husband had rolled over onto his back. I stood up and bathed his brow with Anna's cloth. He opened his eyes for an instant, then sank back into his dreams again. It was not until the middle of the night that I was able to go back to my room, confident that the fever was going down. A curious feeling of intimacy took hold of me, and it took a long time for me to fall asleep.

The next day, everything was resolved as if by magic. The fighters' clothes which had been repaired and washed to rid them of bloodstains, now covered injured bodies. Faces were smiling again, laughter rang loudly in the great hall, and there was no more talk of the skirmish. I was astonished to see just how fighting was a normal part of life at Mallaig. I was equally very impressed by the vigour of the men who had quickly regained strength and, in particular, by my husband's recovery. He met me as I came out of the chapel after the morning service. He was impeccably dressed; his hair was pulled back and tied with a leather lace. His eyes still had the brilliance of the fever, but nothing in his bearing showed that he had a back injury. He thanked me for staying with him the night before. I was embarrassed by this expression of gratitude, especially since such expressions were unusual on his part.

I answered rather stupidly, 'It is quite normal, my lord. I only did my duty.'

Right away, I noticed him stiffen, but he did not say a word. I did not know what to add to make up for my clumsiness. It was too late. At that moment, we were called urgently to see Lord Baltair, who was in the throes of another crisis.

I remained at the door, incapable of entering the old chief's room. I felt powerless, and I was distraught. My husband immediately took control. He relieved Anna, who was on the point of fainting, and took her place at his father's bedside. Someone asked him if the doctor should be sent for, and he shook his head. He had sat down on the bed and was holding his father's two hands in his. He leaned over the old man and spoke quietly. The servants, Nellie and Anna, left. I tiptoed inside and stood against the wall. The cold of the stone went right through me. My husband must have heard the rustle of my dress, for he turned and looked towards me. It was then that he asked me to go for Father Henriot, which I hurried to do, only too happy to be of some help. One would have said the priest was expecting me. I did not even have to mention Lord Baltair. He had prepared what was required for the last rites and calmly followed me. As I walked beside him in contemplative silence, a sense of peace gradually took hold of me and did not leave until it was all over. When we arrived, Iain let go of his father's hands and gave his place to the priest, who sat down immediately beside the sick man. I had withdrawn to the back of the room near the fire and remained available if needed. My husband joined me and sat down in one of the armchairs, his back straight and his head resting on the back of the chair. He closed his eyes. I could see no hint of what he was feeling. I only saw that he was acting like a loving son, and the discovery comforted me.

Father Henriot stayed for an hour beside the dying man whose confession he heard and to whom he administered the last rites. The MacNeil clan chief's final hours were peaceful. My husband and I had not exchanged a single word. The priest had left. Suddenly Lord Baltair called me in a very weak voice. I rushed to his side. He kept his eyes closed but felt for my hand. Gently I intertwined my fingers with his. He was murmuring in a faint voice broken by his wheezing, and I had to put my face up close to hear.

'I will not be saved by your hands this time,' he said. 'I am about to depart. Gunelle, you are the chatelaine Mallaig needed. You are also the wife Iain needs, but he does not yet realise it. Do not give up on him, Gunelle, promise me.'

'My lord,' I answered, 'I never give up. It is not in my nature. I promise to be as good as the chatelaines who have preceded me here. I beg you, have as much confidence in your son. He possesses your qualities as a chief. You have no need to worry about the future of Mallaig.'

I stopped talking as a sob rose in my throat. I looked down at our clasped hands and, in my heart, said goodbye to him. *May God take the soul of this worthy man.* I heard the old lord ask to speak to his son in private. I rose immediately and gave a despairing glance at my husband who was watching us from the back of the room. With two strides, he was beside us, and I placed the old man's motionless hand in his and left the room. A knight stood on duty outside the door, and Mairi was standing beside him. They must have read the distress on my face, for each took one of my arms and led me down to the great hall amongst the castle folk. I raised my head. *To live up to my position*, I said to myself. I ignored my pain to look after others, conscious that this was my last duty for my father-in-law.

The devoted Anna was inconsolable. I quickly noticed that she needed comfort, and I charged Father Henriot and Nellie to see that the people who had come to attend the wake of their chief were looked after and lacked nothing. I undertook to console the old nurse, whom I led to a quiet corner away from watching eyes. During the two hours we sat together, I learned more about Lord Baltair, his wife, and their two sons than I had learned in three months. In the comfort of my two arms around her, Anna poured out her heart of memories, regrets, fears, and doubts. It was through her that the first corner of the veil was lifted, and I caught a glimpse of this family saga. A drama which held the key to understanding my husband's tormented heart.

Thirty years before, at Mallaig, a chatelaine had given birth to a fine heir called Alasdair. In this child, so longed for, all the hopes of a powerful clan in the heart of the Highlands were met, and the chatelaine loved everything about her perfect son. Four years later, she brought her second son into the world, and his difficult birth almost cost her her life. The second son, called Iain, never had the right to his mother's love and it was left to his nurse to care for him. The nurse acted as his real mother during the boy's infancy, but the child desperately tried to win his mother's love which he missed and longed for. His elder brother soon became the main obstacle to be overcome if he were to attain that love. A life of permanent discord and jealousy began at the castle, which only settled down when the elder son left to study for two years in Edinburgh. The younger son was unable to benefit from his elder brother's absence to improve his relationship with his mother and was forced to accept that she would never love him. Life at the castle became unbearable for him, and he tried by every means possible to spend as little time as he could there. He would go off fighting or participating in tournaments at every opportunity. At his father's side, he proved to be a fighter of great talent and the uncontested champion of the equestrian jousts or in the use of arms. On his brother's return to Mallaig, Iain had become number one in these areas. The round of challenges thrown down to the MacNeil brothers to take part in the Highland tournaments meant they fought side by side for a year, at the end of which took place the famous tournament of the isles. Iain was nineteen, and Alasdair twenty-three. Alasdair died there as a result of a dagger blow. Iain, who was suspected of not having helped him, was covered in disgrace.

It was late afternoon when the death of Lord Baltair was announced in the great hall. Father Henriot took charge of the proceedings and invited the faithful to pray together for the rest of the deceased's soul. A knight came to fetch me, and I went upstairs with Nellie, who had offered to prepare the chief's body. Anna, who could do nothing but cry, was left in the care of the Mallaig women who had rushed to pay their respects to their old master. I found my husband prostrate in prayer at the foot of his father's bed. I looked at his head, leaning on his clasped hands, his sagging shoulders, his straight back. It was the picture of a penitent, heart-broken son. I went over and knelt beside him in silence. My eyes went quite naturally to my father-in-law, who looked peaceful and serene. *So*, I said to myself, *the father was reconciled to the son before he departed.* I looked again at my husband. It was then I saw that he was weeping, and my heart melted.

Chapter Seven
The Tide

O n this first day of March 1424, the funeral of the eleventh
chief of the clan MacNeil was marked by an exceptional
gathering of clergy, nobles, and chieftains from every
corner of the Highlands. About one hundred came to pay their last
respects to the chief, testimony to the high esteem and respect
everyone had for this exceptional man.

Torrential rain had been falling on Mallaig for two days, and the
accommodation of a great number of travellers at the castle had
posed some problems. Fortunately, Lady Gunelle was greatly aided
by her personnel and therefore was able to perform her duties as
chatelaine impeccably without calling upon her husband, who, in
any case, would have been of no help whatsoever. Lord Iain was
experiencing the most difficult moments of his life. The death of his
father had affected him deeply. The final moments spent at the dying
man's bedside had been highly emotional and had proved to be
crucial for the peace of mind of one as much as the other. In addition,
Iain was under extreme pressure regarding his succession to head of
the clan, a subject which was not finding consensus among the
lairds. Lord Baltair's reputation in the Highlands meant that all the
other clan chiefs, several of whom were enemies of the MacNeils,
were gathered within the walls of Mallaig Castle. It was a situation
which stirred up in Iain, ever the fighter, a concern which he found
difficult to bear. To cap it all, the searching, questioning eye Sheriff
Darnley was continually casting over the whole business was
beginning to exasperate him.

Father Henriot, Lord Tomas, and the household knights understood
the state of mind of the MacNeil heir and showed him great support

at this time. Father Henriot undertook to receive the condolences on behalf of the young lord so as not to compound his grief. Tomas mingled with the lairds canvassing for expressions of support for his cousin. The Mallaig knights organised close, discreet, and effective surveillance of those guests known to be hostile to the family and made sure that no incident threatened the safety of the castle.

When the day of the funeral came to an end, and his father's tomb in the chapel was closed and the slab put in place, Iain MacNeil felt, for the first time in his life, an immense emptiness. It was even greater than that which had devastated him on the death of his mother. This time he was losing the only man ever to have shown him love and understanding. The words spoken by his father on his deathbed were like a priceless gift, which had restored his self-esteem. One statement, in particular, had lifted the heaviest burden a man could carry: that of killing his brother. *'Son,'* he could hear the words again, *'I know you did not kill your brother. He killed you. He took the castle and all of your mother's love. I know no surer way of killing the man who is being formed in the boy.'*

When the chapel emptied of the faithful who had come to pray for the last time for the eternal rest of Lord MacNeil, Iain remained alone. He was kneeling on the slab, his hands spread flat on the inscriptions. He heard nothing. He felt nothing, not even the throbbing of the wound on his back. He heaved a long sigh and took a very long time to compose himself. So it was that he said his goodbyes to the father he had loved so badly.

Darkness had fallen on the castle when he finally stood up, strengthened with a new strength, comforted by a new sense of peace, and almost happy. He slowly tiptoed out of the chapel. He did not even look at the stone next to his father's which bore his mother's inscription. He had never said his goodbyes to her. For one of his parents, he would remain a son in exile. Among the far-travelled guests, there were two representatives of the Keith family: Daren, Lady Gunelle's older brother, and Lieutenant Lennox. They had heard of the clan chief's death while at the felling site in the Grampians. For the young chatelaine, the rediscovery of two members of her family was an occasion of great joy in the midst of the widespread heartache. Once the visitors had left the castle, and only a small number of guests remained, she could devote herself entirely to her brother and the lieutenant, who were staying for a further three days.

During their stay, Lieutenant Lennox was glad to renew his ties with the place, the inhabitants, and the Mallaig way of life He never took his eyes off the young chatelaine and tried to spot signs of a change of attitude between the couple. He quickly concluded that their relationship was distant. *At least Iain MacNeil has stopped insulting her*, he said to himself. He asked her how she got the scar which she tried to conceal and was disturbed to learn that it was her husband who had inflicted the injury. He was very surprised, too, to learn that, unlike elsewhere in Europe, in the Highlands, the knights' training was not conducted using blunt weapons. Yet another northern practice that shocked him and led him to be wary of the MacNeils.

Daren Keith, too, was watching his brother-in-law's behaviour. At Crathes, young Vivian had informed him of the aggressive character of the young MacNeil and the difficulties she had had with him at the beginning. In fact, that was one of the reasons he and Lieutenant Lennox had ridden day and night to attend Lord Baltair's funeral. The other reason was business: Several matters regarding the exploitation of the forestry land needed be clarified with MacNeil's representative.

Daren Keith was a tall man, broad-shouldered rather than slender. His round face gave him the appearance of a well-behaved child, which was far from what he was. Stubborn and given to trips of fantasy, he sometimes lacked sound judgement, a weakness on occasions compensated by his courage. Curiously, he was a gifted negotiator, which meant he was a great help to his father, Nathaniel Keith. More than anything else he adored his young sister and had suffered greatly during her various absences from Crathes: first in France and then in the Highlands. When he met his brother-in-law for the first time, he found it difficult to not treat him as an enemy. He found him haughty, taciturn, and cold. Like Lieutenant Lennox, he was astonished to hear him express himself in Scots with ease, and both men imagined immediately that his ignorance of the language had just been a ploy at the time of the wedding. Besides that, Lord Daren was worried about his young sister's health. Certainly, the injury to her hand had shocked him, but it was his sister's look of tiredness which really concerned him. He asked Nellie if his sister's complexion was due to early pregnancy, a question which greatly embarrassed the old nurse. He sensed something was going on, and as he was very good at getting information, he ended up learning that his sister was being neglected by her husband. From then on, he began to watch the young chatelaine closely and concluded that she was ill-treated, ill-married, and unhappy at Mallaig. That was all Daren Keith needed to hatch a plan to take his sister back to Aberdeen. As it is not easy to separate a wife from her husband, however negligent he is, Lord Daren had to find an excellent pretext and his inventive mind quickly found a way around the problem: He announced that their mother's state of health demanded the young woman's return to Crathes.

Lady Gunelle was astonished that her brother had taken so long to give her the news about her mother. Why had he not shared this distressing information with her as soon as he arrived? Nor could she understand why Vivian had not written to her about it when they had sworn to write to each other about anything important. She had to admit that life at Mallaig had been so demanding these past two months that communication with her family had taken a back seat. She was troubled. When she tried to learn more about her mother's illness, all she received were evasive answers from her brother, which greatly fuelled her concerns. She thought that he was hiding the seriousness of the situation at Crathes so as not to worry her, and that was typical of the protective attitude her brother had always had towards her. Lord Daren succeeded so well in alarming her that she immediately agreed to his plan when he shared it with her. It was the day before the planned departure of her brother and Lieutenant Lennox. That evening Lord Iain asked his wife to look at the agreement for the Grampian felling rights with the view to discussing it the next day with Lord Daren.

One candle had completely burned out before I finished familiarising myself with the clauses of my marriage contract concerning the felling rights on the MacNeil property. It was dark, and my eyes were stinging with tiredness. The whole castle was asleep. The wind was gusting against the northern walls, and it was still raining. I would have liked to go to bed. How I missed the competence of Saxton, the secretary, that night! Exhaustion was making me agitated. I had difficulty concentrating, and my thoughts kept turning to Crathes. They went round and round in my head, all over the place; all the bits of news I had been given about each of my family members and which I had not had the time to think about. I pictured everyone living at my father's castle: my sisters, Elsie, and Sybil, who were both coming to the end of their pregnancy, my brothers-in-law, my nephews, and nieces. It was Elsie, the eldest's third child and Sybil's second. *'The Keith girls are fertile women!'* my father would always blare out to whoever wanted to listen. He was as proud of his grandchildren as if he had been their father. I bit my lip as I thought of how disappointed he would be if he knew I was not carrying a child. I looked down at my damask coat and then closed my eyes for an instant. Suddenly, Ceit came into my mind: her rosy dimpled cheeks, blue eyes, copper red hair, and that little look of concentration when I spoke to her. I was overcome by a flood of tenderness and sighed.

'I would like to have a child,' I murmured. 'It would give my life here a purpose.'

At that moment, my thoughts turned naturally to my mother and pictures of her flooded my troubled soul, and I realised just how much I missed her. Her sense of justice, her advice, her beliefs, and her wisdom—qualities which would be useful in my new role as wife and chatelaine. I just had to see her again! Mallaig could do without its chatelaine for a few weeks; after all, it had not had one for five years. A log fell over in the fire sending out a shower of red sparks. A shiver ran down my back. I refolded the pages of the contract and gathered up the papers, which were scattered all over the table. I picked up the candlestick and left the study.

The shortest route to my room was via the staircase leading to the chapel on the first floor. As I set off, I noticed a dancing light brushing the wall ahead of me.

'Someone is coming,' I said in astonishment. 'Who can still be moving about at this hour?'

The person coming down must have seen the light from my candle, as I had seen his, for he turned back, and I did not actually meet him. But when I reached the landing, I clearly heard Lady Beathag chuckling from behind the door, which was ajar and from which a beam of light escaped as far as my feet. I immediately stepped backwards. Then, looking towards the end of the corridor, I clearly made out Bran, stretched out outside his master's bedroom. So, it was not my husband who was with her, I concluded. I pouted in disgust at my reaction. I felt as if I was spying, and that troubled me. I turned on my heels and carried on up to my room. I spent a restless night full of mixed-up dreams, and I woke up the next morning absolutely exhausted.

Mairi commented as she combed my hair before putting on my pearl net, 'You did not sleep well, my lady. Are you ill?'

'It is true that I am exhausted but I am well, Mairi,' I replied. 'I would be pleased if you would keep Ceit with you today. She is going to be bored without me. I must go to home with my brother, and I will be staying there for some time. Nellie is preparing my luggage.'

'You are leaving? Today?' she exclaimed.

'My mother is ill, and my brother thinks she needs me. I will certainly be back at Mallaig for Callainn[5].'

I realised from the shocked look on her face that my trip seemed quite extraordinary. At the time, I did not understand why but when the subject was broached in my husband's presence an hour later, I understood all the implications.

---

[5] Gaelic New Year's Day. At this period 25th march

171

Bran was lying outside the study door. He did not lift his head when I arrived, being content with a soppy look and a wag of the tail. When I entered the room, my husband was already in conversation with my brother. I knew right away that something was wrong.

Without getting up from his chair, Iain addressed me dryly and he spoke to me in Gaelic, 'There you are, my lady! I have learned from your brother's lips that you are leaving for Crathes! I imagine you intended to consult me about it this morning.'

'Indeed, my lord,' I said in a voice that was less than assured as I sat down at the desk. 'I miss my family very much, and my mother is ill. You do not really need me in the next few weeks, and I am sure that a few will be enough to reassure us both about her state of health.'

'Dear sister,' interrupted Daren, 'could we not converse in Scots?'

I saw Iain clench his fist on the arm of the chair. He turned slowly towards my brother and replied in Scots, in a tone which did not invite a reply, 'I speak to my wife in whatever language suits me. Her planned trip only concerns you in so far as you will be her escort. I will let you know when we will discuss your business in the Grampians.'

He stopped speaking, obviously wishing that my brother would leave the room. Such was the turmoil within me, I could not move. I suddenly felt very hot. The extreme tension floating in the air was suffocating me. I began to tremble from fatigue, nervousness, or apprehension; I could not say which. Doubtless, all at the same time. My brother noticed and settled back into his armchair; his arms folded on his stomach. He had the look of someone who was about to take part in a long discussion. Then I was horrified to hear him confront my husband, asking if he were in the habit of terrorising

172

his wife, wounding her with a weapon, and neglecting her in the bedroom. This last accusation made me jump to my feet. Iain reacted in the same way. He left his chair, walked straight over to my brother, grabbed him by the lapels of his coat, and lifted him off the floor as if he were a small child. He ordered him to leave the room in such a violent way that Daren complied. Iain had his back to me, but I could well imagine the look on his face as he said it, and a shiver of panic ran right through me. I closed my eyes to stop myself from bursting into tears, silently begging my husband not to do anything irreparable.

'Leave,' I murmured. 'I beg you, Daren, get out! Immediately!'

I heard the sound of his footsteps, the door opening and closing again. 'Daren has left,' I sighed, without opening my eyes. The next instant, I sensed my husband standing behind me. He put his hands on my shoulders to make me sit down. I let myself sink down onto the bench and I leaned over with my arms crossed on the table. He walked around the table and sat down again in his armchair opposite me. After a long moment of silence, he finally spoke to me in a voice that shook with the effort he was making to keep his calm.

'It is true, my lady, that the events which we have just lived through at the castle have not allowed us too much time to talk to one another. I do not know how long you have been plotting to leave with your brother, but this plan will not come to fruition. I will not permit it. That you miss your family, I can accept. That your mother is ill, that is possible. That she is dying, that I doubt very much. I do not know who led your brother to believe that I mistreat you, but I certainly hope it was not you.'

He was waiting for a reply from me, and I looked at him, at a loss for words. *How do you quench the anger of a man who cannot bear to be criticised or crossed?* I thought. First, I had to try and stifle the resentment rising within because of the despicable way he had dismissed my brother. I, too, tried to control my voice so that he did not see my resentment.

'My lord, I would be lying if I said you mistreat me. Here I receive all the respect due to a chatelaine. By nature, my brother is a little unreasonable when it concerns me, and he must miss me a lot for him to arrive at such conclusions about my life at Mallaig. So, I beg you to forgive him. Furthermore, I wish to make my request. I would very much like to see my mother. Now it is the end of winter, life is very quiet, and the castle will not suffer from a short absence on my part. My lord, you have just lost your father, and you must certainly understand the need one can feel for one's parent. Allow this trip if you can...'

'When you visit Crathes, my lady, I will accompany you myself. It will be by carriage, in the summer when the tracks are dry or by boat when the water is free of ice. We will also take a strong escort since, by accommodating the king's sheriff, Clan MacNeil presents a threat in the Highlands. You have my word that you will go to Crathes but not at the moment. You are needed at the castle to support me in the succession to the title of clan chief.'

'I am not surprised by your response, my lord,' I replied after a moment's silence. 'Does it ever cross your mind to think of others rather than yourself? That you should put declarations of loyalty and titles before family duties hardly surprises me. The whole of my family could die if there were a reception to organise here. You would make it my duty to stay. On the other hand, I do not think my safety would be threatened on such a journey, for I do not think I could be better protected than by my brother and Lieutenant Lennox. Not one of your answers justifies your refusal. Your only motivation is lack of consideration for me.'

Thereupon, I stood up. I could hardly breathe because of chagrin, anger, and scorn. I was no longer in control of myself. It would have been better to stop talking, but I carried on in the same vein.

'After having welcomed me here with contempt and then inflicting your moods on me, you use me when it suits you to complete your education, to keep your books, and see to your table, you cheat on me with your sister-in-law in the full view and knowledge of everyone, you deprive me of anyone likely to bring me some friendship, you insult my brother, and prevent me from going to see my kinfolk by keeping me prisoner within your walls.'

I stopped speaking when I ran out of breath, turned around, and left the room. My brother and the dog were waiting for me in the hall. My brother was shocked when I did not even acknowledge him before rushing towards the stairs. I kept out of everyone's way for the rest of the morning. I should not have done that. At lunchtime, Nellie came to find me, and I saw immediately that she had been crying. On questioning her, I was horrified to learn that after I left, my husband had quarrelled with my brother and had chased him from the castle without allowing him to say goodbye to me. As far as I was concerned, no greater affront could be given to a member of my family. I collapsed onto my bed, murmuring, 'He detests me, and I detest him. Almighty God, you have given me a man who is impossible to love!'

'Do not say that, my dear,' said Nellie. 'One must not speak ill of one's husband. It is a sin.'

I could not tell how long we stayed lying in each other's arms. In any case, we did not show up for the midday meal in the great hall. I did not see my husband at the following meal, for he had left the castle.

All the guests who had come to Lord Baltair's funeral had returned to their estates, and only the family members were at the castle. The cold of winter had made way for the rainy season, which watered the whole landscape, increased the size of the bogs on the moors, and swelled the torrent of the stream, which cascaded with a deafening roar from above. The pure water which flowed down from the mountains was due mainly to the melting snow, and it was by far the best for making beer and whisky. That is why we made them and put them in barrels. A good number of the store and cooperage personnel were needed in the cellars to sort the hops and malt into the vats for the decantation and distillation of the alcohol in the pot stills. Just as his predecessor had done, Father Henriot would go down to see if everything was being done according to the techniques perfected in the abbeys. The Mallaig folk knew their job so well that he never had to say anything about it.

This yield is going to have to be a good one, thought the priest. The wedding and the funeral had all but exhausted the reserves of beer, mead, and whisky, which was matured for almost eight years in oak barrels. If the MacNeil son was recognised as clan chief, his duties were going to call for the castle cellars to be replenished. In fact, the local tribunal held in the arms room during Lord Baltair's final active years had been a weekly meeting place for the serfs, housekeepers, and lairds who came to seek justice from their lord and to whom food and drink were provided for days on end.

The prospect of lairds coming and going to Mallaig cheered the priest, for he enjoyed the company of all these little nobles who lifted the castle out of its isolation. In addition, the revival of an active clan life would certainly increase his standing with the other priests. Father Henriot shrugged his shoulders as he went up from the cellar. He strongly hoped that the young MacNeil's approaches to the lairds would be successful.

After Daren Keith's departure, Lord Iain had not wanted to isolate himself in his grief, and he had undertaken to visit his entire estate and its lairds to strengthen the ties his father had established with each of them. The lairds, all older than the young MacNeil, devoted a lot of time to their discussions and listened to him with great interest. They recognised the temperament and qualities of the father in the son. They particularly sensed Iain MacNeil's sincere respect and love for Baltair MacNeil, which made him suitable for the role he was seeking in the bosom of the clan. The young lord had had his cousin, and two knights accompany him on the round of visits. In each house, he was made welcome and offered hospitality for the night with the result that he did not come home for four days.

Mallaig had resumed its day-to-day life. Taking advantage of the escort of the Grant chieftain, one of the last guests to leave Mallaig the day Daren Keith left, Sheriff Darnley had gone to inspect the books in the area around Inverness. Iain MacNeil was in a hurry to return home. He had to admit he felt more at ease at Mallaig when the sheriff was not there. He hoped the constable would continue his mission towards the north without returning to Mallaig. That would give him at least two months for a much-needed rest. He was not proud of the way he had treated his brother-in-law, but his state of exhaustion after the funeral had made him fragile and a slave to his impulses. He should have ignored Daren Keith's insinuations and reproaches in a way befitting his position as host. Lord Iain was especially displeased that he had once again incurred the anger and contempt of his wife by provoking an argument he should have avoided. She, too, had lived through exhausting days during the funeral, and he had not been gentle with her during their last conversation. He strongly wished that these four days of separation would have lessened the resentment Gunelle felt towards him. He sighed with bitter disappointment as he gazed at the horizon when they came out of the forest.

It was a cloudless evening. The wind freshened and increased as they covered the peninsula. The horses were exhausted for Iain had chosen to cross the forest part of his land at a gallop and without a single stop. He was not in the mood to run into a fight. Their trip had passed without incident, which was quite amazing. In the Highlands, the weeks between the death of a chieftain and the succession of another were habitually marred by brawls and local rows. That was not the case following the demise of Baltair MacNeil. The whole clan silently mourned its chieftain and waited for events to unfold. No one seemed to want to force them. Of the five clan lairds, only one had expressed a wish to claim the title of chief. It was Iain's youngest uncle, Aindreas of Loch Morar. He owned several herds, and his income allowed him to train and arm half a dozen knights. However, when it came to his relationships with the other Highland clans, he was not totally trusted. He had asked Iain to allow him time to think before coming to a decision.

Iain MacNeil realised that he had risen in the clan's estimation since his marriage. No one spoke anymore about Alasdair's death, and the reception of the King of Scotland at Mallaig had elevated him to the rank of a major chief in clan circles. Anyway, the young lord was no fool: His young wife had something to do with this renewed interest in Mallaig's reputation. He was returning to Mallaig, assured of the loyalty of four of the five lairds, and he had arranged to meet them the evening of Callainn. He wished the ceremony of homage to take place then, in twelve days' time.

On seeing the castle turrets appear in the distance, Iain spurred on his mount and went across the moors at top speed, followed by his men. He was in a hurry to see his wife and try improving his relationship with her. When he entered the castle, she was not there. He learned from Anna that Lady Gunelle had gone to the beach with Mairi and Ceit at the beginning of the afternoon.

Iain was startled at this piece of news. 'Without an escort, Anna?'

'No, my lord. As a matter of fact, your wife wanted to go walking on her own as she has done since you left, but today we insisted that Mairi and Ceit go with her. She was very troubled. I think she received upsetting news about her family from Father Raibeart, who arrived from Glenfinnan this morning.'

'Where is he?' Iain anxiously asked.

He found him with Father Henriot, who already knew the gist of the Lady Gunelle's family news. Iain learned that it did not concern the mother's health but her son's. On leaving Mallaig, Daren, his guards, and Lennox had been attacked by a group of Camerons in the Grampians before they reached the felling site. He had received a deep wound to the stomach and was no longer fit to fight. They had taken him to Crathes.

So, Iain said to himself, *now Gunelle will know that a safe passage is by no means guaranteed in the Grampians.*

However, he was very annoyed that the Camerons had made such an attack and he was angry that he could not retaliate immediately. He had to first settle the succession to the head of the clan before undertaking such a fight, for he would need to involve all the lairds. Turning his head, he saw Anna, who was anxiously awaiting the end of his conversation with the two priests. He stood up quickly, startling Bran, who was lying at his feet. He nodded to the two priests and went off to join his wife on the shore. He got back in the saddle and galloped towards the village, his big dog in his wake. The sun was beginning to sink into the sea, casting thick powdery rays of mist. The wind had dropped. Those he asked about the direction his wife had taken had not seen her since the beginning of the afternoon when she was heading south towards the caves with her servant and the little girl. Iain had a sense of foreboding as he looked at the sea and the southern cliffs. There was suddenly a knot in his stomach. The tide had been on the rise for three hours, and if they had had the time to reach St. Ninians's cave, they would not have had the time to get out before the water flooded it. That is why no one had seen them coming back. He galloped off along the ice-covered shore, which was shrinking with each wave. On seeing him ride off in such haste, the people he had questioned realised the danger posed by the tide and rushed to the castle to seek help. Iain had to ride further up on the shoreline. The sea had reached the rocks and was cutting him off from the cove where the caves were. Minutes counted. If the water had reached this level near the village, there must only be six feet of fresh air in the grotto. In the distance, he saw a woman and a little girl running to meet him. It was Mairi.

'Good grief, where is Gunelle?' he groaned. He spurred on his horse and joined them within the same minute. 'Where is your mistress?' he asked, his voice tense.

Mairi was in tears; she had lost her headdress, and her clothes were torn. Little Ceit was soaked to the skin, her eyes filled with fear. She clung to the dog's neck while he licked her face.

'My lord, it is terrible!' Mairi said through her tears. 'We had managed to climb onto the rocks when Ceit slipped and fell into the sea. Lady Gunelle rushed into the water and grabbed her, but as she was bringing her to me, it was she who was carried away by the wave. I kept hold of Ceit's hand, but I lost hold of my mistress's.

Oh, it is all my fault. I knew we had to turn back before the tide came in, my lord. Now she is stuck in St. Ninians's cave, and she is going to drown. I… I am damned…'

Iain had not heard the end of the story. If, by some good fortune, Gunelle had reached the top of the cave without being carried off by the wave, he had to lift her out from above and reach Ninians's Peak before that passage too was cut off by the rising tide. The peak was surrounded by reefs which made access by boat impossible.

Since his childhood, Iain knew the cave beneath the peak like the back of his hand because he and his brother had played there, and all too often had risked their lives by betting on the movements of the tide. The north face had an opening which led out onto the peak, but it was often obstructed by debris left by the tide. If he could reach the ridge of the peak, he would find the opening and would be able to get down into the cave, if it wasn't yet underwater.

Almighty God, he implored, *hold back your tide, I beg you. Do not take Gunelle back now!* Iain had dismounted opposite the peak. He ran to the foam-covered rocks. The three points of black rock which gave access to the St. Ninians's peak were still visible when the waves ebbed. Bran was barking with concern. Iain took off his claymore, dropped onto the first rock, waited for the sea to recede from the second, and jumped onto it. His feet slipped, and he almost lost his balance, but he straightened up and threw himself onto the third before a fresh surge of water arrived. This time he had to grip the moss-covered rock and hold on until the wave receded. He succeeded. Wet with the foam and pushing on the uncovered parts of the rock, he heaved himself onto it. From there, he managed to reach the peak. When he turned around, he watched as the sea completely covered the three rocks, thereby cutting him off from the shore. He could hear his dog howling amidst the roar of the breakers.

181

He quickly found the passage between two rocks which led into the cave. There was nothing in his way —in winter, the tides brought in less rubbish. He slid down the opening and was immediately in darkness. The noise of the water against the walls of the cave deafened him. His heart was pounding, and he had to wait for his eyes to get used to the darkness. Little by little, he made out the form of the rocks and the level of the sea. There remained barely the height up to his waist before the water would be licking the roof of the cave. He had jammed his feet between the stones and was desperately looking around the cave as the water receded. At last, he saw her. At first, what seemed like a pile of wet clothes from which emerged a head of long hair floating at the whim of the waves. She was only an arm's length away from him. He quickly stretched across the stones to reach her. It was then he saw her swollen face, her puffy eyes, and her half-opened lips. He grabbed her under the arms and dragged her onto the last rock close to the roof of the cave which was as yet unreached by the sea. *Almighty God, he murmured, tell me she is breathing!* When he put his ear to her mouth, he felt her breath. In the space of a few seconds, with a tremendous surge of energy Iain lifted his wife and carried her out of the cave. Up above, it was now pitch dark; he could no longer make out the coast. The wind had gotten up and was sweeping the rocky plateau covered with scraggy moss. There was nothing, not a tree or a rock, behind which to shelter from the wind. Iain had a moment of panic as he looked at his unconscious wife, whom he had stretched out on the ground with her head resting on his knees. He took her face in his hands and gently whispered her name. She opened her eyes and closed them again immediately. Her cheeks were cold, her forehead and hands too. Iain realised that her blood had begun to thicken. He had lost men this way after they had been in the cold sea. The blood would gently flow from the heart, and they would fall asleep, never to waken again. He cast a frantic look around him—there was nothing with which to light a fire. His own clothes and flint were

182

dry, but there was nothing on the ground to burn. *If I do not warm her up, I will lose her*, he said to himself.

He quickly undid his plaid, which hung over his left shoulder, and took off his leather jacket, his tunic, and his shirt. Bare-chested, he began to undress his wife. The sodden clothes were clinging to her taut skin, and it was no easy thing to remove them one by one. When she was naked, he wrapped her in his own dry clothes, laid her on her back, took her in his arms, and held her tight against him. He wrapped her in his wool plaid and feverishly rubbed her back. He could feel his wife's wet head in the hollow of his neck, her cold face resting on his shoulder.

'My lady,' he whispered to her. 'Speak to me! You must talk to me! You cannot go to sleep. Say something to me!'

He could not bear her silence and redoubled his efforts to waken her from her state of unconsciousness. He desperately kept repeating her name. At last, he felt her lips move against his skin and heard her murmur softly, 'Let me sleep.'

My head was spinning. I no longer heard the deafening sound of the waves tossing me to and fro. I no longer felt the water round about me. *Where am I?* I asked myself. I could not open my eyes, and I could not feel my legs. I had to make a real effort to concentrate on sensing the feeling in my arms, then my body. I did not feel the weight of my sodden clothes, which had dragged me down to the bottom of the cave. *Had I lost them as I drowned?* I heard someone calling me. The voice was very close to me. I concentrated on the voice. I recognised the voice of my husband begging me not to sleep. I opened my eyes. At first, I saw nothing; it was dark wherever I was. Then I remembered the sensation that my body was floating in space. I was stretched out against a body, flesh against flesh, hands rubbing my back, and my husband's voice persistently saying my name just above my head. He was asking me to talk to him. Suddenly I was conscious that I was naked in his arms. So, I was not dead. I would have liked to get free, but none of my limbs would respond to my will. I told him to let me sleep.

'No, my lady! If you sleep, you will never wake again.'

I closed my eyes in exhaustion. I could not help it. I was numb from my head to my feet. I felt him press me against him and again forbid me to sleep. Then he began to say words in Gaelic to me, which he would ask me to translate into Scots and then French. His voice was strained. At first, I did not respond, but as he insisted, I slowly began to translate the words he was saying. The words had absolutely no connection with each other. While continuing to massage my body, he said them one by one—no order, no logical sequence. The idea that this method of learning a language was of little use crossed my mind, but I did not have the strength to protest and docilely repeated the words in Scots and French: *grass, turn pale, tapestry, dagger, fire, drink, trestle, shoulder, otter…* When I hesitated, and there was silence, he repeated the last word as he rubbed my shoulders. The warmth of his hands caressing me and his chest underneath me gradually reached my heart, and I began to shake.

'That is good, my lady. Your body is responding,' I heard him murmur with hope in his voice. 'Tremble, my lady, tremble. You are beginning to warm up.'

'Can I rest now? I am tired of the language lessons, my lord.'

He stopped rubbing my back and began to massage each of my trembling limbs. Finally, he began to gently stroke my face.

'Yes, my lady, you can rest,' he said cheerfully. 'Your skin is becoming warm again. I, too, have had enough of Scots and French!'

His hands replaced the plaid around my shoulders, and he enclosed my legs between his. He put his arms around me on top of the plaid, and I felt his beard brush my temple when he placed a kiss on my wet hair. A strange sense of well-being took hold of me at that moment and calmed the tremors running through my body. I had difficulty thinking about the situation now that my mind was free from the obligation to translate a list of words. One would have said I was sinking again. I felt sleep coming over me, and I could not resist it.

I do not know how long I remained asleep against him like that, but when I awakened, everything came back to me. I lifted my head, rolled over on my side, and sat up. A bright moon shone out through the clouds of mist. I saw his face turn towards me. He was smiling. The cold air hitting my naked body made me shiver, and I grabbed the plaid and covered myself immediately. I asked him, 'Where are we, my lord? Why isn't anyone coming to rescue us?'

'Because we are cut off from the rest of the world for at least another four hours, my lady. We are surrounded by the sea. We are on St. Ninians's peak, just above the cove which is submerged.'

'Where are my clothes? I am cold.'

'They are here. They are drying.' He stood up and held out his tunic. 'Here, put that on. It will keep you warm.'

I put my arms in the tunic and pulled it over my head. I brought my hair, which was stiff with the salt, out over the collar. I stroked my face, which was burning. I had bumps on my temples and a gash on my forehead. The rocks had not spared me. The whole scene of Ceit's rescue and my drowning came flooding into my mind. But I had not drowned. My husband had saved me. I looked at him. I was intrigued. He was sitting with his legs crossed beneath him. He had put on his shirt, which was opened on his chest, and he was looking at me in silence. He held out his leather jacket, but I refused it.

'You take it, my lord.' I said. 'I will keep your plaid.'

'And you are going to come back into my arms,' he added as he put on the jacket.

Trembling, I covered my frozen bare feet with the plaid and brought my knees up under my chin. He moved over towards me and pulled me against him again, encircling me with his legs and arms to protect me from the wind. Once again, I began to shiver and offered no resistance. I settled into the hollow of the welcome warmth of my husband, my head resting on his shoulder. Strangely we adopted the same position as when we had been riding on Christmas Eve, my back against his chest, his arms around my waist. We were going to spend the second part of the night intertwined thus. It was at that moment, above the incessant sound of the waves crashing against the walls of the cave, that I heard him speaking seriously and gently into my ear. He was reproaching himself for not having warned me about the tides in the caves. He gave me news of Mairi and Ceit, apologised for his behaviour during our last conversation, gave an account of his round of visits to the lairds, and shared his concern after the attack in the Grampians in which my brother had been wounded. Without saying a word, I listened as he expressed himself like the most attentive of husbands, and I was fascinated by what he

186

was saying. *Who is this new Iain MacNeil, I do not know?* I thought. When he stopped speaking, I could not stop myself from heaving a sigh.

He tightened his embrace and, after a brief silence, asked me, 'Tell me, my lady, unless you wanted to die, it was madness on your part to throw yourself into the water to save Ceit. Why did you do it?'

'But, my lord, it would have been impossible to do otherwise. Does one know why one acts in a certain way when a life is in danger? Why did you save me? Out of duty? Did you want to kill yourself?' I moved so that I could see his face.

He looked serious; his brow was furrowed. He said slowly, 'I saved you because I did not want to lose you.'

I kept looking at him. *How much this declaration seemed to have cost him!* 'I did not save Ceit so that I would die,' I said to him. 'If you believe me capable of taking my own life, you do not know my faith in God, and you offend me. I am not happy at Mallaig but rest assured, I will not kill myself for that reason.'

At this point, I buried my head in my crossed arms and my hunched knees. *This man has a real gift for annoying me*, I thought. I heard him move behind me.

'I am not happy at Mallaig either, but I would be if I knew how to make you happy.'

I raised my head and looked at him. He had bowed his head, and I could not see his eyes. His silhouette stood out against the dark sky. I saw his shoulders rise and fall to the slow beat of his heart. I looked out to sea, my heart full of confusion. I no longer understood anything about this man, and I gently told him so.

He held out his arms and drew me close to him again. 'I do not understand much either, my lady,' he whispered in my hair, 'but I do know I am tired of fighting with you, and I surrender. From now on, I am no longer going to fight the feelings I have for you. Too bad if one day you reject me!'

This declaration caught me unawares. My heart was beating wildly, and I had difficulty unravelling my own feelings. Barely a few hours ago had I not detested him? In the space of three months, Iain had stirred up in my heart a whole range of contradictory emotions, which went from anger to trust, scorn to pride, and then, tonight, he wanted to awaken love. I did not know where I was with him anymore. I closed my eyes and snuggled into the hollow of his enveloping arms. Silence fell between us without any feeling of embarrassment. We had said a lot of things we had to think about, one as much as the other. I just let myself go, listening to the raging sea which surrounded us and isolated us on St. Ninians's Peak. The tide was ebbing. In a few hours, we would return to our folk. Death had come on the prowl but in the end had taken no one. *Praise God*, I thought, exhausted, as I dozed off again.

Chapter Eight
The Vote

At daybreak the next day, all the inhabitants of the castle, as well as those of the village, were standing on the rocks to watch as the knights went into St. Ninians's Cave. Anxiety and consternation were written all over their tense faces. The sea had completely receded from the rocks, and the gentle breeze announced a good day in prospect. Bran, who had ventured into the cave after the men, suddenly gave a bark of joy that echoed against the rocky walls. A single sigh of relief was expressed from fifty hearts: They were safe.

A huge shout greeted the MacNeil son as he came out of the cave carrying his wife in his arms. The ladies were laughing and crying at the same time. Mairi ran to meet her mistress; Nellie followed with more difficulty, tears streaming down her face. Little Ceit was jumping from one rock to the other to get closer to the young chatelaine who held out her arms as soon as her husband had set her down on the sand. With whoops of joy, the child ran to her and clung to her.

Lord Tomas, who had run to meet his cousin, grabbed him, and gave him a big affectionate hug. He looked into his eyes and was so moved he could not speak. Lord Iain smiled and squeezed his shoulder. Then he looked around at the crowd gathered to witness his return and felt a swell of gratitude more than pride rise within him at the sight of all these delighted faces. *Why have I never felt that the folk of Mallaig loved me?* he wondered. He turned around and saw Anna shaking her head in distress, her eyes red from crying. He went over to her, took her in his arms, and with a lump in his throat, clutched her to his chest as a son would have comforted his mother.

'Oh, Anna, don't cry,' he murmured. 'Don't you know I always come back?'

'Of course, I know, my lord.' she answered with a sob, 'but you are going to end up losing Lady Gunelle if you are not careful.'

'I am going to try from now on, Anna. I promise!' he said to her with a big smile.

While the young lord put his claymore, which one of the knights had handed to him, back in his belt his sister-in-law grabbed hold of him and gave him a big sloppy kiss on the lips, under the looks of embarrassment of everyone present. He pushed her back furiously telling her to control herself. Lady Beathag, who did not like to see her advances rejected, turned around in anger and, muttering away under her breath, went to join her companion. When everyone reached the shore where the horses and a carriage were waiting, she went over to Lord Iain and, within easy earshot of Lady Gunelle, following behind with Nellie, Mairi, and Ceit, reproached him for his coldness.

'You are not very gracious my lord,' she said to him. 'You have just spent more than seven hours alone with your wife. You could spare a few minutes for me rather than keeping me at arm's length as if I had the plague.'

'Ah, so you miss Sheriff Darnley already, old dear!' retorted Iain infuriated.

Cutting off any kind of discussion, he quickly turned around, took his wife's hands, put his arm around her, and helped her into the carriage. Then he hoisted little Ceit up beside her. Grabbing the reins of the nearest horse, he jumped into the saddle and headed straight for the castle with Bran close behind. The other ladies climbed into the carriage, and the procession moved off, flanked by the knights on horseback and all the villagers.

So, Lady Gunelle came home to Mallaig naked except for her husband's tunic over which someone had thrown a fur-lined cape. She was surrounded by her ladies laughing with delight. Two green eyes gave her a look that could kill: Beathag did not take kindly to being humiliated in public.

The whole day was declared a celebration at the castle. In the courtyard, on the young master's orders, kegs of mead and beer were opened. Eggs, little rye bread, and honey rolls were handed out, and someone went to fetch the piper. Highlanders considered that any human being snatched from the sea was a miracle, and each miracle had the power to cancel out a death. So it was that music and song filled the air at Mallaig until evening and no one considered the celebration as an offense to the memory of the late chief Baltair. At the beginning of the afternoon, Lady Gunelle went down into the courtyard and mingled with her jubilant people. She was rested. She had been bathed, had her hair washed, and dressed by her maids, who rejoiced at her safe return home. A discreet smile lit up her pale, swollen face. The castle staff and the ladies of the village were crowding around her, each one trying to say a thousand kind, little words to her. She was surprised to receive so many expressions of affection. At one point, she noticed the hardness of Lady Beathag's expression and wondered if, in her time, Alasdair's wife had received such affection from the folk of Mallaig. Then Gunelle thought back to the last celebration she had attended, that of her wedding and had mixed memories. On this occasion, she had the most sought-after dance partner, according to Beathag, all to herself.

Lord Iain led his wife from one quadrille to another with a great deal of dexterity and gentleness, patiently teaching her steps. He showered her with little gestures of attentiveness, sometimes suggesting she have something to eat, sometimes that she should have a rest, and at others that she dances with him. A beaming relaxed smile never left his face during the whole celebration, and seeing him with his wife on his arm, a stranger would have thought that this was his wedding day. Towards the end of the afternoon, it had become too cold and only some of the castle folk and the knights remained in the courtyard. Everyone else went inside and gathered around the fire in the great hall. The harpist and the piper played sets of ballads and laments to which the ladies lent their voices, and the songs rang out clearly amidst the stone walls.

Lady Gunelle had sat down on a bench with her back against the column, and little Ceit was cuddled up, sound asleep in her arms.

Lord Iain came up to his wife and gently lifted the child from her arms.

'She is too heavy for you, my lady. Let me,' he said.

He put the warm little body on his shoulder and sat down on the ground beside Lady Gunelle. He studied the child's tiny hands as he stroked them with his thumb.

His wife looked tenderly at him. She was surprised when her husband said in a rather husky voice, 'I did not thank you for saving the life my daughter, my lady.' After a brief pause, he added, 'I know this revelation must come as a surprise to you. A man takes no delight in introducing his bastard to his wife, and I am not proud to be doing so, but I owe it to you to tell you the truth.'

Looking his wife straight in the eye, he went on, 'I am taking that risk.'

'May I ask who the mother is?'

'She died in childbirth. Ceit never knew her, but she bears her name. She was one of my mother's companions. She was fifteen years older than me and, with my mother's connivance, seduced me when I was sixteen.'

Lady Gunelle had looked away, her lips pursed.

'I can stop, my lady, if you wish. You have probably been given an idyllic portrait of the late chatelaine of Mallaig, and I run the risk of destroying it if I continue.'

'Is it essential for you or for me that I know the rest, my lord?'

'Only if you wish to know the man you married.'

I looked back at him and thought about this very new picture of father and daughter. I thought of that intense look in Ceit's blue eyes, the same blue as my husband's and my late father-in-law's. *Heavens! If my husband is her father, I am little Ceit's mother....* I thought. Iain was looking at me with a mixture of concern and hope in his eyes.

I held his gaze and replied, 'I want to know the man I married.'

He sighed and looked again at the sleeping child. Bran responded to his master's sigh by coming and placing his black muzzle on his hand. He lifted his hand off the little girl to stroke the dog's head. The animal snuggled up again against my husband and did not move as if he, too, were waiting to hear the secrets he was about to share.

In a muffled voice, his head towards me, but without looking at me, he began to speak, 'That summer, my father had begun my training as a knight, and I went everywhere with him. My mother entertained a lot. I think that the second year without Alasdair was difficult for her, and she wanted some distraction to take her mind off things. She had decided to hold a *cour d'amour* at Mallaig with the Highland lairds' wives and the knights. When we were at home, my father and I attended these gatherings. My father did not feel very comfortable, but he saw how radiant my mother was in that world, and that was enough for him. As for me, these courtly love exercises were torture. My lack of education and experience with women made me awkward and ridiculous, all of which amused my mother. She came to take delight in my embarrassment and first angst as a man and came up with the idea of throwing me into the arms of her companion. I do not know if Lady Ceit really loved me, but I must have attracted her because she did not keep me waiting. She taught me everything a man can learn in bed, and I became hers exclusively. I should have confided in my father at that time, but I was afraid of how he would react to my mother's role in the story. The following spring, Lady Ceit fell pregnant. It was obvious to her and my mother that I was responsible for her condition. The two women completely ignored me. From then on, I could not bear to stay at the castle for more than three days at a time and I took part in every tournament held in the Highlands. Lady Ceit left for the Isle of Rum, where she gave birth to her daughter. She died. My mother mourned the loss of her companion for a long time and bitterly held it against me. That winter, I was completely lost and miserable.

When the Callainn celebration was over, my mother sent me to Rum to fetch the child. She immediately became attached to the little one and forbade me to acknowledge that she was my daughter. I respected her wishes and kept quiet, convincing myself that a little of the great love my mother showed for my daughter was meant for me.'

Iain had said nothing for a while when Nellie, who was retiring for the night, came to fetch Ceit to put her to bed. My husband stood up with the child in his arms, saying he would take her himself. Turning towards me, he took his leave.

'There you have it, my lady, the sad story of your little Ceit's arrival into the world and the more pitiful one of her father's disgraces. I thank you for listening to me and wish you a good night

'Goodnight, my lord,' I replied. I was moved. I watched him slowly leave the room with his little bundle in his arms. I went up to my bedroom shortly afterwards, declining Mairi's help to get ready for bed. I was desperate to be alone.

I entered my room as if I was going into it for the first time and saw it as Isla MacNeil's bedroom. I walked slowly around the room before beginning to undress. The subjects of the tapestries, the colour of the curtains, and the carved frame of the cheval mirror— every detail whether obvious or discreet in this room seemed to speak of courtly love. Suddenly I felt ill at ease. *So, that is how a mother can introduce her own son into a life of immorality.* I thought. How many more such revelations remained for me to hear from my husband's lips? Something told me this episode was just the first of a series and that Iain would only offer himself to me once he had divulged what he judged appropriate for me to know before accepting him. The thought broke my heart. At that moment, words he had expressed on St. Ninians's peak came to mind, *'Too bad if one day you reject me.'*

The following days basked in the calm after the storm. My face was healing quickly, and I soon regained my strength. The work in the cellars was coming to an end, and I watched Father Henriot and the workmen going back and forth to their daily chores. Lady Beathag and Finella had just finished the largest piece of cloth ever woven at the castle and because they asked me to, I went to see it. The very mild weather had brought the garden to life, and Nellie, who showed an aptitude for gardening, began to hoe it with little Ceit's help. In the kitchen, Anna and the servants had begun the preparations for the great feast of Callainn.

As for Iain, two engagements fell on the 25th of March: the ceremony of homage to the new clan chief and the end of his lessons in reading and writing in Scots. As Iain had nothing to see to concerning the succession to the title of chieftain other than await his uncle Aindreas's decision, he put in double the effort to finish his studies. Instead of half the day as we had done up until Lord Baltair's death, he asked me to devote the whole day to the lessons until the 25th of March. So, we began every morning in Alasdair's room and worked until late afternoon. At midday, we often ate a light meal which Anna brought up to us.

The weather was exceptionally mild, and the sun, streaming through the windows heated the room, with the result that there was no need to light the fire. Iain would often work in a linen shirt with his sleeves rolled up, unable to bear wearing a plaid and a woollen tunic. I was sometimes surprised to find myself admiring his broad shoulders, muscular back, and arms as he leaned over the page, quill in hand. I discovered that this visual exploration of my husband's body began to fluster me somewhat.

One morning as he was coming out of the morning service, Iain was called to the estate to solve a disagreement between some of the serfs. He apologised and left with Tomas and four men. Having nothing to do, I went to lend a hand in the kitchens and spent the rest of the morning there. After lunch, my husband still had not returned, and I learned that seven more men had been requested as reinforcements because the situation he had gone to sort out had degenerated into a fight. I found myself alone at the table with Beathag, who, taking advantage of my obvious concern, began to make fun of me under the pretext of reassuring me.

'Dear Gunelle, do not worry. It is just another skirmish. He will come back to you safe and sound, as he always does. My brother-in-law cannot be killed, neither on the battlefield nor in bed.' Seeing my embarrassment, she continued, 'Oh, it is true you are totally ignorant on the last point. Obviously, I am telling you nothing new when I say that I know Iain well in that domain. I could point out his preferences if ever you get the chance to use them…'

Crimson with embarrassment and anger, I had risen to my feet with the clear intention of putting an end to this gossip as soon as possible, but Lady Beathag did not agree and was determined to carry on boasting about the intimate knowledge she had of my husband. She grabbed my arm and forced me to sit down again. As she was much taller and stronger, I could only free myself by pushing her out of the way. At that moment, someone entered the room, and then left again immediately. I felt trapped. If I wanted to break free, I would have to cause a scene that would bring all the servants running, something my position as chatelaine did not permit. So, I stayed where I was and resolved to be patient while trying to remain in control of my emotions.

'Ah, curious little one,' she simpered when she realised, I was not putting up a fight.

'I do not suffer from the kind of curiosity in which you seem to delight,' I replied. 'What you do in your bed is your business, and I have no wish to know. I would like you not to forget that your brother-in-law is married. If he is still your lover, this situation cannot go on forever. So, keep the details of your debauchery to yourself.'

'Dear Gunelle, I do not think you quite understand the limited power a wife has over her Highlander husband. The character of our northern men is summed up in two things: their virility and their authority. If you cannot satisfy the first, you are sure to suffer as a result of the second! Iain is a generous and demanding man in bed. He never knows long periods of inaction, and you do not get bored with him. Last night again, I had the pleasure of biting his neck, which was tense with lust.'

I could not bear to hear anymore, and I rushed out of the room, the sound of my shoes on the floor was drowned by her laughter ringing out as clear as a bell. I left the castle by the first available door and ran to take refuge on the ramparts. It took a long time for me to calm down. In fact, I spent almost the whole afternoon there.

Mist covered the moor. Not a whisper of a breeze came from the sea to chase it away. The landscape was motionless, as if suspended between earth and heaven. There was the smell of a storm in the air. There was nothing to look at, so I had to look within to examine the contradictory feelings vying with each other inside me. With bitter disappointment, I realised that I knew next to nothing about the relationship between my husband and his sister-in-law. My instinct told me that since the incident at St. Ninians's Peak, Iain had not touched Beathag, but what assurance had he given me? None, of course. What happened at night in the wing where they both had their bedrooms? Thanks to Beathag's latest revelation, I was going to go over that question, which tortured me so much, again and again. Despite my great ignorance about the intimacy between men and women, I could not subscribe to Beathag's narrow description of Highland husbands. Physical, carnal exchanges. Was that all that there was between them? But I remembered the 'dirty viper "remark which Iain had thrown at Beathag one day. 'Vipers bite,' I murmured.

A downpour put an end to the fight. Torrents of water fell from the dark sky, and those fighting could not see a thing. Lord Iain and his companions broke up the hostilities with the mutual agreement of their assailants. It often happened that they would begin to fight for no good reason and would bring it to an end for a reason which was no better. *'Just for the form,'* Iain would say to his men. This skirmish had been such a fight. A minor incident of cattle rustling between his serfs and those of the neighbouring clan. It involved two shorthorns. Nothing that called for the deployment of a band of a dozen armed men, but if you looked at it as a fighting exercise, it would have been useful, even enjoyable. No one had been seriously wounded. No insult or threat had been uttered. Each one took what was his and went home to get dried.

Iain sheathed his claymore, got into the saddle, and stretched himself. It was nearly a week since he had ridden and a month since he had had a fight. As he had spent long hours bent over a desk, his muscles were tight, and this little outing had done him a world of good. He smiled at his men, who obviously had felt the same benefit. The little group left the "battle" field, now a veritable bog and headed for Mallaig. It was very dark in the keep when he arrived.

Iain lit every torch as he went. Dripping with mud and water, he went straight up to his room and on the way, he asked a servant to take up hot water for a bath. As soon as the bath was ready, he slipped into it with sheer delight and closed his eyes, a smile of satisfaction on his face. He did not see Lady Beathag come in.

'You seem very happy, my lord,' she said. 'One would say you had a good time on the moor.'

'Not bad,' he replied, closing his eyes again. Beathag was silently walking around the bathtub contemplating her brother-in-law and looking frisky. When she was behind him, she bent over his head, passed her arms over his shoulders, and plunged her hands into the water level with his stomach. Iain sat up straight with a start.

'It appears to me it is a long time since I gave you a bath. Let me, my lord, you will not regret it,' she offered sweetly. Accompanying the offer with a gesture, she put her hands on Iain's shoulders and began to gently massage them. Then kissing his neck, she quickly ran her fingers down his chest. She was about to continue on down when he grabbed her wrists to stop her.

'I would prefer you to do nothing. I will manage on my own.'

'And what about tonight, Iain? Will you manage on your own with that?' she said, pointing to his erect manhood.

'Get out of here immediately, or I will throw you out myself!' he shouted.

'My lord! How violent you are! Are you afraid that your irreproachable little wife will come to inspect the damage caused by today's fight? That would surprise me very much after all the assurances I gave her about your various accomplishments…'

Iain jumped out of the bath and grabbed a towel, his face dark with anger. 'Good grief, Beathag, leave Gunelle alone! She wants nothing to do with all your goings-on.'

'Our goings-on, you mean. I assure you she proved to be quite interested. But you will have a lot of work to do with her before she can satisfy you in bed. She has no idea about what makes you groan… except perhaps this.'

While saying that, Beathag grabbed her brother-in-law's bare shoulders and bit him on the nape of his neck. 'This is one of the tips I gave her,' she said before quickly leaving the room.

Iain did not have the time to react. He felt his neck where his sister-in-law's teeth had left their mark.

When Iain sat down at the table that night, he realised that the discussion between his sister-in-law and his wife had caused a lot of damage. Gunelle was not taking part in any conversation, was hardly lifting her nose out of her bread, and what alarmed him most was that she was avoiding looking at him. On the other hand, Beathag was babbling incessantly and was wearing a little look of triumph, which infuriated him. He would have liked to have been alone with Gunelle and promised himself that he would take her for a walk on the ramparts as soon as the meal was over. The time had come to speak to her about his relationship with Beathag; on that point, his honour was seriously sullied. He sighed deeply, and at that moment, he and his wife's eyes met. He read suspicion in hers. He was the first to look down. *The contest is far from won*, he said to himself

When the meal was over, as Lady Gunelle was making her way towards the armchairs near the musicians, she was aware of her husband at her side. She looked up at him. He looked worried, and she picked up a hint of a plea in his voice when he asked her to join him for a walk on the ramparts. She agreed, and he took her hand to lead her out of the room. The rain had stopped. There was a light breeze, and the air was filled with the smell of wet bracken, marsh, and kelp. The storm had created hundreds of streamlets which slithered across the moor like snakes and which the last rays of sunlight made glisten in the distance. The couple walked for several minutes in silence, with Bran running about in front of them, delighted to have this unexpected walk. Gunelle had placed her hand on the arm her husband had held out to her, and she fixed her eyes on the horizon. Without exchanging a word, they reached the parapet, which looked out over the village and the sea. Gunelle let go of her husband's arm and went over to lean against the stone wall. She peered through a crenel. Her husband joined her and calmly revealed another episode in his life.

'My lady,' he said to her, 'I think my sister-in-law shared things with you today which you would have preferred not to hear. I know her well enough to surmise that they were out of place. However, it would be dishonest of me to claim that they were completely without foundation.'

'My lord,' she interrupted, 'what you and she do or what she does with you is a matter for your conscience. I am no different from other wives, and I am not compelling you to justify your behaviour.'

'You are not compelling me to do anything, my lady. I want to explain myself. I have decided to reveal myself as I am to the one, I wish to deserve.'

Gunelle withdrew her head from the crenel and stared at her husband. She looked at him for a long time without any sign of anger or contempt. She saw a man opening himself wide to the judgement of another. A brave man. She had to show the same courage and listen to another revelation.

'I am listening, my lord.'

Iain offered her his arm again, and buffeted by a spring breeze, they continued their leisurely walk on the ramparts. 'I met Beathag MacDougall at a tournament in the islands the year before my brother returned to Mallaig. She had decided to set her cap at the champion, and that was me. I fell in love with her as one does at seventeen. My father recalled me to Mallaig, and I did not see her again until the following summer when I returned to the islands with my brother. She was immediately seduced by him. Why make do with the younger son when you can have the MacNeil heir? They married that autumn, and with my pride crushed to pieces, I fled Mallaig for nearly a year. I would meet my brother occasionally at tournaments throughout the Highlands. The MacNeil brothers were popular with the heralds and the spectators in the team competitions. Beathag never went with him. After my brother's death, I had to return to the castle, where I realised that my mother was suffering more from his loss than my sister-in-law. Beathag decided to take me into her bed to console herself. I admit I had no hesitation in taking her as my mistress. I did it as much to get my revenge on my brother as to hurt my mother, but I failed on both counts.'

'Were you still in love with her?' Gunelle asked him.

'With Beathag,' he replied, 'it is not about a man's heart. That is not what interests her. She is incapable of exclusivity. The liaison suited us both and lasted five years.'

Iain had stopped to say these last words and was looking his wife straight in the eyes. In them, he read an unspoken question that gave him cause for hope. Taking her right hand, he ran his finger along the pink scar and said, 'I gave up Beathag the day I did that to you.'

'My lord,' she asked, embarrassed, 'what do you mean by gave her up?'

The question took Iain by surprise. A vague apprehension crossed his mind. What exactly had Beathag told her? Should he defend himself against some accusation? And, if so, which one?

'I mean that I have not touched my sister-in-law from that day, my lady. Have you information to the contrary?'

'Yes, my lord. Your sister-in-law told me you were in her bed last night and that you bear the proof of your frolicking on your neck.'

Iain uttered an oath and turned right around, his arms hanging by his side, his head bent back in an attitude of utter helplessness. *So that was it!* he thought. He stood in front of his wife, who maintained the look of someone waiting for a denial. In a sudden move, he threw off his plaid, opened his jacket collar, and opened his shirt as he explained tensely, 'I do have a mark on my neck. It does not date from yesterday but from a while ago, and this is not the kind of mark my sister-in-law should have described to you.'

Gunelle was staring at her husband's bare neck. The red bite mark was imprinted on the skin just where the neck and shoulder meet. She closed her eyes and said harshly, 'Tell me, what kind of mark it is, my lord. I am so ignorant of these matters.'

'Good grief, my lady, do you think I would have accepted this kind of bite if I had known what she was doing? Beathag came to find me in my bedroom when I had just come back from the moor and was having a bath. I will not deny she intended to give herself to me, but I did not take her up on the offer. She bit me to punish me and to punish you for being the one I am rejecting her for.'

I felt my heart leap in my chest as if it wanted to jump out. Had I the right, even for a second, to doubt what my husband was telling me? Everything about his attitude cried out sincerity. I realised that I really needed to believe him. Yes, I ardently wished that Iain would put an end to his intimate relations with his sister-in-law. If what he was saying about her was true, we certainly had an enemy within the castle. This woman was capable of stooping very low to achieve her ends, and I wondered if I was capable of being a match for her. The wish that my husband would drive her from the castle crossed my mind.

Iain must have been worried by the silence which followed his explanation because he anxiously asked me if he had my trust. In a spontaneous gesture that surprised even me, I leaned on his chest and replied in the affirmative.

With a sigh of relief, he hugged me. 'Thank you, my lady.'

When we returned to the great hall, I caught Beathag looking at my husband's open collar. I had to smile, for she gave me one of her fixed smiles. I think that our silent exchange did not escape Iain's notice, for he squeezed my hand tighter. I felt myself blushing immediately and responded to his message the same way. *No*, I thought, *I have nothing to fear from Beathag MacDougall. My husband has made his choice.*

205

The next day a letter arrived from Crathes—the first written news from my family for a while. It was addressed to my husband and came from my father. I learned its content from Iain in the study. My hands were trembling with excitement as I held the sheet of paper. The seal, very like the MacNeils' because of the similarity of coats of arms, gave me the strange feeling of opening a letter that was not addressed to me. Without reading it, I handed it to my husband.

'This can be an exercise in reading Scots, my lord. The handwriting is good and easy to read. Do you wish to?'

'Are you so disinterested to know the contents that you do not want to read it first? It could be a long time before you get it back.'

'My lord, I am obviously in a hurry to find out what my father says but this letter is addressed to you, not me. As you understand Scots, and you can now read, you have the right to be first to find out what your correspondence says.'

Without a word, he plunged into reading the letter. I walked up and down the room to calm my impatience. For the letter to have reached us that day, it must have been written in the days after my brother Daren's return to Crathes. It was no doubt about his and my mother's state of health. But the fact that the letter was addressed to Iain led me to believe there was more. I was awakened out of my thoughts by a terrible bang on the table. My blood ran cold.

'Tell me, my lady, do you wish to ask for an annulment of our marriage through your uncle Carmichael, Bishop of Orleans?'

I was dumbfounded. What was my father up to for him to have written such a thing? I came and sat down opposite Iain and looked him straight in the eye.

'No, my lord. I have never even given it a thought,' I replied calmly.

The anger left him as quickly as it had come. Without a word, he handed me the letter. I took it in my hands and read it, all the time forcing myself to remain calm. On reading it, I immediately felt ashamed. My father was demanding that my husband provide a guard of twenty men on the felling site or else he would stop the payments and the work. On top of that, he was demanding the annulment of our marriage for non-consummation. There was not a word about my brother's or my mother's health. It was purely and simply a list of demands, probably written in a fit of either fear or anger. I was dismayed, and my husband noticed it as soon as I looked at him. He took the letter from my hands and held it for a few moments. Then he got up and paced the floor.

'We are now going to practice writing Scots, my lady,' he said.

'What do you intend to do, my lord?'

'With regard to the felling site or the consummation of our marriage?'

I felt myself going red and dropped my eyes. Inside, I was cursing my reaction. To be sure, the subject always made me uncomfortable. I resented my convent years which had kept me ignorant of that side of life, and my mother, who had not taken the time to rectify the situation. I watched Iain bring a stool and set it down next to mine.

He sat down, put his arm around my shoulder and said, as he looked into my eyes, 'My lady, I am going to address the matter of the site. The other matter concerns only the two of us. Do you agree?'

'Of course,' I murmured.

He got up again, went to fetch paper and ink, and sat opposite me at the table. I watched as he concentrated just as he had during our earlier lessons. His large fingers, little used to fine, delicate movements, slowly traced out the lines and curves of each letter. I could not help smiling at this man who had learned so much in a matter of weeks. He had passed from ignorance to knowledge as a landscape passes from shadow to light with the movement of just one cloud. I was so proud of him. It was at that instant I realised that I could come to love him.

When he had finished, with a knowing smile, he held out the sheet of paper. I took it, returning his smile. Before reading it, I congratulated him on his handwriting, which made him laugh. Thus, I learned his response to my father, the tone was relaxed in comparison to that in which my husband had read my father's letter a few minutes earlier. With Highland directness, Iain assured Nathaniel Keith that there would be order and calm in the Grampians as on all other parts of his estate. He himself would be the judge as to the need for a guard on the site and would decide on the number of men if necessary. He asked about Daren and my mother's health. And he closed with this enigmatic sentence: *'Your daughter will tell you herself when a MacNeil heir is expected.'* Looking up from the page, I met his eyes in which I saw nothing but tenderness.

The signing of the title of clan chief always took place at the castle of the former chief on the date chosen by his natural successor. Iain MacNeil waited until the day before Callainn for his uncle Aindreas's response. The latter arrived late in the evening with his wife and knights. The two men shut themselves away in the arms room where, the homage ceremony was to take place the next morning. After two hours of discussion, Iain found himself at a dead end. During the last few days, his uncle had raised the spectre of Alasdair's death with the four other lairds. The degree of their support for Iain's candidature was no longer so strong. In addition, Aindreas offered to share the responsibilities of the title of clan chief if Iain supported him. *So*, thought Iain bitterly, *Alasdair will never leave me in peace.*

'I cannot support you, uncle,' Iain replied. 'I have no faith in your ability to be chief even with me sharing the burden. My father was the eldest, you the youngest. I know what it is to be second: It either develops the qualities of a chief, or it kills them. I developed them. Not you.'

'There is another way of passing from second to first place in the family. Get rid of the one who occupies first place,' retorted Aindreas. 'You see, nephew, the difference between you and me is that I never detested your father as you so openly detested your brother. And that is the most important thing for maintaining clan unity because the clan is, first and foremost, a family. That is the first thing Baltair should have taught you before giving you a claymore.'

When his uncle got up to leave, Iain reminded him that he had not killed his brother Alasdair, but his words dropped to the floor with a thud. He went up to bed, his heart like stone and his stomach in knots. Raised as rivals throughout their childhood, the MacNeil brothers had never learned to love one another. When Iain saw himself robbed of Beathag by his brother, accumulated grudges turned into pure hatred. Lord Alasdair, jealous of his brother's fighting superiority and the fame his spectacular victories had brought him, took great care in feeding his resentment. The younger never succeeded in retrieving his nobler feelings. The team contests in which they participated afterwards were more like contests between the two brothers with other adversaries involved. Iain would take on the stronger of the two rivals and leave the other for Alasdair. When a contest with the sgian-dubh was proposed, Iain knew that his brother had little chance of winning. If he had not hated him so much, he would have refused the challenge, and his brother would probably still be alive. Isla MacNeil had guessed as much, and with her dying breath, she had accused Iain of fratricide, *'You are nothing, Iain,'* she had declared. *'I had Alasdair, and you killed him. I am no longer your mother, and you are no longer my son.'*

Above all, you must not show that you are hurting, he said to himself. *That is a failing which can make everything crumble around you.* He slept badly, and the next day, when he found himself standing in front of the lairds and their wives, he knew he was about to face a new trial. As he had been warned the day before by his uncle Aindreas, the pledges of support he had obtained from the lairds had melted away. Iain felt very bitter and disappointed.

The council meeting was to be held in the presence of the Clan Macneil wives, who had the right to speak concerning the choice of a chief. The women had been his most violent accusers five years earlier following Alasdair's death. The latter had been a shining star at Lady Isla's courts of love for a whole year and had completely won them over. Iain prepared himself to defend himself on that front. However, what he had not foreseen and something which meant that things presented themselves very differently this time, was the effect Gunelle had had on his family.

The men sat on six armchairs placed around a round table on which lay six claymores which gleamed as the strong sun streaming through the windows hit them. Behind each chair, sat a wife on a stool. The arms room was clothed as it were in the clouds fine dust which hung in the air and looked like beams of sunlight as they hit the ground. When Iain rose to speak, silence fell over the gathering. The men looked solemn and inscrutable. The women were discreetly watching the young chatelaine of Mallaig.

'The time has come to replace Baltair as head of our clan,' said Iain gravely. 'Some reject the heir's succession, and Aindreas has submitted his candidature. In such circumstances, it is customary to hear each one of you before putting it to the vote.'

After a brief pause, he turned towards his uncle Aindreas, whom he invited to speak. Aindreas was stocky and muscular. His brown beard contrasted with his good head of hair in which brown and grey were mixed in equal measure. His staccato voice betrayed a certain impatience. For the benefit of those present, he repeated a speech which everyone except perhaps Lady Gunelle had heard before: the circumstances of Lord Alasdair's death. Lord Iain was once again reproached for not having withdrawn his opponent's sgian-dubh from his brother's chest and for having let him bleed to death without intervening. Aindreas spoke at length of the hatred for one other which the two brothers in fact nurtured and ended his plea with this question: 'Can we put a man guilty of fratricide at the head of clan MacNeil?'

Griogair, the eldest of the lairds, began to speak immediately. He was one of Lord Baltair's two brothers-in-law, the husband of the deceased's eldest sister.

'We all know this story which has already been recounted many times, Aindreas. What I would like to know is why you think you would make a good chief.'

'Because, out of you all, I am the one who has the most knights, owns the largest herd and who lives in the best castle.'

211

'Apart from Iain MacNeil, of course,' interrupted Daidh de Finiskaig.

Struan of Airor and Aulay of Arisaig spoke in turn, expressing their hesitation in entrusting their clan to the youngest among them without the assurance that he was capable of putting the interests of the clan before his own personal feelings. When the last one had finished, Iain started to speak again.

He hated having to recall the daze he was in during those minutes bent over his dying brother after the contest. More than anything, he was concerned about the turmoil the account would cause in his wife's heart. He looked up and decided to tackle the problem head-on. He could not look at Gunelle without turning his head completely, so he was unaware of her look of support. However, looking up at the coat of arms above the fireplace, he felt a very definite sense of his father's presence in the room.

'I am not guilty of fratricide,' he said slowly. 'I did not kill Alasdair. It was not me who stabbed him; even if I had withdrawn the sgian-dubh immediately, he would have died. Anyone who saw his wound can testify to that. I have not regretted his loss because I was not capable of doing so. What I am guilty of towards him and him only is not having loved him enough.'

This confession was followed by a deep silence, which Rosalind, Baltair MacNeil's sister, broke by opening up the discussion to the five wives. They confessed an unbridled admiration for the late Alasdair, whose tragic death had elevated him to the rank of one of Clan MacNeil heroes. Strangely, not one of them, not even his own wife, gave any credence to Aindreas's so-called qualities to take over as clan chief. It was Gunelle's turn to speak last, and every eye, except her husband's, was focussed on her. Iain kept his head bowed. The chatelaine was the youngest and the slimmest of all the

212

women present. That morning, she looked particularly frail in her very sombre garb, her face as pale as her white headdress. From her first words, her calm, confident voice won over several of them and won the silence and respect of them all.

'I know in addressing you that my opinion cannot be considered as impartial. In addition, I do not know Lord Aindreas, my husband's opponent. Therefore, I will not make any pronouncement on his qualifications as chief. Even if I am the one here who has known Iain MacNeil for the shortest time, I think I know him well enough to believe that he will make as good a chief as his father. He is a Scot, loyal to his king, in whose eyes he has won the clan a place of high esteem. He is equal to the task of defending the king against the other clans, for his knowledge allows him to continue the diplomatic role his father played in the Highlands. My husband is a sincere and gifted man. He is capable of giving of himself without counting the cost, and I know he is capable of risking his life to save his own kin. He has his dislikes and weaknesses, as we all have, but I believe that none of them will cloud his judgement as chief.'

'You surprise me, my lady,' interrupted Aindreas's wife immediately. 'Can one have faith in a man who detested his brother and mother and who rebelled against his father? Can one trust him with the responsibility of his entire family without turning a hair? My dear, it is obvious you do not know what the word detest means to give so little importance to the emotion.'

'I agree,' replied Lady Gunelle, her voice trembling. 'I was with Lord Baltair during his last hours and can affirm that Iain MacNeil loved his father and was loved by him. That love was unconditional. What a man feels for his mother concerns him alone. As for the brotherly love between Lord Alasdair and my husband, it was as non-existent in one as in the other. The younger has no obligation towards the elder which the latter does not have towards the younger. It is true that hatred takes over the mind, but as with all emotions, it can change. I know that because I, myself detested Iain MacNeil, but today I believe in him more than in any other man I know.'

Iain looked up and turned towards his wife, his heart was pounding. So, Gunelle had faith in him in face of the rejection of the lairds and their spouses. On catching her look of pride, he knew that for him to become head of the clan was now secondary to the place he wanted to occupy in his wife's heart. He could hear his father whisper, *'Win her love, and she will show you the real Iain MacNeil.'* Rising to his feet, he faced the gathering, which he steered to the crucial business of the meeting. He asked if anyone wanted to say anything else before proceeding to the vote, but no one showed any desire to add anything at all to what had been said.

Intrigued, the five lairds were staring at this little chatelaine, brought from a rich Lowland family, fresh out of a French convent, and yet who showed such sound judgement. As for the spouses, they were subdued by this eloquent testimony of loyalty towards a husband whose reputation as a womaniser was far from being exaggerated. Since only the lairds could vote, on a signal from the eldest present, the wives left the room one after the other. They settled in the armchairs in the great hall to await the result of the vote and began to chatter nervously.

Lady Gunelle, who had only met them twice, at her wedding and her father-in-law's funeral, felt a little out of it. She was thinking of the revelations she had made in the arms room when Lady Rosalind spoke to her, 'Dear Gunelle,' she said as if she were about to share a secret, 'I admire you for having taken Iain as your husband. He is the most courageous yet most tormented young man I know. But you are perfectly right about his qualities as a chief. He is a MacNeil of the MacNeil's great lineage. And I agree you are up to the task despite the fact you are not from the north.'

'Thank you, Lady Rosalind,' replied the young woman. 'I would like to meet up with the ladies of the clan more often. I know I have a lot to learn from you. It would help me to get to know you and to appreciate your gifts whoever becomes chief today.'

With a smile of admiration, Rosalind MacNeil took the young chatelaine's hand and squeezed it as she assured her of her support.

In the arms room, each man picked up his claymore from the table and silently went back to his seat. Iain looked at each of the five lairds, bent over, put his weapon down at his feet, then straightened up slowly. Griogair went forward, placed his claymore at Iain's feet, and returned to his seat. He was followed by Aulay, Struan, and Daidh. Only Aindreas remained in his seat and put his weapon down on the floor in front of himself. The MacNeils had just voted five to one in favour of Baltair's son. A huge sigh of relief and pride emerged from Iain's chest. He looked up at the coat of arms and thought, *Father, I am your successor. I swear that the MacNeils will never have cause to regret this choice.*

Chapter Nine
Ne'er Day

S ince his cousin's rescue of Lady Gunelle on St. Ninians's peak, Lord Tomas had regained peace in his soul. During that fateful night, the prospect of losing the young chatelaine and master of Mallaig at the same time had plunged him into a state of anguish, which their safe and sound return to the castle had dissipated. He would have found it difficult to suffer yet another bereavement after the death of his uncle. When he entered the great hall, he noticed that Lady Gunelle looked concerned. She was sitting with the lairds' wives and was glancing anxiously at the door of the arms room where the vote was taking place. He went over to her and whispered a word of encouragement in Scots in her ear, to which she replied with a smile.

He, too ardently, desired that the title of clan chief should go to his cousin. In the past few weeks, he had found many reasons to change his opinion about Iain MacNeil. He had been forced to recognise his qualities as a man and a leader of men. Since his return from the islands with Sheriff Darnley, what he had seen had confirmed that Lady Gunelle had gained her husband's respect. Iain's sister-in-law would have to be satisfied with just being Alasdair's widow. There was no longer any need to check whose door Bran was sleeping outside to find out whose bed his master was sleeping in. He felt a surge of admiration for the young chatelaine who had succeeded in bringing about such a change in the behaviour of his indomitable cousin.

Bran jumped up when the arms room door finally opened, Tomas stepped forward and noticed that Iain was coming out ahead of the lairds. He heaved a sigh of relief: His cousin had received the majority of the votes. The men followed one another out, with Aindreas coming last. Tomas noticed his look of bitterness and surmised that Iain's uncle was not happy with the clan's decision. The ladies, who had stood up as one, looked with delight at Lord Iain, who was beaming with satisfaction as he came to greet his wife. He walked slowly towards her and greeted her solemnly in the manner of the northern knights. The young chatelaine returned his greeting with a deep curtsy. As if cut off from the rest of the company, the couple communicated with one another with their eyes and without saying a word.

Thunderous applause burst out in the great hall filled with castle folk and the estate serfs, who had all come to swear their oath of allegiance to the MacNeil heir. Every one of them had, in his own way, prayed for this favourable outcome for their master and lord and their young mistress, for the title of clan chief guaranteed them greater security. Vibrating with his shrugging shoulders, Father Henriot crossed himself and gave thanks for the blessings bestowed. On this first day of the year 1425, the sun and Almighty God flooded Mallaig with their light.

In the ceremony, the serfs were assuring their lord of their loyalty and their labour, and he, in return, promised them work and protection on his land. Highland custom required that the successor of an estate received the renewal of the homage given to his predecessor. That is why about forty men were eagerly awaiting the moment to swear allegiance to Iain MacNeil that New Year's Day morning. In the absence of the family secretary, whose task it was to organise the ceremony, it was Father Henriot who directed the proceedings. Each of the serfs and his family were well known to him and he had no difficulty assembling them in the arms room to proceed in the correct order to the swearing of the oath. The men meekly followed the instructions of the little man with the ever-shrugging shoulders.

Little Ceit furtively slipped through the open door of the arms room. Fascinated by the sight of the spiked clubs, axes, crossbows, claymores, armour for the knights and their horses, coats of mail, coats of arms, and plumed helmets, she never missed an opportunity to go into the arms room, which was festooned with them. It was crowded, and in order to see, she had to scramble up on to the platform behind the great wooden chair where Lord Iain had sat throughout the very long ceremony. Full of curiosity, she watched all the men and the labourers come in one by one. With their belt unfastened, they knelt at the lord's feet, placed their clasped hands in the lord's and each invariably pronounced the same words: 'I swear to remain loyal to you against all others and to protect your rights with all my strength.' The lord raised them up by taking them by the shoulders, kissed them, and presented them with a branch representing his promise of his protection. Little Ceit glanced at the basket full of branches sitting beside the great chair and grabbed one, which she examined closely. Her eyes were full of wonderment. *So, this branch is magic*, she said to herself. *It protects people.*

As soon as they had sworn their oath of allegiance, the serfs and the castle men left the room. Soon, only the household knights, the lairds, and their wives remained. Lord Iain joined them. To everyone's surprise, Aindreas came forward, took his hands, and with a bow, he, too, pledged allegiance to him. The other lairds followed suit. Iain movingly thanked each one with an embrace. Then the ladies, falling in behind Lady Rosalind, approached one by one and repeated the serf's oath as they knelt at his feet, signifying that they were putting their castles and their people at the new chief's disposal. Iain was touched by these spontaneous gestures from those who had so fiercely condemned him in the past. He signalled to them to stand up, and he kissed them as he had kissed his serfs. The last to come and kneel before him was his wife, but he stopped her from kneeling by taking hold of her shoulders. When she was about to pronounce her oath of loyalty, he stopped her and, looking into her eyes, said quietly, 'No, my lady, it is I who swear to remain faithful to you before all others.' And without giving her the time to say a word, he placed a gentle kiss on her lips and drew her close.

The tables had been moved back against the walls of the great hall, and the food was arranged so that guests could help themselves. Wine and beer were offered to the castle folk, the serfs, and the lairds who were invited to celebrate Callainn. People joined hands to form several circles, which soon filled the middle of the hall. They began to sing the traditional Callainn song 'Auld Lang Syne,' and several women threw a pinch of salt into the fire to ward off any evil spirits which may be tempted to turn up in the New Year. The musicians began to play a dance tune which everyone welcomed with whoops of joy. The party was soon in full swing, and the laughter, as much as the music, drowned out all other sounds.

In the kitchens, Anna and Nellie were supervising the service of the food, and they were exultant as they held hands. All the emotions they had experienced these past weeks were rising to the surface of their worn-out hearts, and tears of joy ran down their cheeks. Anna, reassured by the dignified behaviour of her young master, felt all her doubts about him melt away. She heaved a sigh of relief on thinking that perhaps this was the moment of happiness for this wild child and that, at last, with his young chatelaine on his arm, he would find his real place in the castle. As far as Nellie was concerned, the change she had noticed in her young mistress since the St. Ninians's cave accident filled her with hope for the fine couple she and Lord

Iain made. Gunelle had stopped being at war with him and looked at him differently. There was neither anger nor distrust in her eyes. They had even noticed affectionate gestures being exchanged between the young married couple. The nurse could now allow herself to hope that she would soon know intimacy with her husband and be carrying his child. Having looked after Gunelle's two sisters during their pregnancies and then delivered their babies, she knew how much joy a new baby would bring. Being an upright woman, she also sincerely believed that of the Keith girls, Gunelle was the one, most endowed with the gifts needed to be a mother.

'Almighty God, do not give up on Lord Iain. At the moment, you are doing wonders with him.' she would pray.

That day I thought again about the promise I had made to Lord Baltair, to never renounce my role as chatelaine of Mallaig and Iain's wife. Each act I was asked to perform was part of that commitment to my father-in-law. I had known him for a short time but had loved him very much, perhaps even more than my own father. The revelations during the lairds' council regarding the death of my husband's brother had troubled me and it was all I could do not to judge and condemn Iain. When I was given the right to speak amidst the general disapproval of the family, I was aware of words of defence coming to mind, words whispered to me by his father. Yes, Baltair MacNeil would have fiercely defended his son. I was convinced of that, and I knew I had to do exactly that in his place. At the end of my speech, when I saw my husband looking overcome with gratitude, I realised that I totally believed every one of my words in his favour. It was no longer my promise to Lord Baltair which inspired me stand up for him. It was a new emotion for me, feelings for his son who had saved me from drowning, not through bravado or duty but simply out of love.

I had to admit that, these past few days, my husband had confided in me as few husbands do. He had bared his heart and soul and had revealed far more than most wives ever hear during their marriage. *That is what is sometimes possible between a husband and wife*, I mused. I began to study Iain and watched him as he mingled with his people who were having a good time. He was quietly moving among them, his head held high, his infectious laugh, making lots of warm gestures with his large hands, sometimes on a man's shoulder, sometimes on a lady's arm or a child's head. Suddenly I wanted to have those hands on me, and I closed my eyes to savour this new and rather disconcerting picture. When I opened them again, I noticed Iain behind a pillar. He was crouched down beside little Ceit and talking away to her. Instinctively I went over to them. I broke in on one of the most touching scenes I ever had the pleasure to witness: a great declaration of love of a father to his daughter. Ceit was trying to hide a little branch behind her back, and Iain asked her, 'Tell me, Ceit, what is the branch for?'

'It is magic. It protects, my lord, but you must give a kiss first. Listen carefully. I will show you.'

Having put the branch on the floor, she took Iain's hands in her own tiny hands, knelt down, and recited, without the slightest hesitation and without omitting a word, the serfs' oath to their lord. 'I swear to remain faithful towards you against all others and to protect your rights with all my strength.' Then she picked up the branch, stood up, and put it in his hand, staring straight at him and waiting for the response to her oath.

My husband's face showed deep emotion, and he had to clear his throat before reciting his part of the vow, 'Ceit, I assure you of my protection and my love since you acknowledge me as your… father.

'No, you have to say, "since you acknowledge me as your lord and master, she corrected him bossily.

Without even waiting for him to correct himself, she placed a kiss on Iain's lips and immediately drew back, scratching her chin and shouting, 'You are prickly! Bran's hair is softer when I kissed him to make my vows.'

Taking her in his arms, he picked her up. 'Yes, I am pricklier than Bran when you were taking the oath, but my protection is greater too. Even more so since today, I am clan chief as well as your father.'

'What are you saying? My father left. I do not have one,' she replied in astonishment.

'No, Ceit, your father is living with you here in the same castle, and he has you in his arms at this very moment.'

At that instant, Iain caught sight of me standing behind his daughter and smiled. Ceit turned towards me in amazement. She held out her arms, and Iain came over with his little bundle, who was tense with excitement at this astonishing revelation.

'Did you hear that, Gunelle? Lord Iain is my father and you; you are married to him. So, you are my mother!'

I grasped her little hands and kissed them, overwhelmed by my little Ceit's utter and perfectly simple joy. I met my husband's eyes and realised that this happiness was shared. *Today everything has been restored to him*, I thought as I smiled at him.

'You must not say Gunelle, Ceit,' began my husband.

'I must say "Lady Gunelle." I know, Lord Iain,' answered his daughter, stressing the word lady.

'No, Ceit, you must say "mother" from now on. And as for me, you must say "father." Now, you are coming to dance with me. The music is good.'

'Oh no, Lord Iain. Everyone is going to look at me,' she protested strongly without using the names she had just been taught. 'They are going to see how ugly I am! Tell him, Gunelle! I want to stay hidden!'

'Who said you are ugly?' my husband said immediately in a tone feigning anger. 'You cannot be ugly. You are my daughter. You know very well that daughters look like their fathers. Do you find me ugly, Ceit, my daughter?'

'No, my lord, but I would rather look like Gunelle.'

'Your brother will take after Gunelle,' he replied, looking at me, amused by the conversation. Ceit gave me a questioning look.

I kissed her hand again and told her to do what her father was asking. 'You should accept the offer to dance with your father, my dear. There are a lot of children here who would love to find themselves in the clan chief's arms. There are also ladies who would like to be in your place... like me, for example!'

'Your turn will come, my lady,' my husband said tenderly as he carried his daughter off to join a quadrille that was forming.

I watched them go off together: Iain's steady step and a little redhead bouncing above his broad shoulders, her thin arms wrapped around his neck.

It was Lady Rosalind who drew me from my thoughts. 'Lady Gunelle, I am beginning to see that you are exceptionally gifted. In a few weeks, you have performed real miracles. You have taught a little girl who was said to be a deaf-mute to speak, and you have taught my nephew to read and write, which was no doubt the more difficult of the two tasks. Everyone knows how impervious Iain always was to education. Anyway, he was always against any activity at which Alasdair excelled. Iain devoted himself to the art of fighting, which obviously served him well.'

'Lady Rosalind, teaching my husband was not difficult. He is an extremely gifted man, perhaps just as gifted as his brother, whom I obviously did not know. The same goes for little Ceit. Besides, it was even easier as I discovered in doing so that I love teaching. I think that is what helped me to settle down to life at Mallaig,' I replied.

I saw she was thinking about what I had said. Her look was full of curiosity and affection for me. I was relieved. I desperately wanted us to become friends. In her, I saw someone who could shed new light on the clan MacNeil, and I wanted to gain her trust. It seemed to me that that way, I could become a real Highland wife.

'What are you going to do now that the studies are all but finished for the little girl and Iain? It would be a pity to lose such a propitious gift for teaching. You should, if you want to take the advice of an old lady who knows nothing about it, re-open the village school. My

224

sister-in-law, Isla, was interested in the Mallaig children's education, and it is sad that Father Henriot is not more involved in it.'

'You are right, my lady. The undertakings of my predecessor as chatelaine are all worthy of being continued, and I will make it my duty to make sure they are.'

'Does that include the *cour d'amour*, Lady Gunelle? You must know that Lady Isla made a name for the castle with such an entertaining innovation for us and our knights. The idea was to give Alasdair's widow the opportunity of proving her talents as a courtesan. No doubt you are unaware, but Lady Beathag shone as brightly as her husband here in the great hall.'

'No doubt,' I replied too hastily. 'With those self-same talents, she also procured my husband as her lover. Unfortunately, I have neither the qualities needed nor the know-how to organise such a distraction at Mallaig, whether it be for the benefit of our knights, the ladies of the clan, or the widow Beathag.'

'Come now, my lady, I did not mean to offend you by bringing up the subject. I see that you see faults which are not as great as you think. My nephew Iain was never simply under Beathag's influence alone. He is, what one would call, a womaniser, as are many men. However, from what I know of him, I can tell you that you are exactly the kind of wife to whom he wants to swear to be faithful. And if he does so, you can trust him. Iain is wholehearted, and that is what makes him so attractive or so repugnant, depending on your point of view. We all know that your marriage has its problems but no more than in most arranged marriages.' When she saw my embarrassment, she took my hands and added, 'I do not know why but I am very fond of you. You remind me of my only daughter, whom I lost when she was twelve.'

I did not hear the rest of her revelation. Iain had come to ask me to dance, and I left her with a smile of gratitude and tacit agreement. I found myself pulled into a frenzy of movement with only my husband's strong hands as support. They were guiding me as deftly as the hands of the weavers on the spindles' constant movement backwards and forwards on the looms. I was following the steps, back and forwards, circling around him, approaching and moving away, my eyes riveted on his eyes, and all the time trying to hear the music so as to follow the rhythm. Lady Rosalind's revelations showed me in Iain, a man receiving the favours of several women and not just of one as I had imagined until now, apart from the affairs he could have had with the castle servants. It was even possible that among the dancers round about us, the daughters of lairds or serfs, there were some of his old conquests. Perhaps those young women who were looking at me with a great deal of curiosity. How could my husband's aunt have concluded that I was the kind of wife for whom Iain would be ready to stop his womanising? I had no idea. It was true that, in the arms room barely a few hours earlier, he had sworn loyalty. Suddenly I clung to that promise as if it had the power of life or death over me. *Iain MacNeil*, I said to myself, *could I have fallen in love with you?*

After several dances with him, I had a hint of an answer to that question when we left the circle to go and quench our thirst. He led me by the hand through the crowd as far as a bench placed against the wall of the arms room. On the way, he grabbed a cup of beer which he offered me first. I collapsed onto the bench, put the cup to my lips, and gulped it down. When I handed it back to him, he smiled when he noticed it was almost empty. As he was getting up to go and have it refilled, Father Henriot came and stood beside me. He was very red in the face and dripping with sweat. *Has he been dancing?* I wondered immediately. As he watched the fun, he began to talk haltingly about the village folk. I realised just how attached the priest was to his faithful parishioners. Then I remembered Lady Rosalind's suggestion and took the opportunity to put the plan of reopening the school to him. At first, he was taken by surprise and then spoke about the organisation, the number of children, the age range, and the building. It was the beginning of a very constructive discussion, as all I really wanted was to talk about it in order to clarify my ideas. When he rejoined us, Iain welcomed the idea with a cautious reserve but without any sign of open disapproval. I smiled and saw that it would not be difficult for me to convince him of the benefits of education for the children. The priest was no doubt thinking the same thing, for he pointed out to my husband that Mallaig was fortunate to number among its inhabitants a well-educated chatelaine who was capable of passing on her knowledge and that it would be a pity not to allow the village children and those in the castle, like Ceit, to benefit from it. He did not reply. He seemed to be following another train of thought, for he asked the priest if the church had a procedure of adoption if someone wanted to recognise an orphan as his heir. The generosity of his question moved me, and I thanked him immediately with a look of admiration. The priest had immediately guessed which child was involved, for he mentioned Ceit's name in his answer to my husband. There was a blessing for adoptive children and parents, but the addition of an illegitimate heir to a noble family's register did not need the church's recognition.

'Very good,' said Iain. 'In that case, Father, I should still like you to bless my wife and myself as little Ceit's adoptive parents. Tomorrow, if that suits you.'

'At your convenience, my lord,' replied Henriot as he stood up to take his leave.

When we were alone, Iain raised his cup and drank to his daughter. Then he held it to me, and I made the same toast but emphasised 'our daughter' before drinking it.

'Forgive me, my lady,' he said to me. 'I did not consult you. Have you any reservations about becoming my bastard's mother?'

'My lord,' I answered as I put my finger on his lips, 'do not call her by that name, I beg you. I am perfectly happy to be her mother.'

He took my fingers and held them against his mouth, slowly kissing them one by one. I drew back a little at the touch of his beard on my skin. He noticed and stopped to look at me, keeping my hand in his.

'You are certainly happier to be her mother than to be my wife,' he quietly declared matter-of-factly.

I tenderly touched his cheek and then his lips with my other hand and shook my head. His face lit up immediately. He jumped to his feet, handed his cup to the nearest person, and led me into the middle of the group of dancers. They were dancing a very slow dance in which couples held the forearm, the men making the lady pass in front, then to the side. Once again, I allowed myself to be led by him while enjoying the warmth of his hands and the nearness of his body as he brushed against me.

He awoke me out of my dream with a question which seemed incongruous and asked in a muffled voice, 'My lady, do you wish to be my wife?'

'I thought we were already married, my lord,' I replied, dumbfounded.

'We are, but we have only fulfilled half of our marriage vows. 'This one,' he said, taking my wedding ring between his fingers, 'with this ring, I thee wed, but I have not yet honoured you with my body.'

'My lord, you have given me no opportunity to refuse to let you share my bed. I would certainly not have done so if you had shown the slightest desire.'

'I am well aware of that, my lady, but had I asked, you would have performed your conjugal duty without any protest at all. After all, have I not married a dutiful wife? But… I do not wish to take you to bed out of duty.'

We could not continue this conversation while doing justice to the dance steps. Leading me gently out of the quadrille, he led me resolutely to the far end of the room. On our way, I caught the looks of surprise on the faces of the men and women who were watching the dancing. My heart was thumping, and I felt myself blushing. When we were hidden by the pillar, he took me in his arms, and before he could say another word, I again touched his lips to prevent him from speaking.

Looking straight into his eyes, I affirmed my desire for him. 'My lord, I shall not sleep with you out of duty. If you want me as your wife, I want you in the same way as my husband.'

By way of a response, he kissed my lips with infinite delicacy, almost reverently. I thrilled at this contact and pressed against him.

The serfs and the castle folk had long since left the great hall when all the torches were lit, and the leftover food was carried back to the kitchens. That first day of the year of grace 1425 was drawing to a close, and tiredness seemed to have overcome everyone. The lairds and their wives who were spending the night at the castle had gathered around the fire and were contentedly listening to the musicians. Suddenly, someone suggested asking the chatelaine to sing. It was Lady Rosalind who encouraged the young woman most, and Lady Gunelle finally agreed, to the great delight of the gathering. To everyone's amusement, Lord Iain, who, after the dancing, had been sitting at the end of a long bench with his wife and holding her close, had had to resign himself to letting her go. Iain had never openly shown such tenderness and affection to a lady in front of his family. All the ladies, except one, were under the spell of the young chief who was so obviously smitten by his wife. Lady Beathag, who was not the kind to champ at the bit, had used every opportunity to take her mind off the spectacle of her brother-in-law, who was so obviously very much in love, and she did not hesitate to run her eyes over the lairds at various times. Lord Tomas had noticed her game and, as a result, was apprehensive about the future harmony of the clan. He was relieved to see her setting her cap at Rosalind's son, Raonall, an unmarried cousin. During the singing, Tomas saw them slip quietly from the great hall with Raonall taking the arm of Beathag and her companion, both of whom were clucking with pleasure. Shaking his head in resignation, he could not help thinking of the young girl he had courted at Duart Castle a month ago. As he poured himself another whisky, he sighed, how he would love to hold a woman in his arm and whisper 'my dearest."

Lady Gunelle was particularly on song that evening. Over time she had put together a very fine repertoire of songs with the clarsach player, and the songs they sang delighted their audience. The piper, who knew several of the tunes, accompanied them quietly from the other end of the room. It was a special moment for everyone. Sitting a little back from the circle of armchairs, Iain had the very clear impression as he watched his wife that she was singing just for him. Anna, who had quietly gone over to her young master, knelt down beside him and could not help taking his hand. She saw on his face the expression of happiness he had had as a child when she would take him on her knees to untangle his hair or simply to caress him as she sang to him.

Iain turned towards her, and squeezing her fingers, he said, 'Anna, listen to the second good fairy in my life singing. The first one was you.'

 She was moved, stood up and reprimanded him brusquely, forbidding him to make fun of her by comparing her to the young chatelaine. She left the room, a tender smile on her lips, her eyes sparkling with joy, and slowly made her way to the room on the first floor which she shared with Nellie and little Ceit. If she had glanced out an arrow slit on the way up, she would have noticed the movement of about a hundred torches coming down from the plateau and taking up positions on the moors surrounding the castle. If she had gone up to the ramparts, she would have noticed the absence of guards. But Anna carried on up as if sleepwalking, her eyes heavy with tiredness.

Once all the guests had gone off to bed for the night, Lord Iain could at last retire. He was leading his wife by one hand, a candlestick in the other. He had taken a pitcher of water, which he had asked her to carry, and he had ordered his dog to stay in the room. After a few minutes of a surprisingly silent walk, the young chatelaine, feeling slightly uneasy, wondered where he was taking her.

'Where are we going, my lord? This is not the direction of my room or yours.'

'True, my lady. We will not go to yours, for the last time I set foot in that room, it was to be rejected by my mother on her deathbed, and I swore I would never go back in there again. We will not go to mine either; I have had too many women there. We will go to my father's bedroom. My parents made love a lot there. Besides, I need something I am sure to find there.'

When he opened Lord Baltair's bedroom door, a heavy smell of dampness filled their nostrils. He sat Gunelle down, took the pitcher from her hands, put it on the sideboard, and busied himself, lighting a fire. Then he turned down the bed so that the heat of the fire would warm the sheets. Still in complete silence, he took the pitcher and the light and put them on the table underneath the window whose shutters were closed. He opened his shoulder strap and plaid and then took off his jacket, tunic, and shirt. His wife was watching in silence, not understanding his behaviour, but not daring to ask any questions. She watched him as he stood bare-chested in front of the table on which there was a little mirror and a shaving kit. Pouring some water into the bowl and rubbing some soap on his face, Iain began to shave. At the same time, he apologised to his wife for making her wait.

'It will not take long, my lady. It will be worth the wait, you will see.'

After a moment, she said, 'My lord, you are shaving off your beard.'

'Isn't that what you and our daughter both want?'

'But I thought Highlanders love their beards!'

Turning around, razor in hand, his cheeks covered in suds, he smiled wickedly.

'Correct, my lady! I am very fond of it, but I am fonder of feeling your kisses on my face tonight. Shaving by candlelight is not ideal, but I am doing my best. You will see the results for yourself in a minute.'

Thereupon he continued the task in silent concentration. Lady Gunelle could not help smiling, delighted with the relaxed atmosphere of this strange second wedding night. She looked at the half-darkness in the room, where the walls and furniture were hardly visible and allowed herself to be invaded by memories of the last moments, she had spent at Lord Baltair's bedside. A wave of happiness took possession of her already pounding heart. She slowly undid her veil and loosened her hair, which she carefully combed with her fingers and put in a single long plait. After a few moments, absorbed in this task, she caught her husband looking at her. He had finished shaving and was looking at her with sheer desire. He stood up, moved towards her, taking care to put his face in the light of the candle, and asked her opinion. Gently taking her hand, he made it glide over his cheeks and chin. Gunelle, leaning her head to both sides, let her fingers be guided over his fresh face and smiled upon discovering a dimple on each cheek, which gave a childlike look to her husband, and which showed another resemblance to his daughter.

'It seems to please you, my lady,' he murmured.

'You are correct, my lord. The wait was worthwhile. You have shaved yourself well.' With a smile in her voice, she went on, 'I think you are now as soft as Bran… It is a pity that I cannot remove what you do not like about me.'

'What is it that I am not supposed to like, I beg you?' he asked, intrigued.

'This,' she replied, opening her bodice to reveal her throat speckled with freckles.

He took her by the shoulders and raised her gently to her feet. He kissed her neck, then her bare throat, and finished up caressing her cheeks and her nose with his lips. He trembled at the touch of his wife's body close to his bare chest.

'You are mistaken, my lady,' he said hoarsely. 'I love your speckled skin. With your brown eyes, I feel as if I am holding a hind in my arms. Can I undress you now?'

He immediately began to undo the laces at the back of my dress, saying it was easier to remove dry clothes than wet ones, thus reminding me that it was not the first time he was undressing me. The memory melted the embarrassment my nakedness in front of him caused me, and I immediately became more relaxed. I let myself go with the kisses and the fondling each part of my body received as it was uncovered. I closed my eyes in ecstasy. It dawned on me very quickly that my conjugal duty would be the least onerous of all my duties at Mallaig. Having removed his breeches, he laid me down on the bed. On touching the cold sheets, my body stiffened. That made him smile, and stretching out on his back, he caught hold of my shoulders and rolled me over on top of him. Once again, our night at Ninians's Peak came to mind. With my forearms leaning on his chest, I looked into his eyes; he was thinking of that too. We smiled at each other, and I kissed his full inviting lips, now free of his beard. I was delighted to see how simple the first experiences of lovemaking were when there was trust. He passionately returned my kiss, and, putting his arms around me, he reversed positions. With my hands and arms now free, they went round him quite naturally, stroking his shoulders and back where I felt the scar of his recent wound. His knees gently opened my legs, and his erect manhood entered to take away my virginity. I remembered the short description Nellie had given me of the conjugal act, and discomfort paralysed me. Iain must have noticed, for he stopped moving and began to slowly kiss my breast, neck, and mouth. I took his head in my hands, stroked his thick hair, and then moved my hands down his neck to his back. When I touched his hips, I felt him shake, and it was at that moment he chose to take me completely.

Contrary to what Nellie had told me, I did not feel any discomfort; no pain when he delicately penetrated my intimacy. Leaning up on his outstretched arms, Iain was looking at me attentively as he moved between my legs. Then he slipped a knee between them and leaned harder. What I felt then between us made me shiver with a sort of impatience. I closed my eyes in a world of incredible sensations, and I soon heard myself moan with pleasure. I lost all sense of reality for a few seconds, and when I became conscious of our united bodies, I felt the skin of my husband's neck quiver. I opened my eyes and saw him stretched out on top of me, his head slightly turned towards the shadow, his lips half-opened, his eyebrows together, and his eyes closed, preparing his body for one last thrust. When we were lying side by side in the damp sheets, slowly getting our breath back, he took my hand, raised it to his lips, and kissed it gently, saying, 'I hope I did not hurt you, my lady. It is very important to me that this wedding night was a success and that you enjoyed it as much as I did.'

'Rest assured, my lord, I could not have enjoyed it more,' I said, snuggling up to him, my head on his arm and pulling the sheets up over us. A wave of gratitude for my husband completely overwhelmed me, and I dozed off in that frame of mind.

I did not know how long we slept before being wakened by Bran's unexpected arrival in the bedroom. The dog put his two front paws on Iain's side of the bed and barked. Iain sat up immediately and grabbed the dog by the muzzle to stop him from barking, but at that same moment, we heard Tomas's panic-stricken voice through the curtains.

'Praise God! You are there. You must get up, cousin. The castle is surrounded. I do not know how many men there are, but I counted about fifty torches on the moor a while ago.'

'Good grief! Why was the alert not given? What are those stupid guards up to again?'

As he spoke, he jumped out of bed and hurriedly dressed in the dark. The candle on the table was only giving a faint light, and Tomas did not have another with him. In the same fearful voice, my husband's cousin continued his account: He had gone up to the ramparts before going to the guardroom with the rest of the knights and in the distance had noticed little spots of torchlight spread across the moor in the form of a circle. Going back down, he had found the guards lying all over the courtyard and reeking of alcohol. Tomas had rushed to his cousin's bedroom, then mine. Not finding us, he had gone to get Bran from the great hall where he had been lying settled down for the night in the middle of the guests. Not wanting to cause alarm, he took the dog out and told him to fetch his master.

Iain was cursing and swearing about the situation. He put on his shoulder strap and was ready to leave the room when he remembered I was in the bed. I had sat up, covered my nakedness with the sheets, and watched the shadows of the two men talking. Iain came and sat down on the edge of the bed, and taking me by the shoulders, told me not to leave the room or make a noise until he came to fetch me. His tone of voice was curt and anxious. I took his face in my hands

236

and reassured him immediately, while attempting to silence the sense of panic I felt rising within me.

'I am not moving, and I will wait here for you, my lord,' I murmured, my lips against his ear. He kissed my hair and went out to join his cousin and his dog in the corridor. I got up slowly as if stunned by the shock. *What is happening at the castle?* I asked myself with concern as I got dressed. It was then I noticed blood on my thighs. I wiped it off with the towel my husband had used to shave himself. So ended Ne'er Day 1425.

Chapter Ten
The Siege

T he first thing Lord Iain did was to go up to the ramparts with his cousin. However, he only saw about ten motionless lights half a mile to the north and northeast of the castle. To the west and south, there was nothing.

'I assure you, Iain, there were five times that number a while ago,' Tomas insisted when he saw his cousin was unconvinced. The circle was very clear. They will have taken up their positions and then put out their torches.

'I believe you, Tomas,' Iain replied, looking grave. 'I can only see the Camerons attacking Mallaig at this time. They will have known that my lairds were all here without their men. What worries me is how many there are of them. They could have joined forces with another clan; they are not stuck for choice when it comes to our enemies.'

'Do you think they are going to attack tonight?'

'Possibly. Let us go. There is no time to lose! We must evacuate the village. They will try to burn it. Bring everyone in by the west footbridge. Leave the men in the courtyard and take the women and children down to the cellars.'

Iain had already set off in the direction of the guardroom. As he passed the sentry on the northern battlement walk, he was tempted to ask him to report on his watch, but he changed his mind. *Later*, he thought, rushing down the staircase to the courtyard with Bran at his heels. On entering the arms room, the soldiers and knights were asleep. He realised just how vulnerable his castle was at night when the guard on the ramparts was less than they might be. Suddenly he wondered if the enemy had already been able to enter the walls, and he broke out in a cold sweat. He curtly gave his orders to his dumbfounded men and hurried to the keep to warn the lairds and organise the protection of his people. It was barely more than an hour since he had left the great hall, and already there was complete silence. Once again, he felt a shiver of concern go down his spine as he contemplated the possibility that enemy soldiers could have slipped in amongst them. When he had wakened his lairds, he gathered them together in the arms room to explain the situation and draw up a plan of defence in the event of an attack on the castle. As for their wives, by now awake and worried, they were at a loss as to what to do, and they were assured of their role only when the chatelaine joined them.

With no sign of her husband coming back, Lady Gunelle left Lord Baltair's bedroom and went to the bedroom of Nellie, Anna, and Ceit. Since their room was above the arms room, Anna's keen ear had picked up the unusual activity, and the old housekeeper was already up and looking grumpy.

'Ah, my lady,' she said to Gunelle when she saw her standing in the doorway. 'It looks like the party is starting up again. Just listen to that!'

'It isn't the party, Anna,' Gunelle whispered. 'They think the castle is surrounded. By whom? I do not know. But the night is over for us. We must get dressed and be ready. Lord Iain is coming to fetch us at any moment.'

Nellie was awake, as was little Ceit. A heavy cloud of fear took hold of the women, and they fell silent. The little girl, still half asleep, said nothing and went along with the young chatelaine, who was hurriedly dressing her. When they were all dressed and ready to leave, they heard footsteps in the corridor, and they saw a light just before Lord Iain entered carrying a torch.

'What are you doing here, my lady?' he said dryly when he saw Gunelle. 'Were you not to stay where I left you a short time ago?' As his wife was about to reply, he put his hand over her mouth, saying, 'At the moment, the last thing I need is to have to go looking for you.'

Turning to the two nurses, he ordered, 'Come, no one is to stay upstairs. We are going down to the great hall.'

While rushing down the stairs, he held Gunelle's hand so tightly in his that she tried to break free. When she asked her husband what was happening, Lord Iain loosened his grip a little and looked briefly in her direction, his brow furrowed, his jaw tense. Gunelle was struck by how hard he looked: his beard would have had the advantage of hiding his chin and those cheeks, which his anger and fear made tense. The young woman had a knot in her stomach.

Before he left her at the great hall crowded with guards, she grabbed his jacket and with authority said, 'My lord, answer me! What is happening? I must know. I am the chatelaine, and I must know what to do with our folk.'

Iain was annoyed with himself, without understanding why. He would have liked to keep quiet about his fears, but it was clear she had to be kept informed of the situation. He freed Gunelle's hands from his jacket while all the time frantically checking the deployment of his guards around them; he was completely preoccupied with the eventuality of an attack. He explained to her that they were bringing the villagers to the castle, and they would have to be taken care of, that they would take refuge in the cellars, and the men would be put to use in the courtyard, that if there were a battle and there were casualties, they would be taken to the great hall to be tended by her and the other ladies.

'My lady, do I make myself understood? I do not wish to see any woman or child outside the cellars or this room. That includes you.' Looking her straight in the eye and adopting a tone of command, he added, 'Does the chatelaine of Mallaig now know enough to be able to fulfil her role?'

'Yes, my lord,' she replied in exasperation. 'It is all very clear, and your orders will be respected as far as it is possible.'

Thereupon, she did an about turn and, in a fury, entered the great hall where the ladies were waiting for her and welcomed her immediately. When she glanced behind her, her husband had disappeared, leaving four guards on guard at the door and his dog on the lookout in the hall. It was a cold night, and the constant north wind was blowing on Mallaig, carrying with it the smells of sea and marsh, and drowning out the sounds from the moor. There was no moon in the sky, which was covered with large black clouds. In a state of extreme nervousness, Iain went straight to the bastion to join his knights and the lairds. The castle had never been attacked in his father's or his grandfather's lifetime. He was furious as he thought about it.

The defence of Mallaig Castle was admirably served by the way it had been built the previous century when the second dry stone wall had been erected. A fortified barbican where four men were posted protected the entrance to the exterior wall. A drawbridge, secured with iron bars and built over the wide moat partly filled with water flowing down from the mountains, led to the second wall, which was twenty-five feet high. This wall, overlooked by the battlement walk, connected five round turrets peppered with arrow windows, which allowed the bowmen to shoot their arrows undercover. They included machicolations, floors that jutted out and could be opened to enable rocks or burning oil to be dropped on the attackers. Finally, each face of the wall was flanked by a stone brattice wide enough to comfortably hold three men whose job it was to guard the access to the wall but who were very exposed to the enemy arrows. The guards who had neglected their duty on the battlement walk the night before were posted there. At the end of the drawbridge was a double door protected by a port-cullis. Above was a stout bastion, the irregular openings of which allowed an easy attack on those arriving. That night, Iain positioned eight bowmen with enough arrows for twelve there. That was where he established his headquarters. Once through the wall, one reached the courtyard surrounded by the castle outbuildings: stables, kilns, water tanks, and the thatched blacksmith and saddler's quarters. Under the command of one of the lairds, about thirty men from the village and the castle were busy working silently by torchlight, drawing reserves of water in case of any fires and also heating two tubs of a mixture of sand and pitch, which would be then taken up to the machicolations. The guard room and the adjoining keep formed a group of buildings adjoining the south wall and looking out onto the cliff. The keep, with a wooden roof above which flew the MacNeil standard, was a massive square tower, thirty feet wide and about fifty feet high, with several windows on each of the three floors. It was the final refuge of the castle. The main access was a wide wooden door set into a high portal overhung by a pediment and usually guarded by a single lookout. Iain had placed two armed guards there. Two other small doors, one leading to the kitchens and the garden in the southwest and the other leading directly to the chapel in the east, had been barred from the inside. Finally, at the far end of the courtyard between two workshops, the west wall had a narrow, thick wooden door opening onto a light footbridge, which could be lowered above the torrent coming down from the cliffs and by which one reached the village and harbour by winding one's way across the rocks. It was through this door that Tomas brought the villagers in single file by the light of torches crackling in the darkness of the night.

I was amazed to see the state of quasi-calm in which the lairds' wives were awaiting the outcome of events. Having no more information than I had, they were speculating about the why and how of an eventual attack on the castle. Some of them had already lived through a similar situation, particularly Lady Rosalind, who seemed to control her nervousness better than the others. I was drawn like a magnet to her. She had gone to the far end of the room and was busy putting wood on the fire. Soon all the ladies joined us. My little Ceit, struggling to stay awake, was hanging on to my dress. I settled down in an armchair with her on my knees. Right away, she snuggled into the hollow of my arm and did not move again. Raonall, Lady Beathag, and her companion came down from upstairs, having been sent down by the guards. Neither of the two seemed to have had a lot of sleep and came over to butt in on the discussion the lairds' wives were having about the castle defence. As for Raonall, he exchanged a few words with his mother and headed off to the guard room. I watched it all as if in a daze. I was thinking of my husband's coldness towards me and it brought a chill to my heart. *What a contrast with the man who had cherished and honoured me barely a few hours ago*, I said to myself dejectedly. I had to give myself a shake to answer the questions Lady Rosalind was quietly asking me.

'What medicines do you have here if there are casualties? Do you have something we could make dressings or poultices from? Should we not ask them to boil water and bring spare blankets and furs here to the hall? I seem to have heard them saying we are going to be confined here for quite some time, didn't I?'

'You are certainly right, my lady,' I replied as I looked around for Nellie and Anna. My two servants had already understood what had to be done to set up a makeshift hospital and had given instructions to that end. They had even thought of preparing enough food to feed the castle folk and informed me of the plan. I had nothing more to do than agree. Wanting to put thoughts of Iain out of my head, I stood up, passed Ceit to Mairi, who was standing close by, and began to make preparations.

I decided to visit the cellars to see how the village women and children were handling the situation. This step was a great help in taking up all my attention. Several torches had been lit, chasing away the darkness which is deeper in these windowless areas. No fires had been lit, and it was very cold and damp. The first person I met was Father Henriot, who welcomed me enthusiastically and gave me a breakdown of the families who were taking refuge: four women were breastfeeding; there were about a dozen old men and women; about twenty boys and girls aged from five to twelve were playing around the copper barrels; ten young women and mothers were patiently waiting to be given something to do. As soon as they saw me, they got up and came over, each one with a smile on her face.

I was moved by their calmness. *How can they smile in such circumstances?* I wondered in admiration. I smiled back at them and asked them what they needed in the way of food and water. Father Henriot joined me, and together, we made a list of what was needed to ensure a more or less comfortable night. While this discussion was going on, the children, out of curiosity, had come over and were carefully looking me up and down. I recognised them, having seen them on various occasions in the village or the castle courtyard.

I could not help picturing them as my pupils, and asked each of their names. The children were delighted and introduced themselves one by one, the little girls with a curtsey. During these introductions, I noticed that I was able to match their parents' names with theirs. And I must have made a good impression when they heard me associate each name with the trade of the man who bore it either in the village or the castle. Then, I took Jenny, a young girl of sixteen, with me to fetch what the families needed, recommending that everyone try and get as good a night's sleep as they could. Father Henriot stayed with them. In the great hall, there was calm. Most of the ladies had gone to lie down, rolled up in their capes. Lady Rosalind had remained sitting by the fire, seeming to want to keep watch during the early part of the night. I put Jenny in Nellie's care for the collection of the foodstuffs and headed for the door to talk to the guards about the possibility of going upstairs to gather clothes and covers. I immediately sensed their reticence. My husband had given strict orders: No one was permitted to walk about in the keep. However, the men thought twice about denying their chatelaine free access, and I took advantage of their hesitation. One of the guards offered to accompany me, and I asked for a second man. We went up by the main staircase, and I could not help looking through the arrow-slits. All I saw was eerily silent pitch blackness. I enjoyed searching the first-floor bedrooms and took as much as my two guards could carry by way of covers, rugs, and furs, and I also took two torches. Our expedition only lasted a few minutes. When we went back down to the hall by the other staircase, we were met by my livid husband berating the two guards who had stayed at their post. Before he even spoke to me, I cuttingly explained.

'Save your reprimands, my lord. Your men obeyed their chatelaine, who is in the middle of organising bedding for those sheltering in the cellars. You have no objection, I hope?'

'Take that to the cellars,' he hissed at the guard, who did not know what to do.

Then, addressing me, he added gruffly, 'You seem to take a wicked pleasure in going against my orders, my lady. I am not in the mood for an argument with anyone tonight. So, try and avoid my having to have one with you!'

I was immediately spared a dirty look. Followed by two knights, he had turned on his heels and marched towards the corridor leading to the guard room. Entering the great hall, I caught a glimmer of interest in me in the eyes of the guards who had just been reprimanded by their master. I bit my lip in bitter disappointment. *Why does Iain speak to me like some stranger who has annoyed him?* I thought. I was worried. *Was I not his wife, his companion, and his helpmeet tonight?* Evidently, the fighter he was had regained control. In his arms, I had tended to forget that side of his personality. It was the only valid explanation, and I had to be content with that for the two days the siege of Mallaig lasted.

Hostilities began at dawn, just when the light was good enough to make out the moor and its marshes. From the top of the bastion, Lord Iain and his lairds were astounded to see the enemy slowly advancing and tightening the circle around the castle. They counted more than one hundred and sixty men, including about thirty knights in armour. They covered the whole east flank, the north, and northeast sides and were equipped with ladders and weapons of war, such as battering rams, catapults, and even crossbows, weapons which the church forbade. However, on the battlefield, Highlanders cared little about what the bishops allowed or prohibited. To each his own business…

'The Camerons!' Iain and his men shouted in unison when they were able to make out the enemy standard.

At that very moment, they saw a thick plume of smoke rise from the village, which was hidden by the mist.

'This is it,' growled Iain. 'It has started. I prefer that to waiting. Everyone in position! Mallaig is under attack!'

Lord Tomas oversaw the defence on the west side of the castle. When he saw the village in flames, his anger rose a degree. For him, Mallaig was as much the village as the castle. What a relief that it had been evacuated before daylight. But the loss of the villagers' meagre possessions broke his heart just as much as if he had lost his own horse.

'Renegades!' he muttered.

He looked up towards the northern plateau and saw the enemy coming down. He recognised the Camerons' standard and was enraged. He checked his men's positions and waited for his cousin's signal to order the archers to start shooting their arrows.

A rather watery sun rose and chased away the morning mist which covered the village and its harbour. It was then that Tomas noticed a flotilla of three ships approaching the coast and flying the clan MacDonald flag. He felt his blood run cold. *Reinforcements already! he thought. How many are there?* It was high tide, which meant they would be ashore in an hour or even less. He sent a soldier to warn his cousin of the imminent arrival of the MacDonalds. Arrows began to rain down on the walls, but the Camerons were not yet within the range of the MacNeils. Almost immediately, shouts arose from the courtyard. Three men had been hit by the first enemy arrows, and so within the walls, they learned that the battle had begun. Orders were given for some of the men to take cauldrons of hot pitch to the machicolations and for others to take shelter in the outbuildings.

The first targets within range were those on the west flank. Tomas knew at what point it was worthwhile shooting the arrows The large yew bows his men were armed with were the height of a man. In one minute, an experienced archer could shoot twelve of the arrows with goose tail feathers and iron tips and pierce the armour or chainmail of their target at eight hundred feet. However, the foot soldiers who were sent ahead carrying ladders just had a helmet for protection. He gave orders to shoot to the first group of bowmen. Almost all the arrows hit the enemy, and the ladders were smashed against the walls. The battle quickly spread to all sides of the castle except the south southwest, which was protected naturally by the cliffs and sea. Large wooden screens protected the positions from which the Camerons could reach the outbuildings and keep with the burning projectiles launched by their catapults and the cannonballs fired by the gunners. From the very first shots, Iain knew that the weapons of war would inflict considerable damage on the castle. Several of the keep windows had been smashed to smithereens, and parts of the outbuilding roofs were already ablaze. The angle was narrow, and it was becoming difficult to hit those who were moving the weapons. Iain put his best archers onto those targets. A cannonball exploded in the face of a gunner and destroyed one of the screens. At the same time, three of the MacNeil archers hit their targets, who had been left unprotected. Three Camerons fell at once. The number of soldiers on the first outer wall was sufficient to push back each ladder that reached it, and none of the attackers reached the moat.

The MacDonald ships reached the shore and about forty men, armed mainly with crossbows, disembarked, and entered the village. There were a few horsemen, not a single knight in armour, and not even a sniff of a clan chieftain. *MacDonald is not too keen on getting involved or compromising himself. He must think Darnley is at the castle*, thought Iain as he watched them coming ashore. *That way, he would be able to accuse one of his renegade brothers if the king were to reproach him for taking part in the attack on Mallaig.* The arrival of MacDonald's men breathed new vigour into the Cameron attack and clearly accelerated the thrust of their assault. The main door was shaken by blows from a battering ram but just about held. A hail of arrows pierced their assailants, and a gush of hot pitch burned several of them seriously enough to force them to beat a hasty retreat. With some apprehension, Lord Iain wondered when his lairds' men would arrive as reinforcements and create a diversion on the northern flank, thereby preventing those manning the catapults and cannons from setting their screens in place. However, he suffered the disappointment of not seeing a single reinforcement until dawn the next day. After several hours of fighting, there was a period of calm. The enemy weapons and battle cries were silent, leaving the air filled simply with the groans of the wounded. There were more outside the walls than inside. In the courtyard, there were about ten wounded and about twenty soldiers on the walls. The castle itself had been significantly hit. All the fires had been put out, but the water reserves had been used up. When the lairds came to report, Iain was relieved to learn that there had been no fatalities in his ranks. He gave orders to hand out food and drink. *My men have not slept all night, the Camerons maybe*, he thought bitterly, looking at the tired faces and exhausted bodies of the soldiers standing around him. Sleep had a certain importance in the siege, for the defenders had to add watches to fighting hours, whereas the attackers used the time as they wished and decided when to rest. This kind of thought never failed to annoy the young chief. He felt much more at ease in an attacking role and preferably on the ground, man to man, rather than in the role of the defender on the top of the wall where the claymore proved to be useless. The wind arose, dispersing the smoke coming from the village and bringing with it clouds heavy with rain.

'God of heaven, pour out a deluge right here!' said Iain.

During the siege of a castle, the rain always favoured the defence: It put out the fires, dampened what would prove afterwards difficult to set fire to, made the ground impracticable for the attackers outside, and, above all, soaked them from head to toe since they were unable to take shelter if they stayed close to the walls. The Camerons realised the same thing for they began to transport their wounded to the edge of the forest half a mile away, thus momentarily interrupting the hostilities. From the top of Mallaig's walls, the soldiers looked at one another with a sigh of relief. They were going to have a well-deserved break. The trembling hands of the soldiers grabbed the bowls filled to the brim with the thick broth of oats and bacon. If they could not sleep, they could at least eat if the siege did not last too long. For cut off as they were by their assailants, all that would be left for them would be to die of exhaustion and starvation if the foodstuffs ran out. How much meat and flour did the castle have? Deep down, each one asked himself the same question as he devoured his ration.

The same question worried Anna as she sat alone in the middle of the store where the provisions were piled up. The first meal for everyone at the castle had exhausted her. Having gone down to the cellars to make an inventory of the foodstuffs, the old housekeeper admitted that the task of feeding all these mouths was beyond her. She began to cry quietly and then let an uninterrupted flood of tears run down her furrowed cheeks. That was how young Jenny found her, in great distress. Completely at a loss as to what to do, the young girl ran to get the chatelaine. Lady Gunelle entered the store and came to kneel beside the housekeeper, putting her arm around her shoulders. She sent Jenny to fetch the priest and to ask him to bring something with which to write.

'Don't worry, Anna,' she said. 'We will come out of this, and no one will die of hunger. It is simply a matter of doing some arithmetic and, if necessary, limiting the rations. This battle will end. It cannot go on for days all the same! Lord MacNeil and his lairds are going to find a solution.'

'They will have to, my lady,' groaned Anna. 'We have almost two hundred people to feed now. That is three times more than usual, and for the castle folk, we only keep fresh provisions for a week. We could bake for two weeks, not more. And soldiers cannot just eat bread.'

His eyebrows raised; Father Henriot entered quietly. He was carrying a board, a single sheet of paper, and an inkwell ready to take the dictation. The young chatelaine stood up and pointed to a spot close to the torch. She began to call out a list of everything in the store, asking Jenny from time to time to move sacks or barrels which were hiding others. Anna, looking dazed, was listening to the numbers while watching the long tresses the colour of ripe corn swinging on her mistress's back with each step she took. Her tears dried up, and she felt her confidence grow the more she saw the priest's sheet of paper become black with columns of figures and words. The exercise was quickly finished, and Gunelle, list in hand, went back up to the kitchens with the housekeeper.

'Come, Anna. First of all, we are going to do some calculations and then make up menus according to what each one can eat. But first, we would need to have an idea of how long this siege could last.'

She sat Anna down at the table, asking her to work out how many loaves she could make with the flour available, then went out the door leading to the garden to look for her husband on the ramparts. She was immediately hit by the smell of smoke floating over the deserted courtyard. Making her way carefully through the debris scattered all over the ground, she saw the burning roofs of the stable and the smithy. Above, a strong wind was driving along clouds heavy with rain without sending a single drop on Mallaig. Looking up towards the eastern rampart, she saw two archers crouched over their bowls and, a little further on, three soldiers sitting with their backs to the parapet with their legs stretched out in front of them. She thought the battle was over, and four steps at a time, she went up the nearest staircase leading to the battlement walk while avoiding the many arrows scattered on the ground. She asked the first soldier about the situation.

He raised an eyebrow and answered soberly, 'They are picking up their meat. It will start again in a while.'

'What do you mean, captain?' asked Gunelle intrigued.

At that moment, a warning shot from outside the walls made the young woman jump.

'You can hear it,' the soldier said to her in no way bothered. 'It is just as I told you.

'Sons of dogs, come and pick up your meat! It is the Cameron war cry. They are going to begin the attack again. If you want my opinion, it would be better to get out of here. We are for it again.'

From the bastion, Iain saw his wife go up to the ramparts, and his heart missed a beat. '

'What the devil is she doing now?' he growled as he hurried out of the room under the stunned gazes of all those present.

He ran without taking cover onto the battlement walk, as far as the first floor and rushed down the steps. He crossed the courtyard and caught up with Gunelle, who had come down quickly, upset by her conversation with the soldier. An arrow landed on the ground a few steps from the young woman. Iain rushed towards her and pinned her against a wall. He did not have time to open his mouth.

'Ah, my lord,' she said straight away, out of breath. 'I was looking for you, actually. I think the hostilities are going to resume. Do you think it is going to be very long? Finally, do you expect a siege of at least several days? We are trying to draw up rations for everyone, and we would like to have an idea of the number of meals we will have to serve before the castle receives provisions again.'

'My lady!' he exploded. 'Are you making fun of me? How do you expect me to answer that question? You do not seem to understand that we are under attack at the moment... and that we will defend ourselves as best we can and for as long as the attack lasts. You would have to ask the Camerons.'

'That's true,' she had admitted, embarrassed. 'But what do they want? Why do they want to capture the castle?'

Lord Iain was boiling over with exasperation. He glanced briefly at the ramparts and the courtyard, and taking his wife firmly by the arm, he strode towards the turret, scolding her as he dragged her along. 'My lady, I do not know what they want, and I do not want to know. On the other hand, I know what I want at this moment, and

I am going to get it—even if I have to lock you up! I do not want to see you outside the keep again. We are at war, and you are going to have to understand that very quickly.'

He went ahead of her up the staircase. Gunelle hardly had time to gather up her skirts than she was climbing the stairs, only touching every second one. When they reached the machicolations, Iain signalled to the three soldiers to leave. Taking their bowls and leaving their crossbows, they obeyed, their eyes wide open with surprise. When the last one had started down the stairs, Iain threw the weapons on the ground and put his wife in front of an arrow window. Looking at her, he leaned against the wall, his arms crossed on his chest, and asked her to describe what she saw. His harsh tone was eloquent enough evidence of his state of mind, and Gunelle broke out in a cold sweat with fear.

I was leaning with my hands on either side of the arrow window as I had done so often at the beginning of winter, but the spectacle which presented itself to me this time froze me with horror. Tens of wounded, dying, or dead were lying scattered on the ground less than a hundred feet from the castle. About ten others were being carried by the enemy soldiers towards the plateau. Then to the northeast, large panels of smouldering wood, peppered with arrows, gave cover to some other assailants. At the far end of the moor, about thirty knights were riding around in circles. I was awakened from my observation by my husband's impatient voice, saying he was waiting for my comment.

'How many have we lost, my lord?' I asked cautiously, looking him straight in the eyes. We had not suffered many casualties this morning.

'No one is dead so far, praise God! But the enemy could well breach the first wall at the next charge. If they are successful, all our lives are in danger. Do you feel in a state of war now, my lady?' he said bitterly.

'Ah, my lord, the carnage must be stopped! You do not even know why we are under attack! Have you at least asked them?' I said, outraged.

'Good grief, my lady! Do you think I would amuse myself by asking the Camerons what they want when they are bombarding us? They want to wipe us out. They want their lands back; they want whisky, salt, anything. There is nothing we can do about it,' he hurled.

'What, my lord? You have not exchanged a single word with your enemy? We are, in fact, in the middle of a battle, which is costing you your village, wounded, perhaps even fatalities within a few hours, which has already slain tens of men in the other camp, and it hasn't even crossed your mind to negotiate a settlement?'

'Listen to me carefully, my lady,' he growled. 'War is not your business but mine. I do not tell you how to embroider, and you will not tell me how to fight.' And on hearing the cannon fire resume, he continued, 'Now you are going to have to leave me to work in peace. And you will return immediately to the keep.'

I was aghast and in despair. A clan chief could not act in this way. It was senseless. Lord Baltair would have tried to talk to the Cameron chief. I was convinced of that. Whatever it took, Iain had to understand that. *But how?* I said to myself. *It is my duty to make him see it. He has the lives of others in his hands.*

We went down the stairs as quickly as we had gone up a few minutes earlier. I noticed his hand was cold. When we came out at the bottom of the turret, the three soldiers looked at us nervously. Iain moved to let them pass, and they went up without a word. If we went out the door, we would find ourselves without cover. My husband pulled me behind him, and standing in the doorway, he checked the courtyard and the ramparts for a minute to determine our chances of reaching the keep without being hit. I gave him a sidelong glance—his thick furrowed eyebrows, his firm profile, his tense jaw, his hair stuck to his wet temples. I suddenly wanted to touch his face to soften the hardness. He turned his head towards me and met my gaze.

'I feel I do not know you anymore, my lord. Where is the man who took me last night?' I murmured to him as I stroked his cheek.

'He is here, my lady. He is the same one, who made love to you, but today he is making war, and his most urgent task is to take you to a place of safety. Come!'

He had spoken these words very matter-of-factly, and his eyes revealed a certain indecisiveness. I felt it was better not to say any more, and I followed him, keeping my sadness and disappointment to myself.

Anna was very surprised to see me come in through the garden door, escorted by Iain. He disappeared without a backward glance and without a word of greeting. I was trembling with fear. I collapsed onto a bench and rested my head on my crossed arms on the table. Then I felt the housekeeper's hand stroke my hair and slowly take it in her hand. I turned to look at her.

'Two hundred and twenty-four loaves, my lady,' she said quietly.

'Good. Let us see to the dividing up of the other provisions now,' I replied calmly.

I lifted the inventory from the table and began to work out some figures. Fire arrows were whistling over the courtyard and reaching the fortification walls without setting anything alight. I rushed to close the door to the garden and put the bar across. Then I took Anna with me into the great hall. The images of the battlefield were passing in front of my eyes, and I had a knot in my stomach. *Sons of dogs come, come, and fetch your meat. How barbaric the Highlanders are!* I thought with a shudder.

Lady Rosalind came over as soon as she saw me and held out a large slice of bread. 'If you are not sleeping, you must at least eat, my dear. Here, that is your share. Let us be economical, isn't that, right?'

'Indeed, my lady. I would like your opinion on this,' I replied, showing her the inventory.

She smiled at me and took the paper, which she carefully perused. I watched her as I bit into the thick bread. At that moment, I found Iain's aunt very beautiful. There was a certain nobility and intelligence about her, and I sensed her support even before she had made a single comment on the provisions available at the castle. I looked around the room. The wounded were gathered in one corner and the ladies in another. Mairi and my little Ceit were soundly sleeping side by side on furs with Bran at their feet. Nellie had gone down to the cellars with the servants to feed their families.

I followed Lady Rosalind over to the circle of armchairs, where we sat down. I listened carefully to what she had to say about the distribution of food, trying to drive from my mind the thought of the outside wall, which could give way to the enemy within the next hour. Her analysis of the provisions was insightful, and I adopted her recommendations without hesitation. I immediately informed Anna, which greatly reassured her and also gave her a lot of authority as a housekeeper. This effort had drained me. I lay down for the rest of the day in the great hall, exhausted but incapable of resting as my people suggested. I no longer wished to leave the keep and was content to listen to the noise of the battle, which was raging outside and imagining the destruction it was causing. We only had four wounded in the afternoon.

At nightfall, the fighting stopped, but I did not see my husband return. With a heavy heart, I went down to the cellars and joined the families at the priest's evening prayers. As always, they brought me peace. Looking at the faces around me, all one in the same faith, I thanked God for the day He had given and the lives spared and prayed for the eternal rest of those souls who had died in combat. Then I went back up to the hall and went to cuddle up to Ceit in the hope of finding sleep. The heat of her little body took hold of me, and I quickly dropped off.

Waking the next morning, when the wounded flocked into the room, I was amazed to learn that the enemy had made a strategic move under cover of darkness. They had succeeded in draining the moat thanks to the dam they had built upstream, thus diverting the waterfall which supplied the water around the castle. They had dismantled the door in the exterior wall and had taken up positions at the foot of the walls; using approach devices, they had attempted to climb them at several places. Alas! We counted our first fatalities: five soldiers, two archers, one of the laird's household knights, and the stonemason from Mallaig. I was devastated. I had the cellar man take Ceit and Mairi down to the cellars and prepared myself to receive my first contingent of wounded. There were mainly burns to the back and arms, arrowheads to be removed, and limbs to be dressed. I did not even think about the condition of the enemy. It had to be catastrophic. I knew that at any moment, we could be invaded, and inside, I was trembling. How could I last a whole morning of relentlessly caring for the wounded without fainting? The lairds' wives were keeping up, as indeed was Lady Beathag, who, with Finella, showed exemplary zeal in getting folk back on their feet. Someone came to announce that knights from lairds in the north had arrived and were having a fierce fight on the plateau with the Cameron cavalrymen. This news comforted us for the moment.

At midday, there was a ceasefire. I saw Lord Tomas cross the hall in the direction of the arms room, enter, and come out a few moments later, with the standard bearing a white cross on a blue background-the cross of St. Andrew, the patron saint of Scotland. He made a detour to my side and whispered in my ear that his cousin planned to negotiate. Then he disappeared out the door. With my heart expectant with hope and filled with pride for my husband, I had difficulty getting up as my legs were numb with having been crouched too long. I left the wounded man I was attending in the care of a stretcher bearer, who led him to the end of the room with the other invalids, and I walked slowly to the door. There was only one guard in the entrance hall now, and he humbly advised me not to go out. I smiled at him, thanked him for his concern, and while I was thinking about going back to my folk, I had the idea of asking him if the MacNeils had a war cry. He had difficulty hiding his embarrassment. As I insisted, he ended up revealing it without looking at me. And in a voice that betrayed his embarrassment, he said, 'Those who have nothing between their legs, lie down.'

I could not help smiling as I went towards a group of wounded men whom Lady Beathag was looking after. She noticed the look on my face and asked me about the pleasantries exchanged with the guard. I did not know how to answer her right away. Then, realising that she was hinting at what had made me smile, I told her. She burst out laughing with her usual guffaw.

'That war cry is typical MacNeil, if you want my opinion. It is quite new. Have a guess at who thought of it,' she said mischievously

'I have no idea. I only hope it was not your brother-in-law,' I replied laconically.

'Almost. It wasn't Iain. It was me! Isn't it just perfect as a war cry on a battlefield full of Highlanders?'

What could I reply to such an idiot? I ended the conversation by turning towards another group and directing all my thoughts to my husband. The go-betweens just had to succeed. It was essential. There was a growing number of wounded, dead were being added to the dead and bereavements to be lived through. I thought of the stonemason's family; his wife was one of the ones who were breastfeeding, and the family had two other boys. My heart stopped, and I had to close my eyes for a few moments to keep control. I then began to pray fervently for Iain.

The afternoon was drawing to a close, and a watery sun was casting its last rays of light on the stone floor covered with bloodstained cloths. The fighting had not resumed. In the room, there hung an atmosphere of "at last a time of respite." The wounded were resting on rugs near the fires; those who could walk had left the room and resumed their positions on the ramparts or regrouped in the courtyard. Father Henriot was mingling among the men, helping some and blessing others. The circle of armchairs had been pushed a little to the side. There was almost complete silence when I heard footsteps in the vestibule and saw Iain appear. He stopped in the doorway and leaned against the doorpost; his eyes fixed on me. I jumped up and ran towards him. I had never seen him so exhausted. Tiredness was etched on every trait of his face, and his look expressed a kind of resignation.

'What can I do for you, my lord?' I asked him compassionately.

'Come into my arms if we are still friends,' he replied in a whisper, stretching out his hands in front of him.

I took his hands in mine and leaned my head against his chest without saying a word. He placed his mouth on my hair and sighed loudly. Then straightening up, he took me into the study at the end of the hallway. I was on edge. Was the fighting over? Had he surrendered to Cameron? The fact he was moving about on his own… Did that not mean the danger was over? He sat in the only armchair in the room and took me on his knees, putting his two arms around me. He leaned his head back on the chair and remained silent for quite a while with his eyes closed. I studied his dirty face ravaged by fatigue—his stubble shadowed his cheeks and chin. I gently stroked his face with the back of my hand. He opened his eyes and looked at me for a long time, with an inscrutable expression.

'My lady, I listened to your advice, and I brokered the peace this afternoon: me in exchange for the restitution of the forests. MacDonald's men retreated at midday and will leave on the next tide. Cameron wants his lands back, but he has only about thirty warriors and about ten cavalrymen. They succeeded in reaching the wall, but they cannot go any further. We are holding them back. In a few hours, we will have killed them all. The only thing is, I am unable to continue. It is sheer butchery. I think Cameron has gone completely mad. He is risking his men's lives, as others bet their shoes in a game. I have proposed a man-to-man combat with him. If I lose, the Camerons take back the Grampians. If I win, they give them up forever.'

But what did it mean, 'if I lose?' I was panic-stricken. Was my husband telling me he was putting his life on the line to spare the lives of all the others? His clan and the Camerons? I slid from his knees to his feet, my hands grasping his, which I feverishly stroked.

'Has he accepted this offer, my lord?' I articulated with difficulty.

'Not quite. He wants a two-handed fight in memory of the MacNeil brothers. It will be the MacNeil cousins. He and his brother Athall against Tomas and me.'

'God in heaven!' I exclaimed.

I buried my head in my arms. I was devastated. How could they come to such a solution? He continued huskily, and I had to lift my head and strain my ears to catch what he was saying.

'Believe me, my lady, I would have preferred to spare Tomas. Even more so because I would have entrusted you to him if things had gone badly for me in one-to-one combat. Now that is no longer possible. If one of the cousins is to die, the great risk is that it is the one you chose two months ago.'

'Keep quiet! How can you talk like that?' I breathed. Standing up as if my skirts were on fire, I grabbed him by the shoulders and leaned over his face. 'I want you to know, my lord, that I have since discovered another man. A man who, from now on, not only is my preference but who completely has my heart. How do I have to say it to you, Iain MacNeil, for you to understand? I love…'

I could not finish my declaration, for he had jumped to his feet and was kissing me passionately on the lips.

'As you have just said it, my lady, it is absolutely clear,' he murmured between two kisses. He hugged me for a long time as our entwined bodies rocked from side to side and he whispered words of hope.

'We will begin the contest at nightfall, and we can win it if we recover our strength. I would like to rest alone with you until it is time. I need you to keep me warm this evening. Will you stay with me, my lady?'

'I would be incapable of leaving you, even for a minute. I have felt so isolated from you since yesterday that I am overjoyed at finding you again. I no longer want to lose you in that way, my lord. Promise never to treat me, ever again, with such coldness as you did today.'

'I promise you, if, in return, you promise never to run into danger at the slightest opportunity,' he replied tenderly.

Seeing me smile, he led me to the bay window, where he sat me down on a rug on the floor. He undid his shoulder belt, which he put at my feet, and he lay down on his side, putting his head in my bloodstained skirt and hugging my knees with his arm. I had my back to the wall and was stroking his shoulder and back as one does with a child one is reassuring. He calmly explained his attitude towards me: His own fear of losing me had thrown him into a state of panic on seeing my safety threatened. I had to admit that I had shown imprudence more than once since my arrival at Mallaig. We recalled those memories, and that made us forget the dramatic situation approaching as fast as the night. Gently, I stroked his untidy hair with my two hands and soon felt him drop off to sleep. A love song arose within me, and I let it flow through my lips in the fresh evening air as I looked out the window at the day coming to its close.

Chapter Eleven
The Hunt

The fight was over. The smouldering moorland around the castle was bathed in the watery late March sun. A light breeze from the sea was carrying the last lingering smells of gunpowder towards the plateau and accompanying the Cameron troops, with their chieftain in front, back to their own territory. Several carts loaded with the dead and wounded went ahead of the column of horsemen and weapons as they left the battlefield behind. Three of the MacNeil men brought up the rear, and one of them was leading a horse for Father Henriot, who was travelling in the cart to tend to the dying on their journey back home. The four men were due to return to Mallaig a few hours later accompanied by the Cameron chief and his brother for the contest with Lord Iain and his cousin Tomas.

Lord Tomas watched the Cameron troops heading northwards until their standard disappeared from view at the edge of the wood. He was still holding the St. Andrew's Cross, which his cousin had used to indicate his readiness to talk. At that moment, he had felt admiration and pride. His cousin had shown a rare maturity in initiating the end to hostilities just when victory was his for the taking. However, remembering the conditions of the agreement he had come to with Cameron and which engaged him in a two-handed fight, Tomas could not help feeling dismayed and apprehensive. *I am not up to the task*, he said to himself as he thought of the men he and Iain would be fighting.

Bruce Cameron and his brother, Athall, were in their late thirties, well-built, and very accomplished fighters. In his time at Mallaig, Tomas had never met Bruce the chief, but his brother Athall had taken part the skirmishes which were forever bringing the two clans face to face. It was always Iain who took on the latter, and Tomas remembered that his cousin found him a tough opponent. As for Bruce Cameron, there was a good chance he was a champion with the claymore. *I am going to lose my life, and Iain is going to lose his lands if I do not win my contest this evening*, he thought resignedly on his way back down from the ramparts. The first person he met in the guards' room was his uncle Aindreas, and, catching his eye, he could not help thinking of how the latter had lobbied the lairds for their support for himself in the vote for clan chief a few days earlier. Totally unexpectedly, his uncle took him by the arm and led him to the far end of the room, where he offered to help him prepare for the contest.

'Come with me, Tomas. You need to rest,' he said. 'If you do not win your fight this evening, your and your cousin's lives are on the line.'

'If Iain dies, uncle, you will become chief, will you not?' Tomas muttered softly between gritted teeth.

Aindreas stopped dead and looked his nephew in the eye. A worrying gleam lit up Aindreas' eyes. He looked around to see who was standing about and, leaning towards the young man, he whispered in his ear, 'And if he dies and you live, you inherit his castle and probably his wife… Fate is strange, Tomas. Think before you draw your weapon. You are risking much this evening, but you can also gain much.'

'Leave me alone, uncle! Your aspirations are unworthy of a MacNeil,' replied Tomas as he turned away brusquely in disgust under the dumbfounded gaze of the knights who were within earshot.

Tomas rushed out of the guard room as if he had seen a vision of the devil himself. His heart thumping, the flag still in his hand, he headed straight for the door of the keep, completely unaware of the looks of all those in the courtyard. Entering the hall, he bumped into young Jenny, who was taking the children outside as they had been shut up in the cellars for two days. He was startled, and as he apologised, she timidly interrupted him.

'My lord, may heaven protect you tonight. I heard that you and Lord Iain are going to fight the Camerons. I am praying for you, and I am going to pray non-stop until midnight. You cannot die.'

Turning on her heels and without looking back, she rushed out to rejoin the children and left Tomas standing in the middle of the hall, completely at a loss for words. He noticed Bran sitting outside the study door and realised that his cousin had shut himself away in there. *I must have a nap. Otherwise, I will lose*, he thought. Clenching the flag in his hand, he headed towards the arms room. Father Henriot was exhausted. On his way back to Mallaig, he just let himself be jolted awkwardly at his horse's slow pace. At his side was Lord Eachann of Lochalsh, and behind him, Sir Eideard and Domnhull from Gairloch. In front were the Lords Cameron and four of their men. The sky was clear, and its starlit dome was pierced by a white, almost transparent full moon. The priest was praying silently for all the souls called home during their short battle. He had never had to give the last rites to so many dying men at one time, and he would, in all probability, have to do the same for others tonight. He prayed with all his heart that it would not be Lord Iain or his cousin.

'Almighty God, who am I that I should beg you to intervene on Lord Iain's behalf?' he pleaded. 'If you must take more men, spare the MacNeils. It was the Camerons who broke your divine law by declaring war during Lent. The Mallaig men defended themselves out of respect for the church.'

As the escort emerged onto the moor, in the distance towards the east, the priest saw a circle of torches stuck in the damp ground of what had been the battlefield a few hours earlier. About thirty men were stationed around the circle. A guard, bearing the MacNeil standard, was circling the area on horseback. *The contest is to take place outside the walls*, he said to himself, surprised but reassured. When he passed the drawbridge, having left the knights and the Camerons behind on the moor, he had a strange feeling that there would be no further deaths to add to the numerous ones which had already marked the day. He shrugged his shoulders nervously. Lord Iain was waiting for him in the courtyard and came to help him dismount. Father Henriot noticed right away that the young chief was clean, changed, and rested. He gave a sigh of relief. 'Father,' he said, 'I would like you to bless me, my wife, and little Ceit before the fight. I would also like you to hear my confession.'

'It would be a pleasure for me to do that, my lord. I was desperately hoping you would ask me,' replied the priest, his heart somewhat lighter.

The two men solemnly entered the chapel by the little door which led from the courtyard. The nave was softly lit by the candles on the altar. Lady Gunelle and little Ceit were sitting waiting, hand in hand, on a pew in the front row. Behind them, Lord Tomas, Anna, Lady Beathag and her companion, the five lairds, and their wives formed a tightly knit group of tense and anxious faces. When she saw the priest and her husband entering the chapel, Lady Gunelle and Ceit stood up and went towards them. She had changed into a very discreet dark-blue dress and was wearing a simple white veil. The little girl was just as plainly dressed, her hair in pigtails under a little bonnet. Her tense little face showed she was fighting sleep. With a smile, the priest took their hands. He suddenly felt dirty and was aware that he smelled of horses in front of this group who had had time to freshen up. Turning round to Lord Iain, he saw he was showing signs of impatience and decided to proceed quickly to the blessing of adoption. He directed the parents and child to a spot beside the altar, then quickly went off to collect his books in the little sacristy.

Iain came and stood beside me. He took my hand and, putting his arm in front of his daughter, drew her close to him. Ceit immediately grabbed her father's hand and put her cheek against it. Iain looked at me and smiled. His eyes were beaming. His cleanly shaved face was relaxed and peaceful. I returned his smile and squeezed his hand. After having slept a long time with his head on my knees, he had wakened refreshed and ready for action. With tender gestures, he had left me to go to the guard room where he had had a bath and spoken with his cousin while waiting for the return of the Cameron brothers.

'My lady,' he had said before leaving the study, 'I must stay with my cousin until our opponents arrive. We must prepare ourselves and focus only on the contest we are going to fight together. I have one thing to ask you: I would like you not to attend.'

'So be it, my lord,' I had replied, my voice trembling. 'I will not attend, but I will be with you.' Putting my hand on his chest, I had added, 'Here.'

When he kissed me on leaving, he had informed me that he wanted to recognise Ceit as his daughter and asked me to be ready with her as soon as the priest returned to the castle.

I had spent all the time until the adoption ceremony with Ceit. I had taken her up to my bedroom and had taken a bath with her. I did not stop talking about Iain and the adoption, for I wanted her to really understand what it meant and for her to be able to call Iain 'father.' I felt that my husband's gesture towards Ceit that evening was very important to him. It was equally important to me. Those intimate moments spent with my little Ceit turned my thoughts from the fight which would take place in less than an hour and could cost the life of one or both men. I listened to Father Henriot pronounce the blessing of adoption in Latin after he had translated the main parts into Gaelic.

Ceit was standing very straight and had let go of her father's hand to get ready to cross herself. When we had all received the blessing, she turned around, looked up at Iain, and held out her arms. He gently lifted her and hugged her. I heard Ceit whisper in his ear: 'I love you with all my heart, father.'

He gave her a kiss and then put her down and took a folded piece of paper from his doublet. Turning towards the little gathering, he opened it and read it aloud.

'In these first days of the year of grace fourteen hundred and twenty-five, I, Iain MacNeil, son of Baltair MacNeil, recognise Ceit as my daughter and my heir as well as the children who will be born in this marriage. May she be raised by my wife Gunelle, who, too, adopts her as her daughter today.'

After a brief silence, he turned to the priest and said, 'I would like you to witness this document, father.' Then, looking at me, he added in the same breath, 'And you too, my lady.'

I noticed an ink well and quill on the table behind the altar. The priest and I went forward together to sign the document Iain was indicating to us. He took his daughter's hand and went to sit down in the pew we had occupied before he arrived. When had my husband prepared this document? It could only have been that evening. It was well drawn up, and I was proud of it. I glanced at the congregation and noticed that Anna and Tomas were deeply moved.

Except for Iain, who remained with the priest, we all left the chapel and returned to the great hall. I was immediately approached by Lady Beathag, who obviously had evil on her mind.

'My dear chatelaine,' she said in her mellifluous voice, 'what have you done to our chief in such a short time? He gives in to those Cameron rogues, shaves like an English man, and adopts an orphan as if he were a man who is not sure of ever having any descendants of his own.'

'I am surprised you know your brother-in-law so little, Beathag dear, to believe that he did not do it off his own bat. My husband did not surrender, but he decided to settle this war with four men rather than a hundred. He does not shave like an English man but as a Scotsman, and he is not adopting Ceit because he thinks I am sterile but because he loves her as much as he loves me.'

'I know my brother-in-law, dear Gunelle, and like all the women here, I can recognise a change in him when there is one.' Turning to the group of lairds' wives, she continued, 'I maintain you have transformed him. Give us the recipe for your potion. I am curious as to how you went about it.'

'If there is a recipe, you do not possess the principal ingredient,' I replied as I turned away from her and led Ceit away. I immediately heard a clear voice rise from the group of ladies Beathag had called as witnesses to her comments. It was Lady Rosalind who completed my response for me.

'Dear Beathag, I think the chatelaine of Mallaig is hinting at love. Not sensual lust, which knows nothing of the actions of the heart, but true love which occasionally grows between couples, strange as that may seem to you.'

I was relieved to hear nothing more from Beathag and sought refuge with Nellie and Anna. I wanted to be with people who loved my daughter and husband unconditionally. Were my nurse and the housekeeper not my double rampart at Mallaig?

I sat down beside Nellie, who affectionately put her arm around me and whispered, 'Pay no attention to Lady Beathag. She is eaten up by jealousy. Lady Rosalind is perfectly right, my dear. A woman who loves can influence the one she loves a lot. I am reassured to see that you are in love with Lord Iain. It suits you and him too! And what can I say about the incredible happiness of our little Ceit?'

I smiled with gratitude and, my heart filled with anxiety, settled down to wait for Iain and Tomas's departure for the contest with the Camerons.

When Lord Iain left the confessional, he noticed Tomas on his knees at the back of the chapel. The latter stood up immediately, came towards his cousin, and, putting his hand on his shoulder, whispered,

'It's my turn, Iain, I will join you soon.' Then he went to kneel by the priest.

Iain left the chapel and went towards the great hall. Every eye was on him when he entered. The atmosphere was charged with emotion. Added to the upset two days of fighting had caused the folk of Mallaig there was now the anxiety of a contest in which the young MacNeil chief was risking his own life as well as his cousin's. Iain decided to cut short the gushing, thereby deliberately depriving himself of several expressions of respect and encouragement. He headed straight to his wife, whom he took by the hand and, after he had stroked his daughter's cheek as she cuddled in Anna's arms, led her towards the door.

'My lady,' he said huskily when he was alone with Gunelle. 'I am going now. I want you to know the most important thing of all. Before you, I have never loved because I was always afraid of having my love rejected. You have lit up my life by showing me how to be happy.' He kissed her forehead and then added, 'Whatever happens, Gunelle, remember that you are my beloved and you always will be.'

The young chatelaine had difficulty hiding her despair. She could not reply to her husband's first declaration of love and collapsed on his chest with her arms around his neck. He clasped her tightly around the waist, put his head on her shoulder and they remained entwined like that for several minutes, silently savouring their intense oneness.

As Lord Tomas came out of the chapel, he found them thus and turned on his heels in the direction of the guards' room. Almost immediately, he heard his cousin's footsteps behind him in the corridor. In the knights' and soldiers' common room, there was a roaring fire and cups of whisky were being handed around by the

272

nervous men. Iain and Tomas did not drink anything. In silence, they took off their tunics and, with the help of two knights, put on their chainmail, greaves, arm pieces, breastplate, and helmets, and then, taking their claymores, they went out into the courtyard. Restricted in their metal straitjackets with the helmet visor raised, they walked awkwardly, in silence towards the drawbridge. They had said all that had to be said regarding the contest.

For almost an hour, Lord Iain had instructed his cousin on the best tactics, speaking to him, not as a master at arms but as one man whose life depended on the other. Never had Iain talked like that with his brother, with whom he had fought all his fights as a team. He felt very close to his cousin. He felt connected to him in the same way he imagined an older brother and his younger brother would be when there was real fraternal love.

'Tomas,' he said as they walked. 'Tonight, I am fighting for my land. I am fighting for both of us to live. If you are hit, I will ask for mercy, and surrender to the Camerons. Do not sacrifice yourself for me. You are the brother I would like to have had, and I do not want to lose you.'

Lord Tomas had a lump in his throat. A terrible dread was oppressing him, and his cousin's declaration tortured him even more. A host of conflicting feelings were jostling together inside him, and ever since the conversation with their uncle Aindreas, he had been unable to distinguish between what he wanted and what he feared. To become master of Mallaig with a widowed Gunelle at his side, was an impossible dream, and he refused to think about it. He knew he would do nothing in the fight to bring that about. Now that he knew his cousin's heart and the feelings he had for his wife, his death became an unthinkable prospect. *Iain must live*, he said to himself. Having arrived at the end of the footbridge, which now led directly onto the moor since the first door had gone, they saw the fighting ring marked by burning torches. It seemed to have shrunk. Almost fifty people had gathered around the edge: the MacNeil lairds, knights and soldiers, Father Henriot, and several men and women from the village, including young Jenny. Further back, the Camerons had gathered around their standard, which had been stuck into the ground near their horses. Everyone stopped talking when the MacNeil cousins appeared. The screech of an owl ripped through the still air, and a shiver ran right through all those present. The MacNeils marched down in step towards the fighting ring. The first person Tomas caught looking at him was his uncle Aindreas.

In a whisper, he said to Iain, 'Iain, if I die and you live, promise me that you will always be wary of uncle Aindreas. He wants to take your place and was ready to betray you a while ago.'

Lord Iain quickly turned towards his cousin and, stopping him with his hand, studied him for a long moment, trying to work out exactly what he was saying from his expression. With a sigh, he said quietly, 'Tomas, if I die and you live, promise me you will always protect her. I entrust her and my daughter to you.'

These words made Tomas shudder. He clenched his fists and his jaw as he looked at his cousin. 'If God is on Mallaig's side, neither of us will die, Iain,' he replied confidently.

The two men smiled at one another and turned towards the ring. Irritated by the delay, the Cameron lords were already in position. In keeping with the conditions Iain had negotiated, the MacNeils had the choice of place and the protocol for ending the fight. The Camerons decided on the time and the amount of protection. When Bruce Cameron learned that Iain was opting for the claymore alone, he opted for reduced armour, halberd, shoulder pads, arm pieces, and iron gloves, and no breastplate, greaves, or helmet. The knights helped Iain and Tomas to discard their superfluous armour. That was the first point in Tomas's favour, since, not having completed his training, he had very little experience in fighting on the ground in full armour.

Once the four men were in position in the ring, Iain facing Athall to leave Bruce for his cousin, the Camerons realised that their chief's wound, although barely visible, had not gone unnoticed. In fact, Iain had noticed the stiffness in Bruce Cameron's right arm during the afternoon negotiations and deduced that he was injured. The fact that his opponent had chosen the pieces protecting the shoulders, arms, and hands as armour, confirmed his suspicions. The cousins had agreed that Bruce would be the weaker of the two and Tomas would take him on. That was the second point in his favour in this two-handed contest. From the first exchanges of blows between Bruce Cameron and Tomas, the evasive tactics used by the latter set the tone for their fight. Tomas parried each blow, struck none, and moved with such speed that his adversary quickly began to get annoyed. Still fired up by his rebellion and destructive madness, the Cameron chieftain was going at its full tilt and progressively losing his cool. He was tiring himself out with attacks which came to nothing, whereas Tomas was conserving his strength by parrying his opponent's blows or avoiding them altogether. In the other part of the ring, after several technical blows Iain had made to gauge Athall's form, the combat was very close. They were of equal strength. Athall was taller than Iain, and so his weapon covered a larger area, forcing the latter to make larger circles with his claymore. On the other hand, the young chief MacNeil had the advantage of having a stronger strike, for he was a lot more powerful than Cameron and quicker. Iain was concentrating on his opponent, but whenever Tomas entered his field of vision, he could not help but be distracted for a second. Athall must have noticed this, for he moved about as often as possible so that Iain would be just at the right angle to see Tomas.

As for Bruce Cameron, he was becoming more and more exasperated. Out of breath, he suddenly lashed out at Tomas, 'You are very brave to fight alongside your cousin. He will let you bleed to death when I wound you!'

Iain shuddered when he heard those words and said between his teeth, 'Shut up, scum!'

Bruce reacted to the insult by making a rash movement, which gave Tomas an unexpected opportunity to strike his right arm. Tomas hit him with such force and precision that it was the only blow he had to land. As Cameron fell to the ground, unarmed and armless, he screamed with pain. He was out of the contest. Taking advantage of his adversary's momentary lack of attention Athall launched a lightning blow and succeeded in disarming Iain.

Just as Iain's claymore fell and he jumped backwards before his opponent's weapon was pointed at his throat, Tomas rushed up behind Athall and placed his sword on his neck, shouting, 'Beg for mercy, Cameron.'

Feeling his skin cut, Athall, stiffened. He lowered his claymore, and then, after a second's hesitation, he dropped it at his feet, muttering in resignation, 'I yield!'

Iain looked at his cousin in amazement. A shout which carried all the way to the castle rose immediately around the ring. Cameron's horses neighed in surprise. The torches were burning bright under the starlit sky, and the Mallaig knights rushed towards the winners.

I watched him go along the corridor through a veil of tears.

'Why must it be like this?' I murmured.

It had taken so long to come to love him, and perhaps he would be taken from me this very evening. When he had disappeared from view, I entered the chapel. An overabundance of emotions constrained me. Pray... that was all there was left to do for him... and for me. There was no fire in the chapel and the coldness of the place hit me immediately. I saw Father Henriot go out by the little door beside the sacristy, which he left open. It was a starry night. I went forward and knelt at the foot of the altar, spirit and body paralysed. I stayed prostrate like that for what seemed an eternity. I heard none of the noise from outside, nothing of the frenzy in the hall which drew the ladies from the great hall out to the courtyard, nothing of Bran's barks of excitement on welcoming his master. It was Father Henriot who found me when he entered the chapel and he lifted me out of my daze by gently lifting me up by the arms.

'Come, my child. It is all over. In his great wisdom, God has not taken the life of any of those fighting. The defeated Camerons are on their way home with their folk, and your husband and his cousin are safe and sound.'

I looked at him speechlessly, trying to take in what he was saying. 'They are both alive!' I shouted.

Overwhelmed with gratitude and without thinking, I threw myself into the priest's arms. I immediately felt him nervously shrug his shoulders and let go of him in embarrassment. As I looked at the altar, I crossed myself and ran out of the chapel without another word. There was absolute silence in the great hall. At the far end, I noticed Nellie and Ceit in the corner lying cuddled up, sound asleep. Glancing out into the corridor leading to the guard room, I saw Bran and deduced that all the others must be there and rushed towards it. My heart was thumping as I went into the room for the first time. Stone walls not quite as thick as the castle's were covered with lime and had black wooden beams. The very high ceiling and floor were wooden, too, and several little windows opened out onto the courtyard. A ladder led to a gallery, covering half the floor, which probably held the beds. Near the door, a large fire with chimney hooks cast a dancing light on the small and noisy group of castle folk. They were buzzing around the victors whom I could not even see. I stood in the doorway, overcome with emotion. Bran came to lick my hands, and I instinctively bent to stroke his head.

Lady Rosalind came to meet me, took my arm and, babbling away, led me into the sweltering heat of the smoke-filled room and towards the group clustered around Iain.

'Where were you hiding, my dear? We were looking for you. The MacNeils won, did you know? And almost without any blood loss! It is incredible, after all! Bruce Cameron has had his arm cut off, and his pride is in bits. His brother Athall is disgraced for having surrendered to a man half his age and he, not even a knight. It is a thrilling outcome for a war that was hardly a war. Good old Henriot thinks it is God's will to punish those who did not respect the holy days. What do you think?'

I had no idea what to say. It was true that the church forbade leading men to war during Advent and Lent and on Sundays, but I had my doubts about the Christian fervour of Highlanders when it came to a fight. In fact, I was hardly listening to Lady Rosalind. I had just caught sight of Iain. He had his back to me, and his sister-in-law was standing close to him, her bracelet-laden arm, lovingly draped around his shoulders. My husband was holding a cup, probably of whisky. Tomas, some knights, and lairds were standing around them, and hearty laughter arose from the group. When Tomas saw me, he stopped laughing, and Iain turned round. My gaze met my husbands in the sudden silence which fell over the room.

Freeing himself from Beathag, he took a step towards me, then changing his mind, he turned towards his sister-in-law, held out his cup, and said mockingly, 'Here, my dear. Get Raonall to drink it. He is a good fighter, and you stand more chance of succeeding with him.'

Immediately Iain was standing in front of me and hugging me close to his chest. He whispered, 'Where were my daughter and wife? Did they not miss me?'

'Your daughter is asleep, and I was waiting in the chapel, scared stiff,' I whispered as I pressed close to him. 'Oh, Iain, I would have died if you had not come back!'

'No, my beloved, you would not have died. You cannot die. You are the chatelaine of Mallaig and Ceit's mother, and the happiness of everyone at Mallaig depends on you.' he replied, looking me straight in the eye, his eyes beaming.

What love I saw in them at that moment! Under the spell of his blue eyes, I could not see the black hate-filled looks Beathag was casting my way. The circle had closed in around her, and Raonall was lustfully looking her up and down in anticipation of what was to come.

Tomas smiled with delight in seeing his cousin's behaviour towards Beathag and could not help giving Raonall a mischievous look.

'You haven't met Sheriff Darnley, cousin Raonall,' he said. 'He is a fine specimen of man, I assure you. Do you not think so, Lady Beathag?'

'He's an interesting man,' she replied sullenly. 'You either like him, or you do not. It depends....'

'It depends on what?' asked Raonall, whose curiosity had been aroused.

'Whether you are a woman or a man.' said Tomas off the cuff.

Leaving Raonall speechless and Beathag furious, Tomas turned around and went towards another group. It was then he noticed young Jenny, who was watching him furtively by the door which opened onto the courtyard. He joined her.

'Good evening, Jenny,' he said. 'What are you doing here? Is your family not still sleeping here at the castle? Tomorrow we will get down to repairing the village houses. Everyone will be needed. You should be with your own folk this evening. Where are they?'

'My father has gone with men from the garrison to remove the dam which is diverting the water into the hillside, or we will have none tomorrow. I am waiting for them to come back. I saw your contest earlier. Why are you not a knight?' she asked, intently.

'Because I have not been dubbed yet. I will be before the summer when everything in Mallaig is rebuilt and the castle repaired, and this accursed conflict will be no more than a bad memory for everyone,' explained Thomas.

'Not for me,' Jenny said quickly. The war will always be a good memory for it allowed me to get close to the mistress... and you.'

Thereupon the young girl fled, running into the moonlit courtyard. Tomas watched her skip to avoid the debris covering the ground and smiled with amusement. Jenny was so small, she reminded him of an elf. The happy reunion around the victorious cousins did not last long. Everyone was exhausted. Since the night was not too far gone, several of the lairds, mentally exhausted by the atmosphere of tension the MacNeils had been living under for three days, decided to go home that evening and gathered their people together. Aindreas of Loch Morar was the one most in a hurry to leave the place. As he was leaving, Lord Iain took him aside.

'Uncle, you did not congratulate me on the contest. Are you pleased with the outcome?'

'It was very exciting, nephew. You are a master at arms without equal. Tomas is as ready as anyone could be to be knighted,' replied a furious Aindreas.

'It is true. Tomas has all the qualities needed to become a perfect knight. He has one, which I have not taught him because it cannot be learned. Loyalty.' Looking his uncle straight in the eye, Iain added, 'I know one thing about Tomas. No one will ever be able to accuse him of treachery.'

'Are you accusing me of something, Iain?' asked his uncle defensively

'No, I am warning you.' Narrowing his eyes to restrain the revulsion he felt rising within him, he continued, 'I am clan chief, and as far back as you can go in its history, the MacNeils have never betrayed one another. I would be very sorry if it were to begin with us, and I will do all in my power to avoid that.'

Aindreas had to turn away to hide his rage. He had misjudged his nephew Tomas and realised his mistake. At least he knew that from now on, he had two men to deal with rather than just one. Two cousins who that night had fought like brothers, the weapon of one in the service of the other.

Not all the lairds left. One of their wives stayed on. In fact, Lady Rosalind offered the young chatelaine to stay on for a few days to help the young chatelaine. She sent her husband home to fetch his stonemason to replace the one Mallaig had lost. Her son Raonall was quick to declare that he would stay too for as long as Mallaig needed his services. His mother smiled rather maliciously.

Addressing Lady Gunelle, she said, 'That is a good idea, my lady. Keep Raonall here. He will be of use to you in many ways. Particularly with the women, will he not?'

Gunelle could not help giving a knowing smile. She really appreciated this strong frank, woman. How she would have loved to have the same self-confidence in certain circumstances! Anna, who had already received her master's instructions regarding the sleeping arrangements for the village folk and the guests, came to inform Lady Rosalind that she would have her late sister-in-law's bedroom. On hearing that, Gunelle gave a start.

'Are you sure, Anna, that Lord MacNeil said that room?' she whispered to the housekeeper.

'Certainly, my lady. And he is giving his to Lord Tomas. He does not want him to sleep in the guardroom any longer.' Rather embarrassedly, she added, 'My master is taking Lord Baltair's bedroom with you, my lady. That is exactly what he said. All your personal things have already been taken there. Mairi took care of it after she put Ceit to bed.'

'I see...' was the only comment Gunelle made.

A few minutes later, when she went into her new bedroom with her husband, Iain noticed her unease.

'You seem upset to find yourself here again, my lady. Did you not like the way I organised your bedroom with Anna? 'Holding her close, he continued, 'From now on, we will no longer sleep in different rooms, and neither will we share our bed with anyone else. I know it is the custom in the Lowlands, England, and France to invite visitors to do so, but this bed is a lovers' bed. Look at how narrow it is! Even Ceit would not be comfortable in it with us. Tell me it suits you, my lady... you can allow your warrior husband this one whim.'

Gunelle had decided to indulge all her husband's whims. The only reply she gave him was to slowly caress his face and kiss him. Returning her kisses, Iain undid her veil and spread her hair down her back. He picked her up off the floor and laid her on the bed, looking at her, desire in his eyes.

'I am dirty, hungry, sore, and exhausted, my hind, but I am also in the mood for love. Do not think badly of me for the way I am going make love to you. It is not the best way, but it is the only way of which I am capable tonight.'

He took her with passion. The young chatelaine discovered with rapture that her husband's passion aroused her own, and she showed it in showering him with kisses and caresses. She was once again satisfied by him, and for the second time that day, she watched him fall asleep, his dark hair on her stomach, his warm hands clasping her breast.

On the west coast the first days of April were sunny and very mild. The lairds had sent several workmen to Mallaig to help rebuild the village and restore the castle. A tour of his property by Lord Iain had allowed him to see that the war had not affected the herds which grazed quite a distance from Mallaig at that time of year. Iain was pleased to know that the livestock was intact as it would be the most reliable source of income for the next year since the saltern had been destroyed by the fire in the village.

Lord Iain oversaw the restoration work of the castle himself: The projectiles had caused several breaches in the outside wall and a few holes in the north face of the keep and the west turret. A brattice had given way, and part of the bastion roof had caved in. The Mallaig stonemason's death had left the young man he had begun to train without a master so Lord Iain asked the mason lent by his laird to take on the boy as an apprentice and paid him the due sum for the duration of the work.

In the village, it was Lord Tomas who was overseeing the work, supervising the provision of the basic materials needed to build the houses and lending a hand when needed. Not everything had burned, but the thatched roofs all had to be replaced. The rest of the winter fodder set aside for the castle stables was used for that. The villagers rebuilt their homes according to a different layout proposed by Lord Tomas, which won everyone's great admiration. The position of the houses in relation to the sea was changed, and the doors and windows installed in such a way as to protect the inhabitants from the prevailing Mallaig winds. As a result of his participation in rebuilding the village, Tomas developed an even deeper attachment to Mallaig and its people. In keeping with the knight's code which demanded that he should help the weakest and protect them, he gave himself unstintingly for days on end. Those weeks were among the most gratifying of his life.

During the early days of reconstruction, the children were kept in the castle courtyard to facilitate the work in the village, and Lady Rosalind took charge of them. In the evening, young Jenny helped her and displayed a natural authority over the children. Jenny was just as useful to Nellie in the garden. Several crops had been sown, and the young girl showed a keen interest in growing vegetables. The chatelaine's old nurse took great pleasure in sharing her know-how with her and even more so because it relieved her of the heavy work. So it was that Jenny gradually carved out a place for herself within the castle walls. Easter Day was a glorious day, and the priest celebrated the mass in the well-cleaned courtyard. All the inhabitants, those of the castle as well as the village, gathered together with great joy since the village chapel did not yet have a roof. It was a moving moment for the young priest to see his faithful flock come together for the service. Taking advantage of the building works going on, Gunelle had asked her husband to build a small room adjoining the chapel in which to hold classes. With the priest's help, she had drawn up the plan for this extension, and, knowing his reservations on the matter, it was with some apprehension that she had presented it to Iain.

'My lord,' she said, 'if the classes are held within the castle, Father Henriot and I will have less need to move about. As well as that, it will be safer for the children to come here, and it will be comforting for their parents to know that they are safe. Besides, nine of the children already live at the castle, and that is about half the class.'

'How many hours per day do you think these children will be in the vicinity of the courtyard? Here we practice archery, combat with all kinds of weapons, and riding! Are you suggesting we do everything on the moor to avoid putting the children in danger?' he answered.

'Could we not share the courtyard? I mean that, that on school days, there would be set times for training your knights and others for the classes. As well as that, I believe that some of your men would like to learn to read and write. They would be welcome during class time…'

'And they would become better educated than their chief. My lady, you are asking a lot! I do not see what benefit Mallaig would gain from this project, although a happy chatelaine is a great benefit for any castle. If it adds to your happiness here, I cannot oppose your idea.'

Lady Gunelle smiled at him. What would this man not do out of love for her! She went over and gently stroked his face as she did so often these days. She thanked him softly so that only he could hear.

'Iain, I love you. I married a man who is not only valiant but also very generous towards his wife and his people. And, do not fear. Your men will not be better educated than you. I will see to that personally.'

'What do you intend to do, my lady? Will you only teach them half the alphabet and to only count to twenty?'

Taking his face in her hands, she declared, 'I am going to devote myself to your education. That is what I am going to do. You are a gifted pupil, and I am going to make a point of teaching you all that I, myself know.'

'If I want to and if I have the time, of course!'

'My lord, God has given you an exceptional gift for learning as well as a wife who is a teacher. To neglect your education would be to offend Him,' she said, as she brought the conversation to a close with a smile.

Two weeks after Lord MacNeil had agreed to his wife's project, three thick walls were built at the far end of the chapel, and a wooden floor was installed. The school opened in mid-April and welcomed twenty-two children and three knights in their thirties. With economic activity picking up again in the village and the beginning of sowing time, the children's education was welcomed by everyone as a blessing from God. To Lady Gunelle's delight, such was her interest in the little school that Lady Rosalind had expressed a desire to spend spring at the castle. Along with the priest who taught the Holy Scriptures in the morning and the two ladies who took it in turns to teach reading and writing and arithmetic in the afternoons, the Mallaig children were given quite a full education for a village school. Lord Iain had paid for each pupil to have his own slate and chalk and had given orders that they be served pancakes and milk for lunch.

So that the books were within easy reach of the school, the entire contents of the castle library had been brought back down from Alasdair's bedroom to the sacristy, where lots of shelves had been put up. With Father Henriot's approval, the young chatelaine and her guest would retire, sometimes for a whole evening, and enthusiastically prepare their lessons. So developed a deep friendship between the two women from which Gunelle benefitted greatly. From that moment on, the young woman gained a lot of confidence, and it became second nature to her to organise a social life largely stimulated by the active part her husband took in the interests of the clan and the running of the estate business.

In fact, Lord Iain reinstated the weekly meetings of the clan council and welcomed a constant stream of serfs, vassals, and clerics who came seeking justice. All these comings and goings at the castle kept Lady Beathag occupied too as she took advantage of the fact that the chatelaine was teaching in the school to play the hostess in the great hall. Lord MacNeil's sister-in-law had hoped for a long time that the social life of Mallaig would pick up again and momentarily put her jealousy on the back burner in order to devote herself fully to the guests who stayed and those who were simply passing through. Every afternoon she came down dressed to the nines and sparkling with jewellery. She was all smiles and would circulate from one group to the next, having plenty to say and gushing in her usual way.

In the final week of April, as the repairs to the castle were almost completed, Lord Iain decided to go to his father-in-law's business in the Grampians. On this trip, he merely wanted to assure himself that everything was going well on that part of his estate and that the Camerons were keeping to the agreement. He gathered together an escort of about ten men, leaving three knights and other soldiers and men at arms under Tomas's command at Mallaig. He planned to be away for three or four days. Lady Gunelle did the best she could to hide her disappointment from him.

When I saw Iain get into the saddle in the courtyard where I had come to see them off, I turned away so that he would not see my eyes mist up with tears. By doing so, I deprived myself of one of those looks of his to which I had become accustomed over the past weeks—tender and arrogant at the same time. *I am an idiot*, I thought. *A chief does not stay in his castle all the time, and Iain no more than the others. I will have to get used to it, or I am going to quickly become unhappy. Isn't it strange? Five months ago, I was unhappy at Mallaig when he was here, and now I cannot imagine being happy when he is not!*

When they had crossed the drawbridge, I went back to the porch and noticed the puzzled look Tomas was giving me. I smiled and passed in front of him without a word. Where was Iain's cousin as far as his emotions were concerned? I knew that he had saved my husband's life in the fight against the Camerons, and that made me uncomfortable although I could not say why. That evening at supper, Tomas, Lady Rosalind and I conversed in Scots, thereby cutting ourselves off from Beathag. She must have resented it, or else she felt free enough from her brother-in-law to allow her animosity towards me to flare up again. She was making cutting remarks, which I did my best to ignore.

The day after Iain left, Sheriff James Darnley returned from the north. As soon as he arrived, he asked to see me in the study, where he kept me for almost an hour. His trip, which had lasted almost two months, had not allowed him to complete his tour of the Highland clans, and he had to summon several of the lairds' secretaries to present their books at Mallaig. This meant he was requisitioning the study for the rest of his stay and asked me to remove our papers and effects. I could not refuse him, nor had I any intention of doing so. Since he only had two months left to conclude the mission the king had given him at the beginning of winter, he was afraid he would not succeed and did not hesitate to share his concerns with me. During our meeting, which was conducted in Scots, I found him very bitter and angry at not being able to conclude his business with Iain. He clearly showed his discontent when the next day, we learned that my husband would not be back for at least ten days because he had decided to deal with the matter of the felling site directly with my father and had left for Crathes with Lieutenant Lennox.

I was very hurt on hearing the news and had to muster up a lot of patience to put up with the king's representative who was making our lives a misery. He was in a foul mood, particularly at mealtimes with Lady Rosalind, who obviously despised him. Only one person found favour in his eyes. It was, of course, Beathag who followed him right into the study where he had established his quarters. As unpleasant as it was, the sheriff's return within our walls had the advantage of diverting the attention of my husband's sister-in-law, and that did me a world of good. A visit from uncle Aindreas was just as successful in distracting the sheriff and Lady Beathag for a whole day. They discovered a host of common interests, one of which was falconry. Aindreas owned a falconry and suggested organising a hunt on his estate, which adjoined Mallaig.

Several days after Darnley's return to the castle, Lady Rosalind tired of his presence and decided to return home. I was upset at her departure, but we left each other with the promise to see each other again regularly.

'Do not be upset, dear Gunelle,' she said. 'I will accompany my husband each time he comes to the castle. I cannot just abandon you, you and all our dear pupils! But for the moment, I need to breathe in air other than that of that detestable constable. I am too old to allow myself to be harassed by such a horrible man.'

'I am really sorry his presence is driving you away,' I said as I kissed her, 'but I understand. I think I would do the same if it were at all possible.'

It was one of those mild spring days when the rays of the sun came to warm you despite the fresh sea breeze. We instinctively looked skywards as we stood in the courtyard to say our goodbyes to my guest, whom Tomas was going to escort. My little Ceit, bareheaded and sleeves rolled up, was running about laughing with the schoolchildren. I loved seeing how she had blossomed in just a few months—no longer hiding, loving to play with the other children, even making friends, and above all, expressing herself with such

290

confidence. Her position as the lord's daughter had certainly contributed to her acceptance by the little Mallaig society, who no longer dared to make fun of her deafness or her looks. As Lady Rosalind and Tomas's party was about to set off, I heard Lady Beathag call to them from the stables.

'Wait for us, Lord Tomas. We are going to travel with you. Sheriff Darnley and I are going to Loch Morar to hunt with the falcons. The weather is ideal! It is going to be a marvellous day.'

Accompanied by two of the sheriff's personal guards, she was running in front of the grooms leading the horses into the courtyard. Just at that moment, he himself came out, dressed like a prince. I could not stop myself from gasping when I saw how outlandish his attire was. *How could he travel with such clothes in his trunk?* I asked myself in astonishment. Lady Beathag was not far behind, elegance without equal. Suddenly I heard her addressing me cheerfully.

'I think you should come, Lady Gunelle. You have never seen the MacNeil lands at Loch Morar. It is a magnificent forest, and Lord Aindreas and his wife would be delighted to have a visit from the chatelaine of Mallaig, would they not, Tomas?'

'I do not know,' I said hesitantly. 'I am going to keep you back. Everyone is ready to leave.'

Not knowing what to do, I looked at Tomas and Lady Rosalind, who seemed to find the invitation quite in order. In addition, the fact that the sheriff was about to visit a part of the estate, which was still unfamiliar to me, made me accept the offer. When Beathag assured me that the party had time to wait for me to get ready, I slipped off and changed as quickly as I could. After all, I really wanted to go riding in this glorious weather, and it seemed the perfect opportunity.

The road to Loch Morar was beautiful, and I rode beside Tomas and Lady Rosalind, who were chatting in Scots with the sheriff. I soon stopped concentrating on how I was sitting in the saddle and so could listen in on their interesting conversation. I learned that the former chatelaine of Mallaig had loved falconry and had even owned a bird which Lord Baltair had given her. On the death of Lady Isla, the falconry had been abandoned since my husband preferred hunting bigger game.

'My cousin,' Tomas explained, 'hates having animals do what he sees as the work of a real hunter. He will not even allow his dog to raise the game. He loves finding his prey himself and watching it for a long time before killing it. He is a redoubtable hunter because he respects the animals he kills.'

After an hour our paths separated and I slipped into the silence of the small group formed by the sheriff, his two men, and Lady Beathag. I continued to take in the scenery. We had left the moor and were moving towards a thick forest with a dominating smell of pine. It was cooler, and the horses dripping with sweat were soon plagued by flies. Lady Beathag was leading the way, following a path which, from time to time, was not very clear. At the end of the morning, we came out into a vast clearing with about ten paths leading off it. Lady Beathag must have ridden there often, for she began to follow one without any hesitation, assuring us that we were not very far from Morar Castle. Iain's uncle's castle was a modest size: a high, wide fortified tower took pride of place in the middle of a walled courtyard. Stables, a washhouse, and outside ovens were the only outbuildings. The interior was well-lit by the natural light coming in through glass windows just below ceiling height. Three large galleries, all with doors facing south south-east, made up the upper floor. Aindreas's wife seemed impressed by my presence and was very attentive, which annoyed Beathag. We had a very quick lunch since the men were impatient to go hunting. I would have preferred to stay with my hostess, but uncle Aindreas was so insistent that I attended the hunt that it would have been impolite to refuse. I joined the hunting party and we set off again on horseback into the heart of the forest. Uncle Aindreas was obviously an avid falconer. He bred several birds and even sold some to other Highland lords. I learned that you could spend two years training a young falcon to hunt—more time than needed to train some young men to be knights. The allusion made me smile. I could not get interested in the intricacies of falconry at which the sheriff and Lady Beathag appeared to excel, and so I stayed behind the party all afternoon. When the sun began to sink, and it was time to think about leaving, the hunters gathered and counted the bag to share it out. Aindreas invited us to supper, but we were apprehensive about returning to Mallaig at night and declined. He retrieved his birds, and we said goodbye in the clearing.

On the return home, the men took the lead, and I stayed behind with Beathag. She seemed tired because there was no talk from her. I noticed she was slowing her horse down so much that the distance between us and the group ahead grew greater. Suddenly without my expecting it, she spurred on her horse and set off at a gallop and disappeared out of sight into the thick wood. My horse, which, since we had left Mallaig, was gently following the group without my having to guide him much, did not have the reflex to set off after Beathag's mount. I did not dare make a move which would unseat me, and I let him carry on at his own pace in what I hoped was the right direction. After quite a while, I noticed that I had lost the trail of my companions. I could not hear their horses, and the forest was getting darker and darker. I stopped my horse and dismounted. It was pointless to continue in a direction which risked being the wrong one, as that would complicate any search to find me. I noticed a mossy rock jutting out slightly and sat down. I let my horse graze around about me as Iain did so often when we were out riding together.

An hour must have passed, an hour of waiting which deepened my fear, before I realised that no one was coming to look for me. *It is not possible!* I brooded nervously. *They cannot simply abandon me here!* Then I remembered the strange look Beathag had given me before galloping off. *She is capable, and she has done it*, I thought suddenly. From that moment on, I was certain that my husband's sister-in-law had hatched this whole plot to abandon me in the wood, and her plan would succeed if I could not find my way, if not all the way back to Mallaig at least to return to Loch Morar. I called my horse. I looked up and noticed that darkness had fallen. I could neither see him nor hear him. I was now completely alone. Anxiety overcame me and crushed my heart. All I could hear was my own heartbeat.

Chapter Twelve
The Forest

L ord Tomas was very fond of his Aunt Rosalind and Uncle Griogair. He had never got to know their three sons very well, but at Mallaig, he had talked to Raonall, the eldest and found him pleasant company. Being about ten years younger than Raonall, he admired his quiet confidence and openness, and he had greatly enjoyed watching the game of seduction between him and Beathag. When they arrived at the castle, his aunt invited him to supper and to stay a while, which he could not refuse. So, he and the Mallaig men spent several pleasant hours relaxing, and they almost accepted the invitation to stay the night. However, his responsibility for Mallaig in his cousin's absence constrained him to return home.

It was well after dark when he left. The full moon was particularly bright and lit up the path which wound along the plateau going down to Mallaig. Not a breath of wind disturbed the greyness which surrounded them. They rode in silence. When they entered the confines of castle in the middle of the night, everything was calm. The guards were at their posts, and an old groom met them to take their horses to the stable. Only too pleased at the prospect of getting to bed soon, the old man did not exchange a single word with the party. The men hurried to the guardroom, briefly bidding Tomas good night, their voices revealing their tiredness. The latter did not go to the stables, so he did not notice that Gunelle's horse was missing. He went straight up to his room without speaking to a living soul. The castle was completely plunged into the quietness of the night, which immediately overcame the young man and sent him off to sleep.

I calmed myself down. I had to think and not panic. Turning in circles, I looked desperately in every direction. The only sound was the rustle of my dress. I could not make out a single path anywhere. I was shivering. Having set off this morning in hot sunshine, I had brought neither a cape nor a hunting jacket. I had nothing with which to light a fire. I looked up to the sky, where the stars were beginning to light up one after the other. I began to hope that the moon would be full and not be veiled by a single cloud. *What must I do? Get my horse back or find a way back to Loch Morar?* I wondered. *Perhaps my horse will be able to go back to its stable on its own. On the other hand, there is no doubt I am closer to uncle Aindreas's castle.*

There was certainly no point trying to call my horse, for I was not familiar enough with him to hope that he would respond to a whistle or a call as Iain's would have done. However, it costs nothing to try, and my cries would signal my presence in the forest. I began to look for the path, all the time calling out in a voice which became stronger the further I went. All kinds of obstacles hindered my movement and ripped my dress. My shoes got caught in the thorns and stones. After a while, I was in a sweat, my heart was thumping, and my hands were cold and scratched from catching hold of the branches, which hit me in the face as I went along. *Where was the damned path?* Suddenly I realised I had missed it and was going deeper into the heart of the forest. I stopped, unable to breathe. I leaned against a tree trunk and tried to listen for sounds. If I could hear the sound of the water of the loch, I could head in a direction likely to bring me on to a path. Nothing. Was it fear? Anxiety? The only sound I heard was my pounding heart. Suddenly the screech of an owl ripped through the air above me. I collapsed at the foot of the tree and began to weep in despair. 'Help, come and save me,' I groaned weakly. 'Someone! Please! Do not leave me here!'

I must have remained in that position of total abandonment for a long time. A cloud of midges had spied me and surrounded me. They were soon attacking my cheeks and my neck, which were wet and salty with tears. I just had to get up and continue my frenzied, erratic walked through branches and foliage. I saw that the moon was full. If I really thought about it, it could help me to head in the right direction. But was it north, south, east, or west of Mallaig? Of Loch Morar? I was incapable of finding the answer. You would have said that my mind was utterly confused by fear. One question came after another. Which animals were about at night? Were they man-eaters? Should I find a place to hide? In terror, I realised I had very little experience of the forest. I had hardly ever been riding there with Iain, who chose rather to take me over the MacNeil property by the moors and the shore during our riding lessons. During my trip through the Grampians last autumn, I had never wandered far from the party, and I had never asked Lieutenant Lennox or the men about life in the forest. In utter disappointment, I had to admit that my complete lack of curiosity about the woods had deprived me of the knowledge I now needed to survive. The only things I could remember in my frenzy were the stories and fables teeming with monsters and villains of the night, which we told each other, tucked up in the warmth of our dormitory in Orleans.

I bit my lips until they bled to stop myself from crying. It was just then I heard the sound of what seemed like breaking branches and snorting coming towards me from quite far away to my left. I froze on the spot and strained my ears. Then I distinctly heard a neighing.

'My horse!' I exclaimed with all my senses on the alert.

I concentrated on the sounds to direct me. The moon, now very white, was lighting up my pathway, and I quite easily avoided the obstacles. I was walking with hardly a sound. I was able to distinguish more and more the sounds which were becoming louder coming from the direction I was heading in. I was making out the sounds of growling mingled with neighing, and the thought suddenly struck me. *There is another animal!* I stopped, speechless. *A fight*, I quickly thought. *Between a horse and another animal. Which animal? A bear, a wolf, a wildcat?*

I began to tremble from head to toe. I had absolutely nothing which would serve as a weapon. Thinking I should have something in my hand, I feverishly looked around for a stick. Instinctively I picked up the first branch I found on the ground. It was absolutely rotten and broke as soon I picked it up. Right away, I saw another, which seemed more solid when I hit it against a rock. The thud of the blow on the rock filled me with anxiety. The sounds of fighting stopped, and a threatening silence closed in on me on every side. Then a long whinny rent the air in two and froze me to the marrow. After a few minutes, I reached the spot from which there now were coming only faint rustlings. I was horror-struck, and it was all I could do not to scream. In a ravine lay my horse, ravaged by several wolves which were still tearing at his neck, now black with blood. His body was writhing in agony. The moonlight filtering through the dense trees lit up his white head. His eyes rolled upwards, wide open and lifeless. His twisted bridle was caught on some branches. In sheer panic, I turned away from the horrific sight and made off into the woods, tightly clutching the branch as my last weapon of defence. I ran, spurred on by the only hope I had—that I would not be chased and that I might find refuge. How far did I run to get away from the carnage? It seemed a long way. Exhaustion hit me when I stopped running, and I began to stumble more and more. I tried to concentrate my mind on what I knew about wolves. *Do they prefer horse flesh or human flesh? Have some of the pack followed me? How can I protect myself? Can I kill them with this stick or with stones? Can they swim? Can they climb trees?*

The last question was the correct one to ask. I remembered that bears climbed trees but not wolves. I started to look for a tree in which I could manage to hide and I saw a larch whose branches I could easily reach. Dropping my stick, I started to climb. My tired legs were heavy and got entangled in my tattered dress.

'Almighty God, help me,' I pleaded softly.

My right hand caught hold of a branch, and I lifted my head to hoist myself up a bit. At the same moment, I heard a growl. Looking down, I saw fangs snapping at the air near my foot which had just reached the next branch. I let out a scream of terror, and something made me climb up several more levels towards the middle of the tree. I reached the main branches to which I clung desperately, all the time screaming non-stop. Down below, part of the pack was gathering, and they were growling incessantly. My fingers grabbed tightly around my support.

Tomas was surprised not to see Gunelle at the morning service, which he attended with only Nellie and Ceit for company. His surprise turned to a vague concern when he was told that the young chatelaine had stayed the night at Loch Morar. Mid-morning, when Beathag came down to breakfast with Sheriff Darnley, and he noticed the strange look she gave him, he knew something had happened at the hunt. When he asked her, the account she gave of the day said nothing about any mishap suffered by any of the people who had taken part in the trip. However, something in Iain's sister-in-law's attitude rang the alarm bells. *Iain would not have left Gunelle on her own at Andreas's!*

Turning to a knight, he announced, 'I am going to fetch Lady Gunelle at Loch Morar. I am taking two men with me, and if we are not back for supper, it means there is a problem. Send reinforcements.'

'Why such a hurry, Tomas dear?' whispered Beathag. 'It is raining. You are not going to make the chatelaine travel in the rain, are you? You are not thinking straight. She is safe with Aindreas and can easily spend another day there. Poor thing, she has so little opportunity to get out…'

It was strange, but on hearing Beathag's comments, he sensed an urgency to act immediately and got up so quickly that he knocked over his stool, hitting Bran's paw.

'My uncle will be delighted to offer me hospitality too. If Lady Gunelle does not want to brave the bad weather, I will bring her back later, and I will send a messenger to let you know,' he replied cuttingly.

He had never ridden as he did that day. He covered the whole distance like the wind, giving no thought to his horse's well-being. His escort had difficulty keeping up. He saw nothing of the forest as they were going through it at this lightning speed. When, on arrival at Loch Morar, he learned that Gunelle had not returned there as Beathag had said, he was livid and let out such a shout of rage that he frightened everyone. With his long, wet hair stuck to his forehead, his eyes burning with rage, his wet clothes dripping on the floor, his voice clipped and almost spitting out the words, this was no longer the same Tomas. Aindreas was shocked. When it dawned on him that the young chatelaine had not returned to Mallaig with the party the night before, he realised the danger she had been in if she spent the night in the woods. Without any hesitation, he offered his men's help in the search Tomas had organised. The party set off from the clearing where the two women had probably separated.

It was a little after midday when the men discovered the remains of Gunelle's mount at the bottom of the ravine but not a trace of the young woman. When they saw the wolves' handiwork, they feared the worst. Tomas could hardly control his panic. The rain had not let up, and every track had been washed out. There was only one way of finding the young woman—put the dog on her scent.

'Bran!' shouted Tomas, and he galloped off under the stunned gaze of Aindreas and his men.

The search continued without success until Tomas came back with the dog, which they took to the bottom of the ravine. Exhausted from so much running, Bran slowly sniffed the horse's carcass. His tail was tight against his hindquarters, the hair on his back was standing on end, and muffled growls filtered out from his turned-up chops. Agitated, his senses on alert, he got the scent of the wolves. Tomas dismounted and took one of Gunelle's shoes from his bag. He grabbed Bran by the scruff of the neck and pulled him away from the carcass, then he gave him the shoe to sniff.

'Bran, sniff! Gunelle! Seek, dog! Seek Gunelle!'

Bran stuck his long muzzle inside the shoe, and his tail began to wag. He gave a short bark as he looked at Tomas, from whom he seemed to be waiting for something. Brokenly pleading, the young man repeated his order to the dog, which grabbed the shoe being held out to him and sat down, still wagging his wet bushy tail. Suddenly a note of despair in Tomas's voice seemed to be what set the dog off. To the relief of everyone there, Bran dropped the shoe and, muzzle to the ground, began a frantic search of the wood. He found her scent at the top of the ravine and followed it for about three hundred yards, straight to the larch in which the young woman was perched. It was then they saw her, looking totally lost and totally distraught. Tomas, who was completely beside himself, had the greatest difficulty persuading her come down from her refuge. She did not answer to her name, did not recognise anyone, and grabbed hold of every branch as he helped her down. She opened her mouth to utter cries which did not come. Her face was covered with bites, her hair full of twigs and sticky with resin, her hands covered in scratches and her black eyes as if she were looking upon a never-ending horrible spectacle. When she reached the ground and Bran came to lick her, she uttered such a piercing shriek that everyone stepped back. Tomas realised instinctively that when she looked at Bran, she saw a wolf, and he asked the guard to take the animal away out of her sight. He took her in her arms and shielded her face. He choked on words of comfort which would not come.

Aindreas suggested to Tomas that they take her back to Loch Morar but received a prompt and categorical refusal which offended him. Tomas was adamant. He had his horse unsaddled and wrapped Gunelle in a large cape which slightly calmed the rigors of terror which were shaking her. Then he mounted his horse and took the trembling young woman in front of him, holding her close as he had seen his cousin do. The journey home was spent in silence, at a snail's pace and in constant rain. Iain's angry face haunted Tomas. 'I have failed,' he repeated over and over. 'I no longer deserve his trust.'

On leaving Crathes Castle, Lieutenant Lennox was watching Iain MacNeil out of the corner of his eye as he rode beside him. He had to admit that the young clan chief impressed him. The way he had conducted his business in Scots with Nathaniel Keith showed a maturity which had surprised him. When Iain MacNeil had turned up with a small company of men on Ben Braenach on the Grampian felling site a week earlier, just like any lord visiting his property, Lennox had immediately felt reassured. Even if Iain MacNeil's laconic reply to his master's letter complaining about the attacks on the site led them to believe that the MacNeils did not intend to provide protection, the very presence of the chief on this part of his estate and so soon after the siege showed his willingness to respect the contract. In his discussions with the young chief, Lennox had discovered that the contract did not apply to the banks of the river Dee, by which the cut timber was taken to Aberdeen. The slopes of Ben Braenach overlooking the Dee belonged to the MacPherson clan, who did not want to give a right of way to the Keith workmen. This revelation seemed to reassure Iain MacNeil, who had thought that it was the Camerons who were threatening the site. The crux of the dispute lay in a misunderstanding of the boundaries of the MacNeil land in the Grampians. The wood was indeed cut in accordance with the felling rights given by the MacNeils, but it remained blocked at the site if they could not cross the southern slopes of the mountains. Maps of this part of Scotland were non-existent, so you had to take the word of the various clans who owned the land in the Grampians. The two men had quickly concluded that the situation had to be explained to Lord Keith, who would probably have to come to some agreement with the clan MacPherson.

At Crathes, it was not quite as simple as that. As an opinionated businessman, Nathaniel Keith held it against the late Baltair MacNeil that he had not indicated the exact boundaries of the land subject to the felling rights, thereby leaving him ignorant of the fact that it did not include the southern slopes. Never was a son-in-law received in such a cavalier fashion by his father-in-law. The whole Keith household was mortified in the face of the flagrant lack of manners shown by their master. Even Gunelle's mother, already ill-disposed to her son-in-law, through the good offices of Daren and young Vivian, had to admit that her husband showed a shameful lack of respect. The young Lord MacNeil had already figured out his father-in-law and was prepared for a cool reception at Crathes. He would much rather have met his in-laws with his wife, and he missed her a lot. At the end of the first discussions, Lieutenant Lennox was forced to admire Iain MacNeil's coolness in the face of the barely veiled insults coming from Lord Keith. For the two days of his visit, Iain kept his composure and maintained a keen analytical approach, thus making him an adversary equal to the task of doing business with his merciless father-in-law. Iain decided not to mention the fact that not a single payment for the felling rights had reached Mallaig when the contract stipulated that the first payment should be made following the marriage. The MacNeils were not hard up, and the castle was managing even after having lived through the siege. Iain was proud of that, so it was out of pride that he chose to keep quiet about this failure. The young man got nowhere with his father-in-law, who insisted on having his wood go by the south when the MacNeils owned the northern slopes, culminating in a river flowing into the North Sea. He ended up proposing that he himself would negotiate with the MacPhersons for the right of way for his father-in-law's wood, but there was nothing doing and the discussion ended abruptly.

'MacNeil, we will come to a better agreement with the Lowland lords,' replied Gunelle's father. 'Be content with protecting your lands during the felling. The wood is costing more than was agreed. So, rest assured, I will not lose a single day's work because my men have to wield the crossbow rather than the axe.'

Although very unpleasant, the visit to Crathes had been fruitful for Iain. It had allowed him to satisfy much of his curiosity about his wife's family, of whom he had only met Daren. He was just as pleased to be able to take fresh news to Gunelle since her mother had entrusted him with some letters. In addition, the journey with Lieutenant Lennox had brought him closer to this man whose dignity and sense of justice he admired. They were travelling together again, he to Mallaig and Lennox to the worksite. Their conversations were conducted in Scots.

'We heard about the attack on Mallaig, my lord,' said the lieutenant. 'The village was destroyed, I believe, but you did not lose as many men as the Camerons, as far as it is reported.'

'That is true,' answered Iain. 'It was a mistake for Cameron to try to take Mallaig. I think he wanted to weaken us enough to negotiate the retrieval of his forests, and he almost succeeded.'

'I did not know that you had come to the point of surrendering.'

'We did not. I agreed to negotiate to put an end to what had become mere butchery and to spare the men who were left... on the advice of a certain chatelaine.'

Lennox turned to him and caught a glimpse of an enigmatic smile. In the silence which followed this revelation, the lieutenant realised that Iain MacNeil's feelings for his wife had to be very strong for them to have played a part in a conflict he was conducting.

'I see, my lord,' continued Lennox. 'There comes a time when it is pointless having a great battle plan. Neither camp has anything to gain. The attack by the Camerons was a waste of time. Do you think he will stay away from the site from now on?'

'I cannot be sure. So, I am going to leave one of my men to patrol the west and northern flanks of Braenach. Lennox, it goes without saying that if you are troubled by any clan at all on our lands, you can appeal to me, and it will soon be sorted out. I consider the security in the Grampians as an integral part of my part of the contract.'

'Thank you very much, my lord. However, I am afraid that Lord Keith will withhold the second payment of the felling rights as long as he has not succeeded in getting the timber to Aberdeen.'

When he heard this, Iain turned around in the saddle. He stared at Lennox, and looking intrigued, he asked calmly, 'Did you talk about the second instalment, a moment ago, Mister Lennox?'

This time, it was Lennox who looked in utter surprise at the young lord. He carefully chose his words before expressing the doubt the question had raised in his mind.

'My lord, are you trying to tell me that you did not receive the first payment Lord Keith sent in January after Lady Gunelle's marriage to you?'

'Do you know who delivered it?'

'I took it as far as the site, and then three other men delivered it to Mallaig. It was a small white leather casket with lead mountings. Besides the bag containing the payment, there were letters addressed to Lady Gunelle from her mother, her sisters, and Vivian. There was also a gold cross given to her as a wedding gift by her uncle, John Carmichael.'

Deep in thought about the questions this revelation raised, the two men remained silent for a long time. Lennox became uneasy. Was he to believe the casket had been stolen without the Keith family's knowledge? How was that possible? He had recently seen the men who had been given the task of delivering it to Mallaig, and if they had stolen it, they certainly would not be still in the family's employment. He then heard his companion make a strange statement.

'I do not regret the loss of the money so much as the loss of news from Crathes for my wife. She missed her family very much. Those letters would have given her great joy at a time when she had none.'

'This casket must be found, my lord. Your father-in-law's integrity is in question. I know he paid that instalment in keeping with the contract. What happened to it? You and I both need to know.'

'We will, Lennox. Believe me, we will finish up finding out.'

The investigation would have to wait. As they were beginning to climb Braenach, they were met by a messenger coming from the site. He was bringing news of the wolves' attack on the chatelaine in the forest. Iain hardly found out anything from the messenger, who had no details of what had happened. The event had been recounted by a man sent from Morar. The young Lord was seething, torn between helpless rage and the torture of not knowing. He left Lieutenant Lennox and his guard and set off on his own after a hasty goodbye. Iain MacNeil had become a man of action again, a warrior. Lieutenant Lennox watched him galloping off into the distance in a cloud of dust. A sharp pain pierced his heart. His precious protégée attacked by wolves? What had happened?

During the early days of my return to the castle, when I would wake from one of my all too short sleeps, I could, just for a few minutes, sort out my thoughts. I gradually understood which room I was in. Lord Baltair's! Then one day, I recognised Nellie's voice but not the old woman who was speaking. Another time, through the half-open door, I glimpsed a little red-haired girl who was watching me and crying and calling me 'mother,' but not a sound left my mouth in response to her call. Those moments of lucidity eased my heaviness of heart for a short while and loosened the knot in my stomach.

Alas, they were all too brief, and I would always drift back, fully awake, into my nightmare until the moment exhaustion finally overcame me. It was only then that sleep put a stop to my terrifying thoughts and ended my torment. My nostrils were no longer filled with the smell of my horse's blood; I no longer heard the growls of the wolves rumbling in my ears; I no longer saw the yellow fangs snapping at my ankles. When I woke up in the middle of the night, my heart would sink as soon as I opened my eyes. The darkness intensified tenfold the fear which occupied my whole being. I think that the people who were keeping watch over me understood that, for one night, they lit a multitude of candles around the bed, bathing it in a large ochre halo. Arms which cradled me in my agitation held me so that I could see the bright light. I tried to focus on it for as long as possible before the gulf would reappear before my eyes and the tears flowed once more. From then on, they made sure that the room was never in darkness when night fell.

I had stopped calling out. As no sound left my mouth, it was pointless exhaling the air so forcefully from my lungs and risk being unable to breathe afterwards. I had stopped crying too. There must have been no tears left. My moments of consciousness became longer and longer. I think that those looking after me saw signs of an improvement in these changes. A man was forbidding them to mention the word 'madness' in the room. I think it was a priest, for on one occasion, he was wearing a wooden cross on the leather cord around his neck, and he blessed me before I left for the abyss again. When I came out of it, my fingers were tightly clutching a wooden cross now free of its cord. They left it with me. The contact with the roughness of the wood sometimes made me hit it against a hard surface. They would take it from me and return it to me after I came back from yet another absence.

Sometimes at midday, a young man called Tomas would bring me some cut flowers. He would silently place them by my bed, being content to bow, his hand on his chest. He never stayed long. His gentle, pain-filled eyes never met mine. I would dearly have loved to speak on those occasions. I would close my eyes and put my hands over my ears, fearing that the sight of an object or the sound of a single word would thrust me back into my nightmare. It took so little to send me off again. I tried with all my strength to remain motionless, present, and simply there.

The night was pitch black. A salty, constant breeze was sweeping the ramparts and driving away the thick clouds which veiled the moon and stars. Like a drum roll in the distance, the muffled sound of the sea breaking against the rocks to the east was the sign that the tide was rising. Tomas had begun keeping watch from the north turret as soon as night fell. He wanted to be the first to speak to his cousin on his return. He knew his uncle Aindreas had sent a messenger to the felling site. Unless he was still delayed at Crathes, Iain should be back in the Grampians by now. *Oh, that I could be free*, he thought. *The guilt is too heavy to bear. Iain, come home. Everyone at Mallaig is waiting for you.*

As was the case for several days now, he again pictured Beathag fleeing every time anyone spoke of his cousin's return. He heard the obvious note of anxiety every morning when she asked for news of the chatelaine, whose recovery she seemed to fear more than she hoped for. No doubt about it, Beathag was acting like someone who was dreading something. What? Tomas would have paid a lot of money to find out.

When Iain dismounted, the courtyard was already full of people, all strangely quiet. Everywhere, on each face, the same anxious and distressed look. His cousin, Tomas rushed over, his arms by his side and his head bowed. He was at a loss as to what to say but confessed his failure in deep contrition.

'Iain, I failed in my duty. You had entrusted her to my care, but your wife was not in my care when she left the castle. I am responsible for her misfortune and am no longer worthy of your trust.'

'She is still alive then!' said Iain as he pulled his cousin to his feet. 'Where is she? I want to see her.'

Father Henriot came over and, taking his young master's arm, led him towards the keep as he, with calmness and gravity, described the young chatelaine's condition. The priest's explanations slowed down Iain's rush to be near Gunelle. He listened attentively. A vice tightened around his heart as the word madness became clear in his mind to explain the behaviour the priest was describing. The latter ended his report, affirming that according to him and Doctor MacDuff, who had examined the chatelaine, it was rather a state of shock which would pass with time.

'My lord, I have formally forbidden anyone to speak of madness or demon possession. Your wife is not possessed. I affirm that before God,' added the grave looking Henriot.

Iain shook his hand vigorously. The whole group around the young lord had gone into the great hall. The fire lit during the evening was still crackling in the hearth and Iain sat down in front of it. Suddenly,

310

Bran burst in and threw himself against his master, who took his head in his hands. Iain, his features drawn and looking preoccupied, looked up at those gathered and asked Tomas to come over beside him. Quietly he asked the young man about the circumstances surrounding the tragedy, and he was not quite satisfied with the account given.

'Do not hide anything from me, Tomas,' he said. 'Something in your account is not quite convincing. What is it?'

'Listen, Iain, I do not know. I cannot believe what your sister-in-law says. That Gunelle should decide to return to Loch Morar alone is very unlikely. She is not an experienced enough horsewoman, and, more importantly, she does not know the way to your uncle's estate well enough for her to decide to backtrack without an escort. You can question Beathag tomorrow. You will get more out of her than me.' Shaking his head, he added, 'Nevertheless, the fact remains. I should never have let the chatelaine of Mallaig go hunting without a bodyguard.'

'Darnley's men were more than enough for that kind of excursion, Tomas. What was there for you to fear? They were not to know about Gunelle's inexperience. They could not oppose her returning to Loch Morar on her own.' After a brief silence, he let out a shout and shook his head. 'Good grief! That traitor, Aindreas! That is the last place to send my kin!'

'That is exactly what I am guilty of, Iain. If Gunelle wanted to take part in a falcon hunt with Aindreas, I should have been at her side, for I know the threat he is.'

Iain MacNeil no longer had the heart for conversation. Despite his tiredness and anxiety, he did not want to sleep that night and stayed in the great hall. Anna came to tell him what was happening in the castle, gave him news of little Ceit, and informed him that Lady Rosalind, who had come to visit the chatelaine, had decided to stay to help the priest with the education of the children. She ended her report by suggesting he wait till the next day to see his wife as she would have woken out of her nightmare. Before taking leave of her master, the old housekeeper could not help stroking his head which was black with dust and sweat.

'Why does such misfortune dog our chatelaine?' she groaned. 'She is so good and has great faith in God. Could He not protect her better?'

'My dear Anna, alas, it is up to me to protect my wife. God gave her to me, and I did not deserve her. That is all there is to it...' Iain murmured as he grasped his nurse's hand.

'Do not say that, my lord! You deserve her. If ever there was a Highlander made for her, it is you, a MacNeil!'

Iain smiled weakly. As he watched her leave, he noticed how stooped she was becoming. *The problem is*, he thought, *that Gunelle Keith is not made for the Highlands or a Highlander.*

The next day when Nellie and little Ceit came out their bedroom, she was astonished not to find Bran lying outside her mistress's door as he had been in the habit of doing since her return. *What kind of night had they had?* she wondered, thinking of Lady Gunelle and Mairi, who sat with her each night. As she did every morning, she went down to the kitchen to have a bite to eat before relieving the young servant at the patient's bedside. Nellie was exhausted from the growing number of sleepless nights and all the pain and concern she had for her mistress. Suddenly she heard a shout of joy from Ceit, who had run ahead of her into the great hall. She heaved a sigh of relief and relaxed her shoulders when she entered: Lord Iain had finally come home.

Ceit had thrown herself at her father when she discovered him stretched out on a bench near the fire at the far end of the room. She was stroking his bearded face, kissing his hands, and laughing.

Iain sat up and hugged her. 'Good morning, my daughter. You are very happy this morning. One would say you missed your father.'

Her smile disappeared. 'Father, it is terrible,' she replied. 'The wolves took mother's voice in the forest. You must go and kill them! Today! If you do not, she will not be able to talk to me ever again. I want her to speak to me again, to sing, and come to class again. Oh, father! You are the greatest knight of all. Tell me you can kill those wolves.'

'I will kill every wolf in Scotland if I must, my dear. I want her to talk to me too. Do not think about it anymore, and come, have some some oatcakes with me.'

When he noticed Nellie standing at the door smiling as she watched them, he was taken aback. His wife's nurse seemed to have aged ten years. Under her headdress, her hair, already grey, was completely white. Her face was thinner and furrowed with deep wrinkles. He greeted her briefly and hurried to the kitchens, holding his daughter's hand. There was real apprehension in his heart. He put off his visit to Gunelle for as long as possible. He went to the service, had a bath and a shave, looked over the garden with Anna and young Jenny, went to class with Ceit, and spent a moment with Tomas and the knights in the guardroom, but he avoided his sister-in-law. He did not feel ready to question her. He barely greeted Darnley when he saw him on his way back to the keep. He went up on the ramparts and inspected all the sentry posts. With his hair blowing in the wind, he spent a long time on his own just watching the sea. A host of memories with Gunelle flooded back to him and upset him. His dog brought him out of his dream by licking his hand.

Good grief, he said to himself. She is not dead. Come on. It is time to go and face the wolves.

He hesitated for a second before opening the bedroom door. When Nellie saw him come in, she looked at him despairingly.

'She has not come out of it yet this morning, my lord. I mean, she is not conscious, but she is not agitated. Mairi said she had a calm night.'

Iain glanced at the bed. His wife, wearing a light night dress and with her hair in two long plaits, had her back to him. She was curled up in a ball and clinging to the bedpost.

Intrigued, he asked Nellie, 'Where are the curtains?'

'She ripped them off by clinging to them. We had to take them down. She clings to anything she can find. My lord, she must come out of this nightmare. It is bad for the child,' she replied as she wrung her hands.

'What child are you talking about, Nellie?' he asked eagerly.

'I do not think I am mistaken, my lord. I know the Keith girls well and am certain my mistress is pregnant even if she does not know it herself. And the child will not be normal if it grows in the womb of such a tormented soul.'

In astonishment, Iain stared at Nellie, who had stopped talking with embarrassment. After a long moment, he turned towards his wife and, with a lump in his throat, gently spoke her name. Gunelle did not turn a hair. He carefully moved forward and went around the bed to face her. He was struck by her deathly colour and those wild eyes scouring the floor at his feet. He glanced at Nellie, who was watching anxiously.

'She is always examining the floor like that, my lord. It is as if it is seething with snakes,' she explained nervously.

'Not snakes, Nellie,' he murmured, turning his attention back to Gunelle. 'But wolves.'

He went closer and held his hands out towards Gunelle's white arms, which were entwined around the bedpost. He slowly stroked them and then began to open her fingers, rigid with fear, one by one. As he did so, he spoke to her in a very gentle but sad voice.

'Gunelle, my beloved, it is me. I am here. Do not be afraid. It is all over.'

With a lot of perseverance, for she continually resisted his movements, he managed to free her from the bedpost without her having looked at him once. Her eyes were still glued to the floor. He bent down so as to be in her field of vision, all the time holding her two hands firmly. He caught her eye and spoke to her again, trying to coax her.

'My love, come back. I beg you, come back.'

Nellie shuddered. The scene she was watching filled her heart with hope. She saw her mistress react to such a call for the first time. In fact, Gunelle was screwing up her eyes and examining her husband's hands as he held hers. Then her breathing quickened and became noisy. She looked into her husband's face and hoarsely pronounced his name.

Nellie crossed herself. 'Almighty God, she is speaking! She recognises you, my lord. It is a miracle!' Then she hurried out of the room, leaving the couple on their own.

Suddenly, I felt the branches scratching my arms. Down below, the wolves were silent. No matter how hard I looked, I could not see them anywhere. The tree was moving to free itself from my grasp. *I am going to fall*, I thought. But it was strange; I was not falling. Suddenly I saw my own hands, then two others. *How is that possible?* I said to myself. Then I distinctly heard a whisper. *Someone! At last!* A white flash of light blinded me, and I came out of the abyss.

'Iain!'

I had spoken his name with a voice I did not recognise. My husband was there. He was holding my cold hands and calling me 'my beloved.' He was looking at me with his blue pleading eyes. A drum roll was beating in my head. I forced myself to focus my attention on Iain's eyes and begged heaven to keep me here a little while before sending me back to the abyss. With every ounce of strength in me, I wanted to stay with my husband, who was pleading with me to come back. I freed one of my hands and moved it over his tense face, and I knew I was safe with him: His skin was clammy, smelt of shaving soap, his lips trembled slightly, and he was holding his breath. I leaned my head on his outstretched arm and he tensed up.

'They are going to come back, Iain. We must not climb down out of this tree. They are dangerous. They killed my horse. They are wolves, Iain. The wolves Beathag set on me.'

'Where is Beathag now?' I heard him ask me as if there was an echo.

'She went galloping off to join the others and left me. They are not coming to look from me, Iain. I should have tied up my horse,' I answered, gasping for breath, without taking my eyes off him.

'And what about Loch Morar? Why should you want to go back there?'

'It is closer to here, but I would prefer to find a way back to Mallaig. What direction is it in? I have no idea.'

To my astonishment, I felt the tears flow down my cheeks. Iain took my face in his broad hands and, without a word, began to gently wipe away each new tear with his thumbs. I looked over his head and recognised the décor. All I could hear was our breathing. I was not wallowing in my abyss. I stayed close to my husband, whom I had found again. I closed my eyes, leaned against him, and welcomed my feelings as they returned one by one: first the weight of my hair on my back, my hands opening flat on his wool tunic, my shoulders tightly enclosed by his arms, the warm scent of his body, his tender voice which continued to wrap me in endless declarations of love. By now, I was sobbing, shaken by long bouts of hiccups.

'Cry, cry, my love. The terror will leave as soon as your heart is empty. I heard him saying in the same whispering voice.

I was rocking back and forth in his arms when he lay back on the bed and cradled me in the hollow of his shoulder. The vice of terror loosened its grip, and a soothing calm swept through me. I think we stayed motionless like that for hours. I was vaguely conscious of people entering and leaving the room one after the other. Neither Iain nor I took any notice.

'Do not leave, Iain,' I would say to him from time to time.

'I am staying, and I am holding you, my beloved,' he invariably replied.

I soon began to fight against sleep, afraid of plunging into my nightmare again. Physically drained, I begged him to help me stay awake. On the contrary, he enjoined me to sleep. Assuring me that there was nothing to fear, he promised to watch over me as I slept.

'My love, you must let yourself go to sleep. You need it. When you awaken in a while, I will still be there. We will dine together, and we will drink the last bottle of wine from your father's cellar. Then we will read the post from Crathes, and you will reply. Then we will go downstairs and listen to the clarsach. If you want, I will sing with you, or you will sing for me. We will do all that but only if you are rested.'

I smiled; my nose pressed into his neck. That was just like Iain with his one thousand and one plans. How good it was to feel completely lucid again! *I am healed*, I thought joyfully. I could not resist the desire to sleep in the comfort of my husband's arms. I dozed off, completely enveloped in him.

The first thing I saw on opening my eyes was Ceit's puzzled, little face. With her chin resting on the mattress, she was looking me up and down. A strong smell of barley soup filled the air. I took a deep breath and smiled at my daughter.

318

My daughter, I thought. I had the feeling I was coming back from a very long journey. I raised myself up on one elbow and saw Iain sitting at the foot of the bed with a pewter bowl in his hand. He turned around and smiled.

'I apologize, my lady. I was too hungry. I did not wait for you. How are you feeling?'

'Well enough to undertake the programme you proposed a while ago,' I replied, delighted to see his white teeth and big broad smile.

'Mother!' shouted Ceit, jumping to her feet. 'Your voice is back. I knew that father would do it.'

Iain interrupted her immediately rather sternly. 'Ceit! We said that we were not to talk about it. Remember, daughter!'

Seeing the tears well up in her little eyes and the dimples appear in her pink cheeks, I held out my arms to her and drew her close to me in the bed.

'My lord,' I said softly to Iain, 'be indulgent with our daughter. She missed me as much as you did.' Seeing him look down, I added, 'Iain, do you not know that I love you?'

'I know, but it comes as news every time you tell me, 'He replied huskily. 'You have no idea what power those words have over me when they are spoken by you.'

I held out my hand, and he squeezed my fingers. For a long time, he contemplated the picture we presented, our daughter and I cuddling up together, and he heaved a strange sigh. So many emotions were coming and going within us, like the untiring movements of the tide.

There was a procession of joyful, tear-stained faces through the room in the moments following my awakening. Aunt Rosalind, Nellie, Anna, Father Henriot, Tomas, Mairi, and Jenny came to visit me. Fortunately, Beathag, her companion, and the sheriff did not appear. On Tomas's advice, Iain had given orders to that effect and warned me so that I would not worry needlessly about it. The bottle of wine Iain had promised was shared in as many glasses as there were visitors. Nellie set a little table where I sat down after she had helped me put on a dress. Iain refused to have my hair put up under a veil and he sat beside me, with Ceit on his knees. I was surprised to heartily eat everything Nellie and Anna offered me. Later the clarsach player joined us, and we all agreed to stay in the bedroom. My voice, which still was not very strong, was supported by the combined voices of the others and the songs followed one after the other, joyful, and hearty, until nightfall. Casting a worried look towards the windows, I noticed them gradually getting darker with the approach of dreaded nightfall. Iain must have suspected my growing fears, for, at one point, he took my hand, whispered in my ear, and offered me a drink of whisky from his cup.

'You would give me great pleasure, my lady, if you shared some of the water of life with me. I do not know of a better drink with which to start the night when one does not want to sleep.'

I would have done anything he asked me to do, such was my trust in him that evening. I took the cup he was holding out to me and took several mouthfuls, my eyes gazing into his. Not one wolf came to haunt me. Later, I was barely aware of my visitors leaving or when I went to bed.

Lord Iain helped Nellie to put his wife to bed and stayed for a long time in the room, looking thoughtful and preoccupied as he watched her sleep. Nellie was coming and going, picking up and tidying. The master had asked her to stay by Lady Gunelle's side during the first part of the night. She watched him furtively as she tried to work out the reason for the worried look on his furrowed brow. He did not seem to have been swept along by the general euphoria which had spread through the castle on the announcement of the chatelaine's recovery, and she would really have liked to know why. Did he fear a relapse? Was he afraid for the health of the expected child? Not knowing what to dread, she too began to worry again.

Iain could not put off his meeting with his sister-in-law any longer. If, as he supposed, she had deliberately abandoned Gunelle in the forest and planned it so that there would be no help or rescue, he must consider her as a deadly enemy, whether she was conscious or not of the power her jealousy had over her. He noticed that he was clenching his fists as to almost break his fingers as he went downstairs to the great hall. Several knights were still at the table and were playing dice amidst a great deal of laughter. They turned around when they heard Bran's paws sliding across the flagged floor and animatedly greeted their chief. Iain smiled and greeted them as he went over to them, clapping several on the back as he passed. Then he headed for the far end of the room towards a circle of armchairs where Tomas and the sheriff were sitting.

'Good evening, Darnley,' he said in Scots. 'I see my sister-in-law has abandoned you. Fortunately, we have Tomas. He is a very good stand-in for me as a host at Mallaig.' Taking a chair, he went on, 'If you have no objections, I would like to know your version of the events which caused my wife such a great trauma. According to you, how did it happen?'

'Your sister-in-law would be of most help. She was the last one with Lady Gunelle, my lord,' he answered calmly.

'I know that. I will hear her version. But yours interests me.'

James Darnley had nowhere to hide. He fidgeted about in his chair. Without being able to explain it, he was overcome by a certain nervousness as he related the events from the start of the hunt. From time to time, he caught the two cousins looking at one another, but neither of them commented; both listened with intense concentration. When he had concluded his account, he was struck by the hardness of the look on the young chief's face and felt obliged to justify his behaviour.

'I confess that Lady Beathag's desperation to leave the forest seemed suspicious at the time. When she galloped up and passed us without slowing down to give us even the briefest explanation for your wife's absence, I hesitated and turned around to see if your wife was in sight. Now that I know she did not find her way back to Loch Morar, I reproach myself for not having offered one of my men to escort her. But your sister-in-law spoke as if she herself had accompanied her. You see, MacNeil, it is just an unfortunate accident.'

'Thank you, Darnley,' interrupted Iain as he quickly stood up. 'It is indeed unfortunate. Now, let us see if it was an accident.'

'Hold on, MacNeil!' said the sheriff, who stood up and grabbed Iain's arm. 'I know that the circumstances surrounding it may give rise to suspicions about your sister-in-law. She is a woman of a rather lively temperament who does not hide her feelings, but I do not think she is so blinded by jealousy that she would commit an act of such—'

'Listen to me carefully, Darnley,' replied Iain as he broke free. 'You are here to examine books. I am the one who judges affairs at Mallaig. If I esteem that my wife is the target of someone in the castle, it is an intolerable situation which I will deal with my way, whether it pleases you or not.'

Iain MacNeil did not see the look of scorn on Darnley's face because he had turned away so quickly. He left the room which had suddenly become silent. The final words and the anger of the chief warned of a formidable storm approaching. Tomas signalled discreetly to a knight who caught up with him and they both climbed the stairs behind the master of Mallaig. When Beathag saw Lord Iain come into her room and signal to Finella to leave she put on a broad smile and got up to meet him.

'It has been a very long time since I saw you on your own,' she said as soon as the door closed behind her companion. 'I see your wife is not up to having you.'

She was about to put her plump arms around her brother-in-law's waist when she received a terrific slap in the face. She jumped backwards, her hand on her jaw, her eyes wide open in shock. Her brother-in-law grabbed her by the shoulders and threw her against a chair.

'Sit down and do not dare lay a finger on me,' he spat at her. 'I have come to hear your confession, you viper, and I do not intend to stay here forever. Tell me what happened between you and Gunelle in the forest before you left her.'

'You already know,' she hissed between her teeth. 'Tomas told you. It is pointless threatening me. That is all you are going to get.'

Beside himself with rage, Iain grabbed the necklace hanging around his sister-in-law's white chest and wound it around his clenched fist.

'We'll see about that,' he whispered.

Without paying attention to his sister-in-law's hands which were trying to free herself, he slowly turned his fist.

'That's enough,' she choked immediately.

Iain let her go, and she rubbed her neck where the chain had left its mark on her skin. Regaining her composure, she concealed her hatred with a look of enticement.

'What do you want to hear, my lord?' she whispered, now lowering her eyes.

Iain sat down on a stool facing her and stared at her for a moment, his look icy cold. 'The words exchanged between you and my wife before you left her to re-join Darnley's group.'

'There was not a single word spoken, my lord. We did not talk to one another. I thought she did not want to return to Mallaig in the dark and preferred the hospitality offered by uncle Aindreas. I left her do what she thought best.'

'Lies! She preferred to come back to Mallaig.'

Lady Beathag smiled at her brother-in-law, a slight gleam of scorn in her eyes. 'Ah, I see, our chatelaine has found her voice again, my lord. How can you believe the claims of a person as demented as your wife? Does she even remember going to the hunt that day? Be careful about the accusation you might be tempted to make based on such a doubtful testimony. You cannot make wild accusations without proof. Darnley would not permit it...'

White with rage, Iain jumped to his feet. 'Let the devil take him if he even lifts a finger. He is certainly the last man to prevent me from dealing with affairs in my castle my way!' Walking towards the door he said, 'You are confined to this room until high tide when you will return to your island. Your things will be sent with your companion on another sailing.' Turning towards her, he continued, 'Never come back to Mallaig, Beathag, for it would be the last piece soil you would set foot on.'

Iain went out and banged the door behind him. In the corridor he noticed Tomas and a knight standing guard, weapons at the ready. He gave his cousin this brief order, 'Watch that door! My sister-in-law must neither leave nor can she receive anyone. And that is until I come and fetch her myself to take her to the harbour tomorrow. Is that clear?'

'It is,' replied Tomas promptly. At that same moment, through the door, the three men distinctly heard Beathag threaten her brother-in-law in a voice sharpened by anger.

'You bastard MacNeil! You will pay for this!'

Chapter Thirteen
The Tournament

Nellie was pleased to see the young lord return to the bedroom. He seemed calmer and gave her a smile as he took over from her. Her mistress had not wakened. Having wished her master a good night and advising him to leave several candles burning near the bed, she heaved a sigh of relief as she closed the door behind her. Iain undressed, washed his face and hands in a bowl of water, and gently slipped into bed, taking care not to waken his sleeping wife. It took him a long time to fall asleep. Beathag's expulsion from Mallaig would turn over a new page in the saga, which was his life, the conflict with his mother being the backdrop. A new life was going to take root in the castle: the child Gunelle was carrying. Would it be a son or a daughter? Was his wife strong enough to go full term? Would the child live? And above all would Gunelle survive childbirth? The torturing questions haunted him and dampened the joy which the imminent arrival of an heir brought him. His last thoughts were about the theft of his father-in-law's payment, but the suspicions which were beginning to arise in his mind faded in his sleep.

I turned my sleepy head sideways and touched his warm shoulder. I woke up. Daylight was filtering through the shutters. Two candles were burning away at the foot of the bed. My husband, only half covered, was breathing slowly, his tanned face and dimpled cheeks marked by a smile as he slept. Despite slight nausea, I felt full of joy. *I had slept the whole night without a single nightmare*, I thought

326

in amazement. I sat up and watched Iain emerge from his sleep. He opened his eyes, looked at me, and gave me a radiant smile. I stroked his face, my fingers brushed against his stubble, and I whispered my thanks for not having abandoned me to my madness. He sat up, put his arms around me, and pulled back on to his hairy chest.

'Gunelle, my love, you have never been mad,' he said seriously. 'You lived through some horrible moments, and in your condition, that could only lead to deep distress.'

'What are you referring to, my lord?' I asked, intrigued, without turning to look at him.

'The condition of a pregnant woman, my hind,' he said, putting his nose in my hair and tightening his hug.

'Who told you that? Nellie?' I eagerly asked. I turned towards him and looked him straight in the eyes.

'Nellie... and your body. I have never seen such full breasts, my lady,' he said as he caressed them hesitantly.

'Iain,' I cried, 'how is that possible already?'

By way of an answer, he stretched me out beside him and gave me a mischievous smile before beginning a complete exploration of my tingling body with his lips. I clung to his muscular shoulders and received him with exquisite pleasure, all the time hoping that Nellie would not come into the bedroom.

By the time she appeared Iain had left. He asked me to stay in the room until he came back. He had to go to the harbour to see to his sister-in-law's departure. He had been very clear in his explanations on the subject and I made no comment, preferring to think of anything but Beathag, and particularly her role in my nightmare although I was not quite sure what exactly that was. Nellie, her usual quiet self, started preparing the bath. I looked at her out of the corner of my eye and noticed how she had aged. I was moved to the point of tears. *Ah, Nellie, how you must have worried about me in recent days*, I thought.

'We will have to put the drapes back on this bed, Nellie,' I said to her after a moment. 'And cover a cradle with the same fabric. Since you are bound to know, tell me when I shall have this child my husband has just announced.'

By bringing up the question, I could not have made her more pleased. She quickly came and sat down beside me. With a laugh and a look of relief, she grasped my hands. I could see in her eyes the great joy she felt in her heart.

'My lovely, this child could well take the focus off the baby Jesus. According to my calculations, you will give birth around Christmas. You will see, it will be as beautiful a child as has ever been seen in the Highlands! A boy to succeed the master when the time comes or a little sister for Ceit… this castle is entering a period of perfect happiness. I am sure of that.'

I smiled at her overflowing enthusiasm and rediscovered my old nurse, always resolutely optimistic. A little later, Aunt Rosalind brought me my lunch. My chat with her put me completely at ease. Her calm assurance and her friendliness comforted me. We made no reference to my illness and quite naturally talked of my pregnancy. I was struck by her affection and interest, and I remembered she had neither daughter nor daughter-in-law. *I think she and my mother would get on very well, I thought. For my part, I was very tempted to adopt her as my confidante.*

Iain came back a little before midday. He smelled of the sea, and his hair hung tangled on his shoulders. He looked distracted and came and sat down beside me while examining what was left on my tray. 'You have had a feast, my lady! I am pleased. You must always eat well if you want to give me a big strong MacNeil boy.'

'Or a MacNeil girl,' I corrected him gently while stroking his hair which I began to untangle. I guessed he had had problems with his sister-in-law, and I wanted to take his mind off it. 'Did you not speak to me yesterday about post from Crathes, my lord?'

'Indeed, you are right, my lady. I have it here,' he said, looking in the inside pocket of his doublet. 'I can assure you that your whole family is doing marvellously well, including your mother.'

I let go of his hair and took the letter he was holding out. It was my mother's handwriting, and my heart leapt for joy. I feverishly unsealed the envelope and read the long letter. Iain had moved over to the window.

Most of the letter contained family news. My mother was informing me of the birth of my sister Sybille's daughter in March and Elsie's, the eldest's second son. Like all the others, these grandchildren were infants blessed with a good constitution. She assured me of her own state of health which had never given any cause for alarm that winter as Daren had invented. The latter had fully recovered from his injury but remained with my father in the business in Aberdeen, leaving the management of the felling completely to Lieutenant Lennox. She finished with a strange comment about my husband.

'Of all the northern men I have ever met, your husband is the least wild.'

This hurtful little phrase took me aback. I suddenly realised that Iain had had dealings with my father and no doubt had met the whole family. I looked at my husband with concern and asked several questions about his visit to Crathes. His evasive answers led me to believe that the welcome had been quite chilly. I bit my lip with disappointment and, for the first time ever, felt a touch of rebellion towards my father. Not content with having packed me off to the far end of Scotland to a husband our family did not know, he affronted me by lacking good manners when he did meet him. I asked Iain about the outcome of the dispute, which had taken him to Crathes, but with little satisfaction. I concluded that my husband and my father were not on the best of terms, which upset me, but I hid my hurt.

'Would you like to go downstairs with me, my lady?' he asked simply to change the subject. 'If you are up to it, I think that a short appearance in class would please the children and reassure everyone in the castle. Father Henriot, too, is in a hurry to talk to you.'

'With pleasure, my lord. I could go to the ends of the earth on your arm unless it was through a forest,' I replied as I got up.

'My love,' he said quietly, 'we will visit a forest together but not now.' He wrapped me in his arms and kissed my brow.

After a whole night spent guarding Beathag's door with Domhnull, Tomas was sore and stiff. Apart from Alasdair's widow's companion, no one had appeared all night. The hostage had not even tried to leave, nor had she spoken to them. When Tomas heard his cousin's footsteps in the corridor and saw Bran appear, he heaved a sigh of relief. At last, he was going to be relieved of his post. Iain greeted them. He was wearing his claymore and had a rope in his hand. When Tomas noticed it, he was startled. Iain ignored his reaction and, with a nod of the head, signalled to him to open the door. Lady Beathag was lying naked on the bed. The covers had not been pulled up, and she had a provocative, tempting smile on her lips. Without any preamble, Iain entered and looked around for his sister-in-law's clothes.

'Get up and get dressed! Hurry, I am not in the mood to wait for you,' he growled between his teeth.

He saw a dress hanging in the alcove, took it down, and threw it at her. Tomas and Domhnull were standing at the door, unsure what to do. They were waiting for their chief to dismiss them, but he seemed to have forgotten they were there.

 'If I cannot have my companion's help, you will have to help me, my lord. I will not manage on my own… well, not as quickly as you want,' whispered Beathag from the bed as she picked up the dress which had fallen on the floor beside her.

Impatiently, Iain turned towards the two men and signalled to Dohmnull to go over to his sister-in-law.

Beathag burst out laughing and said bitterly as she winked at the knight, 'Look at the virtuous MacNeil, incapable of touching the woman whose bed he has wallowed in for five years! Domhnull, come on, get your hands on a well-built woman instead of your chief. Marriage has robbed him of his virility.'

Iain clenched his fist to stop himself from jumping up, and he turned towards his cousin. Tomas smiled and shrugged his shoulders.

Without even looking at his sister-in-law, he said: 'I am counting to thirty, and then I will take you out as you are!'. 'If you want to leave Mallaig in a dignified manner, you are going to have to comply, Beathag MacDougall. Do not give me a reason to spoil your fine body. I am already having great difficulty stopping myself from doing so.'

'Count, count, my lord, since it is all you are capable of doing now,' she replied, as she slipped her hand under her pillow.

With the speed of lightning, she produced a pair of scissors and hurled them at Iain, who had his back to her. Tomas anticipated the move rather than saw it and pulled his cousin towards himself. With a thud, the scissors hit the open door, just missing the young chief's sleeves. A heavy silence fell over the room. Dohmnull rushed towards the young woman to overpower her. Never had Iain felt such hatred, and never had he had such a taste for murder in his mouth. When he turned to his sister-in-law, his face was white with rage, and his screwed-up eyes burned with shafts of anger. He grabbed his cousin's sleeve, hoping to be held back rather than to hold back. Tomas sensed the urgency, understood the implicit appeal, and led his cousin out into the corridor. Beathag's companion was standing with Anna and the ridiculous-looking Sheriff Darnley, who was staring with his mouth wide open at the scissors embedded in the door. The two women rushed in and started to dress the sister-in-law, who was shaking and laughing nervously. After taking a few steps, the two cousins stopped.

Iain, livid and as tense as a crossbow, put the rope in his cousin's hand and whispered harshly, 'Take her out bound. I will be waiting in the courtyard.'

Then he turned to his cousin and looked him straight in the eyes. 'Tomas, keep me from killing her. At the harbour, stay beside me until she is on board the boat for Skye.'

That is just how it happened. In brilliant sunshine which would last for several days on the west coast of Scotland, Beathag MacDougall left the castle under close escort and to the general indifference of the people of Mallaig,

The weather in June 1425 was magnificent throughout Scotland. It rained very little, and the heat of that early summer gave all of nature a boost. The clumps of blooming heather gave a purple tint to the plateau, which ran down to the Mallaig Peninsula, and the dried marshes were surrounded by a green blanket of luscious grass. In the fields, the crops were high, waving about in the misty breeze from the sea. Bareheaded men and women came and went, each carrying the implements they needed for their particular task. The flocks of black-faced sheep and the cattle brought down from the winter pastures covered the moor around the castle, their numbers augmented by lambs and ungainly spring calves.

Every day, the village children came up to the castle for their classes and benefitted from a new teacher in the person of Tomas. The MacNeil cousin had taken over from his Aunt Rosalind who had returned home. He was given the responsibility of teaching writing and arithmetic, and, discovering a real love for teaching, he put his whole heart into it. Young Jenny assisted him, and together, they made a team capable of captivating for hours on end, not just the children, but also the few adults who attended the classes. Father Henriot extended his range of subjects to astronomy, geography, the Holy Scriptures, and the great heroes of antiquity. As soon as morning service was over, he would gather the castle children together, and they would all go to meet the village children who arrived by the southern footbridge. The chatelaine only taught Scots and reading. At her husband's request, she only spent one hour a day in school. Even though it did not seem enough, she contented herself with it.

Gunelle spent several hours in her large bedroom, dealing with the family accounts and continuing her husband's education, to which the young chief began to devote most of the morning and always with the same degree of interest. The folk in the castle were delighted to see the connection between the couple. Their tenderness and obvious compatibility made all the women, from the youngest to the oldest, dream. They were also the focus of the clan and the small groups of highland society which frequented the castle. Her duties as chatelaine called for Gunelle to maintain a constant presence in the great hall to welcome her husband's and Sheriff Darnley's guests. The latter was in the final months of his stay at Mallaig and received a lot of people in the little study. Several tardy secretaries paraded through one after the other as they came to present their books and obtain the king's representative's discharge. With the assistance of some of them, the sheriff remained in touch with Beathag MacDougall, who was holed up on her island. At the castle, no one missed Alistair's impetuous widow. On the contrary, the whole atmosphere of the place had improved since her strange departure with neither luggage nor farewells. She was just a vague memory for everyone, and her name was rarely mentioned. Darnley was the only one who would occasionally speak of her to the servants who made sure that neither the master nor the mistress was within hearing distance. Everyone respected the unspoken agreement not to discuss that particular subject. The chief and the chatelaine acted as if Lady Beathag had never even existed.

Anna and Nellie were roped into the preparations for a big new celebration—the dubbing of Lord Tomas, which was to take place at the Feast of St. John. A variety of pies, breads, preserves, and liqueurs were prepared during the hot days of that month. Lord MacNeil had sent invitations to every clan member and was determined that the event would be memorable. To that end, he decided to organise a tournament in which Tomas would be the star attraction. The two cousins had never been so close. Their training sessions invariably ended in banter and pranks in which all the knights revelled. Iain noticed that young Jenny's presence at the back of the courtyard during these exercises had a positive effect on his cousin, and he arranged that she should be there as often as possible. He began to picture the couple these two shy people would make if his cousin thought of opening his eyes and looking at the pretty young woman even though she was a servant. On one occasion, he shared his thoughts with his wife, who was very surprised by his revelations. It amused him to see her blush: talk of games of seduction between men and women embarrassed her as much as ever.

Those days were equally happy for Ceit, who had suffered a great deal from her young mother's illness. She was now in her eighth year and had developed physically as well as intellectually during the spring. The little girl was delighted about the arrival of a little sister or brother and, without any shyness, revealed her curiosity in the matter to her mother. Seeing the pleasure her mother derived from walking in the garden from time to time, with Nellie's help, Ceit had discovered a love for gardening. Occasionally abandoning her little friends, she would go there at the end of the day and follow the old nurse around. In the middle of June, the two delighted pickers harvested a fine crop of green beans for the kitchen. The old rose bushes, which had been pruned back, came into bloom and produced enough flowers to provide beautiful table arrangements in the great hall for weeks.

I quickly discovered that my illness had taken a lot out of me. When evening came, I was incapable of sitting up with my folk and retired very early with Ceit. I would take her into my bed, and we would talk for a long time before we fell asleep. How I loved those simple little chats. When Iain came to bed, he would pick up his daughter and take her into the bedroom next door without waking her. Occasionally I would wake up at that moment and often heard him whisper tender, loving words to the sleeping Ceit, which filled my heart almost to bursting point with love for him.

I do not know whether there was ever a time in our life when we were closer than at the beginning of that summer. Every moment of the day I felt myself surrounded, protected, and loved by him. When he was not walking with me on the ramparts, which remained a favourite place, he was with the estate folk in the arms room for the court or in the great hall. Every morning after the service, we would go back up to our room, where we had continued the habit of working for a few hours. He had had a large table brought upstairs. One end of it was piled high with the account books which I took care of each week. The other end was for our work. We would sit opposite one another and enthusiastically continue the completion of his studies.

I tackled the most difficult of works with him and had others sent from the monastery at Melrose. He was always eager to begin the lesson. He was more relaxed and his thirst for knowledge had deepened. Since my illness, he had begun to speak in Scots to me in private, and he extended its use to his visitors. I was so used to living in Gaelic that I was almost surprised and seduced when I heard the words of love, he lavished on me in Scots. It was as if he had entered the world of my childhood and occupied it completely. *I love this man passionately!* I surprised myself thinking more and more often.

It was with a great deal of emotion that I informed my family of my pregnancy in a letter addressed, on Iain's advice, not to my father but to my mother in reply to hers. I told her I wanted to call my child Annabel after her if it were a girl or Baltair, Iain's father's name, if it were a boy. I was very positive about my state of health, keeping from her the dramatic weeks I had lived through in May. I was not stingy in my comments about the irreproachable husband Iain was and how I was completely in love with him. I spoke to her too about Ceit, my adopted daughter and the school I had set up at Mallaig. With all my heart, I wanted her to know how happy I was and that I did not wish for any other life than my life in the Highlands. I think I succeeded.

I took advantage of an unexpected visit by Lieutenant Lennox and asked him to deliver the letter to Crathes. He arrived during the first week of June, accompanied by a single guard. I surprised him in the great hall when I went down for lunch, and he rushed to meet me, his face beaming.

'Oh, at last, my lady! How happy I am to see you again! I was so upset when I heard about your accident.'

Overcome by emotion, I took his hands and looked affectionately into his eyes. *My dear Lennox*, I thought thankfully. I invited him to eat with us and sat him between Iain and myself. However, he only stayed one night at Mallaig and spoke for a long time in private with Iain. I thought they were discussing the felling and left them alone. I felt a pang of sadness watching him leave the next day. This man had the gift of making me miss him the moment he left. Seeing Lennox's attitude towards my husband, I began to desire his presence permanently at the castle, for he displayed respect and even a certain attachment towards Iain. I did not think his feelings for my husband were influenced by the affection he had for the wife. They seemed to have developed during those few days the two men had spent together in May. I went as far as to imagine that Lennox had acted as an ally for my husband during his visit to Crathes. I was not wrong.

As he was leaving, Iain invited him to the Feast of St. John and suggested he bring some men willing to take part in the tournament and able to wear the Keith colours. I smiled with joy when I heard him answer affirmatively. *I am going to see him again soon*, I rejoiced. *He will bring me the latest news from Crathes.*

When Lennox and his companion were no longer in sight on the track, taking them back to the felling site, I noticed Iain's thoughtful look. His eyes were fixed on the horizon. He took my arm to lead me back inside and confirmed what I had sensed between the two men.

'The lieutenant is a man of great maturity such as I would like to have here at Mallaig,' he said to me. 'If I were in your father's shoes, I would not waste him by having him oversee a work site. I would have him beside me as my advisor.' With a wistful and teasing smile on his lips, he added, 'Truly, my lady, Lennox is the only southern Scot in whom I would have complete faith.'

'You are right to appreciate Lennox, my lord,' I replied, 'but your statement obliges me to defend the Lowland Scots. They are as good and loyal as the Highlanders.' I hesitated for a moment, then continued, 'Do not base your judgement on some irascible character from Aberdeenshire.'

After Lennox's visit to Mallaig, Iain MacNeil became very reflective and often thought of his father. How would he have reacted to the theft of Keith's first payment? His conversation with the lieutenant left him in no doubt. Since one of the three men to whom the delivery of the casket had been entrusted worked at the felling site, Lennox had begun his investigation with him. He had learned that the three riders had got lost on the banks of Loch Morar during a snowstorm. They had been spotted by a group of MacNeils who had taken them to one of their homes. The latter, who introduced himself as Lord Baltair's brother, had made a good impression on them from the start. The MacNeil coat of arms which hung everywhere in the castle confirmed that he belonged to the clan, and Lennox's men had had no hesitation in accepting his offer to take the casket with its unknown contents to Mallaig. They handed it over to him and returned to the work site the next day without thinking any more about it. They had not thought it necessary to mention the matter to Lennox.

'My lord,' Lennox had said to Iain, 'I have no reason to doubt the story. It means that the casket was no longer in possession of Keith representatives after the middle of January. Who has it now since it has not been delivered to you, and why are we just discovering now, after such a long time, that it has been stolen? I am extremely perplexed. Finally, can I ask you what you have found out here?'

'Nothing at all, Lieutenant. Nothing, because I have not looked for any answers since my return. You see, Lady Gunelle's state of health has completely preoccupied me. All other matters were relegated down the list. Perhaps I am surprising you by saying that, and I am surprising myself. I am going to confide something to you, Lennox. I love my wife passionately. If I had lost her, I do not know what would have become of me.'

After a long silence, he continued, 'Thank you for this information. You have done your duty in carrying out your own investigation, and rest assured, from today, I am taking up the matter of the delivery of the casket. I believe it is in MacNeil hands. From now on, it is up to me and only me to find out whose.'

'Good, my lord. However, allow me to remain at your service in settling this question. And if I learn anything else, I will see it as my duty to pass it on to you.'

'I appreciate your gesture, Lennox. I ask just one thing from you— that this matter remains just between the two of us. I am clan chief, and it is my responsibility to maintain the unity of the clan before the other Highland clans and our king. I appeal to your loyalty to my wife, who is now a MacNeil.'

'My lord, I give you my word that I will say nothing to anyone about the disappearance of Nathaniel Keith's casket,' the lieutenant solemnly promised.

Lieutenant Lennox's revelations had really staggered Iain MacNeil. The details of the story implied that the casket was kept by one of his lairds. If it was his father's brother and his lands touched Loch Morar, it could only be his uncle Aindreas. A cold sweat ran down his neck, and a cramp gripped his stomach as he reached that conclusion. There was no other explanation or a valid reason for diverting the suspicion that was settling on his uncle. What astonished him was that the theft had taken place before his father's death. In vain, he searched his memory for anything old Baltair might have said which could have led him to believe there had been an argument or a dispute with his young brother Aindreas. However, he remembered with sorrow that at that time, he avoided his father as much as possible and knew nothing about his business. He and his father may have shared secrets after Guilbert Saxton had left the family service, but he had preferred to let his wife take care of the running of the estate and keep his father company. What was his father's relationship with his youngest brother like? He had no idea, and he reproached himself for his lack of thought at that time. Now he should judge his uncle based on the relationship he himself had had with him since March. *To me, Aindreas is a self-seeking and treacherous man. But could he have been disloyal to his brother?* Iain continually wondered about that. In the days following Lieutenant Lennox's departure, the young chief MacNeil's deliberations led him to the certainty that his uncle Aindreas had stolen the casket.

Right up until the feast of Saint John, he lived constantly with these dark thoughts. He hid them as best he could from his wife, with whom he shared everything else. He thought at one moment of opening up to his cousin but changed his mind. The only thing which should occupy the aspiring knight was his dubbing. A man is knighted just once, and the engagement is for life. He decided to forget about the affair for the moment and devote his time to Tomas. As master of Mallaig he must attend the dubbing ceremony. Since the aspiring knight had to be accompanied to the ceremony by his parrain, Iain must find a replacement for himself. He opted for Sir Dohmnull and paired him with his cousin for the final stages of his training. Dohmnull was the oldest of the knights and, like Tomas, had arrived at Mallaig with neither father nor mother. The castle had become his only home. So it was that, in the weeks leading up to festival of Saint John, outside on the area bordering the east wall of the castle, Tomas could be seen training in full armour under Dohmnull's watchful eye. Around them, workmen were busy erecting the platform and constructing the tournament arena. From daybreak on, through the wide-open windows, one heard the carpenters' hammers mingle with the noise of weapons striking equipment or armour. Young Jenny took them light meals, which they hurriedly ate before resuming the training. In the heat of the day, they would take off their armour and dive into the pool at the foot of the waterfall which cascaded down the cliff. In the icy cold water, Tomas and Dohmnull would sometimes fight hand-to-hand so as not to miss a single opportunity to train in all kinds of combat. Their naked dripping bodies shone like bronze in the sunshine.

When the twenty-third of June arrived, Tomas was ready and looked magnificent. His long blond hair had bleached in the sun and gave him what seemed like white mane. His sun-tanned skin brought out the blue of his eyes. Under his tunic one could see a muscular chest and shoulders, which gave him a proud and strong bearing. Dohmnull stuck out his chest with pride as he prepared his protégé for the next day's ceremony. First came the aspiring knight's purificatory bath, which he took in the guardroom. He immediately dressed him in a white shirt, the symbol of purity and the red tunic, representing the blood which the knight sheds in defence of God and honour. Throughout the hours of preparation, they spent together, Dohmnull reminded him of the knight's undertaking.

'Tomas, may your weapon be at the service of the church, the poor, and the weak: women, children, and peasants are included. You will commit no act contrary to the code of honour. When your lord calls you to war, you will present yourself before him dressed in armour and on horseback. Heroism and bravery will be the motivation behind each blow you strike on his behalf.'

When darkness fell, Dohmnull took Tomas to the chapel. He placed the young man's claymore and spurs on the altar and left him alone in prayer and meditation all night. In the early hours of the morning, it was Father Henriot who met Tomas first. Unable to hold back his emotion, he embraced him for a long time. Tomas was the first man to be knighted at Mallaig since he had been responsible for its souls, and the young knight's sacred commitment represented a step of great faith. As was the custom, he heard his confession and then said the mass for him in front of everyone.

The morning meal in the great hall was particularly joyful. Members of the family, the knights and several guests who had already arrived were standing around Tomas, who was looking relaxed and calm. Iain, in full highland dress, was watching him with a glint of tender pride in his eyes. *The first man I am going to dub*, he thought. *What a blessing that he is the one I am closest to.*

When he entered the sunlit arms room, Tomas felt a rush of joy flood his heart. At first, his gaze was drawn to all the happy faces looking at him, then his eyes turned to the coats of arms and banners in the MacNeil colours, freshened up and hanging from poles. Dohmnull, who was walking behind with his hand on his back, directed him towards Iain. Thomas felt the warmth of Dohmnull's hand through his tunic and, deeply moved, closed his eyes for a moment.

Then he heard the soft voice of his new parrain whisper, 'It is a great honour to be received as a knight in the MacNeil household, Tomas, and I am particularly proud to be the one to present you for that title...'

Tomas gave him a look of gratitude over his shoulder and said quietly, 'Thank you, Master Dohmnull!' before walking on his own towards his cousin, who was waiting for him at the far end of the room. The murmuring hushed when Tomas stopped, standing straight, his eyes fixed on his chief's. The latter drew his claymore and raised it above the blond head with both hands as he pronounced the dubbing aloud.

'Tomas of Inverness, son of the clan MacNeil, in the name of God, I make you a knight. Be valorous, valiant, and humble. Remember where you come from and whose son you are.'

Tomas felt the flat of his cousin's blade on each of his shoulders. Then Dohmnull approached him and slipped his claymore into his belt, greeting him with a bow, then knelt to attach his spurs to his boots. That done, Tomas turned around and received the ovation of the whole gathering. Amongst them, Jenny's radiant face caught his eye, and he smiled.

A flood of joy ran through me when the roar went up in the arms room. I could not take my eyes off Tomas, who was beaming. I noticed the smile he gave Jenny and made up my mind to arrange a seat for her amongst the ladies on the platform. *Iain is right*, I thought. *There is something going on between those two hearts.*

Every invitation sent by my husband had been accepted, for I noticed no absentees when I began to seat everyone at one of the three tables set under Anna and Mairi's direction. The atmosphere was jovial, and already the fiddlers and pipers were hotly vying with one another, plunging the whole gathering into a lively din while everyone sat down and the meal was served. I noticed that Iain was abandoning the lairds' company for that of the knights, particularly Tomas, to whom he was clinging like a leech. The group consisting of Nellie, Ceit, and Jenny was continually joined by Aunt Rosalind, who seemed happy to meet up with the castle ladies again. I had to look after the lairds' wives who, having learned of my pregnancy, talked of nothing else, and I graciously prepared myself for their questions and lots of advice. Sheriff Darnley was in deep conversation with the lairds, and several times, I caught him obviously sharing secrets with Uncle Aindreas. Lennox had come down from the Grampians that morning with two men whom I recognised as being from my father's personal bodyguard. I invited him to sit beside me. As I hoped, he had brought my mother's reply to my letter.

Grouse, salmon in pastry, pate, gigots of lamb with haggis, beef stew—the dishes were placed on the table, and everyone was invited to help themselves. The thick slices of brown bread placed in front of each guest were soon soaked in the meat juices, and greasy fingers regularly disappeared under the table to be hastily wiped clean on the tablecloth before coming back up to pick up a juicy piece of meat here or there a cup of mead or beer which the servers kept filling up. As I watched the joyful faces as the banquet progressed, I knew that this Mallaig table was living up to the memories my husband and the guests, who had known the last chatelaine, still had of days gone by.

Everything was going perfectly until the moment when Aindreas's wife noticed the absence of her great friend Beathag. She obviously knew all about the affair, but she wanted to put the master of Mallaig ill at ease by asking questions about her friend's departure. From his aunt's very first words, I saw him stiffen, and I began to shake. To our great relief, Rosalind came to our aid.

'My dear Morag,' she interrupted, 'why ask here and now what you have learned from your friend's own lips? Did you not visit the MacDougalls last week with Aindreas? Remember, you met my son Raonall who had business on the island.'

Aindreas looked furiously at his wife, something which did not go unnoticed by my husband. I saw beads of sweat form on Iain's brow, and I gently squeezed his arm. He looked at me, and I saw a look of suspicion in his eyes. I did not know why. As for myself, I felt my face getting redder and redder. With a furious look on her face, Aunt Morag had stopped talking, and after the silence which followed Rosalind's intervention, the conversations resumed. My shoulders relaxed. The threat was over. I concentrated on breathing normally. I heard Iain whisper in my ear, 'Everything is all right, my lady. Keep calm.'

Beside me, Lennox looked intriguingly at Iain, who did not react. In the middle of the afternoon, we all left the great hall to go and watch the tournament. It was so hot outside that, for a moment, I almost fainted, and I grabbed Iain's arm. Looking worried, he asked me if I preferred to stay in the coolness of the keep with Anna or Nellie.

'Not at all, my lord. It will pass. I must have drunk too much mead. I would not miss the first tournament at Mallaig for six years for anything in the world,' I replied with a smile.

'It is a pity I have to preside over it, my lady, for it would have given me great pleasure to joust for your favour,' he teased.

As he led me up the stairs and sat me down in the place of honour in the ladies' section of the dais, I squeezed his hands warmly. Before he went to the rostrum where the lords and distinguished guests were sitting, I very quietly asked him to ensure that Jenny, my companion, had a seat among the other ladies just behind me. He raised his thick eyebrows in surprise, then gave me a smile of agreement. He went down and looked

for Jenny, but as she was not there, he had a few words with one of the guards before going to the jousters' tent, which was erected against the wall. A steady breeze coming from the sea unfurled the standards which were flying at the four corners of the arena and on the awning shading the platform. Their vivid colours gave the whole plain a great look of celebration. The piper was walking up and down the rail which divided the arena in two, drawing strident notes from his instrument. Rosalind, who had sat down on my right, identified the different shields held by the horsemen on duty near the tent. I was amazed to hear her recite the family names and their connections simply from the designs and colours on the escutcheons. In an uninterrupted and captivating flow, she enthralled me with her knowledge of coats of arms which was equal to that of the most competent harbinger. It meant that I, who had never attended such an event, was able to benefit from her vast experience of tournaments. A little before the jousts began, I saw Jenny come out of the tent and come skipping towards the platform.

She made her way towards me, flustered with emotion, and said, 'Here I am, my lady. I have just been asked to join you.' As she slipped in behind me, she whispered quietly, 'You are goodness personified, Lady Gunelle.'

At last, we heard the trumpeters announce the spectacle. Thirty-six knights emerged from the tents, visors raised and marching in procession to the accompaniment of the jingling of their armour. They walked towards the horses held by the grooms, and, putting one hand on the horse's back, they jumped into the saddle. Before they were handed their shields and lances, they lowered their visors. I immediately understood the importance of the coats of arms. Without them, it would be impossible to recognise the jouster once he was enclosed in his iron suit. To our frenzied applause, the knights slowly entered the arena, where they stopped in front of the platform to greet his lordship. The row they formed in front of us was impressive. In a profusion of colours each knight's coat of arms was repeated on his halberd, helmet, shield, and horse's cover, which swayed elegantly with every clip-clop of the hooves. Their lance, which was the same colour as their coat of arms, was pointing forwards and slightly dipped. On a signal from Iain, the lances were raised vertically, and the horsemen shouted a resounding 'For honour!' Then they left one by one, leaving two knights who trotted to either end of the arena where they took up position. Without further ado, the trumpeter sounded for the first joust to begin. In a voice which excitement rendered trill Rosalind explained the procedure. I guessed my elderly companion was very fond of this kind of entertainment. In this tournament, we were only going to see single bouts with the lance. The Mallaig representatives always kept to the right-hand side of the arena. It was Uncle Griogair, Rosalind's husband, who was acting as harbinger announcing the jousters' names. When the two contestants had come to a stop, his strong voice rang out.

'For Mallaig, Sir Ruad against Sioltach MacNeil of Arisaig.'

Arisaig Peninsula was the domain of Aulay, one of the clan lairds. Rosalind informed me that Sioltach was the eldest son, and, pointing with her chin to a big red-haired woman wearing an extravagant hennin, she added that he was married with two daughters. I watched the opponents lower their lances, and on the short blast of a trumpet, they galloped towards each other. They met almost in the middle without colliding. Then they went to the end of the barrier, turned their horses around, and set off again. Each time they were met with shouts of surprise from the crowd. I noticed that in my excitement, I had taken hold of Rosalind's hand. She smiled at me fondly and reassured me.

'Do not be afraid, my dear. They are well protected. When they do clash, it will make a lot of noise and dust, but there will be no blood.'

'It is said that the point of their lance is blunted so as not to cause injury, Lady Rosalind. Is that true?' I asked her, trying to sound assured.

'Not in the Highlands, my lady. Here weapons are never blunted. The Highlanders would not wear them. It goes against their beliefs whether fighting in a tournament or not,' she answered calmly.

A shout from the crowd drew my attention back to the joust. Ruad had been unseated by his adversary. Having lost his shield and lance and with his armour damaged, he was having difficulty getting up. He lifted his visor, and, turning towards the rostrum, he greeted Iain with a deliberate and noble gesture. The winner trotted to greet his lady with a bow over his horse's neck. The two competitors left the arena to applause while the next two appeared. So, throughout the afternoon, there were jousts between representatives from Mallaig and those representing other members of the MacNeil clan or, indeed, my own family with the two men Lieutenant Lennox had brought with him. I did not keep a tally of the winners and losers and only learned later that of the eighteen contests, Mallaig had won eleven. Sneaking a look at Lennox's reaction, I was pleased to see him smile as the Keith men hit the dust at the first blow.

If the jousts and their degree of sameness quickly bored me, the preamble, and the exits captivated me. In fact, the favours pledged between contenders and ladies interested me intensely. Glancing around me, I saw I was not alone. A buzzing sound like a swarm of bees arose from the ladies' section each time a fighter came to declare the name of the lady for whom he was assuming the role of servant. Some showed the crowd a scarf or a ribbon the chosen one had given him as a favour. A thrill went through me at the thought of these openly declared allegiances, and I could not help imagining how I would have felt if Iain had called on the tournament audience as witnesses to his love for me.

Tomas had been kept until the last joust, and I jumped up when I heard his name being called. I had almost forgotten he was taking part. He was up against Dughall of Loch Morar. *How strange!* I thought. Without being able to explain why, I would not have imagined any other opponent for Tomas than one of his Uncle Aindreas's men. Apart from the background of the escutcheon, which was blue for Mallaig and purple for Morar, both shields were very similar. Dughall turned his horse around twice before lifting high the favour of Thora, Aindreas's daughter. Every eye was on her while, scarlet with embarrassment, she untied the long green shawl covering her shoulders and threw it at the feet of the knight's horse by way of assent. Dughall bowed to her and went to his corner of the arena. Slowly advancing his horse towards the dais, Tomas stopped in front of me. I gave a start. My hands became cold, and I let go of Rosalind's. I was hypnotised by Iain's cousin's focused and silent demeanour. The whole audience fell silent at the same time, waiting for the new knight's declaration of love for a lady. It was then I noticed a white ribbon attached to his right glove. Tomas said nothing. He leaned over his horse's neck, turned towards me, then sat up and spurred on his horse and galloped to the far right of the arena.

I was blushing with embarrassment and noticed the looks of astonishment from the other ladies. I did not dare look up from the ground; I barely heard the trumpet signal the attack. When I gathered myself together, I looked furtively at Iain. What a surprise when I saw him smiling over at me. Concentrating on his blue eyes, I realized that he was staring at Jenny behind me, and it hit me like a flash of lightning that Tomas was jousting for the young girl's heart and that his greeting had not been meant for me. I forced myself not to turn around and stare at the girl whom I had just designated as my companion.

'You seem to be enjoying yourself, my dear,' whispered Rosalind, which made me jump. 'Our new knight possesses great charm, which seems to shine right through his iron suit. One wonders how. Let us wish him good luck.'

I could not help bursting out laughing at her remark. When I turned to watch what was happening in the arena, a first clash of the lances had taken place without result. On the second attempt, Tomas left a second later than his adversary and with longer strides. His lance, which he was holding very straight, hit Dughall's shield with a thud and unbalanced him for a second. His horse sidestepped, unseated him, and he dropped his lance.

Tomas, who had turned back, shouted to Dughall as he dropped his lance to the ground, 'Dughall, hand-to-hand.'

Rosalind leaned over and whispered in my ear, 'And chivalrous into the bargain! Tomas is proposing to continue the joust, which was his to claim since his opponent was disarmed. Dughall does not know how fortunate he is and Aindreas must be delighted.'

I watched the two horsemen turn their horses to face one another and try to grab hold of the other's right arm. Then after several attempts, they let go of the reins and shields and, grabbing each other with both hands, pulled as hard as they could to try and make the other fall. It looked to me as if Dughall did not have a good grip, and his gloves were slipping on Tomas's chain mail. Taking advantage of that, Tomas pushed his adversary off his horse with a hefty shove. I jumped off my seat at the same time as most of the audience and added my voice to the thunderous shouts which greeted the result of this final contest.

Tomas took off his helmet and put it under his arm. His blond hair, which was sticking to his head, shone in the sunshine like a golden helmet. He nodded in Iain's direction, then in my direction, and at Jenny behind me. I glanced over my shoulder at her and, in so doing,

351

noticed Lennox who was sitting further along. An inscrutable look was written all over his face, and he was staring at the gold cross and chain around Thora's neck. I had not noticed it when she had untied her shawl to throw it at her jouster. *What is he doing staring at Aindreas's daughter like that?* I thought for a moment. I was moving forward, drawn along by the ladies who were leaving the dais.

As soon as I got down, I was joined by an overexcited Ceit who had watched part of the tournament with Nellie and Mairi at the edge of the arena. Bran brushed against my skirts with a bark, and Rosalind came and took my arm to accompany me to the courtyard. Jenny had disappeared, no doubt into the combatants' tent where I saw Iain follow his cousin. A last look in his direction informed me that Lennox was on his heels.

Iain MacNeil was as pleased as could be with the whole of the tournament and in particular, his cousin's joust. *Decidedly, Tomas has a sense for the spectacular!* he thought as he went into the tent. Before he reached the circle of riders, who were surrounding Tomas and helping him off with his armour, Lieutenant Lennox stopped him.

'My lord,' he said tensely. 'Could I speak to you in private… outside?'

Without any hesitation, Iain nodded and followed him quickly towards the door. When they were away from all eyes and ears, Lennox told the young chief what he had discovered; the cross Aindreas's daughter was wearing around her neck was the one in

Nathanial Keith's casket and had been Uncle Carmichael's wedding gift to Gunelle.

'I am not mistaken, my lord,' affirmed Lennox. 'I recognise that gold cross. Examine it closely when you can. You will see it is the work of a French goldsmith, characterised by the absence of the circle found in the middle of the Celtic crosses.'

'You are undoubtably correct, Lennox. The casket ended up in my uncle's hands, and for some time now, I have no doubt about that. That cross is perhaps the proof I need, but I have not made up my mind yet as to how I am going to proceed. I do not want to make any accusations now. Therefore, I am asking you to say or do nothing. I will let you know when I need your help.'

Grabbing his arm before taking his leave, Iain thanked his father-in-law's servant, who seemed more and more devoted to the service of Mallaig. He re-joined Tomas and the knights, who had all worn his colours during the tournament and warmly congratulated them for their contests, whether victorious or otherwise. The grooms did not have to be told twice to open a cask of whisky for the jousters. Dohmnull and Tomas were holding one another by the arm, each heartily congratulating the other. It gave Iain great pleasure to see them so close. As he also had to look after his guests, he left the tent soon afterwards and went to the courtyard where refreshments were being served.

From the minute he saw them, he guessed that something was being hatched between his Uncle Aindreas and Sheriff Darnley. Cups in hand, the two men were having a private conversation, and they turned away when they saw him enter the room. The young chief ignored them and walked straight to his wife's group. There was still the evening meal to deal with and he wanted to make sure that she was feeling up to her role as hostess. The radiant smile with which she greeted him, her fresh complexion, and the absence of a headdress and veil were eloquent testimonies that she was indeed feeling well and enjoying the day.

'My lord,' she exclaimed, holding out her hand, 'what an unforgettable day you have given us all! I thank you on behalf of all our guests.'

The ladies and gentlemen surrounding them echoed the chatelaine's words, each wanting to personally express his or her delight to the young Lord of Mallaig. Iain had taken his wife's hand and squeezed her fingers affectionately as he listened. He seemed delighted by the testimonials she had aroused.

Intoxicated as much by the praise showered upon him as by the whisky he had drunk in abundance, Tomas finally approached young Jenny and drew her aside, taking absolutely no notice of her embarrassment. He took out the white ribbon from inside his shirt and held it out to her, claiming her favour.

'I remind you I won the joust, and therefore, I claim the forfeit. You gave me this ribbon, and I accepted it.' Grabbing her by the waist, he whispered, 'You owe me a kiss, Jenny.'

'My lord,' she said, 'I have no intention of refusing but...'

The rest of her sentence was swallowed up by Tomas's lips. Clumsily with one hand, he fumbled for the laces of her bodice. Breathless, she managed to break free and took a few steps backwards. She was very upset. Tomas was stunned and he stared at her.

'You do not like kissing a knight, Jenny? Yet it seemed to me as if you could not wait for the moment I became a knight,' he commented.

'You are making fun of me, my lord. A knight acts with honour, and what you are expecting from me has nothing to do with honour. Would you behave in the same way with one of the young ladies in the courtyard? I doubt it. But I am only a servant girl, so your knightly code does not apply,' she replied with tears in her eyes.

She ran away so quickly that Tomas did not have the time to react. Sheepishly he returned to the festivities, his heart heavy from having made such an unforgivable mistake. Which one? Having claimed her favour? Or the way he had done so? *The heart*, he thought miserably. *I did not talk about my heart which could not care less about her being a servant... what an idiot! Oh, Jenny!*

The festivities ended very late on that day of 24 June 1425 at Mallaig. After having eaten a meal as copious as the first, the guests had the great pleasure of hearing the chatelaine singing as they sat in the moonlight in the courtyard. For a long time, the strains of the fiddle and the pipes rose towards the skies and were masked only by the sound of the tide dashing against the cliff as darkness fell. Lord Iain accompanied his wife when she said she wished to retire and he carried his soundly sleeping daughter in his arms. As they reached the door, Sheriff Darnley approached them.

'My lord, what a perfect evening,' he said churlishly. Looking at Gunelle, he continued, 'What an exhausting day for you! You do well to go to bed now. I will need your help tomorrow morning.'

'To do what, I beg you?' an on-his-guard Iain asked dryly.

'For the books, of course,' replied the sheriff slyly. 'There is something I would like to verify… a sum I did not notice in January when I examined your finances with Saxton or perhaps it was with Lady Gunelle. I do not know which of the two were keeping the books when the sum of money was paid.'

In astonishment, Gunelle was about to answer, but her husband stopped her immediately.

'Leave it, my lady. We will see to that tomorrow. I am sure the sheriff is not expecting us to clear it up tonight. Isn't that right, Darnley?'

'Of course, that goes without saying. I wish you a good night, Lady Gunelle, and you too, my lord,' replied the sheriff who was gently stroking Ceit's cheek, which Iain brusquely turned away from him.

Chapter Fourteen
The Plot

Although I was utterly exhausted, occupied as I was by the question of monies received which did not appear in the estate books, I could not get to sleep. Iain had walked with me to the bedroom and left me to get ready for bed with Mairi. Followed closely by Nellie, he carried Ceit to her bedroom. He must have gone straight to the courtyard, for I did not see him until much later, after our guests had all left.

Earlier, I had asked Mairi to light a candelabra before she left. The candles were still burning when I heard Iain come in. I rolled over to the edge of the bed and looked out through the curtains. I watched him take off his belt, which he looked at for a moment before he put it down. He looked annoyed. Once he was undressed, he noticed me watching him as he went to blow out the candles.

'My lady, I know you're asking yourself questions,' he said as he slipped in beside me. 'Let me tell you, I am asking the same ones, but I have a vague idea of the answers. The sum of money darkly hinted at a while ago was paid to my father in January but it had not arrived at Mallaig, which explains why it does not appear in our books.' Surmising my questioning look rather than seeing it, he put his arms around me and told me to go to sleep. 'Things are not very clear at the moment but do not think about it. I will talk to you about it again in the morning, my love. Sleep well …'

'What!' I exclaimed. 'Do not think you can put me off so easily, my lord. You started a story about the books, and you are going to finish it immediately, or else I will not sleep.'

I had thrown my leg over him and was firmly holding myself on top of him, my hands leaning on the mattress on either side of his shoulders, my stomach touching his.

'Really?' he murmured as he kissed my breasts.

I could not help smiling as I looked at him. *What a man!* I thought. *At least he is no longer angry!* I joined in his game and slid gently over him, forcing him to let go. His lips moved from my breast to my neck. When my lips could reach his, I kissed him passionately. I felt the skin of his arms tingle.

Breathless, he took my face in his hands and, breathing deeply, he murmured, 'Leave me alone, my lady or I will not sleep either.'

In fact, we went to sleep very late that night. After we made love, with a satisfied grin on his face, he told me at length everything he knew about the incredible business concerning my father's first payment as stipulated in the marriage contract. He told me about Lieutenant Lennox's help, the suspicions about Uncle Aindreas and the contents of the casket including Uncle Carmichael's gold cross now hanging around Thora's neck. Finally, I understood Lennox's strange behaviour at the tournament and the equally strange behaviour of Aindreas and his wife throughout the day. I was stunned. *How could I sleep after such revelations?* I thought as I snuggled up to the warm body of my husband, who had fallen asleep after having told me all. *It is my own fault*, I told myself. *He did his best to spare me a sleepless night.* My curiosity got the better of me. I felt a thrill go through me as I thought about how I had managed to get him to tell me everything. It was on that note that I finally fell into a deep sleep.

The next morning after the service we went to the study with Darnley. Iain had brought along the accounts book, and with a look of defiance, he placed it on Darnley's table. I stood in front of him and waited for the questions. Darnley, who did not seem to be in very good form, silently scanned the pages looking for the contentious information.

'Lady Gunelle, can you find the entries for January for me?' he said after a while. 'I do not understand Saxton's dates.'

I took the book, which he turned towards me, and leafed through it for a few moments. I easily found the place where I had taken over, and I put the book back in front of him, open at what must be the January entries. He ran his greasy finger across the pages looking for a figure. Iain, who was standing behind me, had not turned a hair from the outset. The sheriff began to read out a column.

'Millet seed, Red Manas, three shillings; fifty pounds of salt, MacLeod of Harris, seven hundred and fifty shillings; twenty-three pounds of smoked herring, MacNeil of Loch Ness, fifteen shillings.' Without looking up from the page, he asked, 'What amount are we speaking about, my lord? About one hundred pounds if I am not mistaken?'

'One hundred and twenty,' said Iain through his teeth.

'Let us see… twelve shillings, forty, five, sixty-seven, fifty-five shillings. There is no sum which reaches one pound until this one in April: three-year-old mare, eight pounds, Marshall of Kyle,' continued Darnley. 'Is that not so, Lady Gunelle? That is your writing is it not?' Without waiting for my answer, he slammed the book closed and continued, 'Now then, MacNeil, did you or did you not receive the first instalment of the felling rights?'

Iain began to walk the floor, taking pleasure in making the sheriff wait. I felt my face gradually turn red with embarrassment. Iain and

I had not discussed what attitude to adopt. I knew that, above all, he wanted to preserve the unity of the clan and that he had nothing but contempt for the king's unpleasant representative. He was not sure what to do: Divulge the theft of the sum of money and open an investigation within the clan or give no explanation at all?

I shuddered when, after an interminable silence, I heard him say from the other end of the room, 'Neither my father nor I, after his death, received the sum in question. I have learned that Nathaniel Keith had paid it but the purse must have been lost en route. That is why neither Saxton nor my wife has entered it as part of our meagre income this winter.' Going right up to the sheriff until the point of his claymore touched him, he continued, 'Darnley, I am not in the habit of losing what is owed to me. I am going to find this money, and I am prepared to enter it in the books immediately so that our books tally with my father-in-law's. Obviously, I shall pay the tax on those one hundred and twenty pounds along with the rest of my dues to the Crown. Will that suit the king of Scotland?'

'Let us hope so, my lord,' the sheriff replied dryly. 'As far as I am concerned, a fictional entry of a sum of money after the books have been audited is absolute proof of embezzlement. So, I strongly advise you to recover your father-in-law's payment before I leave for Stirling in two weeks' time.'

Without a word or even a nod, Iain picked up the book with one hand and took my arm with the other and we hurriedly left the room. We were just like the many other secretaries who had not obtained exemption for their masters. My husband was trembling with barely controlled rage, and I was careful not to mention our conversation with the sheriff right away. He left me in the great hall to have breakfast and I was immediately cornered by Ceit who was waiting for me. I turned around just in time to see him disappear upstairs with Bran at his heels. I did not see him again all morning.

It was late morning when Tomas opened his eyes. He suppressed a look of disgust. As if in a daze he looked around his bedroom where he had not touched a thing since his cousin had slept there. *What a poor knight I make*, he thought, thinking back to the night before. Having been extremely drunk, he had gone to bed without undressing, and he had no clear memory of the events which had ended St. John's Day, a day blessed with his dubbing and his victory in the tournament. The sight of Jenny in tears was the only clear memory he could remember. He struggled out of bed, trying to ignore the vice which was crushing his temples.

'Rotten whisky,' he murmured.

Filled with utter contempt for himself, he looked at his soiled doublet with the once-white ribbon sticking out beneath the collar. When he entered the great hall, Domhnull greeted him with that frank, knowing smile of a father when faced with his son's indiscretions.

'Our young knight won his spurs yesterday,' he shouted, 'but I think he polished them in whisky!'

This remark made the three knights, who were present, laugh. Tomas looked gloomily at the group and sat down on a stool.

'Don't take it so badly,' Domhnull said as he sat down beside him. 'It is only a well-deserved little drinking session which will not tarnish your honour. To reassure you, I can tell you that the lairds drank as much as you and they all had difficulty getting into the saddle when they left the castle.'

'Everybody except Uncle Aindreas, I suppose,' muttered Tomas.

'You are right. Come to think of it, he was very well behaved. Ah, you see, you were not as drunk as you seemed last night. Come, my boy, there is no school today. The children are off for the day. Come and spend the day in the guard's room. We are playing dice. Luck favours a champion the day after a victory. You can prove it to us.'

Thereupon, Domhnull stood up and waited invitingly for his protégé's acceptance. Tomas had neither the desire nor the strength to argue and stood up. *Do not run into Jenny today*, he thought as he followed Domhnull into the corridor leading to the guards' room.

The young groom was making a mess of girthing Iain's horse. He was flustered by his master's impatient look and the gruffly delivered orders. For months now, Iain MacNeil had lost the habit of being grumpy with the servants. That morning, however, he was giving his groom a hard time for no good reason. The young boy did not know where he was with it all and was making one mistake after the other. He breathed a sigh of relief when the master finally left the stable and rode off across the drawbridge with his big dog behind him. Iain rode across the moor towards the western plateau, going around the fields and the grazing herds. He spoke to no one and made do with a brief nod in response to folks' greetings.

'Nothing like going for a ride on your own to be able to think,' he said, spurring on his horse which was already dripping with sweat.

The sky was full of fluffy clouds, which a strong breeze was blowing from the isles towards the leafy green mountains.

When he reached the viewpoint at the edge of the forest from which he could had a good view of the harbour and the castle, he stopped and dismounted. Bran, hot and with his tongue hanging out, came and lay down beside him. Iain crouched down and stroked his dog's head. Staring at the dog's red coat, he concentrated his attention on the sounds around him. The wind in the treetops mingled with the distant sounds of the workmen's hammering as they dismantled the arena and the platform. Iain heaved such a loud sigh that Bran stood up and came to put his wet muzzle into the open collar of his master's tunic.

'Where am I going to find the missing one hundred and twenty pounds?' he said aloud. 'The castle repairs have almost emptied the Mallaig coffers. Damned war! Cameron reprobates! Infamous Aindreas!'

He stood up and looked towards the horizon. 'I cannot borrow it from my lairds. I must settle the matter with my uncle without them getting wind of the affair if I am to keep the clan together. But who can lend me such a sum in fourteen days?'

'My father, Iain!' Lady Gunelle exclaimed when he shared his concerns with his wife that evening. 'I am sure that if I ask him, he will not be able to refuse me. Come now, my lord, money is so short. Only a rich merchant like my father can raise such a sum in a hurry. We do not have to say why we want to borrow it. I beg you, let me try our luck with him.'

Iain would have liked to keep his father-in-law out of it, but he had to admit that he would not be able to present one hundred and twenty pounds to grouchy Sheriff Darnley without someone else's help. Why not Nathaniel Keith's? So it was that he reluctantly told Gunelle to write her father. The letter was entrusted to Tomas the next day. The young knight left with three men, including Domhnull, who did not seem to want to let him out of his sight.

As the little group left the castle under a fine drizzle, Jenny was watching them from a window, her heart full of questions and doubt. Lord Tomas had not sought her out since St. John's Day. Her hopes of receiving an apology for his conduct had evaporated forever. *Why would a lord get close to a servant?* she said to herself. *Are we not just there for their good pleasure?* However, something deep within was clearly saying the opposite. *Not at Mallaig! Not anymore! Not now, that we have our new chatelaine!*

I was in the classroom teaching Tomas's arithmetic class when someone came to tell me he had returned. The last fourteen days had been tense in the castle. Iain was taciturn and forced himself to swallow his rage although he tended to allow it to erupt when he was in the sheriff's company. Since he found it difficult to be interested in anything other than this, his prime preoccupation, we had suspended his lessons, and I had devoted several of my free mornings to the children.

Young Jenny, who accompanied me more and more often, had a great gift with the children, and I left her with them before rushing, my heart thumping, into the corridor leading to the keep door. While Tomas was away getting the answer, I had never doubted my father's help. He was arriving as we had planned since the sheriff was due to leave the next day. When I reached the gate, I met Iain and his cousin, who was dishevelled and covered in dust. The two men looked at me impatiently.

'Tomas, at last!' I whispered, taking him by the hand.

Never has a letter from my father been so eagerly awaited at Mallaig. Ever watchful, my husband looked around and led us up to our bedroom to find out the results of his cousin's mission. As we went upstairs, he tried to calm the excitement which had taken hold of me.

'I remember my father and me waiting very impatiently for a letter from your father. My father wanted an affirmative response and me a negative one…' he said tongue-in-cheek.

I was surprised by his easy-going and even playful tone. I thought about what he had just said and violently blushed when I realised, he was referring to my father's consent to Lord Baltair's offer of his son in marriage. I looked sideways at him and saw that he was looking at me with a smile on his lips.

As we entered the room, he bent over and whispered in my ear, 'If I had to do it again, knowing you as I now know you, I would not wait for an answer, but I would go and fetch it myself and demand that it should be in the affirmative.'

Looking up at his cousin who had gone to sit down at the desk and was opening his doublet, he continued, 'Let us pray that this one is.'

Tomas was exhausted. Wearily, he took out the letter and whispered as he held it out to me, 'What a charming family you have, Lady Gunelle.'

I took the letter which I had difficulty in opening as I was all fingers and thumbs with emotion. I saw that Tomas had two other letters, which he put down on the table in front of me.

'From your mother and your sister Sybille.'

Then he stood and walked to the door. My husband, disappointed at not seeing a purse, caught him by the arm and thanked him for the diligence and discretion with which he had carried out his mission.

I looked at my father's very short letter and could not help thinking of the very lengthy ones he used to write to me when I was in France. At that time, I was his little girl whom he loved tenderly. Today was that affection waning for me who had become a Highlander's wife, the 'least wild' Highlander they had ever met? I read my father's reply aloud. It proved to be neither positive nor negative. He was only lending half the sum and would have Lennox bring it in the next few days at the same time as a payment to the MacPhersons for the right of way through their land. The forty-six pounds would be deducted from the second payment of felling rights, which was to be made at the end of the summer when all the timber would have been cleared. He ended his letter with good wishes for my health and that of the child growing in my womb. Not a mention of Iain and not a bit of news about the rest of my family. When I finished, I looked up at Iain. He had sat down on a stool and was hanging his head, his arms resting on his hips.

I heard him give a deep sigh and mutter, 'Forty-six pounds. Too little too late.' I took the stool Tomas had been sitting on and drew it over beside Iain. I sat down, put my arm around my husband, and put my face on his drooping shoulders. 'I am sorry, my love,' I said gently. 'I really thought my father would release the money immediately and send it. We must hope now that the king will maintain his trust in the MacNeils and not doubt our good intentions.'

'I am really afraid that that will not be enough,' he said as he straightened up. 'I am expecting Darnley to show no mercy or grace in presenting Mallaig's accounts to the king.' Smiling pitifully, he continued, 'I beg you, read the other letters, my lady. I am sure they will be more uplifting.'

I smiled back and began to read my letters. Iain went over to the window and remained there deep in thought the whole time I was reading. Both letters were brief. They had been written in a hurry. My mother was delighted about my pregnancy and bemoaned Sybille and her family's imminent departure from Crathes. My brother-in-law had bought a large house in Aberdeen, and they were moving at the end of the summer. There was a lot about the house in Sybille's letter. Reading between the lines, however, she was reproaching me for my lack of correspondence, which reminded me that the casket which had been stolen in January contained a letter from her. The silence Iain imposed on this whole affair was beginning to depress me. I missed the letters from Crathes more bitterly than Uncle Carmichael's cross, which had been lost. I was especially outraged at the idea that those letters fell into the hands of strangers at Loch Morar. *Is there even anyone there who can read Scots?* I thought in despair. I gave a jump when I heard Iain speaking after a long time of deliberation.

'I can try one more thing even if it disgusts me to do it. Find the money at the home of the thief… if he has not already spent it on bribes for the lairds and their wives last March or to arm his knights.'

'Iain!' I exclaimed. 'How could Uncle Aindreas have dared?'

While rejecting this outrageous idea, I knew my husband was right about his uncle's motives. In silence, I watched him rummage in his trunk, undress, and put on a black leather hunting suit. He did not have to tell me where he planned to go and what he planned to do when he got there. A shiver of fear ran down my back, and hearing the rattle of his claymore in his belt as he strapped it to his hip, I wished from the bottom of my heart that he was not going to Morar alone despite the secrecy he insisted on regarding the affair.

As he passed the guardroom Iain had second thoughts.

'Bran, stay!' he ordered his dog, who was following him. He signalled to Sir Eachann, who was looking out of one of the windows.

'My lord?' he said when he joined his young master.

'I am going to Loch Morar on business, and I would like you to accompany me,' he whispered. 'Hurry! I will wait for you up there,' he added, nodding towards the plateau.

The heavy humid weather was making his horse skittish. The sky above showed signs of a storm. *There is going to be a storm on the islands*, thought Iain, looking towards the horizon as he waited for Eachann. His thoughts turned naturally to the Isle of Skye and his sister-in-law. Iain knew that his death threats the day before her departure would stop her from coming back to Mallaig, but it did not mean that she would stay on her island or give up any thoughts of revenge. He knew Sheriff Darnley had kept in touch, and there was no doubt he would help her if she asked him. He frowned. He could defend himself against an enemy when it was a man. *I thought I would have no more women problems. Even at a distance, Beathag is capable of surpassing even my mother if she makes up her mind to poison my life*, he thought bitterly. He turned his horse around as soon as he saw Eachann approaching, and he rode into the bushes at the edge of the north plateau. When his knight caught up with him, he spurred on his horse. The two men covered the whole distance to Loch Morar in silence.

Iain had thought of several ways of approaching the matter of the theft with Aindreas and had prepared himself for all kinds of reactions but not for his uncle's absence. When his aunt told him that her husband was out on the estate with his falcons, Iain was disappointed. But when she added, smiling rather perversely, that his sister-in-law Beathag was with him, he was frankly disconcerted.

Opening his eyes wide in astonishment, he let slip, 'Beathag! Here?'

'And why not, Iain?' she replied calmly. 'We are free to welcome whoever we wish here, even someone the clan chief has disowned. Beathag MacDougall is my good friend, and we found it sad that your wife could not get on with her at Mallaig, for there is no doubt that it was Lady Gunelle who asked you to throw her out.' Scrutinising his expressionless face, she added, 'I admit that it must be embarrassing to have one's wife and mistress living under the same roof.'

'Beathag is not my mistress, Aunt, despite what she may have told you. And I will have you know that my wife never demanded that my brother's widow leave,' Iain growled as he rose to go. 'On the contrary, I think she would have allowed herself to be threatened by her before she would have asked me to intervene. If Beathag had controlled her jealousy, she would still be holding forth in the great hall at Mallaig. Good evening, Aunt.'

Iain was absolutely furious. Just as he had found it difficult to rid himself of the label of being Alasdair's murderer so he would have the same problem with the label of being his brother's widow's lover. He strode towards Eachann in the yard and mounted his horse.

369

Worried by the look of anger on his master's face, the knight had to ask, 'Where are we going now, my lord?'

Without even looking at him, Iain said in a rage, 'Hunting with falcons.'

By following the flight of the falcons, Iain and Eachann found Uncle Aindreas's party half a mile from the castle. In a little clearing, three knights, his daughter Thora, and Beathag, all dressed to kill, were hunting with him amidst a joyful noise of laughter and conversation. Iain saw Beathag first, and a shudder of hatred ran right through him. Almost instinctively, his sister-in-law had turned towards him, and their eyes met before she could inform the others of his presence.

'Here's the MacNeil chief himself!' she exclaimed. 'He is coming to honour us with a visit in the middle of the wood, Lord Aindreas.'

Turning quickly toward her companion, she continued, 'How impressive your cousin from Mallaig is, all dressed in black, my dear Thora. With his look of evil, he reminds me of an avenging devil!'

'I say, I say, my dear nephew,' Aindreas said immediately. 'We have not seen you much since your visit in the spring! To what do we owe the honour?'

Iain had stopped his horse and was sitting upright, not saying a word. Eachann was close behind him. He surveyed the party with a look of thunder and avoided his sister-in-law. Raising himself slightly in the saddle, he answered his uncle harshly, 'This is not a family visit of a nephew to his uncle, Aindreas. It is Mallaig business which brings me here. I need to speak to you alone and right now.'

He turned his horse around and went back along the path. He signalled to Eachann to stay in view. With his falcon perched on his arm, his uncle mounted his horse and followed him, a hint of a smile on his lips. When the two men were out of earshot of the group, Iain dismounted. Aindreas took the time to hood his falcon and place it on his shoulder before getting down from his horse. He walked measuredly up to Iain, a hand on the pommel of his claymore.

'If you have come on business, Iain, I do not like the way you spoke to me. You do not treat lairds like serfs...'

'Enough, Aindreas!' Iain interrupted with a voice of authority as he placed his hand on his claymore. 'You know very well what I have come here to reclaim: Nathaniel Keith's casket.'

'So that's it,' said Aindreas, smiling wickedly. 'Not before time! I had it in my hands last January... for twelve hours, I would say. I learned quite recently that it contained a nice sum of money, something to do with your marriage. It would appear that your charming wife considered it as her own property and did not tell you about it.' Noticing his nephew's tense expression, he continued, 'If you are here, it is because she has hidden the existence of this casket all this time... that is what comes of having a Lowland merchant's daughter for a wife. If I were you, I would not trust her with my books.'

Aindreas had barely finished his sentence when he felt the point of his nephew's claymore under his nose. Too engrossed in his little game, he had not paid attention to Iain's movements and did not have time to counter the move. He looked over Iain's shoulder and smiled when he saw Eachann and one of his own knights watching them from a distance.

'Calm down, my lord,' he simpered. 'You are being watched. It is not nice.'

'You dare to accuse my wife?' hissed Iain without lowering his weapon. 'How can you hope to have me swallow such a lie?'

'You, I will certainly never get you to swallow it,' articulated his uncle as he turned slowly towards his horse. 'It is simply enough that others believe it, particularly Darnley.'

'Scum! You are admitting your crime!' shouted Iain, almost choking, his feet firmly on the ground and his hands clenched around his claymore. 'It is my wife's word against yours. Are you sure you know what your word is worth?'

'My dear nephew, it is no secret that you and your wife absolutely detested one another before my brother's death. There is nothing more plausible than to believe that she wanted to avenge herself for her unhappy marriage at that time. The casket came from her father, after all, and it is perfectly normal that she kept it for herself. As for my word, it is corroborated by a witness.' Calmly getting into the saddle, he continued, 'In fact, your sister-in-law was present when I gave Nathaniel Keith's casket to your wife. Think carefully, Iain, before making accusations against your own clan. You do not know what harm you will cause the MacNeils.'

Iain's face was like flint. He watched his uncle trot off towards the clearing and closed his eyes in pain. He resignedly put his claymore back in his belt. Proof. There must be evidence to glean besides the testimonies.

'It is a plot,' he said. He held out his hand to his horse, pulled it towards him, and leaned his head on his warm neck. Looking up to the grey clouds, he said painfully, 'Father, what kind of brother did you have? He could not have loved you any more than I loved Alasdair.'

The return journey to Mallaig passed in a heavy silence which the young chief maintained, and his knight did not dare break. When they entered the castle, the evening meal was over in the great hall, and the evening was beginning as usual with songs and music. The young chatelaine, though a little tense, joined in. Tomas looked on. He was intrigued. No one had given any information or, indeed made any comment on the young master's trip. The folk in the castle were used to his secrets. They were more afraid of the look of concern on his chatelaine's face. Young Jenny felt that something was wrong but did not permit herself to question her mistress. She was pretty sure that Lord Tomas's return from Crathes had something to do with the situation, but the young man was the last person she would have asked for an explanation. On the contrary, she did her best not to speak to him more than her duties demanded. *I am stupid to still find him so handsome*, she would say to herself every time she spied on him, without him seeing her. *He is not for me. Almighty God, stop me from loving him!*

Tomas ended up worrying about his cousin's absence. The knowledge that he had gone to Loch Morar alarmed him. He had gone to his bedroom to have a wash and a few hours' sleep and as he came back down, Lady Gunelle had stopped him and told him where Iain had gone. Had he known, he would have gone with him. When his keen ear picked up the sound of hooves on the drawbridge, he discreetly stood up and went out into the courtyard. He caught hold of Iain's bridle before the groom got a chance.

'Well, how did it go?' asked Tomas, relieved to see him dismount safe and sound 'What has happened?'

'What are you talking about?' growled Iain. 'Has Gunelle told you anything?'

The note of suspicion surprised Tomas and opened an old wound. 'No, Iain, I know absolutely nothing about what you went to do at Loch Morar. What I do know is that you certainly did not go hunting with falcons.'

'Wrong! Aindreas hunted all afternoon... and in charming company. Have a little guess who was there?' In his cousin's silence, he answered it himself, 'My ineffable sister-in-law! Beathag, the traitor! Beathag the wicked.'

Iain calmed down on seeing his cousin's puzzled, wounded expression. Putting his arm around his shoulders, he led him towards the keep. 'Sorry, Tomas. You do not know the difficulty I am in. How is Gunelle? She was not too anxious today? Let us go and find her. I will tell you everything later.'

'Listen, Iain, you do not owe me an explanation. It is just that I do not like you going to Uncle Aindreas's on your own without me.' Tomas glanced over at Eachann, who was walking towards the guardroom, and added, 'I would have gone with you if you had asked me.'

'I know, Tomas. I wanted to let you rest. You have already done a lot for me. I promise I will take you next time.'

Silence fell when they entered the great hall. The young chatelaine stood up and ran to meet her husband, who took her in his arms and buried his face in her hair. Little Ceit, who was playing with Bran on the rug, not wanting to be left out, let go of Bran's neck and rushed towards her embracing parents. The dog followed suit with a bark, and everyone burst out laughing, which lightened the atmosphere. Tension had eased with the return of the master of Mallaig. Standing in the doorway behind the reunited little family, Tomas was looking at the circle of armchairs by the fire and the happy faces of the castle folk. He met Jenny's evasive look and decided to walk over to her before she thought of slipping away. He arrived just in time to cut off her retreat.

'I know you have good reason to avoid me, Jenny,' he said breathlessly, 'and I am ashamed of that. I beg you to accept my apologies. I made advances which were unworthy of the respect I have for you and in breach of the knightly code of conduct I have just embraced. I want you to know that I would be the happiest man alive if you remained friends with me.'

He had expressed this last sentence almost as a desperate plea. Jenny lifted her head and looked at him with growing unease.

'Really, who am I,' she stammered, 'to deserve an apology, my lord? Because I am in the garden and school a lot with my mistress and after having a seat on the dais with the ladies, I almost considered myself as one of them. But I am not a lady, and you will always be a lord. I played a game of forfeit with you, but it was out of place. I deserved the reaction which I aroused in...'

'Shhh, Jenny!' interrupted Tomas as he put a finger on her lips. 'Do not speak to me about ladies and lords! Our friendship makes a mockery of those titles. Nothing gives me the right to offend you in any way. I was delighted to joust for you, and I went about gaining your favour very badly. Do not think of me as the horrible caricature of the lord who abuses his privileges, Jenny... I beg you.'

Jenny felt herself blushing as she remembered the feel of Tomas's lips on hers. She looked down to avoid his eyes and murmured, 'If I had drunk half the whisky you drank that day, I am sure I would have gone along with what you seemed to want, Lord Tomas. The other girls think I am mad to have resisted. But not my parents.' She looked him straight in the eye and added, 'And me neither. I wish you a good evening, my lord!'

With a curt nod of the head, she turned around and bounced out of the room, her heart rejoicing. Tomas watched her, relieved of the pain his behaviour towards her had cost him over the past two weeks. He, at last, felt his head reconciled to the title of knight and his heart delighted with the title of lover.

Iain had never seemed as preoccupied as he did that evening. I silently watched him, waiting for him recount the meeting with his uncle. After spending some time with Ceit, the knights, Mairi, Nellie, Anna, Tomas, Father Henriot, and Darnley in the great hall, we went up to our room. As he often did when we dispensed with the servants' help to get ready for bed, he absentmindedly went through his nightly routine. He lit the candles, turned down the sheets, and opened the curtains to air the bed. He closed the rush blinds, which stopped the midges from getting into the room in the summer. He poked the fire we kept burning to heat water and came to undo the laces of my dress.

'My lady,' I heard him whisper, 'your clothes seem tight. Are you sure the baby has room to grow?'

'My lord,' I replied in amusement, 'it is very small at the moment. My waistline has not altered. Do not fear. I will not allow myself to be strangled. Nellie thinks I will not have to wear a smock until September.' I turned to him and added, 'It seems that men do not like bellies sticking out very much.'

'I could not care less what men like or do not like, my lady. As for me, I will always love this belly for it holds my treasure…'

As he said that, he placed the palms of his hands on my belly and gently moved them around in circles. His blue eyes were fixed on mine, and I saw in them a great tenderness. I put my arms around his shoulders and placed my mouth in the hollow of his damp neck. I closed my eyes and whispered, 'I love you, Iain MacNeil.' Little by little, he relaxed and began to recount his visit to Loch Morar in detail. I noticed his clenched fists and a slight tension in his arms when he mentioned his sister-in-law's name. The words he used to describe her, his tone of voice, the fire in his eyes, everything told me that the only feeling he had for her was a fierce hatred which almost frightened me. It crossed my mind that he would be capable of killing her. He had stopped talking and was slowly pacing the floor, lost in thought. I began to consider my own feelings towards this woman I had lived with for seven months. This woman, who at times had exasperated me and at other moments, horrified me. One thing was certain and was deeply embedded in my heart every time I pictured her face in the Morar forest: *Beathag wanted me dead… she hates me.*

Her recent treachery proved that her hatred had now spread to her brother-in-law and former lover. Suddenly I felt vulnerable. For the first time in my life, someone hated me. And faced with this realisation, I questioned whether my Christian faith could control the resentment growing within me. When I thought about Beathag's lies, I almost shook with revulsion. Who was behind the plot against the master and chatelaine of Mallaig? Beathag or Aindreas. Which one of them could have invented such a story about me?

'It is madness, Iain,' I said suddenly. 'Even if I had detested you, which is not the case, I would never have stolen a casket meant for your father, whom I always loved. Everyone knows and will testify that I loved Lord Baltair very much.'

'My darling,' he replied, 'I do not think it was ever about my father. It will always remain plausible that you assumed that the casket from Crathes was meant for you. It does not matter anyway! If I take Aindreas to court, he will need greater proof than Beathag's word alone.'

'You must go to court, my lord. You cannot allow yourself to be robbed by a member of your own clan. No matter the size of the theft, it is inadmissible,' I said in outrage.

'As far as Aindreas is concerned, there is another motive for the theft. Indeed, I think the theft is only a move to challenge my title as chief. If Iain MacNeil is accused of embezzlement against the Crown, they may want to replace him as clan chief. That is why the only thing which matters for the moment, Gunelle, is to convince the King of Scotland regarding the missing one hundred and twenty pounds into our accounts last January.'

'Convince them of the loss or the theft, my lord,' I said.

'Since Darnley is involved, it is better to talk about the loss.'

This did nothing to reassure me. For a long time, I had understood that my husband placed the honour of the MacNeils above everything else to the detriment of his own interests and even to the risk of his own freedom. If he were found guilty of embezzlement, he was certainly going to prison... and perhaps worse. My heart stopped beating at the thought, and I felt I was going to faint. I looked closely at my husband. He had walked over to the fire and was leaning with his hands stretched out on the mantelpiece. I could see his straight back, broad shoulders, and narrow hips, which were

378

shown off to greater effect in the light around him. *The king will not take him from me*, I said to myself. *I will fight with all my strength.*

The next morning when Sheriff Darnley was leaving, Iain showed a great deal of self-control. A slight drizzle covered the courtyard and everything looked damp and grey. With a calmness which worried me, my husband checked the sheriff's team with a smile on his face. He inspected the horses, carriage, and the standards. Adopting a benevolent tone, he gave his instructions to the Mallaig guards he was sending as the sheriff's escort as far as Stirling, the seat of the Scottish parliament for over a year now.

I was standing under the porch with the ladies and Father Henriot, waiting to wish him a good journey as the hostess does on these occasions, and I observed my husband's behaviour rather anxiously. I could not help remarking how Iain had changed since the day he welcomed Darnley in the place of his father. First and foremost, his mastery of the Scots language. I remembered with emotion the king's visit and how I had been ashamed of my husband and his ignorance. The thought of that suddenly reminded me that the King of Scotland no doubt had the picture of a young and uneducated lord in his mind. The look of self-importance on Sheriff Darnley's face as he came to bid me farewell made me realise that that image would be reinforced thanks to the latter. I was to learn later that I was not wrong. Once the sheriff had left, you would have said that Mallaig breathed easily. I discovered the joys and the blessings of life at Mallaig during the summer months. The harvesting, the threshing, the work of the mills, the presses and the salterns, everything seemed to fill the castle and the village with a joyful but tiring effervescence which often went on for several hours.

A week after the sheriff's departure, Lennox delivered the forty-six pounds just as my father had promised. Once again, he could only stay one night, but together with Iain, we had long discussions during which he reiterated his help to solve the mystery. From that day, I knew that a very solid friendship had been forged between the lieutenant and my husband and that his role as my protector was as strong as ever.

July immersed the castle and the courtyard in an uncomfortable heat, and I began to seek the coolness of the chapel and the great hall from early morning. Fortunately, I no longer suffered the bouts of nausea which had begun to depress me. As far as Iain was concerned, I had a sort of respite. Neither completely carefree nor overly anxious, we tried to forget the spectres of Darnley and Aindreas as best we could. At this time, my husband found a distraction in his studies which did him good. He would plunge himself into his reading early in the morning and only stopped in the middle of the afternoon. Then he would go riding on the moor with one of his men and they covered a good part of the estate each time.

As for me, I took my mind off things by making my baby's layette. I spent most of my days at it, helped by Nellie, who was gradually giving up the hard work in the garden. My good old nurse had begun to suffer pains in her legs and back, which gave her little peace and which I did not know how to relieve. During the many hours we worked together, Nellie would speak to me about the confinements she had experienced with my mother and sisters. That way, I learned a great many secrets about being a new mother and about nurses. Those marvellous conversations gradually led me to decide to breastfeed my child.

It was at this time that the diocese of Barra, under the supervision of the Bishop of Kisimul, sent two monks to assist Father Henriot. It was an answer to a request made by the priest before my arrival, which the foundation of the school at Mallaig at the time had rendered urgent. The two young men of God immediately assumed a great deal of responsibility for the children's education, thus freeing Father Henriot and Tomas from their long hours in the classroom. Having settled very quickly into life at the castle, they proved to be pleasant company for everyone. One of them, a very good gardener, spent a lot of time in the kitchen garden; the other taught Anna and Mairi the technique of making goat's cheese. So it was that at the end of the month, I tasted the first goat cheese made at Mallaig, which from what I remembered of that served in the refectory at Orleans, turned out to be of excellent quality.

At the end of August, when the envoys from Stirling began to travel the Highlands summoning lairds and lords to appear before the chancellor, we knew that Mallaig would not escape. Hardly a clan could claim that all its accounts were perfectly in order as regards the taxes. To be sure, the sheriff had done a good job, and the Crown's coffers were filled with a substantial contribution from the Highlanders in that year of grace 1425. We learned very quickly that the prisons at Scone and Stirling were filling. The summonses were simply the preliminary step to imprisonments of shorter or longer duration of lairds, secretaries, and little nobles on whom suspicion of embezzlement weighed heavily. Most were released after just a few days. Others, of whom the king wanted to make an example, were kept in jail all autumn and even a part of the winter. Camerons, MacDonalds, Sinclairs, Frasers, and MacKenzies were such.

During the final week of August, while he was out riding, my husband met the king's emissary who was delivering a summons for Mallaig. The stocky and morose man was travelling with a young guard. As it was the end of the day, Iain brought them back to the castle and offered them a bed for the night. I was in my bedroom when I saw them through the window coming into the courtyard, the royal coat of arms on their halberds. I began to fear the ordeal for which I had been preparing myself. *Iain is going to go away… when will he come back?* Several minutes later, I was completely stunned when I learned from my furious husband's lips that the chancellor was serving the summons on the Mallaig secretary, me, its chatelaine, as it so happened.

'It is quite unthinkable,' he raged. 'It is absolutely out of the question that you go. That devil of a Darnley knows about your condition. What a cheek! I would give my right hand to prove that Beathag has something to do with this.'

We had indeed learned from Rosalind that, a week after Darnley's departure, Iain's sister-in-law had gone to Stirling escorted by a group provided by Aindreas. She had not returned. What had she gone to do there? She did not even speak a word of Scots. Now we had a vague idea. She must have gone to seek refuge with the sheriff and she did not need to speak Scots to indulge in the activities she was involved in. Iain was crimson with rage and thumped every surface within reach. When at last he looked at me, he must have seen my fear, for he calmed down, came towards me, and gently took my hands.

'Do not be afraid, Gunelle. You will not be going. I will give an account of Mallaig's income. No man, not even the king, can demand such a journey of you at the moment. Your condition is obvious and the matter is not up for discussion. I assure you I will have Darnley's hide for this summons. And if my damned sister-in-law has had a part in it, and it is obvious she has, I will have her hide at the same time.'

'Iain, I beg you,' I pleaded, my voice trembling, 'do not go and wage war against a sheriff on his own territory. You have no chance of winning. What use would you be to anyone if you are locked up like so many others? You will prove Aindreas and Beathag right, and you will not see the birth of your child. Oh, Iain! Promise not to do anything irreparable!'

He let go of me and looked at me. I could see in his eyes that he had just realised that a long term of imprisonment could see him miss our child's birth, as I had just said. He heaved such a deep sigh that I felt him tremble when he closed his arms around me again.

'No one on this earth will keep me from being with you the day our child comes into the world,' he whispered.

It was a very weak promise, but I had to make do with it. When Iain left for Stirling three days later, I was exhausted. Right up to the last minute, I had hoped that Tomas would be able to go in his place. In fact, as soon as he had heard the terms of the summons, Iain's cousin had expressed the desire to go to Stirling to represent him, as it is a lord's prerogative to choose a representative from his people when he is unable to attend the court.

But typically Iain, he remained inflexible. 'It is up to me and me alone to represent Mallaig before the king of Scotland's chancellor,' was his only reply.

I think the grace I asked God to give me to bear that departure was given, for a great trust filled and remained in my heart from the moment I saw Iain's party go out of sight on the plateau that fifth of September 1425. The unshakeable courage which undergirded me at that moment never left me until my husband's return.

Chapter Fifteen
The Plague

The road Iain took crossed through the Trossachs and along the shores of a multitude of lochs towards Stirling, a six days' ride from Mallaig. With him, he had brought Eachann and Domhnull, who spoke a little Scots, and two armed men. Father Henriot was accompanying them since he wished to visit Cambuskenneth Abbey, the monastery of his order, the order of St. Augustine. The journey, his first since he began his ministry at Mallaig, filled him with joy, and the excitement of travelling such a distance meant that he did not stop talking. In fact, he was the only one who spoke, and it did not worry him in the slightest that no one else was joined in the conversation.

Because of the stifling heat, the party had decided to travel in the mornings and then in the evening until nightfall, when they looked for a spot to set up camp. At midday, the travellers would stop near water, unsaddle their horses, and let them graze in the heather. The men quenched their thirst from the nearest stream, had something to eat, and rested for a while. Then they started off again when the sun was not as hot. That particular morning, Iain was deep in thought, and was allowing himself to be rocked by the gentle pace of his horse, uninterested in the scenery or the wellbeing of his party. As he had done since they had left Mallaig, Domhnull was at the front and, from time to time, he glanced at the inexhaustible little man of the cloth to make sure that, from his position in the saddle, he was not showing too many signs of tiredness. Father Henriot was a very mediocre horseman, and they had set the speed at his pace. For two days, the weather had been fine and dry. The rugged ground meant that the riders were constantly climbing and descending alongside the numerous lochs with their wooded banks, which formed this part of the Lowlands. They began their final descent towards Loch Lomond, known as the king of the Scottish lochs because of its size and majestic setting, surrounded by green mountains. Domhnull stopped and pointed out the river Leven in the distance.

'If we follow that river, my lord,' he said for Iain's benefit, 'we eventually reach the river Clyde near Glasgow. If we go round by Ben Lomond, we join the Forth near Stirling and Edinburgh passing through Doune, the former home of the Duke of Albany. That is where several of the Highland lords stop on their way to or from Stirling. At a steady pace it is a day's ride. Having taken the cattle to the market these past few years, I know this is the easiest route.'

'And no doubt the busiest,' added Iain. 'Those unfortunate Highlanders who are returning from prison would be absolutely delighted to come upon Iain MacNeil's little party, Iain MacNeil who so obligingly accommodated the inflexible Darnley at Mallaig. But we will go all the same. I would like to see how we are received now that the castle is in the possession of the Crown.'

They did not meet a soul. At nightfall, they had their first view of Doune Castle. There were battle walks on three sides of the courtyard; the fourth was formed by the keep, a magnificent building with four floors. The last rays of sunset formed a pink halo over the crenels. At first, the lack of movement around the walls surprised Iain. Then, the fact that they had not met anyone on the road north to the Highlands led him to surmise that no one actually stopped at the castle. There had to be a very special reason for a chatelaine to refuse hospitality to travellers, and Iain thought it more prudent to stop his party two hundred yards from the castle and to light a fire to show that they were there. The group did not have to wait long to find out the reason. A young horseman rode to meet them. He looked distraught and his greeting was extremely brief. He was only interested in Father Henriot.

'My master sent me,' he mumbled in Iain's direction. 'He saw you from the ramparts and is asking for the priest. Ours died yesterday. You cannot come in. Only the priest. I cannot stay. I must return immediately, my lord... with the priest.'

Immediately, he abruptly turned his horse in the priest's direction to get him to follow. The questions Iain shouted at him remained unanswered, nor did they even slow down the guard's progress towards the castle or stop his desperate gestures aimed at getting the priest to accompany him. Iain resignedly signalled to Father Henriot to follow him. There was no way of finding out more. The priest, looking intrigued, remounted, and set off after this strange messenger. As he left his friends, he gave them one of his reassuring smiles. An hour later, with no sign of him coming back, Iain decided to go back up closer to the woods and set up camp for the night. *What is going on in there?* he wondered.

That evening, around a meal of dried meat and without their talkative travelling companion, the men, deep in concerned silence, found themselves very much at a loss as to what to do. As he took over his watch, Domhnull began a conversation with his lord, hoping to ease the burden which had seemed to be weighing him down since their departure. He was surprised to receive his confidences so spontaneously. As a man of experience, he had judged the young chief's state of mind very well. In fact, Iain took advantage of the opportunity and opened his heart to his knight, welcoming all his questions and even appreciating them. Away from Mallaig, the conspiracy was taking on a different dimension. He was surprised when he found himself mentioning the fact that his sister-in-law was in Stirling, a piece of information he thought it better not to keep from Dohmnull.

'My lord,' suggested the latter carefully, 'if you are afraid of trouble from your sister-in-law, why not take her and lock her up where she can do no harm? She tried to kill you. Even Sheriff Darnley is a witness to that. It was very good of you to simply throw her out of Mallaig at that time.'

'I certainly did not do it out of goodness,' replied Iain. 'I was more concerned for myself than for her, and I realise today that it was not a wise thing to do.' Staring into the fire, he continued, 'You see, Dohmnull, for me and everyone at Mallaig, my sister-in-law is the incarnation of my bad side. To take her to court is to accept the revelation of the despicable man I was. The only way to purify Mallaig of her presence was to throw her out. I know that that does not get her out of my life. To do that, I will have to kill her.' Looking again at his knight, who was hanging on every word, he added, 'She must not give me the opportunity.' Then, after a long silence, he asked point blank, 'Tell me, Dohmnull, did she ever have you in her bed?'

The direct question startled Dohmnull. After the chatelaine's death, there was not one knight, captain, or man at arms at Mallaig who had not sought and won the favours of Lord Alasdair's widow. Lord Iain was not ignorant of that and had never felt any jealousy. If he was asking the question, it was no doubt to discover any connection which could have existed between the widow and his knight.

Looking into the fire rather than at his master, he replied, 'Like all the others, my lord, but no more than any other. When you were away, Lady Beathag did not favour one man over another. It was always she who chose whom she would have in her bed and when.'

'I know, Dohmnull,' Iain interrupted with a laugh. 'Even with me, it was she who decided. If your services were not required, best not to insist, or she would put you in quarantine and starve you... you could say she knows how to control a man... or at least his desires.' Iain uttered these last words with a real note of bitterness.

Dohmnull realised his lord was ashamed and would say no more on the matter. In fact, Iain lay down, rolled himself in his blanket, and gloomily said good night. Dohmnull looked up at the starry sky and silently prayed for everyone who would arrive at Stirling the next day as well as for Beathag, who was perhaps spending her last days there.

However, they could not leave the camp until late the next day since the priest was only relieved of his duties at the castle late afternoon. They saw him leaving the castle on his own and trotting to join them. Iain had never seen Father Henriot look as he did at that moment. The little man looked exhausted and completely drained. He slid down off his horse, knelt on the ground, crossed himself as he looked at the castle walls, and prayed for a few minutes. Not knowing what to say, the men looked on in silence, a vague apprehension gripping their hearts. When the priest finally spoke, it was to give them the distressing account of what he had experienced inside the castle.

'My lord,' he said as he looked at Iain, 'it is the plague. In the castle, seven people died last week, then their priest the day before yesterday and three other men last night. The first was Hamish Fraser, who was coming back from Stirling and heading home; the second was his knight, Ailean. They contracted the disease in the king's prison, where it is spreading like wildfire.'

'That is why we are not meeting anyone heading for the Highlands,' murmured Iain in alarm.

'And why the castle is no longer open to travellers,' continued the priest. 'And why I stink of vinegar! They covered my clothes in it. A precaution which their own priest had not taken, but I doubt its effectiveness.' He looked towards the south and explained, 'It's the south wind which is bringing this sickness… and it is a judgement from heaven.'

Kneeling again, he invited the others to join him. 'Let us pray, brothers. God will hear us if we are repentant, and in His great wisdom, He will spare us.'

I was busy admiring the vase of flowers Anna had placed in the study window. She had done it ever since I began spending most of the day there entering the numerous end-of-summer accounts in the books. I had had no news from my husband since his departure about three weeks ago, and none of the Highland clans waiting for a family member to return from Stirling knew any more than me about what was happening.

There was a knock at the door, and I jumped. A guardsman showed in two of the estate serfs who had come to deliver their part of the harvest to the castle storehouse. According to my reckoning, these had to be the last. The recording of the foodstuffs would begin again at the end of the next month with the slaughter of the cattle which would not be wintered and those destined for the salting, so I would see them all again. One of them, a big strapping red-haired fellow, took a folded handkerchief out of his pouch and put it down on the table in front of me.

'That's from my wife,' he mumbled. 'She made it herself, and it is for the little one, my lady. The heir of the good young lord, your husband. May God protect him from the illness at the king's palace.'

I did not pay attention to the end of his sentence and opened what I knew to be a small present made by a woman from the village for my baby's layette. I smiled as I held up the little woollen bootees to the light. It was the seventh pair I had received since Jenny's mother had started the ball rolling at the beginning of the month. I was touched by these affectionate gestures on the part of the people who often could not put shoes on their own babies. I made up my mind in the future to find out about every new baby in the village and give them swaddling clothes and fur covers.

'Thank her for me, Gavin. They are very pretty,' I said to him. 'If we have a harsh winter this year, my baby will not have cold feet.'

When I had entered the details concerning the two serfs, they left, and I sat in silence, slowly turning the little soft woollen booties over and over in my hands. Suddenly Gavin's words came back to me: *'Protect him from the sickness at the king's palace.'* I looked thoughtfully towards the window. What sickness can Gavin be referring to? By the end of the day, all I could think about was that illness.

We were all sitting at our evening meal by the light of four candelabras. We had started to light them since the nights were drawing in, and it was dark by the end of the afternoon. Never had Father Henriot made such a remarkable entrance as he did that night. With Sir Eachann at his side, the little man, looking tired and distraught, came towards the table amidst total silence.

'Good evening, Lady Gunelle,' he said immediately. 'I know you are waiting for a letter from your husband, but we could not find anyone to deliver it, so he charged me to bring it to you. Lord Iain only kept Dohmnull at Stirling.'

I had stood up, deadly pale, my heart thumping. I feared bad news. I held out my hand to the priest and, in so doing, knocked over a cup. With a blank look on his face, he was staring at the ever-growing damp circle on the tablecloth. Then he looked back at me, taking a moment to look at my belly. His mouth was open, but the words would not come. I saw Tomas rush towards the priest and take him over to a bench, thus preventing me from touching his outstretched hands.

'Sit down, father,' he said. 'We can wait a little for the news about my cousin. You seem so worn out.' Turning to me pleadingly, he asked me, 'Is that not so, my lady? Father Henriot can finish the meal with us and rest a while before telling us about their journey.'

'Of course,' I murmured. 'There, father, have a drink and give us your coat…'

Tomas was already taking it off before I suggested it, and a knight poured him out some beer. When he had drunk several mouthfuls, Father Henriot gathered himself together and looked around at those gathered. He looked like someone who had just survived a terrible ordeal. I was alarmed. It was difficult to pick up the conversations again, and the atmosphere remained tense. It was only later that the priest, although totally exhausted, was able to withdraw with Tomas and me beside the fire and tell us about the weeks spent in Stirling, and I learned with alarm that the plague was raging there. Without a doubt, the vision of horror I had of Stirling on hearing it described in detail, greatly surpassed what I had experienced after my night of terror in the forest. The more Father Henriot told us, the tighter my feverish hands clutched Tomas, who was having difficulty hiding his own fear.

So, Iain, like so many other Highlanders summoned to Stirling, had come face to face with a greater enemy than the king's chancellor. The Black Death. The priest told us that the horrible sickness had broken out among the prisoners and had quickly killed about fifty people in the town within a month. The king was receiving no one, was summoning no one, was imprisoning no one, and with pitiful resources, was calling all his people to fight the epidemic, which they were not sure would burn itself out.

While in Orleans, I had read so much about this terrible plague that had been blamed for decimating the population of France in less than one hundred years! Like everyone, I feared the plague which travelled back and forth across the whole of Europe and never seemed to have had its fill of victims. At will, it claimed one hundred souls here, twenty there, in villages as well as towns. When he arrived in Stirling, Father Henriot, protected by the grace of God like all men of God, had been summoned to help the many dying souls being brought to the abbey. I learned that Iain and his men had taken refuge in an inn outside the town while they waited for the chancellor's orders. He had helped as much as he could with the work of burying the dead, burning the victims' houses, and guarding the wells which were out of bounds to the stricken for fear they would contaminate the water. When the town experienced a period of respite and ten days passed without any new cases, the work of the chancellery resumed, and with it the summonses. Iain was called to the parliament, and he sent a message to the priest asking him to return to Mallaig without waiting for him. Sir Dohmnull had refused to leave Stirling.

'I really do not believe that your husband's life is in danger, my lady,' concluded the priest. 'In any case, he is not in irons, although he is not free to go where he wishes. I do not know if he was able to defend himself or if he was able to see the king as he very much

392

hoped. Perhaps the letter says more about how things are going. As for me, he added, looking at each one of us in turn, I am extremely happy to find you safe and well here at Mallaig. God is gracious…'

I could hardly breathe, I held the letter the priest had given me to my breast, impatient to know its contents. Meeting Tomas's pleading gaze, I stood up and took my leave. I hurried up to my room with Jenny on my heels. She had difficulty keeping up, and the candle flickered with each of her footsteps. I sat down in an armchair and opened the seal. Jenny stood by the table, ready to help me undress when I was ready. There were two sheets of cheap paper written in Gaelic. One for me and another very brief one for Tomas: instructions Iain was giving him regarding clan business, in particular, the attitude to adopt if Aindreas took it into his head to attack during his imprisonment. I felt a dark cloud come over me at sound of the word imprisonment. I asked Jenny to undo my bodice and to take Tomas the letter I had just read.

'I will manage the rest, Jenny. There is no need for you to come back. Good night,' I said to her.

My heart was thumping. I took the time to take off my dress and plait my hair before reading my husband's letter. I was astonished when I read it. Iain had not given me any real news but had penned a love story.

My dearest,

It is my turn to live through a nightmare. The wait to be received is endless, and I think of you all day. In doing so, I manage to forget the horror of the plague, which is on the rampage here in Stirling.

Once there was a wolf which the rest of the pack had kept at a distance for, although he was a strong and fearless hunter, he was not loved. This lone wolf became sad and bitter. And then, one day, while roaming his territory, he came across a hind which had been separated from her herd. He was starving, the prey was easy, and he stalked her. The hind fled. She was disorientated and did not know where to run because the territory was so unfamiliar to her. It was then she decided to face up to her predator and spoke to him in his own language. Never did a wolf feel less hungry than that day.

I knew that wolf, my lady. The wolf which fell in love with a hind. The wolf returned to his pack and became its leader. An invincible wolf… invincible because he is loved by that hind. Gunelle, do not forget me. Be with me as I am with you. I love you more than it is possible for any man to love.

Your beloved

Iain MacNeil

I closed my eyes which were stinging and held the paper against them for a good minute. I was welling up with tears. I stood up slowly, walked over to the bed, and put on a night dress. To help me get to sleep, I left a candle burning as if I was waiting for Iain to come home. I placed the letter on my stomach and, in the secrecy of my heart, began to plan my reply to Iain's love story.

My dearly beloved, how well I recognise you! You transform all my fears. This way, with your story, you turn the wolf of my nightmares into a cherished being, for you are this loving being, who has my heart. And the territory which seemed wild, savage, and hostile to the hind has become her best refuge and safest nest. What need has she of her herd from now on? Not now, since she is loved by a wolf.

Lord Tomas retained Eachann in the great hall after Lady Gunelle and Father Henriot left. He wanted to get more details about the conditions of his cousin's confinement. The two men did not notice Jenny arrive. She was not carrying a light and waited hesitantly in the corner. She was listening to their whispered conversation and turning the letter addressed to Tomas over in her hands. A strong curiosity took hold of her. It was almost unbearable. Barely two months ago, a letter would have left her indifferent, but since then, she had learned to read, and the letter was burning a hole in her hands. *Would I be able to read it?* she wondered. *If it is in Scots, I will not be able to, but if it is in Gaelic, I think I could make out the master's handwriting. Apparently, he is a good writer... Lord Tomas is so secretive when it comes to anything about his cousin. He never says anything about him. Lord Iain could be writing that he has the plague, and Tomas will not breathe a word. I would so love to know.*

Unable to resist any longer, she slipped out silently and went and stood under a torch in the entrance hall. After a brief look around, she unfolded the note and was relieved to see from the first words that it was in Gaelic. She began to read laboriously. She was so engrossed that she did not hear Tomas arrive. Crimson with embarrassment, her hand trembling, she immediately held out the folded sheet of paper. Tomas frowned and gave her a questioning look.

'There you are, my lord,' she whispered to him. 'It is for you. It was in with Lady Gunelle's letter. I was going to bring it to you.'

'Did you read it?' he asked her reproachfully as he took the letter.

'I did not want to read it... that is... I wanted... I should not have...I know it is bad to read someone else's letter. Please forgive me, my lord. I could not help it. I am so afraid for my mistress… that her husband…'

Tomas did not answer. He gestured to the young girl to wait and quickly read his cousin's note; then, looking at her, he could not help gently scolding her.

'You could be and should be punished for what you did, Jenny, but I won't.' After a moment's thought, he looked away. 'My cousin has several problems at the moment, some of which, as you have discovered, having read the letter, are with members of the clan. It may well be that those are the cause of all the others. Your mistress is strong, but she will need looking after more than ever. Now that you are in the know, I am counting on you to be with her at all times and not let her out of your sight.'

'Thank you for your trust, my lord! But just tell me why we should fear Lady Beathag's return.'

Tomas sighed. Of course, the question was to be expected. Among his other suggestions, his cousin wrote that they must be wary of Beathag being in the vicinity of the castle. Iain had heard she had left Stirling as soon as he had been confined to the Ministry of Justice, and he was afraid that she might try something against Gunelle in his absence. Tomas reread the passage, folded the letter, and put it inside his doublet. He decided to answer the question by sticking to the essentials. Without a word, he took Jenny's hand and led her up to the ramparts. The young girl followed willingly, her heart bubbling with joy, her hands clammy. When they arrived at a dark spot well away from the guards, he sat her down against the wall and sat down beside her.

'Jenny,' he began tensely, 'contrary to what was said, my cousin's sister-in-law did not leave Mallaig of her own free will. She was thrown out. For one reason which on its own deserves the death penalty: She tried to kill Lady Gunelle and then my cousin.' Seeing Jenny put her hands on her heart in shock, he continued more gently, 'She is dangerous, and we believe she is capable of anything. She has cunningly won over Sheriff Darnley. That is why my cousin is not in the king's good books and is unable to protect his wife himself.' Looking her straight in the eyes, he added, 'Do you understand why your mistress must not be left on her own, and why Beathag must not be allowed anywhere near the castle?'

'My lord, does that apply to Lady Beathag's companion? Is the castle out of bounds to her also?'

'Finella? Probably. But I doubt very much that she would come here on her own.'

'Yet she was here the day of the tournament. I met her upstairs when I rushed up to get my ribbon.' On remembering that, she hesitated, looked down with embarrassment, then continued, 'She was going into the bedroom Lady Rosalind uses when she stays. I found it surprising but thought no more of it. There were so many people at Mallaig that day. Besides, I did not see her again afterwards.'

Tomas had stood up. These apparently insignificant details set him thinking. What the devil had Finella come to do in such a secretive way at Mallaig? It was no doubt for her mistress?

'Tell me, Jenny, did Finella see you, or did anyone else apart from you see her at the castle on St. John's Day?'

'Everyone was outside, and the castle was empty when I went upstairs. I do not know if she saw me, but at least one other person saw her that day. Your cousin Thora, for Finella was carrying her

397

shawl on her arm or rather in her hands. In fact, it was the shawl Thora threw as a forfeit later in the tournament.'

Finella, Flora, shawl, Rosalind's room. Everything was beginning to add up for Iain's cousin, but he did not yet quite understand how. Jenny tiptoed over to him. 'My lord, have I just said something important I should have said earlier?' she asked timidly.

'You have nothing to feel guilty about, Jenny.' Wanting to reassure her, he put his arm around her shoulders before adding, 'What you have just told me is certainly important, but I am not yet sure how. I forbid you to worry about it until…'

He was unable to finish his sentence. The words stuck in his throat, and his pulse was racing. Jenny had quite naturally cuddled up against him, taking advantage of his reassuring gesture. He felt the softness of her hair against his cheek and smelled her light lavender perfume. Jenny gently moved closer. It was sudden: He took her in his arms, tightened his grip, and put his lips on the head resting on his shoulder. *My love, do not put me to the test yet*, he thought. After a short moment of awkward silence, he slowly moved free and led her by the hand to the keep. He had to clear his throat to say goodnight to her in the entrance hall.

'I know that I can count on your discretion, and you will keep everything you have learned this evening to yourself. Won't you, Jenny? There, have a good night, and I will see you tomorrow.'

'Goodnight, Lord Tomas! I am going up to my mistress. I will not leave her day or night. I will tell her those are your orders, and she will keep me by her side. Have no fear about the rest… I will say nothing… and I will never read your correspondence again.'

Jenny lifted her skirt and ran up the dark staircase without waiting for Lord Tomas to hand her the torch he had lifted as he came in. His heart was racing, he turned around in the opposite direction, and went to his room to reread his cousin's instructions.

The next day the whole of Mallaig had heard from the travellers who had returned from Stirling that the master was the king's chancellor's prisoner in a town where the plague was rampant. Dismayed by the news, Aunt Rosalind and Uncle Griogair were the first clan members to turn up at the castle. Lady Rosalind was, as usual, coming to the rescue of her dear little chatelaine. She was surprised not to find the young woman distraught. On the contrary, she found her rather calm, if not serene. The same sense of calm seemed to inhabit Father Henriot. *Those two have either been touched either by divine grace or by foolhardiness*, she couldn't help thinking to herself when she saw them together in the courtyard on her arrival. *Their welcome was warm and gently eased the tension she and her husband Griogair had felt for some days at Glenfinnan.* In the course of their conversations, Lady Rosalind soon learned to her astonishment that her young friend feared her husband's overthrow in the clan more than the spectre of the plague raging around him. It was not the first time she had seen a pregnant woman invent such a fantasy to take her mind off imminent misfortune. It could only be that. *How could Gunelle honestly believe that the simple fact of Iain's confinement would bring his position as clan chief into question?*

However, the following weeks proved her fears to be justified. Apart from a short visit at the beginning of October by Aulay, the laird of Arisaig, not one other laird came to ask for news of the young chief nor even showed any sign of helping or defending him. On the other hand, Rosalind learned that Struan of Airor and Daid of Finiskaig had gone to see Aindreas. By all appearances, secret negotiations had taken place between them to isolate Mallaig from clan affairs. In mid-October, Raonall, who on the pretext of a falcon hunt was sent to Morar to spy, came back with the distinct impression that he had been excluded from several conversations between his uncle and the other lairds. As well as this, he had seen no trace of Beathag and had been given no news of her when he asked. A short time later, Griogair learned that Alasdair's widow had not returned to the islands.

Where can she be hiding? Tomas anxiously asked himself every day.

On the Mallaig Peninsula, as along the whole west coast, the harvest was gathered in, the butchery and salting finished, and the cattle markets were past. The Highlanders were preparing for winter again. Several clans still had no news of their kinsmen imprisoned in Stirling, for most messengers refused to enter the parliament town, which was still in the grip of the plague. Sir Eachann became the Mallaig messenger, taking Iain letters from the chatelaine and spices and aromatic plants to purify the air so he could be protected from the sickness in his lodgings. Eachann travelled alone by the mountain tracks to be safer. Unfortunately, he had no access to his young chief throughout October and even had difficulty finding Sir Domhnull, who was moving from one inn to another as each closed because of the plague. In early November, it was Lieutenant Lennox who was able to make a connection between Mallaig and Iain. Having brought Lord Keith's second payment from Crathes, he had been given permission to remain with the chatelaine for a while. Since the agreement with the MacPhersons meant that the tree felling in the Grampians was going smoothly, Nathaniel Keith had put his younger son Robert in charge.

Lieutenant Lennox was barely at Mallaig two days when he decided that he must go to Stirling right away to find out more about the young chief's situation, a step which should have been taken right at the start by one of his own lairds. During his conversations with Lady Gunelle, he guessed the precarious position of the young chief as far as his clan was concerned and suspected the laird of Loch Morar. When he passed through Glenfinnan, he received and accepted the unexpected offer from Lord Griogair to accompany him. Lady Rosalind loaded them with such a quantity of food and bottles of vinegar that the two men had to discard part of it before tackling the first hills in the Trossachs.

Being the same age, Griogair and Lennox had adopted a rather pragmatic approach to the plague: To protect oneself against infection, you simply had to maintain stringent personal hygiene, no women, or indeed, any activities requiring heavy breathing. The journey to Stirling provided all of that with its abundance of lochs and rivers to wash in, a complete absence of encounters of any kind and a leisurely ride demanding no excess of effort. When they finally reached Loch Lomond, they decided to go around the west side of Ben Lomond. By doing that, they missed the only traveller returning to the Highlands by the track along the eastern side: Sir Eachann.

I did not see Nellie at the service that morning. My nurse was finding it more and more difficult to walk, and it grieved her that she could only attend the morning service every other day. I looked at Anna, who was no longer young either, and I said to myself that as chatelaine, I would soon have to find a new way of dividing the housekeeping duties the two old women had shared since my marriage. *Mairi can take over since Jenny is attached to me*, I thought. So it was that after the service I asked Anna and Mairi to join Nellie upstairs with the idea of putting my plan to the three women. I anticipated having a few difficulties with the nurses who saw it as a matter of honour to remain active at the castle. I banked on my pregnancy to convince them to move from the care of the house to the care of the future baby, telling them of my intention not to take on a wet nurse but to feed my child myself. I took my time and shared my plan without hurting their feelings. At the end of the meeting the tear-filled eyes of my two old servants confirmed that I had succeeded. Mairi agreed to leave the kitchen and join Anna, who, between now and Christmas, would teach her everything about running the house. Mairi would then take over as housekeeper. I went downstairs and ran into Tomas, who was coming from the guards' room with a bundle of papers in his hand. He looked emotional and downcast. I recognised the letters I had entrusted to Eachann several weeks before. They had not been opened. I took them from him.

'What's this, Tomas?' I said in a choked voice. 'They haven't been delivered?'

'Follow me, my lady,' he said, leading me into the study. 'We have just received a piece of bad news.'

My heart gave a jump. 'Iain is dead,' I could not help muttering. My eyes, full of fear, must have struck Tomas, but he was quick to reassure me.

'My cousin is well, my lady. Calm yourself, please.'

Having sat me down in an armchair, with tears in his eyes, he announced the news: It was about Sir Domhnull. He had died a few days ago… of the plague. Dropping the bundle of letters, I put my hand to my face, stifling a cry of despair

'Our faithful Domhnull, the oldest of us all,' I said, distraught.

Tomas waited until I was composed before continuing, 'Eachann arrived a while ago. He stayed at Cambuskenneth Abbey until Domhnull's death, and he left Stirling as soon as he had buried him. Eachann is well, my lady. He has not contracted the sickness. However, he could neither deliver nor have anything delivered to Iain. The men detained at the chancellery and waiting to be tried can no longer receive messages for fear of contamination. However, they are better protected from the plague there than those found guilty and in prison or, indeed, even the townsfolk themselves. The king has gone to Scone with his family, and he is dealing with royal affairs without setting foot in the parliament. That is why it takes so long to obtain a hearing.'

On seeing how heartbroken I was, my husband's cousin stopped talking. What could be done now to help Iain? I thanked Tomas and asked him to send Father Henriot to me to arrange a requiem mass for our dead knight. I heard him leave and quietly ask Jenny to come in. I did not have to wait long for our man of the cloth. Looking at Father Henriot's face, full of emotion as he suggested the order of service for the funeral, I remarked how he, too, had aged in a very short time. *Ah, Lord Baltair, Mallaig is ageing too quickly since you left*, I thought. After the priest left the study, I looked at the letters lying on the floor and picked them up. So, Iain had no news of us. I doubted whether Lieutenant Lennox and Uncle Griogair would succeed where Sir Eachann and Dohmnull had failed. To *whom can I write to if no one opens the letters at Stirling?* I wondered. I walked over to the window and stared at the clouds passing above the turrets. The thought struck me: *Write to Scone Palace! Of course! Why not go straight to our king whom I know and who knows me? If I write to him in French and none of his staff who open the*

correspondence know the language, there is a chance that he will
read the letter himself... or his wife.

With an intrigued Jenny looking on, I immediately sat down at the
desk and pushed the accounts book out of the way. I took several
sheets of our best paper and threw myself into the execution of my
plan: to obtain Iain's release and get him out of Stirling as soon as
possible. To achieve that, he first had to be heard, and then no
accusation be made against him. I had to find the right words to
plead his case without appearing to meddle in the chancellor's
affairs. I thought long and hard about each sentence, trying to find
the degree of friendship I had had towards the king last winter. The
words flowed with simplicity and precision. Regarding the case
concerning our books, I decided to stick to the version of the sum of
money lost and not stolen, a version which Iain, too, was going to
stick to if he were heard. How had James Darnley presented his
report on Mallaig? Impossible to know that. However, it was
obvious that Iain would have to defend himself on several points and
contradict the sheriff. Also, my husband's defence would have to be
supported by the king's opinion. Therefore, I pointed out the loyalty
and service to the Scottish Crown which the clan MacNeil had
shown in facilitating the work of the king's auditor in the Highlands.
It seemed equally opportune to remind the king that my own family,
the Keiths, were serving the Crown's interests, on the one hand with
my father who had provided the oak for the ships of the royal fleet
for over twenty years, and on the other, my Uncle William, who was
the Marshall in Edinburgh. When I finished, I thought of my replies
to Iain in the letters he had not received, and I remembered his love
story. I looked down at my stomach, which was sticking out under
my dress. Suddenly I felt the baby move like the gentle movement
of the waves. At that moment, it was clear to me that I needed Iain
with me. That was more important than getting my husband out of
the plague-ridden town, more important than foiling the plot in the

heart of the clan, more important than thwarting Beathag's plans of revenge—more important than all of that.

'Your Majesty,' I sighed aloud, 'I desire to have my husband back here with me. Can you understand that?'

I caught Jenny's look of amusement, smiled, and continued my monologue, 'You may not be able to understand but your wife will.'

I took a new sheet of paper and began to write to Queen Jeanne, praising her husband with whom I had had the great honour of conversing here at Mallaig. I pointed out how much she was loved in the royal court and that he, himself, was aware of it. Addressing the mother of the little Princess of Scotland, I wanted to send a gift for the little girl. *The Lone Wolf and the Hind*, I thought. *A story! Of course!*

'Jenny, dear,' I said to my servant, 'would you go and bring me the Gaelic tales we used to teach the children to write? I am going to translate one of them and send it with my letter. The Queen of Scotland will have a Highland tale to read to her daughter in French.'

Buoyed with enthusiasm, I worked with Jenny on the letter to Scone for a good part of the afternoon. As she was a good artist, I asked her to illustrate the tale, which she dotted with little figures in the margin just like the illuminations in an ancient book. The page was very pretty and quite irresistible when she handed it to me. I ended the letter to the queen by informing her of my condition. I said I was hoping for a little girl and thinking of the princess. I did not tell her that my husband wanted a son. I mentioned that he hoped to be home from Stirling for the birth of our first child. I guessed that the queen's heart would want to know more and that she would find out what I wanted her to find out.

The upper wooden bar of the four-poster bed split in two under Lord Iain's weight. The young lord immediately, landed with a thud on the mattress. His body was pouring with sweat. The bed in his lodgings was small but had solid posts which had at one time, no doubt, supported a canopy. He had been using the crossbars to do his daily exercises, which sometimes lasted more than three hours. He found this the best way to pass his endless days of captivity. Having had his weapons confiscated, he had quickly realised that his body would seize up with lack of exercise and so had decided to work at it any way he could. As soon as he had begun to train, he realised that the exercise kept him mentally alert and settled the anger he had felt since the summons. He pouted in disappointment when he looked at the two pieces of the broken crossbar. Leaning backwards, he examined the other crossbar.

'Well, I still have that one,' he muttered.

As he was musing, there was a knock at the door, which opened to reveal Lieutenant Lennox wearing a long coat but no weapon in his belt. The lieutenant came in, and as he waited for his eyes get used to the darkness, he anxiously looked at Iain for a moment. Iain jumped up, smiling.

'Lennox! Marvellous! How did you get through?' he said, walking straight to him, his arms outstretched.

'My lord,' said the latter, staring at the young man's shining body and backing towards the door which had just shut behind him, 'are you ill?'

'Oh, that! Pay no attention to that,' answered Iain as he lifted his shirt. 'I was doing a few exercises to keep my back supple. I am in perfect health. I do not have the plague if that is what you are thinking. I have neither a temperature nor a headache. I am never ill even though what I eat here is often disgusting. I have no boils. But look at that, though.' He pointed to the four walls adding. 'No south-facing window, just those arrow windows facing the northwest, and the healthy, fresh air of the Highlands.'

Lieutenant Lennox could not help smiling at the young chief's contagious humour. He went towards him, holding out his gloved hand.

'It is a pleasure to see you, my lord! It is no small feat to obtain permission to visit a Highlander at the moment, but I played my master's card. The Keiths have a good name in the Lowlands, particularly with the people in the chancellor's office. One must make use of that.'

'You would be lying if you told me my friendly father-in-law sent you, Lennox,' retorted Iain, smiling wickedly. 'I wager you have come straight from Mallaig. Am I wrong?'

'Touché! I have come from your home, my lord. Your laird, Lord Griogair, is with me, but he could not come in. I have only been given a little time to talk to you, so I will give you news of your wife immediately, and you can tell me how we can get you out of here.'

By the time someone came to fetch Lieutenant Lennox, the two men had had time to share the main news and concluded that there was very little room for manoeuvre to free the chief.

'I either escape, or I await my turn,' explained Iain. 'From what I hear, the hearings are long, and there are no more than three a week.

I have not been given the list of the detainees, but I am counting on Darnley to suggest I be kept until last. If you can do anything, that is where you must work.'

'My master's brother, Marshal William Keith, is in Edinburgh, my lord. I am going to go and see if he can intervene on your behalf. But before I leave, Griogair is asking if you know where your knights Dohmnull and Eachann are staying in Stirling?'

'I do not know, Lennox. It has been two weeks since I had news of them. They found a boarding house near the Church of the Holy Rude, I think.'

That very afternoon, Lieutenant Lennox, and Lord Griogair's enquiries led them to Cambuskenneth Abbey, where they were informed that one of the Mallaig knights had died and the other had returned to the Highlands. They did not dare ask which of the two had succumbed to the plague. The damp cold weather which went right through their woollen clothes to their very bones just added to their misery. The wet deserted streets, the persistent wind which surrounded them, and the sky heavy with rain forced them to leave the town before nightfall. Lord Griogair, who had become fond of the lieutenant, decided to accompany him to Edinburgh. The two men only returned to Stirling twelve days later with a letter of recommendation for the chancellor from Marshal Keith. Imagine their surprise to learn that Lord Iain MacNeil had been taken to Scone palace the day before.

During the two days' journey under escort to Scone, Lord Iain had had to stop himself from singing on several occasions. Once the surprise at being transferred to the king's palace had passed, and his many questions proved fruitless due to an absence of answers, the young chief allowed himself to be filled with hope and joy. First, his weapons and horse had been returned to him, indicating that the king did not consider him to be a threat. Secondly, the chief escort was reluctant to discuss the transfer, for there had never been one since the first Highlanders had been summoned to the chancellery. Iain began to hope that he had been summoned to an audience with the king. He had never been to Scone but had heard a lot about the town on the right bank of the river Tay and of its impressive palace, which dated from the time of the Pictish king Kenneth MacAlpin. When the bell tower of Scone Abbey came into view, Iain knew that he was close. And there it was, the palace just visible in the dense mist and opposite it, Moot Hill. The captain in charge of the escort man gruffly gave the order to dismount. Minutes later, Iain accompanied him within the walls of the magnificent palace. At the heart of the palace, he was shown into a vast anteroom where he was kept waiting for an hour. There was no fire, and it was dark and damp. Iain felt very cold as much by nervousness as the lack of heat. There were about ten other people, for the most part, little nobles who, like him, did not know what to do with themselves and were wandering around freely. There was no guard at the door, and Iain was amazed at that. *Is someone finally going to tell me what I am waiting for here?* he said to himself. At one point, he thought he saw Sheriff Darnley in the next room when the door opened. Later, it was Saxton he thought he recognised. *I am seeing things*, he thought. *What would Guilbert Saxton be doing here? For two months I have seen so few people and now, I think I am seeing them all at once.*

Then he heard his name being called from the other side of the room and rose to his feet. A little priest, a pinched smile on his lips, came over and invited him to follow him. He led him silently along a long corridor to an alcove guarded by two soldiers. The priest bowed and left him with a simple 'My lord." One of the soldiers opened the door and let him in. Iain entered a room brightly lit with candles and sulphur lanterns. A large fire gave off a welcome heat. Two other guards were on duty at the door. Iain passed them and slowly went forward. It was then he saw the king stick his head out around his armchair, which was placed in front of the fire. The king turned towards him and looked him up and down for a moment before beckoning him forward.

'MacNeil of Mallaig! Come, my lord. I did not think I would have to summon you here. This is Kenneth Simpson, who speaks Gaelic,' said the king in Scots, pointing to a red-haired man, whom Iain had not noticed.

'Your Majesty, I do not need an interpreter if that is what Mister Simpson does,' said Iain as he stopped in front of the king, whom he greeted with a deep bow.

'I see, I was misinformed,' replied the king, with some annoyance. 'Take a seat, MacNeil. We must talk.'

Looking up at Simpson, he dismissed him with a simple nod. 'First, we are going to lay aside my sheriff's report. Although his instincts rarely deceive him, I have concluded that, in your case, they have. I prefer to believe that the MacNeils are Highlanders whose dealings with the Scottish Treasury are honest. They are perhaps the only ones, but I want to believe that they are. It would indeed be embarrassing to doubt the word of the chief on whom I relied for my campaign of checking the books last winter.' After a brief pause, he continued, 'So, Mallaig has lost a considerable amount of money, my lord?'

'Indeed, your Majesty. It is a matter of one hundred and twenty pounds, last January when my father was still alive. I have not yet made any enquiries into the matter.' Iain prudently replied.

'Good. Good. The important thing is that you paid what you owed in full. The rest does not interest me. However, my lord, I would like

410

to know if Darnley was aware of your wife's condition when he left your castle. For if he did know, the summons he issued for Mallaig is at the very least disgraceful and it is not in keeping with the way our chancellery works.'

'He was not ignorant of it, your Majesty. Can I ask my sovereign how he learned of my wife's condition?'

King James smiled enigmatically and stood up to stretch his legs a little. Iain immediately rose to his feet and stood waiting for his reply. It came after a long moment of reflection.

'Lord MacNeil, the truth is you have a very intelligent and even astute wife. I see that you are unaware that Lady Gunelle has corresponded with the queen. The queen intends to reply to your wife's letter, dear fellow. We received her letter a week ago. She informed us of her pregnancy as well as giving us other interesting information about your books. May I offer our congratulations? I have fond memories of your extremely brilliant wife and her impeccable French. The queen would be extremely disappointed if you were not back home for your heir's birth.' He smiled at Iain's look of astonishment and continued, 'Now, MacNeil, you can relax. I do not know why Darnley is trying to do you harm. Sadly, I believe that, excellent auditor though he is, he has no time for any of the Highlanders. Go, my lord, have a good journey and may God protect you from the plague!'

Iain knelt quickly before his sovereign, hand on his chest and head bowed, unable to say a word such was his surprise. It would have been pointless anyway, for the king had already turned on his heels and was rushing out of the room. Before he went out the door, the king said over his shoulder, 'Give my regards to your distinguished wife, MacNeil.'

'My beloved wife, your Majesty. My beautiful... my adorable hind!' murmured Iain, overcome with emotion, in the quiet of his heart.

Chapter Sixteen
The Return Home

Iain had not slept much. Like him, many visitors had enjoyed the king's hospitality for the night, and the narrow room in the north wing of the palace, which had been set aside for them, was crowded. The foul smell of sweat and damp wool filled the air Iain was breathing in through the plaid in which he had wrapped himself. The coughs and snoring had conspired with the beating of the rain on the shutters to keep him awake all night. Yet he was worn out with exhaustion and excitement after his conversation with the king. With his eyes wide open in the half-light, the young chief had been surprised to find he missed the solitude and silence of his lodgings in Stirling. While there, he had thought a lot and, despite everything, had slept well. At daybreak when he finally got up, he was overcome with impatience to leave. *I cannot wait for Lennox and Griogair, and I do not want to go back to Stirling*, he thought as he went into the room where food was being served. He joined some other visitors who were leaving that morning and spoke to them about the road going north. As he was leaving, he noticed Kenneth Simpson standing in the corner near the door and nodded to him.

'Are you going back to Mallaig, Lord MacNeil?' he said affably in Gaelic.

'Yes,' Iain replied in the same language. 'I plan to take the road along the Tay as far as Rannoch. Are you just passing through Scone? I think I recognise a northern accent, Mister Simpson.'

'Sorry to disappoint you, I am not a Highlander. But my late wife was from Wick, and I learned Gaelic from her. I own an inn in Scone. I act as an interpreter when needed at the palace. But it is very rare. The Highlanders manage on their own or use their own folk. But it turns out I have been coming to the palace every day for over a month for a lady in Sheriff Darnley's entourage. Perhaps you know her. She comes from the Isle of Skye: MacDougall, Beathag MacDougall. She does not speak a word of Scots, and the sheriff spends the weekdays in Stirling.'

Iain froze. *So, she did not go back to Mallaig during my confinement.*, he thought quickly and with a certain sense of relief. A shiver went right through him. He relaxed before continuing, 'I know her, Mister Simpson. I would like to see her before I leave. Do you think that is possible? Can you take me to her?'

I, who had been sleeping like a log since my second month of pregnancy, was beginning to wake now in the middle of the night, soaking with sweat, encumbered with my stomach, and often having cramps in my legs. I could not get back to sleep again afterwards. I would get up and, being careful not to waken Jenny or Ceit, who slept in my bed, I would put on a dressing gown and slippers and take a walk along the corridor. I would quietly sing lullabies or spend those sleepless hours praying for Iain and the baby yet to be born.

Ever since Lieutenant Lennox's departure for Stirling, I had begun to worry a lot. Visions of the plague floated through my dreams, and once again, I felt isolated. I rarely saw Tomas now as he was coming and going all day and often had his meals on his own. He had retreated into a world of silence as he did every time he was preoccupied. There was plenty to preoccupy him. Since Grigoair had left Glenfinnan, we had heard about several plots and schemes aimed at gathering the clan around Uncle Aindreas. Iain's cousin expected a coup by the laird of Loch Morar and did not know how to prevent it. His handsome face was continually downcast, and even Jenny could not get him to smile during our long evenings together. In addition to all of this, he lived in constant fear of an appearance by Beathag, whom I had managed to efface from my memory. We did not receive many visitors at that time of year. It was mid-November, and the mountain paths, rutted by the steady autumn rains, were already difficult. Lady Rosalind remained at Glenfinnan, ruminating over her concerns for her husband. I was surprised to find that she spoke of her uncontrollable fear of the plague in her letters. As I was not up to visiting her to reassure her, I wrote to her. Despite the slowness of the post, letter writing had become my main activity and was very effective in occupying my mind. I sent little notes to members of my family, my Uncle William Keith, the Marshall, and John Carmichael, the Bishop of Orleans. I had replied to the friendly letter I had received from Guilbert Saxton, Mallaig's former secretary at the time of Lord Baltair's death. As a result, we had started to correspond, and I wrote to him often at that time. I also wrote letters to the queen and hoped to give them to Eachann when he returned from Scone. I had also begun translating all the Gaelic tales in the castle library into French for my own pleasure and eventually for the little Princess of Scotland.

Estate business did not take up a lot of time. All the crops and provisions were gathered in. All the herds had returned to their winter pastures and the proximity of the other clans gave me no cause for alarm. I think fear of the plague had temporarily dampened the Highlanders' desire for a fight. Even if we lived far from the source of the plague, it was always possible that the infection could be carried by sea or otherwise. So, everyone stayed in their own homes, avoiding as much as possible any contact with travellers and those arriving by sea. If it had not been for Iain's absence which was becoming more and more difficult for me to bear, I think I would have begun that winter of 1425 quite serenely.

How times have changed, how everything has changed, I could not help thinking as I remembered this time last year. At that time, I was a young convent schoolgirl, daughter of a rich merchant, cast out, as it were, into the wild Highlands, not knowing its language and customs, awaiting a marriage with a hostile and stubborn man. I smiled at this memory, and a sentence from Iain's story came to mind: 'This lone wolf became unhappy and bitter.'

One evening just before supper, as I was looking out the window, I saw Tomas and Raonall come into the courtyard. They looked serious, and when they dismounted, Tomas looked up and noticed me at the window. He looked away and said something to Raonall, for he, too, looked straight up at me and gave me a little nod. My heart missed a beat without me knowing why. I went down to the hall to meet them. Raonall looked very like his mother. He had fine light-coloured hair, a high forehead, and a long nose, and he was very tall. He took my hands and gave me a smile which he wanted to be convincing.

'Good evening, dear Gunelle. I have no news of my father, so there is no change with my mother: She is depressed and is not saying anything. You seem to be well.' Looking discreetly at my waist, he continued, 'You seem to be coping with your husband's absence. Better than my mother, in any case. I admire you, my lady!'

'You are kind, Lord Raonall, as always. I am very well, but you are mistaken. I miss your cousin dreadfully. I try to keep my concerns to myself, that is all.' Leading the way into the great hall, I continued, 'We do not see anyone these days. I am going to keep you for supper, and you will spend the evening with us. If you are good, I may even have a room for you.'

His infectious laugh chased away the unease I had felt a few minutes earlier. I watched Tomas, his jaw set, head towards the guards' room, without even a glance for poor Jenny, who had been watching him from the moment he arrived. When I sat down with my guest, I noticed the young girl had not followed us. Before we sat down to eat, Raonall had given me the news I feared: Uncle Aindreas had convinced the lairds to overthrow Iain and help him take over the clan's leadership.

'He is making it look as if there is a rebellion against the MacNeils among the other Highland clans who lost men in the prison in Stirling. They are blaming the sheriff and the fact that our clan supported him in his work. Evidently, the MacNeil honour is tarnished by the fact that the books are said to be wrong, and there is also Aindreas's hatred of Iain,' he explained. 'Aulay, Struan, and Daidh are behind him. They are all but blaming Iain for the plague from which a good number of Highlanders died in Stirling! I have just come from Loch Morar, and I was not even able to speak on my father's behalf. They did not want to hear what I had to say. I am sorry, my lady, but it is possible that the four of them are hell bent on a change of chief. If only my cousin were free or my father would come home.'

'They cannot do that! Iain has not been found guilty! Come on now, Sir Raonall, it is too soon! This charge of embezzlement is completely false. You know that full well!' I exclaimed distraught.

'Come, my lady, you know Aindreas. He acts on a rush of blood to the head. The others would not have followed him if he had not brandished his famous tale of the stolen casket. The story is implausible from start to finish, but the lairds are full of it. You tell me why. My mother is up in arms... the very idea of implicating you so disgracefully in this whole affair. She thinks they are all jealous of you and my cousin… Lady Rosalind always sees emotional problems everywhere. You know what she is like. As for me, I had to stop myself from crossing swords when I heard Aindreas's accuse you. It is best if I do not set foot in Morar ever again.'

I was dumbfounded. What an evil man Aindreas was! How deceitful. So, there were still surprises to learn in the MacNeil family. Rosalind was probably right. Thinking back to the vote in the spring for Iain's nomination as clan chief, I could still sense the animosity towards him. There must still be traces of it in the lairds. I also suspected that the siege by the Camerons and the McDonalds, which they had had to resist, had cooled their ardour towards their young chief. Finally, I even wondered if the defeat of their representatives by Mallaig in the tournament did not also have a part to play in their flagrant animosity. In your absence *your pack is growling against you, my love.* I thought with a sigh.

The supper and the ceilidh which followed were not very joyful despite the efforts Randall and I made. Jenny, however, seemed to have made some progress with Tomas. I saw them pass each other loving glances several times and they stayed very close to each other all night. *Good little Jenny,* I said to myself as I watched. *Make him smile a little, or else our dear Tomas runs the risk of buckling under the weight of his powerlessness to help his cousin.*

Sheriff Darnley's apartments in Scone palace were up at the top of the west tower, and Iain and his guide had no difficulty reaching them. *This palace seems poorly protected*, Iain could not help thinking as they climbed the stairs and walked along the corridors without ever seeing a guard. Kenneth Simpson was leading Iain in silence, simply giving him a knowing smile from time to time. He seemed accustomed to coming and going freely in the palace. Iain wondered how he could lose him once they reached Beathag's room. He wanted to know every detail of the plot against him and was keen that his meeting with his sister-in-law should not be witnessed. Well, he did not have to wait long. When they reached the sheriff's apartments, he noticed that there was a soldier at every door.

When he saw Iain's surprise, his guide felt he had to explain. 'The sheriffs are important men but unfortunately, they have a lot of enemies… I wonder why…' he said with a mischievous smile. 'Their apartments are guarded. Besides, I will not be able to accompany you to Lady Beathag's room. Sheriff Darnley forbids her to receive more than one person at a time. There is always a servant with her.' Indicating a door with his chin, he said, "There you are. I will wait for you if you wish. I will see to my duties after your conversation.'

The guard had already opened the door to Beathag's room when he saw Kenneth Simpson and he let Iain in without any hesitation. When he entered the room, Iain was trembling with rage.

I am not going to kill her today, he quickly thought. On seeing her, every shred of his hatred for his sister-in-law invaded his heart. He smiled with satisfaction when he saw Beathag's look of astonishment when she saw him enter the room.

'Iain MacNeil.' She almost choked. 'You are not in Stirling?'

'As you can see! I see no one has told you about Darnley. He lied to the king about me and has swapped places with me in jail,' Iain replied nonchalantly.

'You are lying! Do not try to trick me. You would not be here if what you say were true.'

'Strangely enough, as your brother-in-law, I have been asked to escort you home. I do not want to, and I do not think I will do it,' Iain continued without dropping his offhand manner. 'If I refuse, you are being sent back to Stirling to be near your darling prisoner who, it seems, is desperate to see you. No doubt that is what you prefer. The plague should be powerless against a woman as strong as you.'

'I have the strength for a good many things, Iain, not the least of which was being your mistress.' Slowly moving closer to him, she whispered, 'Tell me what I have to do for you to agree to take me back to the Highlands... Supposing I dropped Darnley for you.'

'Don't come any closer, Beathag,' whispered Iain, as he glanced at the servant who was watching them from the other end of the room. 'Let me be very clear. You are not leaving Darnley for me! I have lost two months with your little schemes, and I want to bring them all out into the open before I go back to Mallaig. I am not going to make any trip with you if you have not a clear conscience regarding me or any member of my family.'

'My dear Iain, always passionate about fairness from what I can see. You are not in your guards' room here. It is my bedroom,' she answered with a slight tremble in her voice.

Iain was looking at her and could see doubt making its way into his sister-in-law's twisted mind. On his warning, she had moved

420

backwards towards the fire and was staring at the flames and stroking the pleats of her damask dress with a hand dripping with rings. She had lost none of her haughtiness or her elegance. Her white neck and bosom shone with the brilliance of her several necklaces. Her flamboyant hair, which hung down on her bare shoulders, shone in the light of the fire. The silence was growing longer and Lord MacNeil began to feel rather uneasy. To break it, he walked over to look out the window before turning his attention back to his sister-in-law. The sound of his footsteps made Beathag turn around. She looked at him for a long time. Her captivating green eyes, lustful and full of desire both disturbed and shocked him.

'You must miss your charming wife. You are not the kind of man to go without for a long time. She is surely very fat now.' Seeing him stiffen on hearing these words, she continued in a more fawning tone, 'I could remedy that, you know, Iain. I am capable. I am desperate. Darnley keeps me rather isolated here… and I am deprived of such pleasures. I am disappointed with him and with Scone. I thought that life at the palace would be delightful, but I have been just as confined in this bedroom as you in your lodgings at the chancellery. We both have a lot of lost time to make up. Why waste time in futile talk when we have better things to do?'

Iain stepped back instinctively. *She is mad*, he thought immediately. *I will get no information out of her. She has one thing and one thing only on her mind, and it is always the same. I either kill her or I flee from her.*

He took a deep breath, turned towards the servant, nodded to her, and strode towards the door.

Beathag reacted immediately. She rushed to the door and stood with her back against it to stop him from leaving. 'One moment, Iain MacNeil! Do not go! I will tell you what is waiting for you at

421

Mallaig. You are right. I have nothing to fear from you, for as we speak, you are no longer chief of the MacNeils. It will not be me who will be facing the court but your wife.'

'What are you saying?' Iain interrupted, almost choking. At that moment, the door suddenly opened, and Beathag was thrown against Lord Iain, who had barely time to catch her.

A guard stuck his head inside the room and announced authoritatively, 'The queen is asking to see Lord MacNeil.'

Iain roughly pushed his sister-in-law away and followed the guard into the corridor. Through the open door, Kenneth Simpson had had time to see what happened and falling in behind Lord Iain before letting him and the guard pass, he commented, 'A charming lady, isn't she? She asked me to teach her Scots, but I find it very difficult to concentrate when I am with her. Do you know what I mean?'

Iain smiled tensely. *She is anything but a lady*, he thought, *but you're right, Simpson. It is difficult to get rid of her.*

The guard and Iain took another set of stairs and corridors to reach the wing containing Queen Jeanne's apartments. Without any formal introduction, he was immediately shown into the room. It was long and bright, smelt strongly of wax, and was full of carpets and tapestries. Three ladies and two lords, who were standing by the window, made up the queen's entourage. They barely interrupted their conversation when Lord MacNeil arrived. Pride of place was given to a large marble table beside which the queen was standing, wearing a ruby red dress bordered with ermine. The same height as the king, she had a thin face and very expressive brown eyes. She welcomed the young clan chief with a lively curiosity, for that was why she had sent for him. She scrutinised the knight as he knelt before her.

422

'Please get up, Lord MacNeil. I could have had this given to you for your wife, but I wanted to meet you for myself. The king enjoyed the conversation he had with you yesterday and recommended that I should receive you. We were afraid you might have already left Scone.'

Iain looked up and slowly rose to his feet. The queen was holding out a letter sealed with the royal seal. Iain approached her and took the letter with a smile. She must have liked him, for she returned his smile and, with a simple move of her hand, invited him to sit down on one of the armchairs.

'We found your wife very charming, my lord. As you know, our relations with England are more difficult at the present time. That means, among other things, that we must discontinue our correspondence with our people there for a while. It means that I hardly have any opportunity to write in French now. Your wife allows me to do so, and we are grateful.' She continued, 'As well as this, I find it amusing to send letters written in a European language to the north of Scotland. The Highlands are much closer to Scone than Toulon, Nantes, or Orleans at present. However, the most interesting part of this correspondence is that Lady Gunelle is highly educated, and what she has to say is intelligent and even engaging. In particular, we share the same reading preferences. That is why I intend, as I have said in my letter, to continue corresponding with her. You do not see a problem with that, I am sure, my lord.'

'None, of course, your Majesty. Permit the house of Mallaig to guarantee delivery. It will be a great honour for the MacNeil family to maintain the royal correspondence between you and the Highlands,' Iain answered seriously.

'That is perfect,' commented the queen. 'We learned that the Crown has dealings with your wife's family through Marshal William

Keith. You see, the more I find out, the more I discover links which warrant an exchange of letters between Scone and Mallaig.'

'Since you are speaking of connections, my Queen, if you permit me,' Iain dared cautiously, 'I would like to point out another of which you will learn the existence sooner or later. My brother Alasdair's widow, Lady Beathag of the MacDougalls of Skye, is staying here at the palace. My sister-in-law is part of Sheriff James Darnley's entourage. He met her during his long stay at Mallaig. Even though she only speaks Gaelic, she has great ambitions for her life here. As a matter of fact, I am not sure she is the kind of person who has any place in the Scottish court if she ever succeeded in worming her way in.'

The queen turned away and thought for a moment. She looked serious and annoyed. She then stood up to indicate the end of the audience and said with a constrained smile, 'Lord MacNeil, you are surely mistaken. James Darnley has certainly not brought any lady from the Highlands since he is married to my companion at Stirling castle and is a father of four.' Assuming a look of complicity and looking Iain straight in the eye, she added, 'You understand, don't you? Let us say no more about it, my lord. Come, I will not detain you any longer! Take this letter to your wife and accept my congratulations on your imminent fatherhood. May heaven give you the daughter you wish for.'

Iain felt his face go red. Had he displeased the queen with his revelation? Noticing his sovereign's frank look as she dismissed him, he realised that the consequences were not disastrous for him and that the disclosure of the sheriff's relationship with Beathag had achieved its purpose. The queen would certainly make enquiries as soon as he had left Scone. He rejoiced on thinking about what would become of Darnley and Beathag when their relationship was

424

revealed. *That old devil Darnley! A father of four!* Iain thought as he left the queen's apartment.

One would have thought that the queen's letter tucked inside his doublet gave its carrier wings. Iain MacNeil had galloped out of Scone's walls, delighted to be able to ride freely and at his own pace. After a few miles, however, he had to slow down, aware that the lack of care and exercise his horse had suffered during the confinement meant he could not push him as he usually did.

Iain leaned over and patted his horse's black mane. 'It is all right, Mungo. Walk on, boy. We are going home to Mallaig,' he said in Gaelic. Like many knights, the young chief loved his animal and had no plan to change horses on the way. If he wanted to make the whole journey on him, he would have to look after him. The horse pricked his ears and neighed a few times as a sign of pleasure, pleasure at finding his master again and being ridden by him.

Iain had never travelled through the Lowlands and had hardly ever travelled on his own. The first day the solitude barely troubled him. He had so much to think about: the end of his detention and all the events surrounding it, and not least his wife's unexpected intervention. However, on the second day, he realised that ignorance of the paths exposed a lone traveller to the possibility of attack. He was ambushed by a small, badly armed group of brigands, and it was only by using his horse's skill in clearing the stone dykes that he had been able to escape. He also knew that at night evil spirits inspired terror in Highlanders as much as in Lowlanders and that robbers only ever operated in daylight. He had learned to overcome his fear of ghosts a long time ago, so he decided to ride as much as possible during the night. The autumn weather favoured him too as it poured all day and the breeze at night swept away the clouds. Horse and rider discovered that it was extremely pleasant to ride for hours, almost without interruption along deserted, moonlit tracks, wafted by the breeze. Deprived of conversation and company as he had been in Stirling, Iain began again his heart-searching, as he crossed Scotland deep in thought, meditations, and even prayer. After travelling eleven days in this frame of mind, he was perfectly calm when he reached Ben Nevis. He was convinced that the many problems he had envisaged would be resolved as soon as he reached home. Subsequent events almost proved him right.

The castle was in darkness. There was not a sound. I looked at Bran, who had stopped on the doorstep, his nose against the door and his tail wagging as he looked at me pleadingly. Just as always when I wanted to feel Iain near me, I had gone to sit in his armchair at the far end of this room which reminded me so much of him. I had brought along my coat, knowing there would be no fire. I was not sleepy, and a wander in the corridor outside my bedroom had not been enough to calm the nervousness which gripped my heart. I had such a desire to have someone to talk to but had not dared wake anyone to satisfy it. I decided that Bran, who never left my side, would be my confidant. I spoke to him from the far end of the arms room. I was always fascinated by the unique way the dog had been trained. He was only allowed to enter the great hall or the kitchen. In all the great houses I had visited, the dogs and cats wandered about freely just as they did at Crathes. Bran was finding it difficult to stay at the door of the arms room and became restless each time I spoke. He looked so sad. I was ashamed at the way I was tormenting and soon took pity on him. I stood up, stopped speaking and moved towards the chimney, which was faintly lit by the torch I had placed on the mantelpiece. I looked up at the MacNeil coat of arms and smiled sadly as I thought of the tensions which were splitting the family. I was deep in thought when I heard a noise coming from the great hall. Bran was no longer at the door but I heard his muffled barking and the sound of his claws on the flagstones. My heart missed a beat.

'Someone is there,' I said trembling.

Rigid with fear, I went to the door and looked into the great hall. I could not see anything and wanted to call Bran back but could not utter a sound. I was there, paralysed, my eyes scouring the half-light and my ears buzzing with the sound of what seemed to me to be a struggle between the dog and someone. It was at that moment I distinctly heard a man's voice speaking to Bran.

'Lie down, no! Enough! There you are, you big softy, calm down… Good dog! What are you doing in here in the middle of the night?'

The man must have noticed the light of the torch in the arms room, for his voice had suddenly stopped, and I heard the footsteps coming slowly towards me.

'It cannot be an intruder,' I said quickly. 'Bran would not let him past. It must be someone from the castle.' I thought I was going to faint, and I recognised the man when he was about ten steps away from me: it was Iain.

Time stood still in the long moments which followed. I was in his arms at last, and nothing else existed. I felt the blood pumping in his neck where I had placed my lips. I inhaled deep breaths of his odour impregnated with wind, forest, and horse. We were motionless, his arms holding me tightly.

He gently rubbed his bearded cheek against my head and after a long time managed to say in a trembling voice, 'My love, what are you doing in the arms room in the middle of the night? What is happening?'

'Nothing,' I whispered, tightening my arms around his neck. 'I think I was waiting for you. Oh, Iain! How I was waiting for you. I could not stand it any longer... waiting for you. It is over! You are here! Tell me I am not dreaming.'

'If you are dreaming, my love, then so am I... So is Bran,' he replied, sticking out his chest to look at my face. 'And outside, there are four other people who are dreaming: the three guards and the groom.'

I gently let go of him to look at him. His voice was no longer trembling. He was happy, safe, and well, back at Mallaig, on the quiet. He turned around and, in so doing, exposed both of us to the feeble light in the arms room.

His blue eyes met mine for a long moment, and he murmured before gently kissing me, 'Gunelle, my marvel...' His beard jagged me, but I could not take my lips from his. I was pressing against him, and he must have felt the roundness of my stomach, for he slowly freed himself and lowered his head without letting go of my shoulders. He moved around and came to stand at my back, his hands lightly on my stomach, his arms around my hips.

His lips brushed my ear as he softly said, 'As I had promised, I have arrived in time, my beloved. And that is thanks to you. To your pen. But tell me, what did you write to the Queen of Scotland to make her think that I want a daughter!'

I could not help laughing as I put my hands on his so that he really felt my stomach under my dress. 'You will never know what I wrote, my lord. It is our secret. Be happy with the outcome. But do you not want another daughter? What would you do with me if I were to present you with one at the end of the month?' I turned around in his arms and pretended to look worried as I gazed into his eyes. 'Will you still love me?'

'I will never be able to stop loving you, my lady. For one thing, I am incapable, and secondly, if I want to have a son, I will have to continue to keep on making love to you,' he said as he took my face in his hands and started to kiss me passionately again.

In his desire to prolong our moment of intimacy and not wanting to let anyone know of his arrival, Iain refused to go up to our bedroom and he brought all the furs from the great hall into the arms room to make us a little nest. He placed them in front of the fireplace, had me lie down, and he lit a fire. Then he took off his belt and lay down behind me, putting one arm around me and letting me rest my head on the other. He drew my coat over us and put his head on his which he had rolled up in a ball. We remained like that, cosily huddled together until the first rays of daylight, quietly telling each other about life during the time we had spent apart. He, in torment and imprisonment, me in the long wait for him and our baby. How right he was to isolate us like that! The next day, as soon as the news got out that he was home, he was accosted by all our folk who were happy and overexcited to see their master again, and I did not have another tender moment with him until the evening.

I spent the following days in a kind of numbness I could not explain. I could not take my eyes off my husband, happy to see him moving about, speaking, eating, and drinking, going in and out of rooms, undressing, dressing, shaving, and praying. Every one of his gestures and words was significant, was valuable, and he did not cease to amaze me. *The plague had not taken him, and the king had returned him to me*, was my constant reflection.

After a long conversation with Father Henriot who informed him of Dohmnull's death, Iain spent all his time with the knights and his two cousins, Tomas and Raonall, who never left his side. The desire to be doing something had quickly captivated him again. As expected, his lairds' rebellion was first and foremost in his mind as his resumed life at the castle. Iain continued to act and think like a clan chief, and it took the arrival of Lennox and Griogair a week later to make up his mind to call the crucial meeting with his lairds. I was surprised to sense his self-confidence and conviction in the situation. *Whoever would have said that he needed to face prison to acquire such calmness before a battle?* I thought as I watched him.

The conspiracy, instigated by his uncle Aindreas to relieve him of his title, was indeed a rebellion. When I listened to the conversations of the elderly Lieutenant Lennox and Uncle Griogair, I noticed the sense of outrage during their heated exchanges. At times, it was clear that my husband was showing great wisdom. He remained balanced in his proposals and was preoccupied more with clan unity than with what should happen to the traitor. I was present at all their discussions, sitting by the window, needlework in hand. Sometimes Ceit would sit beside me, but she did not have enough patience to spend a long time at her little pieces of embroidery. Once, when I looked at Iain, I thought I was seeing Lord Baltair. The same way he holds his head, the same serious voice, the same attention paid to those speaking to him, the same quality of reflection. I smiled with joy, and Iain caught me just at that moment.

He left the circle of men and came to kneel and ask, 'Did I say something funny, my lady? Or something wrong for you to smile at me like that?'

'Nothing amusing, or wrong,' I said, stroking his face with my hand. 'At that moment, I saw your father. You are like him, my lord: a proud MacNeil, imposing, infallible and an extraordinary man in my loving eyes.'

Moving his face forward to touch my stomach with the point of his nose, he took my hand, squeezed it, and looked at me for a long time, his blue eyes full of wonder. 'And as for you, my lady, I do not know whether it is your pregnancy or the fact that you have missed your husband but your beauty has grown to the point that in the space of a few months, you have become the most beautiful woman in the Highlands…and the most magnificent hind a wolf has ever seen.'

The Airor Peninsula was being swept by a cold north wind when Tomas left Struan's estate with two men at arms. He had delivered the last of his cousin's messages to each laird and was returning to Mallaig, unsure about the outcome of the exercise. Iain had sent him to inform them that if they wanted to rescind the vote taken in March, they had to come to Mallaig in person, for he refused to recognise any vote removing him as chief. Aulay, Struan, and Daidh had replied individually that they would consult the other lairds before meeting with Iain. As for Aindreas, he had been categorical.

'Tell your cousin that I am happy he and Griogair have returned. I was waiting for them so that I could organise the oath-swearing ceremony. If they do not intend to divide the clan, they will respond positively to my summons. Tell him too that I am going to wait until February to allow Lady Gunelle to recover from the birth. Clan business can continue without the ceremony until then.'

Chapter Seventeen
The Trial

Tomas turned up his collar and spurred on his horse. He was in a hurry to return to Mallaig. Heavy rain accompanied the rest of his journey. By the time the three riders entered the courtyard, they were soaked through. They handed over their horses to the grooms who had come out to meet them. The men ran to the guards' room to get out of the rain, and Tomas hurried through the keep gate. Jenny, who had been rather worried, had been watching and waiting.

'Lord Tomas! At last!' she said immediately. 'Did you see Lady Beathag at Loch Morar? It seems she has left Scone. She could be back in the Highlands.' When she saw his amazement, she continued, as she took his arm, 'You are soaking wet! It is unforgivable of me to keep you outside. Come, my lord, let us get you dried…'

The knight allowed himself to be led without any resistance. He was tired and disappointed from the journey. There was no one in the entrance hall when he went into the keep. *I must change first.* he said to himself. *Then report to Iain about my trip.*

Jenny, who had him by the hand, led him up the staircase to his bedroom. With the assurance of a servant who knows what to do for her master's well-being, she lit the fire and heated the water in the basin for a bath. As she did so, she told him everything worth mentioning about events at the castle during the two days the young man had been away. When she turned towards him, she gave a little start. Tomas, naked from the waist up, was sitting on the bed, taking off his boots. He had hung his wet jacket, doublet, and shirt on the bed posts, and little puddles of water were beginning to form on the floor.

'My lord, don't put your clothes there,' she said, trying to hide her embarrassment. 'They are going to drip on your bed. Hang them in front of the fire.'

Wanting to reach the dripping wet clothes, she stretched up above Tomas, who, without even thinking, put his arm around her waist and drew her close, making himself topple over onto the bed. The young girl became tense when her breasts touched the young man's chest. She remained motionless above him, looking into his eyes and blushing with embarrassment.

'My lord, what are you doing?' she managed to stammer.

'I simply want to tell you I missed you… and I am pleased that you are looking after me the way you are. I am not asking for anything else, Jenny,' he replied masterfully, letting her roll over onto her side.

She was speechless and remained stretched out beside him, devouring him with her eyes. She gently ran her fingers through the young man's long wet hair, and he closed his eyes with pleasure. Jenny was emboldened to slip her hands slowly from Tomas's face to his chest, holding her breath as she did so. She saw the goose pimples rise on his skin at the contact and her awkwardness increased.

'Tomas,' she whispered, 'don't let me … I must not… it is not right… if you knew how much I want you! You are older. It is up to you to make it easier.'

'With pleasure, Jenny. Tell me how.' he replied as he leaned over to kiss her.

That evening the wind was bombarding Mallaig with sheets of freezing rain. In the heart of the keep, the castle folk had gathered in front of the large fire, which lit up their happy faces with its golden rays. The evening was coming to an end, for the chatelaine was tired, having sung a lot with Anna and Nellie. She could not get comfortable, and again changed position in her armchair. She tried not to waken Ceit, who was curled up sound asleep on the ground, one half of her on her mother's feet and the other half on Bran's stomach.

'You're tired, my lady,' whispered her husband. 'Go up. I will join you later.'

After asking Mairi to take Ceit, he turned to Tomas and Jenny, who were sitting close together on the bench and said, 'Tomas, let us have Jenny for a bit, just the time to help her mistress get to bed.'

The orders were given with a smile and willingly obeyed with a smile. Since his return home, Lord Iain was enjoying blessed times in his castle: Everyone was ready to respond to his slightest whim.

'What do you think, Father?' he asked when there was just Lennox, Tomas, the priest, and himself in the hall. 'We heard my cousin and the lieutenant at supper. Now I would like to know how you view the group of lairds and how you think my father would have reacted.'

Father Henriot would have preferred to keep his opinion to himself. With a shrug of the shoulders, he shifted about in his chair for a moment and stared into the fire. The men were saying nothing, allowing themselves to be mesmerised by the movement of the flames along the logs. Iain stood up and went to fill a large cup with whisky, which he then passed round, giving the first sip to the priest. It was most unlike him but he took a good mouthful, screwing up his face as he swallowed, before passing the cup to Lennox, who was beside him.

'My lord, he began, I knew the late Lord Baltair better than any of you. I have to say that I have difficulty imagining him in your situation…'

'Do you mean that the lairds would never have supported Aindreas and his plan if he had made a move to depose my father?' Iain cut in bitterly.

'I mean that Lord Baltair's influence extended not only to his lairds, brothers or not, but to all the Highland chiefs and even to the king's envoys. My lord, your father had one of the longest reigns as clan chief in the history of the MacNeils. Correct me if I am wrong, but he was named chief after the death of his father in 1398, which means he was chief for twenty-seven years. You have not yet completed your first year, my lord.'

'So, my problem is my youth,' Iain said as he emptied the cup Lennox had handed him.

'My lord,' the priest continued gently, 'the problem is that your lairds are twenty years older than you, and the fact that they belong to the clan MacNeil does not remove their aspirations as mature men to lead the young and not to be led by them. I share the opinion of

Lord Griogair and his lady: They are jealous of you, and Aindreas is merely the bellows fanning the feelings of the others.'

In the silence which followed, the priest rose to his feet and, showing a great deal of respect, stood behind the young chief's chair. He caught Lieutenant Lennox's look of approval and put his hand on Iain's shoulder. 'Worth what it is worth, my son. But I believe very sincerely that your faith in the clan is your strength and that your lairds are sensitive to that. They are all fine Christian men who do not find it easy to go back on their word. Trust and pray,' the priest concluded with assurance.

Iain would have liked to have shared the priest's confidence in Struan, Daidh, and Aulay. As he thought of them individually, he doubted whether they would go back on their word, but as a group, their loyalty was diluted.

Deep in thought, he turned the cup in his hands then he gave a start when he heard Tomas beside him ask with a smile, 'Can I have some too? Leave it. I will help myself.'

'My lord,' Lennox looked serious as he went over to Iain, 'what is needed is something which will prove that you are still clan chief before your lairds have the time to go back on their word. For example, summon them to a clan meeting for a reason none of them could or would ignore.'

'I see exactly what you mean, Lennox,' Iain replied after a short silence. 'Begin proceedings against Aindreas for the theft of the one hundred and twenty pounds last January. They will all come running without even questioning who has the right to exercise justice in the clan MacNeil. That is probably the best idea, but I would have preferred not to use this affair which involves my wife, who is so near her time.'

436

'I understand, my lord, but I am afraid that with your sister-in-law's return to the area, it would be difficult to avoid talking about or hearing about it. If you act tomorrow, Lady Gunelle would be able to take part.'

Iain stood up and leaned on the mantelpiece, deep in thought. He was comfortable with the idea of such an action, but there were so many things missing that the trial could collapse. The men were watching him in silence, each one trying to imagine what the others were thinking.

After a lengthy sigh, Iain came over to the lieutenant and asked him matter-of-factly, 'Tell me, Lennox, honestly, what would you do in my place?'

'Honestly, my lord, that is what I would do.'

The trial took place the very next week. Iain went to Loch Morar with Tomas to inform his uncle of the trial in the presence of the clan. Lieutenant Lennox remained at Mallaig to guard the castle since Iain still feared an attack by Beathag on his wife. Iain did not see her at Aindreas's, but he caught sight of her servant, Finella, just long enough to see the panic his presence created in her. *That one has a guilty conscience*, he said to himself without knowing why.

Lord Aindreas was neither surprised nor angered by his nephew's visit. On the contrary, the prospect of the trial seemed to please him and even serve his plans, for he affirmed to Iain that he would be able to convince the other lairds to attend the meeting.

'What a twisted mind,' Iain said to his cousin on the way back.

'He seems sure of his evidence, Iain. I would not be surprised if he had not invented it with your sister-in-law. There is no doubt that is what Finella came to do at the castle the day of the tournament. Jenny saw her on the third floor, coming out or going into your mother's bedroom.'

'I did not know that Beathag's servant had set foot in Mallaig! Good grief! We are going to have to search the bedroom from top to bottom, Tomas, and quickly' Iain concluded as he spurred on his horse.

#

Among the different opinions expressed by the people at Mallaig about the affair, that of Father Henriot and Lennox proved correct from the outset of the clan meeting in the arms room the following Tuesday.

The high windows let in so little light on that dark December day that all the torches were lit so that all those present could be seen the clearly. Iain had put on the old robe his father wore to preside over the court, and contrary to his custom, he wore a hat. Seated in the carved chair which had served four MacNeil chieftains, the lairds saw a calm man in control of himself, a man whom the events of a single year had matured considerably: Iain MacNeil bore his youth as nobly as his title of chief. The only ladies to be allowed into the room were the lairds' wives. They were sitting together at the front of the room near the fire in an embarrassed silence. Lady Gunelle and Lady Rosalind were sitting together, both with a smile and looking confident.

'I called you here today,' announced Lord Iain in an almost solemn tone of voice, 'because I cannot accuse a laird of an offence against the chief without the case being heard in front of the whole clan. I know that this laird has conspired with certain of you to take over the position as chief during my absence, but for the moment, he is

438

not being accused of treason. Aindreas MacNeil intercepted a sum of money which was meant for my father. Until this day, it has not been returned to anyone at Mallaig. You have come here in answer to my summons to hear this case and by doing so to reaffirm your faith in me as one who rights wrongs and as chief.'

A deep silence followed his introduction. The lairds Auley, Struan, and Daidh were squirming on their chairs, ill at ease and with their eyes fixed on Aindreas.

The latter's face lit up, and he began to speak without waiting to be invited, 'Very clever, nephew. Congratulations! But let us not muddy the waters so quickly. Aulay, Struan, Daidh, and Griogair have not come to thank you for having exposed clan MacNeil to the suspicions of the king and the wrath of the Highlanders, nor to retake their oath to you. We are here to listen to the witnesses and to examine the proof of my alleged theft.' Looking angrily all around the room, he asked, 'Am I not correct, my lords?'

'My lord,' interrupted Griogair as he turned towards Iain, 'I am here to say to this gathering how much I regret that such a situation exists at the heart of our clan.' Looking at Aindreas, he added, 'My presence here pays homage to Baltair and to his son for their total devotion to the MacNeil family, one of the most powerful and most loyal to King James. Whatever the outcome of this case, I will not rescind my oath to Iain MacNeil. He has my total allegiance and my unfailing support.'

When Iain saw the lairds of Airor, Finiskaig, and Arisaig look down on hearing these words, he knew Father Henriot had read their hearts correctly. He took a deep breath and began the account of his accusation…ending with a question to Aindreas, 'Uncle, what do you know of the contents of my father-in-law's casket which was given to you by Lieutenant Lennox's messengers last January?'

439

'Nothing! The casket was sealed and even if it had not been, I would not have opened it. Who do you take me for? I helped those men who were frozen and only wanted one thing—to return to the felling site. There!'

'In that case, how did you learn that the casket contained the sum of one hundred and twenty pounds, the first instalment of the Grampian contract, information which you passed on to James Darnley?' retorted Iain.

'This is going to enrage you, my dear nephew, but all my information on the contents of this casket comes from someone who was chased from Mallaig and who, if she returns, will be killed on your orders. I am referring, of course, to your sister-in-law, who was forced to exile herself at Scone. It was Lady Gunelle who told her the amount in the purse locked in the casket after I delivered it to her.'

'You are declaring that my wife received the casket.'

'I swear in front of this gathering: I placed this famous sealed casket in Lady Gunelle's own hands, and she was with Lady Beathag at the time. In my opinion, they are the only two witnesses to the handing over of the casket. After a short pause, he went on, 'This casket, about the size of two hands, is in white leather. The corners, the tips, and the locks are made of lead. The Keith coat of arms was stamped on the seal.' Turning rather majestically towards the lieutenant standing at the back of the room, he asked, 'Is that correct, Mister Lennox? From what your messengers told me, you had been in charge of the casket from Crathes to the site?'

'That is exact. I was even present when it was sealed at Crathes,' Lennox confirmed calmly.

'Here we have someone who saw the casket before anyone in the Highlands,' Aindreas said pompously. 'It is my word and that of Lady Beathag, who unfortunately cannot have her say here, against that of Lady Gunelle, nephew. For I imagine that your wife denies ever having received the casket from me?' Without giving Iain the time to answer, he continued, 'Here is what I propose: a search of the castle. If we find this casket, which Lennox will recognise, we will have the proof that it was indeed delivered to Mallaig.'

'The castle is huge, it could take us all day to search, but I am not against the idea. You take charge of the search party, uncle. Only those directly involved in the case will take part,' Iain said calmly as he rose to his feet.

The gathering rose as a wave. Looking sly and smug, Aindreas took charge of the group of lairds, followed by Iain and his wife. All the castle folk were asked to wait in the great hall so as not to interfere with the search or complicate the situation. Under the confident direction of the accused, the search began in the study where the family assets were kept. Nothing was found there, nor in the other ground floor rooms. It was the same on the first floor, notably Iain and Gunelle's room. However, the leader of the search party was not going to be put off, and he did not seem surprised to find nothing. *It is certain that Aindreas knows where he is going to find what he is looking for*, thought Iain.

It came as no surprise to hear him announce after a while, 'I propose we continue the search in the room which Lady Gunelle was occupying in January, in other words, the late Lady Isla's bedroom.'

He turned towards the young chatelaine, a fixed smile on his lips. 'There is no point in searching the entire castle, my lady. That will be tiring for you. I happen to know that you slept in that room on the third floor for several months before and after your marriage, did you not?'

'That is true, my lord,' she replied calmly. 'Let us go. Climbing the stairs is good exercise for me.'

When the whole group slowly climbed to the top floor of the keep, Aindreas was the first to enter the room which his sister-in-law, Lady Isla, had occupied. As he had done in all the other rooms, he pushed chairs and curtains out of the way and lifted cushions and even the mattress.

Standing in front of the east window, he addressed Iain haughtily, 'There was always talk of a hiding place your mother had made in the wall. At least the ladies spoke about it among themselves. Do you know where it is, nephew?'

Letting go of his wife's arm, Iain went to stand in front of his uncle, and, leaning on the stone seat formed by the window ledge, he slid the flagstone along, saying, 'It is here.'

Aindreas's usual ruddy complexion turned white when he looked into the hole, which was about an arm's length and completely empty. He looked up and met his nephew's icy, cold stare. The two men looked each other up and down, scarcely containing the rage gradually rising in their hearts. The lairds did not understand where the accused was leading, but by all accounts, he was not getting anywhere. His failure was such after this search which led to nothing, that, looking furious, he gave up. Lieutenant Lennox offered to take over what soon appeared to everyone like an exercise doomed to failure. Having examined the third-floor rooms without any enthusiasm, Struan proposed ending the search, and no one opposed his suggestion. They all returned to the arms room for the rest of the trial, which had reached an impasse.

When they were all seated, Lieutenant Lennox asked if he could continue the interrogation. 'Since I know what was in the casket, with your permission,' he said, 'I would like to ask a few questions which could cast some light on the matter.'

With Iain and Aindreas's consent, he continued, 'Lord Aindreas, did Lady Beathag tell you what, apart from the money, the casket contained?'

'I don't think there was anything else,' the accused replied with a little hesitation.

The lieutenant made his way through the crowd of men standing around the lairds and stopped in front of Dughall, the knight from Loch Morar and Thora's fiancé. The man was looking left and right, wondering what on earth they wanted from him.

'Mister Dughall,' Lennox said slowly, 'doesn't it trouble you that your fiancée wears jewellery you did not give her? For I imagine it was not you who gave her a piece of gold jewellery made in France.'

'Ah, you're talking about the gold cross, Lieutenant,' he replied immediately. 'Thora no longer wears it. It was not me who gave it to her but her parents for her eighteenth birthday in January.'

'Thank you, Dughall,' the lieutenant interrupted him. Then, turning to the chatelaine, he asked her, 'Lady Gunelle, did your uncle, Bishop of Orleans, not write to you about a gold cross which he had sent you in your father's package last January?'

'He did indeed write to me about his wedding gift. I have the letter here in my bureau,' she replied, staring at the bright red Aindreas.

'I affirm that the gold cross made in France and easily recognisable, was in the casket Lord Aindreas had in his hands in January and that the last time I saw that cross was in June around Lady Thora's neck at the St. John tournament,' loudly declared the lieutenant as he turned to face the lairds.

A murmur of surprise rose from those gathered and grew louder. Large drops of sweat were forming on the accused's brow as everyone was looking at him.

Lord Iain rose to his feet again and addressed the assembly in a voice muffled with anger, 'I now think it would be an opportune moment to proceed with the search of Aindreas's castle, my lords. Obviously, you have no objections, uncle, since apparently, you have nothing to hide.'

So it was that several minutes later, this time under Iain's leadership, the group of lairds followed by Lennox set off in the direction of Morar. At the back of the line were Aindreas's wife and the knights from the different houses. With a smile, Tomas, and his cousin Raonall walked as far as the drawbridge to watch them go and then the cold wind drove them back into the keep, where they joined the ladies gathered around the fire in the great hall. When Tomas saw Gunelle hunched into her armchair and looking pale, he thought she was worried about the outcome of the trial.

'Do not worry, my lady. My cousin has things well in hand. His uncle will not be able to get out of this one…' he said gently.

Gunelle forced a smile, then suddenly dropped the dossier, and put her hands on her back, her lips pinched.

Rosalind, who was sitting beside her, leaned over and put her hand on her arm. 'Are you not feeling well, my dear?' she asked.

'It is only the baby kicking, my lady. Do not worry,' she replied, catching her breath.

'In the back, my dear? It is not the baby kicking… Come on, the baby is coming,' she said resolutely.

Under Tomas's panic-stricken gaze, Gunelle stood up and leaned on Rosalind's arm as she led her slowly up to her bedroom.

Persuaded by her authoritative bearing which pacified me more than it alarmed me, I had no desire to resist and allowed her to lead me. As we crossed the room, I saw Nellie leave Ceit to catch up with us. Then Anna appeared at the kitchen door, and, seeing the procession we were forming, she joined us, beaming from ear to ear.

Tomas came and stood in front of me, and walking backwards, his eyes like saucers, asked, 'Should I send for my cousin, my lady? Do you want him to come home?'

'Not for the moment, Tomas. Thank you. I will send for him later,' I replied.

It was a long time before I could think about my husband again and what was happening with the trial, for the hours which followed cut me off completely from the rest of the world. Only Nellie, Anna, and Rosalind existed in the enclosed universe of my bedroom and my belly, which, it seemed to me, took up the whole space. Attentive, busy, competent, and so reassuring, they accompanied me throughout the incredible exploit which is bringing a child into the world. It took the rest of that gruelling day and part of the following night.

The biting wind was thrashing the horsemen who rode faster the closer they got to Morar. They were gripped by impatience and nervousness. Aindreas was not leading the group but stayed at the back with his knights. When Iain dismounted in the courtyard, he looked towards a bottom window of the keep and caught sight of his cousin Thora and Finella, who were staring at him in disbelief.

The lairds dismounted and gathered around Iain, who began the search as soon as everybody was there. They went into the castle through the guardroom, then hell for leather along the corridor leading to the living quarters. In contrast to what his uncle had done at his home, Iain did not touch anything, being content to look at the objects and audibly naming all the new things the family had acquired that year: there a table, here a cupboard, a sideboard, tapestries, and a set of fine glass goblets. The lairds who were listening in astonished embarrassment understood full well what their young chief was insinuating.

Arriving in the living room, Iain dryly greeted his cousin, and with a wink at Finella, he whispered, 'Did you enjoy the St. John tournament last summer, Finella? I did not know you were as big an enthusiast.'

On these words, Aindreas jumped up and rushed towards the young woman whom he harshly grabbed by the neck, his eyes sending daggers in her direction. 'Fool! I told you to be discreet... They found out because of you!'

Iain immediately grabbed him by his doublet, which caused him to let go of the girl. He threw him towards the lairds who were standing around. Trembling with rage, he approached Andreas who was being restrained by two of the lairds, drew his claymore and pointed it at his uncle's bare chest.

'How interesting, swine,' growled Iain. Without taking his eyes off his uncle, he raised his voice to call Finella. 'Now, my dear, you are going to explain what my uncle means to these lords who have come to hear you.'

The young woman began to tremble all over. She looked frantically at Thora and her mother who were standing to the side, staring, their eyes bulging with fear.

'Well, Finella! Do not make us waste our time,' continued Iain, the moment of astonishment over.

'Keep your mouth shut, *girl*!' Aindreas shouted to her.

With his eyes still fixed on his uncle's, Iain gave Lennox a nod of the head in Finella's direction and murmured between clenched teeth, 'She needs some coaxing, Lennox.'

The lieutenant drew his sword and placed it on the young woman's chin. Aindreas tried to struggle free and ordered her to keep quiet, but Iain cut the cord of his uncle's jacket with the point of his blade, which made him stop in his tracks. His eyes were now bloodshot.

Utterly beside herself with fear, Andreas' wife screamed, "Look, speak up! He is going to kill him.

Her eyes fixed on Lennox's weapon, which he was gradually lowering, Finella jumped on hearing the order and almost fainted. She closed her eyes a moment and breathed deeply before starting to confess in a quivering voice, 'Lord Aindreas and Lady Beathag had planned to hide a white casket in Lady Rosalind's room at

Mallaig during the tournament. They offered me a little purse of money to take it and hide it in the window seat in the bedroom. I was not to be seen even though there was nothing in this casket. I can swear to that. I opened it before I left it.'

'A little purse…' Iain repeated as he lowered his weapon. He walked around the group. 'The rest of what was meant for my father, and from what I can see, you used the rest well, Aindreas. In fact, how much of the sum is left? And what about the other objects? The letters and Lady Gunelle's uncle's wedding present?'

'I am pleased to inform you, nephew, that there is nothing left,' Aindreas replied wickedly.

He had relaxed since he was not under direct threat from Iain's weapon and had nothing more to lose after Finella's confession. 'I burned the letters and spent everything…. as for the cross, it was a mistake to wear it in June, but we have disposed of it.'

Aindreas's declaration hit the gathering like an anchor hitting the seabed. Every eye turned towards Iain in the deep silence. The young man was shooting daggers at his uncle, his fist clenched around the pommel of his sword, which he was waving about in the air.

'Listen, Iain,' Aindreas articulated tensely, 'it was nothing particularly wicked. It was a sum of money which Baltair did not really need, and no one at Mallaig seemed to be shouting about it. I probably would not have kept it if it had not been for the way you treated Beathag…'

The uncle was unable to finish his sentence. Iain had pounced on him. He caught him by the lapels of his jacket and dragged him towards the entrance, nodding to Lennox, who had let go of Finella.

Lennox went over to hold the uncle, who was protesting mildly, not knowing what his nephew was going to do. He did not have to wait long to find out. Iain pulled his doublet sleeve so violently that he tore it off in one go, leaving his arm bare to the shoulder. He then grabbed him and pushed him against the back of a chair. Lennox came over immediately and prevented him from moving. With the speed of lightning, Iain raising his claymore above his head, aimed a violent blow just at elbow height and cut off the arm in a splash of blood which sprayed the lieutenant's face. Speechless, the uncle looked at his forearm lying on the ground in a puddle of black blood. His wife had fainted. After an initial gasp of horror the rest of the gathering fell silent.

Iain's words resounded with a strange note of indifference. 'In ancient times, a robber's hand was cut off. When treason is added to theft, half of the arm goes.' Turning towards Thora, he said, 'Bandage up your father, Thora, or else I could be accused of leaving him to bleed to death.'

The ride back to Mallaig in the darkness was rapid and silent. The knights did not dare comment on the punishment meted out for Aindreas's betrayal. His face inscrutable and hard, Iain was at the head of his men beside Lieutenant Lennox, who respected his silence. Lennox knew what it had cost the young chief to divide the clan with this affair, and he knew there would be no sense of victory. As they began the descent from the plateau to Mallaig, they met Sir Eachann, who was returning from Scone, bringing the post from the queen to the chatelaine. The knight spurred on his horse towards the party with the joyful look of someone bringing good news, and without noticing the chief's serious demeanour, he launched into a babbling account of his journey. So it was that by the time they reached Mallaig, Iain had learned from his messenger that the king had removed Sheriff Darnley from his position at the chancellery at

Stirling. Beathag, having been evicted from Scone palace by the queen, had taken refuge in Kenneth Simpson's inn, where she seemed to be happy.

At least that is one threat that is distanced from Mallaig for a while, Iain said bitterly to himself as he thought of his sister-in-law. Would to God that she would find she was happy enough to stay with Simpson and never set foot in the Highlands again.

I was exhausted. The interminable sequence of contractions had increased, affecting my lower back each time. How long had I been pushing with very little result, at least as far as I was concerned? Nellie never left me. I felt her hands on my knees, and I still heard her calm and encouraging voice. Between two contractions, I managed to see what was happening around us.

'She is very narrow, my lord, and the baby seems to be a good size,' I heard Anna explain to Iain in the corridor where he was pacing up and down.

Iain has come back, I said to myself in the fog of my pain. At another moment, I heard Bran howl.

Seeing my distress, Anna leaned over to me and said reassuringly, 'Keep going. Do not pay any attention. It is the dog replying to your screams. He has as much sense as his master. Ah, these husbands who lose all sense of control when their wife is giving birth! It is a real pity to see otherwise valiant, courageous men go to pieces like this. Do not stop screaming. It does you good and helps you to push! Too bad if my master cannot bear to hear it.'

I had barely heard her explanations. Scream! I could not have stopped myself; the pain was so great at the end. A little after midnight on this third Wednesday of Advent 1425, to my greatest joy, I gave birth to a son. Through my tears of joy and exhaustion, I recognised Iain in the little wrapped-up bundle which Nellie placed in my arms—his beautiful black hair, his little clenched fists, and his voice so powerful for such a small body... and the eagerness with which he took my breast.

I felt a tremendous feeling of achievement after the birth. Once I had been cleaned up, Anna showed in Iain, who with great care and concern came to look at his son lying asleep in my arms. At that moment, I felt his emotion like a message of gratitude. He was screwing up his thick eyebrows as he passed his trembling hand under our baby's head without daring to touch him. I took his fingers and put them on the little warm, down-covered head. I saw him close his eyes a moment, and when he opened them, a tear escaped.

'He is magnificent, my beloved. What did I do to be so blessed by you?' he murmured, looking deeply into my eyes.

'You were just yourself, my lord. And as such, you deserve this son, just as much as my love,' I replied.

For a long time, we studied our baby together, then seeing my obvious need to rest, my husband made to leave and leave me in Nellie's care, but I kept him there. I wanted to know how the trial had ended. Now that my son was born, no tiredness would have made me change my mind. He must have realised that I was going to insist, for looking sombre, he reported concisely. So it was that in the space of a few minutes I learned of the terrible punishment inflicted at the scene of his crime on uncle Aindreas My husband's hatred had found closure in inflicting this punishment. That was the price he had paid to win his case and in so doing, he had recovered his full authority as chief of the MacNeils.

'Do not be bitter, my love,' I whispered. 'You did what had to be done. I am proud of you.'

'Today, it is you we have to be proud of,' he said, caressing my hand. 'I am infinitely so, Gunelle, and I thank you.'

I slept very little and woke up with the first rays of daylight feeling stiff and sore. I sighed with relief, for my great joy had not disappeared. Nellie and Anna had taken turns watching over me and my son. They welcomed my awakening with such a radiant smile that I burst into tears.

Later while I was feeding my son, I had a visit from Ceit. With her little face full of curiosity, she carefully tiptoed over to my bed.

'Father told me I have a brother, and Jenny says I can come and see him. Can I, mother?' When she discovered the baby wrapped up in his covers, she exclaimed, her eyes wide open and full of wonder, 'He is tiny, and he has a black head! I was told he would look like you! Look at his little hands! How could they ever hold a claymore? Father will have a lot to do if he wants him to become a knight,' she concluded with the air of an expert.

I had all the difficulty in the world not to burst out laughing in the face of my daughter's air of superiority. Nellie and Anna burst out laughing as one. *And yet he will be a knight one day*, I thought as I looked in wonder at my little Baltair who was sound asleep.

Manufactured by Amazon.ca
Bolton, ON